# THE PLACEBO
# EFFECT

*First Book of the Junction Chronicles*

# DAVID ROTENBERG

A TOUCHSTONE BOOK
Published by Simon & Schuster
New York   London   Toronto   Sydney   New Delhi

Touchstone
A Division of Simon & Schuster, Inc.
1230 Avenue of the Americas
New York, NY 10020

First Touchstone trade paperback export edition February 2012

TOUCHSTONE and colophon are registered trademarks of Simon & Schuster, Inc.

For information about special discounts for bulk purchases, please contact
Simon & Schuster Special Sales at 1-800-268-3216 or
CustomerService@simonandschuster.ca.

Manufactured in the United States of America

10  9  8  7  6  5  4  3  2  1

ISBN 978-1-4391-7006-9
ISBN 978-1-4391-7011-3 (pbk)
ISBN 978-1-4391-7264-3 (ebook)

FOR SUSAN, JOEY AND BETH

The earth hath bubbles, as the water has, and these are of them.

Macbeth, Act 1, Scene 3

# ACKNOWLEDGEMENTS

I'd like to thank Alison Clarke and Kevin Hanson at Simon & Schuster Canada for their support and valuable input as this manuscript took shape. As well I owe a debt of thanks to Michael Levine, my agent and friend, who has been in my corner for many years now. In addition I'd like to acknowledge the talents of the teachers who work with me at Pro Actors Lab: Bruce, Rae Ellen, John, Marvin, Melee and Glen. Last, and most important, I want to thank the many gifted actors who have submitted to what were at one time my experiments and are now common practices in the profession. This book could not have happened without their talents.

# PROLOGUE

*You can't understand how a man lives his life until you understand what he thinks is going to happen to him after he dies.*

—ATTRIBUTED TO DAG HAMMARSKJÖLD,
FORMER SECRETARY GENERAL OF THE UNITED NATIONS

DECKER FELT HIMSELF SLIPPING. HE TRIED TO PULL HIMSELF back—to make it stop. But he felt the cold, and knew there would be blood on his right hand if he looked.

"We do what we do to find our place in the universe," someone said.

Decker knew where he was. It was 1988; he was twenty-two years old.

He was on the obligatory European promenade between second and third year at university and on a whim had hitchhiked one night down from Paris to Chartres. At dawn he found himself on the steps of the ancient cathedral beside many other back-packed vagabonds. He watched as the day's first light brought the twelve figures above the massive front doors to life. Each figure's fine facial features slowly awakening and accepting their job of both welcoming and warning the faithful.

"It never fails to thrill me," the same high-class male British voice said.

Decker turned and was surprised to find the voice belonged to a tall, gaunt, middle-aged man wearing a threadbare suit—and not sixteen inches from his left ear.

"Do you know them? Can't understand the message unless you know each statue's story. The left side of the central door has five figures. From outer to inner they follow a chronological order. Outermost is Melchizedek, then Abraham (holding Isaac, whom he is about to sacrifice—note the trapped ram on the pedestal), then Moses holding a tablet and pointing to a brazen serpent, fourth is Samuel sacrificing a lamb, and finally King David carrying a crown of thorns. In some way they all prefigure Christ's sacrifice and passion. You see," he pointed expansively to the figures, "all the Old Testament prophets lead to the arrival of the King Himself."

Decker was going to counter that the Old Testament had been rearranged by the newly formed Christians so that it appeared that the prophets and the line of David led directly to the arrival of Christ, but the original order of the Old Testament did nothing of the sort. But before he could speak, the man put out his hand. "Brother Malcolm. I lecture at ten and one and four every day except Sunday, naturally." Then he said the oddest thing. "Yes, the testaments have been rearranged. But sometimes the truth—His truth—needs to be bolstered by a bit of trickery. The falseness does not make the truth any less valid."

Decker spotted Brother Malcolm again just before ten that morning. He joined the small crowd around the man and listened intently for the hour plus of the man's lecture about the flooring of the east transept and its door leading to what used to be called the Rue des Juifs. At the end of the lecture Brother Malcolm cupped his hands in front of his chest and announced, "I am a mendicant. I live on the generosity of others." The thirty-odd people who had taken in the lecture put coins and notes into his hands.

At one o'clock that afternoon Decker listened for almost two hours as Brother Malcolm explained in great detail the workings of a cathedral's flying buttress system.

Then at four o'clock he heard Brother Malcolm, brilliantly and in remarkable depth, shed light on the carvings, drawings and paintings at the first three stations of the cross. Surprisingly, at least to Decker, Brother Malcolm passed right by a newly bricked-in doorway. Beside the door was a small covered opening just large enough for food to be passed through. Decker was about to ask about it when Brother Malcolm shook his head, as if he knew the question before Decker asked it, and he wasn't going to answer.

Decker didn't remember where he slept that night or the next or the next. But he did remember in vivid detail Brother Malcolm's next nine lectures. At the end of the ninth—on the steps of the west transept entrance—he went to put some coins in Brother Malcolm's cupped hands when the man said to him, "Stand beside me with your hands out as mine are."

Decker never forgot the feeling of the first coin landing in his palm or the feeling of a burden laid down. Later that night, Decker found himself on the front steps of the cathedral again. And as he slept on his backpack he heard Brother Malcolm ask him, "So, have you decided to stay? I've waited a long time. I'm getting old and someone has to take over my ministry when I'm gone. I'll teach you what I know and this great place of faith will be your home." Then he added with a knowing look, "It is another path, a way to avoid the room with no windows—and the hanging man."

In his dream that night Decker closed his eyes—deeper darkness within the darkness of sleep—and watched his retina screen. Two identical cubes entered from the left side and slid majestically into the centre—perfect geometric shapes. Brother Malcolm was telling the truth.

Decker felt the cold envelop him and the slime of blood between his fingers. He opened his eyes within the dream and begged the dream to end.

Decker left Chartres before daybreak—but he never left it very far behind.

## THE DANGEROUS VOYAGE OF
## MIKE SHEDLOSKI BEGINS

ON THE SIDEWALK, ACROSS THE STREET FROM THE MASSIVE headquarters of Yolles Pharmaceuticals, a six-foot stack of bottles of all sizes and shapes were miraculously balanced, one upon the next, creating the most unlikely tree under the heavens.

Mike Shedloski, a pear-shaped man wearing a dirty Michelin Man coat and frayed bell-bottoms, stood, fat fists pressed against his nonexistent waist, admiring his handiwork. A few feet away, another miracle of balance, this time made from random stones and twice the size of the tree, was clearly a representation of an office tower of some sort.

Mike picked up a hand-painted sign that, in angry red letters, asked "What's Your Ratio!" then began to shout across the road, "Tell the Enemy I worked here. I worked here, I worked here, tell the Enemy that!"

Two security guards, one big the other bigger, raced across the street, nightsticks at the ready.

Mike repeated his claim—"I worked here!"—as the bigger of the security guards grabbed him.

"I worked here."

"Sure you did," the security guard said as the other one knocked down the office tower statue with one simple push. When it fell it revealed another hand-painted sign: "Who's Jumping Now?"

"Move it along and don't come back. This is a public sidewalk, not your damned toilet."

"The Enemy knows that I worked here," Mike whimpered.

The big guard grabbed Mike by the fleshy part of his upper arm.

"Hey, that hurts."

"Yeah, it does. Now move along and take your damned signs with you."

Mike took his "What's Your Ratio!" sign but left the "Who's Jumping Now?" sign against the retaining wall.

The guards watched Mike Shedloski amble away, then one of them kicked at the balancing bottle structure. The thing momentarily resisted and then crashed to the ground, clearly no adhesive of any sort had been used, just balance—incredible balance.

## IN THE CASTLE OF THE ENEMY

HENRY-CLAY YOLLES, CEO OF YOLLES PHARMACEUTICALS, stood at the floor-to-ceiling window of his office with his hands clasped behind his back, watching as his guards dealt with the freak. Then his attention was drawn to the "Who's Jumping Now?" sign, which led him to stare at the Treloar Building on the other side of the Ohio River. Why didn't he just buy it? He had the money. Yes, but there was something else—something hidden from him—stopping him from just plunking down the cash for the damned stack of steel, glass and stone.

He pulled his eyes away from the building and looked back at his newly refurbished, massive office. The place made him smile because it had all come about from what he first thought of as a stupid fucking mistake on his part. From the idiotic impulse to be helpful. To think like a doctor, a damned healer—not like a businessman.

He had been approached at an ushy-cushy charity banquet by a Mrs. Francis Xavier—who could forget a woman named after a male saint? Her daughter was suffering from an extremely rare disease that afflicts fewer than sixty people in North America. And the pesky thing principally attacks preteens. The only treatment available—as unreliable as it was—required that the children endure painful and lengthy procedures in the hospital three times every week of their young lives. Mrs. Xavier had begged him to devote some research time to developing a treatment that would save her daughter from "this torture."

In a moment of weakness he had publicly committed his

company to finding a better way to treat the disease. The research had proved to be incredibly expensive—vastly more than he had budgeted—and his stockholders were furious. What kind of return could be made with so few people having the disease? Finally, after applying tremendous pressure and truckloads of cash, his scientists had come up with a simple injection that could be administered once every six weeks.

His marketing department wanted to make a splash, figuring at least on some great press for the company.

He found two doctors who had been dealing with the victims of the disease and got them to agree, on compassionate grounds, to test the new treatment—it wasn't hard to convince them, since the doctors were deeply troubled by their young patients' pain. The only proviso was that the doctors were to forward all records of side effects directly back to him, rather than publishing them in medical journals like *The Lancet*. Positive results he would pass on; negative ones he would send back for a second opinion. It seemed only fair to him, since his company had gone to such expense and there was no way to make money with the treatment.

One of the two doctors found the drug to be "efficacious and with only minimal and acceptable side effects and a great advance over the old procedure." The other doctor, using a sample of only five patients, found one had a potentially dangerous reaction to the drug, and rather than reporting that back to Yolles Pharmaceuticals, she went to a reporter who just happened to be her lover, and the headlines rolled out: PHARMA COMPANY BUYS RESULTS! RIGGED DRUG TESTS! NEED FOR ARM'S LENGTH BETWEEN DRUG COMPANIES AND RESEARCHERS! GOVERNMENTS NEED TO ADDRESS PHARMA MALFEASANCE! Never once did the newspapers or television reports mention that the new treatment worked in 92 percent of the cases—nor did they bother to write about the incredibly painful procedure that the new drug allowed the children to avoid. Or, by the by, the only 64 percent effectiveness of the old treatment. No. Just headlines about how venal his company was. It had cost him a 38 percent drop in the stock price. Scientists deserted the company, and his balance sheet became a daily source of terror.

No good deed goes unpunished.

Two days after the shit hit the fan, Henry-Clay retreated to his Puerto Rico condo on the beach at Isla Verde, fully intending a three-day drunk. He hadn't needed this kind of escape in years, but he wanted to get away from the board members and stock-holders who were furious that his investment in the new treat-ment had darn near drowned the entire company.

God, if they got this bent out of shape over this, what would they do when they found out about the problems he was hav-ing with his new antidepressant. And when they heard about the money he'd already spent . . .

The company's new antidepressant drug was making its way through the ludicrously long FDA approvals process at record speed—a bit of grease from his wallet had helped the process. But the drug was still too expensive to bring to market—almost twice its competitor's price point. And no matter how hard he pushed his scientists he couldn't get that price point down. The actual R & D had been expensive but manageable. The problem was the raw materials themselves needed for the drug. They were extremely hard to find in nature, and the process to produce them synthetically used viciously expensive chemicals. No matter what combination they tried, the price was too high to market.

He awoke late in the afternoon of his second day in Puerto Rico with the post-rain sun streaming in the window. An empty rum bottle was on the floor, a second half-empty bottle tilted off the side of a copy of *Maxim* on the coffee table refracting a tiny spectrum of colour toward his fifty-two inch plasma TV tuned to a documentary on the Discovery Channel.

What he saw made him sit up and question just how drunk he was. On the screen was a Cincinnati street scene that he recog-nized, and in front of an impossibly balanced pile of junk stood a pudgy middle-aged guy. A voice off the screen asked, "And there's no glue or nails holding this together?"

"Why would there be? There's no need for adhesives. Balance is just a matter of ratio. Up to down; left to right; forward to back. Everything has a ratio."

The interviewer asked, "Everything, Mike? Everything has a ratio?"

"Absolutely," this Mike person said. "Light to dark. Smart to stupid. Honest to dishonest." He smiled mischievously. "Pens to pencils, Macs to PC's, rainy days to sunny days, truth to lies, things that work to things that don't." He giggled and added, "Fat to muscle." Then he placed what seemed to be four random pieces atop the balancing act.

The interviewer asked, "And you know where to place the next piece by what you call its ratio?"

"Yep," Mike said as he added two more pieces to his balancing miracle.

"But how do you know the ratio?"

Mike looked at the camera and smiled, his face suddenly luminous, almost handsome. "I just know—I just know."

*I bet you do, I just bet you do,* Henry-Clay thought. *And aren't you just a big ol' lonely dog, yeah, a lonely dog—that's what you are, aren't you, Mikey, a big ol' lonely dog who needs a juicy bone, a pat on your fat belly, and a fluffy bed to call your own.*

"I just know," Mike repeated.

Now it was Henry-Clay who was smiling his version of a luminous smile. He hit mute on the remote then picked up his phone. He hit number 3 on his speed dial. The first two were escort services.

Kreger, the scientist who headed Yolles Pharmaceuticals' research, answered before the second ring. "Hey boss, where are you?"

"Away. Don't ask where away, just away."

"Okay. So how's away?"

"More interesting than I thought. How're the trials going on the new antidepression medication?"

"Good. Yeah, good. It's passing all its trials with incredible speed. It's been five years, but I think we're close to FDA approval."

"How close?"

"Really close. But there's a problem."

"Which is?"

"You know the problem. You've known it from the beginning. Price!"

"But the science is okay?"

"The science is terrific. Terrific."

"So how expensive is it?"

"It comes to almost forty dollars a pill. So, just to amortize the R & D, you'd have to sell them for at least seventy dollars a pill."

Henry-Clay whistled through his teeth—but he was smiling.

"What's the whistle mean, boss?"

"It means—unless."

"Unless what?"

"Unless we know the ratio, Dr. Kreger—unless we know the ratio."

"The ratio of what to what?"

*Of placebo to real,* Henry-Clay thought; *of placebo to real.* "Patch me through to Evelyn."

His secretary's sultry voice came on instantly. "Sir?"

"I need someone to find someone for me. Do we have someone who can do that?"

"Sure. Who're you trying to find?"

Henry-Clay told her. He already thought of Mike Shedloski as Ratio-Man.

Henry-Clay moved to his condo balcony. A parasurfer was taking off from the beach, the ratio of uplift to gravity clearly in uplift's favour, so he soared, as did Henry-Clay's hopes for the future.

And within six weeks of hiring Michael Shedloski, aka Ratio-Man, and treating him like a prized St. Bernard—clumsy but beautiful—he had the knowledge that allowed him to float a few strategically placed rumours about his new—and now not so expensive—antidepressant drug that sent his stock roaring back to new highs. He and his business were in flight, aiming for the stars.

Ratio-Man had, for a few belly scratches and a dozen *Aren't you a fine doggy, aren't you*'s not only stocked Yolles Pharmaceuticals' coffers with gold but supplied something even more valuable: a way for Henry-Clay to find other freaks like Mike—one of whom claimed he could tell when people were telling the truth.

Then of course he'd fired the fat moron. Mac had suggested a more permanent solution, but Henry-Clay was not a murderer—he was a businessman jettisoning a used-up asset.

Easy to do now that he had a new asset on the horizon. *One whose gift I'll have to test,* Henry-Clay thought as he poured himself a drink. *We'll see the reach and breadth of this new freak's gift. You never know when such a skill could be of great value to Yolles Pharmaceuticals—and, of course, to me.*

He raised the crystal glass and saluted the Treloar Building across the Ohio River. Then he downed two fingers of the most expensive scotch whiskey that money could buy—and wished that he could tell the difference between it and five-dollar hooch.

Then he looked down and across the street. Mike Shedloski, aka Ratio-Man, was gone.

## 3

## MIKE GETS THE URGE FOR GOING

MIKE WAS HIDING BEHIND THE RETAINING WALL ACROSS from Yolles Pharma, trying to watch the Enemy standing way up there in his castle window. All around him was the detritus of the statues he'd so painstakingly balanced from nothing into things of beauty. He started to rebuild the stone building, but the voices in his head were confusing him—teetering him dangerously out of balance. And the store didn't have dill pickle chips and that had upset him so he'd thrown over the whole rack—what kind of store doesn't have dill pickle chips? And the store owner had gotten angry and called the police so he'd run, and the voices in his head were confusing him. So many voices. He thought about taking his meds, but they just made it worse—made the voices soft and silky, female, but still there. And even if he couldn't hear them accurately, he knew they made fun of his small penis—and besides, he wasn't sure if the meds came from friend or foe. General Tso's chicken worked better than meds. But where could he find an open Chinese restaurant in Cincinnati at this hour of the night? And he needed to stop the voices, 'cause they were screaming at him now: "You're just a fat idiot. An obese cluck. A tiny-dicked moron in bell-bottoms!"

"Shut up, shut up, shut up, shut up! Natasha didn't think that—didn't!"

He knew he was screaming, and that the teenagers across the street were watching—smiling—ready to jump him. And suddenly he found himself in front of the weird building on Plum Street. The synagogue that looked like a mosque—covering a portal—a danger—he was out of balance—out of balance—out of balance! He really needed dill pickle chips. Right now—or General Tso's chicken—or both—yeah, both at once—the chips crushed on top of the chicken. He began to move along Plum Street, to get away from the teenagers, to get away from the yawning portal, from that weird building, from the voices. The voices that kept on shouting, "Give it up. Give it up. This is too big for a fat boy like you. Give it up!" But he couldn't give it up, couldn't give up. He owed it to himself and the others like himself that he had betrayed to the Enemy. He'd pretended to be nice, given Mike a job, put him in charge of a lab. And Mike had betrayed his own kind. Been used by the Enemy who he thought was going to be his friend, a real friend who understood how special he was— and now that friend was the Enemy and was going to try and use Decker. He had to warn him. He had to get to the place called the Junction and warn Decker, warn him that the Enemy was getting ready to test then use him—him and his gift—just like he had used Mike.

"You can't do this, fatso!" The voice screamed.

"I can," he said under his breath. Then over and over, "I can, I can, I can."

Then he wondered where the airport was. He'd never been on an airplane. He wondered how much it would cost to take an airplane to the Junction—where Decker lived.

# 4

## *TEACHER*

DECKER LOOKED AT THE FORTY OR SO ACTORS ASSEMBLED in his studio and decided where to begin. "Evolution is blindly cruel," he said. "It remorselessly removes the unuseful. Yet it has not done away with actors. Your profession is the second most consumed of all the arts—pop music being number one.

"And the iconography of your art form has never changed. Those who have voyaged have earned the right to be up in the light. Those who have yet to voyage sit in the dark."

An older actor raised his hand.

Decker nodded. "Voyaging?"

"Yeah, go over that again."

"Sure. The first actor was no doubt some extraordinary woman who stood up by the campfire, and because she had gone to the valley, found something there *and* brought it back—voyaged—she had the right to speak, to act while the others stayed in the dark and listened. Without voyaging you have no right to stand in the light. You have to chance the danger of going to the valley, then you have to find something there (the fleece is the mythic expression of this), understand what you have found, then bring back your new-found knowledge to the fire. Only then you can stand in the light."

Decker thought of his twelve years in New York City, his two Broadway shows—and the ALS death of his wife—as going to the valley and his teaching as standing up by the fire.

"What if you've never traveled?" Tawtiawna, an incredibly talented light-skinned black actress, asked.

"Emily Dickinson never went anywhere, but she voyaged. The

Brontë sisters never met anyone like Rochester in their lives, but they voyaged, they explored their world both real and imagined, or they couldn't have found him and brought him back to the fire."

Decker smiled then turned to the blond actress in the front row. "Hold out your hand, palm down." She did as Decker asked, then Decker put his hand out, palm down, six inches from hers and turned to the class. "So two people go to a bar and they flop their hands on the table—about six inches apart—like our two hands. And over the evening they magically join." Decker moved his hand forward and interlaced his fingers with hers. Her hand was remarkably soft, the fit perfect with his fingers—biology saying yes. For an instant he caught the actress's eyes looking up into his, as his wife had done so long ago as she demanded, "Do you know what you are doing, Decker? Do you know?" Decker pushed aside the memory, held the actress's interlocked fingers aloft, and announced to the actors watching, "Two kids, a mortgage, and a car." Then he dropped the actress's hand and said, "And they don't know how it happened." Decker smiled and added, "How it happened is what they learn from actors." He turned back to the actress. "Put out your hand again."

"You going to marry me a second time, Decker?"

Decker paused, then said, "No. Just put out your hand."

She did.

He turned to the class and said, "The six inches between our hands is actor territory. No writer, no director, no cinematographer can guide you across those six inches. That territory belongs to you. It's the reason that evolution hasn't removed you and your kind."

Without segue Decker turned back to Tawtiawna. "Did you have a private name for yourself when you were a little girl?"

The actress looked around—wary—as if Decker had seen into a secret place. Finally she said, "Yes."

"I'm not asking you to tell me her name. But she's your artist, and she wants to voyage, but you protect her because you think she's frail. She's not—she voyages all the time and is waiting to take you along with her."

After a few more questions Decker put the first of the evening's twelve scenes (the Venice sequence from Pinter's *Betrayal*) on its feet—completely unaware that he was being watched, every move noted, every word recorded then transcribed.

Class ended just short of midnight. The actors packed up and headed for cheap beer at Squirly's up on Queen Street. Decker stored the cameras in his office beneath his sixth-grade report card, which he'd tacked to the wall. Long ago he had circled his teacher's comment: "Does not play well with others." Beside it was his son Seth's sixth-grade report card. The comment circled there—"Does not fully participate in group activities"—was more politically correct but meant the same thing. He looked at the two reports, thought about taking them down, then decided, as he usually did, to leave them where they were.

Back in the studio he picked up Tawtiawna's diary—she always left her diary. Decker had been tempted to leaf through it the first time he'd found it but quickly realized it was Tawtiawna's effort to reach out to him. It was tempting, but Decker wasn't ready—perhaps would never be ready to risk hurting those he cared about again.

He had caused enough pain.

He put Tawtiawna's diary on the monitor cart, locked up the studio and headed down the block to his "office," an upscale bar called Politica.

Sitting at the bar he ordered bourbon with water on the side— a holdover from his time directing in regional theatres in the American South.

The waitress knew him and didn't hurry him. But when he gave over his Visa card he was surprised that the bank rejected the plastic.

He apologized, made a mental note to check on this, paid in cash and headed home to the Junction—never suspecting that his personal voyage was about to take him to places of which even he had never dreamt.

# 5

## *YSLAN HICKS*

YSLAN HICKS HATED WASHINGTON. THE CENTRE OF HER HA-
tred was Congress. And the very epicentre of that hatred was the
congressional oversight committee before which she now sat,
waiting for the last plump rump to squattle down into its assigned
chair for the morning session. She hoped that both the early
hour and the esoteric name of her NSA file would scare away
reporters, few of whom were really thinkers. Most weren't really
even newshounds anymore; now they all seemed like wannabe
infomercial guys—"For the next twenty minutes we'll double the
offer. All you pay is the extra shipping and handling. Call right
now. Don't wait. I can't do this all day—and by the way, the synaesthetes oversight committee met today, and the oversighters . . .
oversighted."

Then she saw Emerson Remi enter the room and she felt
herself shrink. Emerson Remi was—as his name implied—old
Princeton all the way to his argyle socks and red suspenders. And
more important, he was a smart guy reporter for the *Times* with a
nose for a story and enough intelligence to find his way through
the murk of this committee—and, at one time, into Yslan's heart.

Yslan forced herself not to look in Emerson's direction and
glanced down at her notes—unnecessary as they were, but ap-
pearing without notes before a congressional committee implied
a kind of arrogance that a woman couldn't afford to show these
old guys. Yslan even thought of the two women on the committee as old guys.

The head of the oversight committee, a congressman from

Texas—in his parlance, "the Great State of Texas"—banged his gavel, the doors were closed and, after he finished his self-congratulatory opening remarks, turned to her. "Ms. Hicks, we'd like to thank you for making an appearance this fine morning before the committee."

"It's not a problem, Congressman. I'm prepared to answer any questions you might have."

"Good. Very good. To begin with, could you pronounce your first name for those in the room who don't come from the South."

"Certainly. It's spelled Y-S-L-A-N, but pronounced like the word 'island,' as in 'island of Manhattan'—but without the 'd.'"

"It's a fine southern name for those of you who are curious. You are welcome here, Ms. Hicks."

"Thank you, Congressman."

So much for the niceties.

"We'll start with questions from Louisiana congressman Villianne. Pass him over the microphone there." A fresh-faced congressional page did as the congressman requested and moved the old-fashioned thing on its heavy stand to the far end of the raised table.

Yslan followed the movement of the microphone along the table to Congressman Villianne. Trim and tanned, the man was handsome in a foxish kind of way. There'd been rumours about a connection between him and the infamous Darryl Marmalukes, but they were unsubstantiated. Yslan reminded herself that this man was no Louisiana back-bayou yokel.

"Ms. Hicks, let me repeat my colleagues' thanks for making the time to appear before the committee."

Yslan nodded and moved the microphone on the table in front of her closer to her face. The old mic made Yslan feel like she was Pacino in *The Godfather,* demanding an apology.

"Now we on this committee are charged with making sure that the taxpayers' money is not unwisely spent."

"I understand that, Congressman."

"Good. I hope you do. So let's all be sure that we all *understand* what we are talking about here. Your file at the NSA, which costs the taxpayers well in excess of five million dollars annually, concerns what some people would call freaks but you call synaesthetes, is that correct?"

Yslan did her best not to flinch. "It is."

"And could you—just so we're all on the same page here—describe exactly what a synaesthete is?"

"Well, Congressman, there is not really an accepted medical definition of the term."

"I am aware of that." His voice had taken on an edge that said, I am no fool.

"Yes, Congressman, I assume you are. I meant no disrespect."

"Good, it would be unwise to be disrespectful to a congressional oversight committee."

For a moment, Yslan was thrown by the tenor of the conversation, then she asked, "Would you like me to give you the working definition of synaesthesia?"

"Yes, I think that would be helpful."

"Fine. The term comes from the Greek. For a comparison, amnesia refers to someone who has lost brain function. *Amn*—lost. *Esia*—brain. Whereas synaesthesia is from *synaesth,* having to do with mixing, and *esia,* having to do with the brain. Synaesthesia is when the brain mixes two or more functions."

"Functions or senses, Ms. Hicks?"

Yslan paused for a moment. Did he know what we're really up to at the NSA? "Senses, Congressman."

"And how does this mixing of the senses happen?"

"Well, that too is a subject of debate. Some researchers believe that we are all synaesthetes for the first six to sixteen months of our lives until the brain sorts out the distinctions between the senses and then divides their recognition function into distinct sections of the brain. Much like a computer's hard drive can be partitioned into distinct zones—often one for storage files and another for operating systems."

"Yes. Well, thanks for the analogy, but how do these 'distinct sections of the brain' as you call them suddenly stop being distinct and leak into one another, if I can put it that way?"

She hesitated, trying to hear if there was real knowledge behind his question.

"Ms. Hicks, would you like me to repeat the question?"

"Often by an injury to the head," she said softly.

"Speak up, Ms. Hicks."

Yslan leaned in closer to the table microphone and said clearly, "Often from an injury to the head."

"Ah. I see. So the government is supplying large sums of money for you to oversee people who have been hit on the head?"

"It's not the way I would put it but—"

"I'm sure you'd prefer to put your work in a better light. But let's be honest here. Your work concerns people who have been hit on the head and as a result of that trauma the walls between the sections of the brain have come down and they can't help mixing up things from one section with things from another section."

She warned herself to be careful—to find the right balance to defend her work without giving away exactly what her work was. "Synaesthetes are able to do some remarkable things by what you call mixing up."

"Like knowing the smell of colours?"

Yslan took another deep breath to calm herself. "Yes, some synaesthetes have that odd crossing of the senses."

"Now the NSA is concerned with national security, isn't it? After all NSA is short for National Security Agency, isn't it?"

"Yes, Congressman, it is."

"So how exactly is the smell of colour useful for national security purposes? How does it merit all the money in your budget to keep track of such important individuals?"

Synaesthetic crosses like the smell of colours were what Yslan called silly synaesthetes—and clearly of no value to national security. They provided a blind, a cover, for what the NSA was really investigating, because there were other, far more important "crossings" out there. And some of the people with those important crossings called themselves synaesthetes, although most went by no name except their own. Yslan thought of these people as the inner circle of the synaesthetic world—and these rare individuals potentially had real value for the NSA. There were only a few they had identified at this point, and Yslan had been keeping close tabs on them. They were the truly gifted. Maybe they were a kind of synaesthete. She didn't know—or really care. But they possessed extraordinary talents—of that she was sure. As sure as she was loathe to speak of them or their unique abilities in a public forum, especially one that might get news coverage. So she grinned and pretended that she was interested in people who could tell you the weather and the day of the week when you gave them a day of any year, or tell you the sounds of smells—silly synaesthetes.

"So, let's be honest here, Ms. Hicks, this file that you look after is a bit like the dolphin experiments of the seventies, wouldn't you say?"

The congressman was referring to the vast sums spent trying to train dolphins to attach explosive devices to enemy warships. The public got wind of the experiments and pilloried the department for its abuse of animals and its vast expense—and, oh, yes, for its failure to produce a single dolphin willing to attack enemy ships.

"No, I don't think it's like the dolphin experiments of the seventies."

"Why not?"

"Because synaesthetes could prove to be extremely valuable in our efforts to keep the American public safe."

"How? By reciting twenty thousand digits of pi?"

Yslan wanted to smile but didn't as she leaned closer to the microphone and said, "Actually, Congressman, we should be exact since this is on the record, I believe it was twenty-two thousand five hundred digits."

There was a brief laugh behind her. She knew it was Emerson.

He even laughed like a Princetonian—a little too high for a man, a bit intoxicated even at this hour of the morning.

"As you will, Ms. Hicks, but what earthly purpose does reciting numbers have in the defense of the United States of America?"

"None, Congressman."

"Ah," the congressman said with obvious satisfaction.

"The man you are referring to is a citizen of the United Kingdom, so I doubt he has any place in the defense of the United States."

The congressman was hard put to keep the anger from his face. "Fine. But let's be honest here. The skills these poor benighted souls have are akin to the ability to keep dozens of plates spinning on sticks, aren't they? A feat to be sure, but a useless one, and in your case an expensive one. And while we're being honest, Ms. Hicks, aren't you just defending your file because it's the only niche you've been able to find at the NSA?"

She heard the nasty curl in his voice and recognized it for exactly what it was. Old sexism at work. But she wasn't going to fall into the trap. She wasn't going to say that he would never question a man about his work this way. Then she saw the odd smirk on his face and recognized that too. And it hurt her. No matter how far she had come from the dingy tobacco fields of North Carolina, people from the South still saw through her citified disguise—like Hannibal Lecter had seen through Clarice Starling, in *The Silence of the Lambs.* She had taken one thing from that movie to heart—the quote from Marcus Aurelius that everybody and everything has a true nature and that nature is betrayed by what he or it does. For an instant she wanted to turn to Emerson and say, "Make him stop it!" An old instinct to rely on men—one that she thought she had erased from her being long ago—but there it was. She ignored it and said, "Although I never thought I would quote one of your heroes, Congressman, I find myself having to agree with Donald Rumsfeld. Synaesthetes allow us to understand what we don't know we don't know. They can point us toward new places to explore—new vistas in both human experience and human potential."

"Now you sound like NASA in the nineteen-sixties."

"As I recall, Congressman, NASA in the nineteen-sixties actually put a man on the moon—a feat to be sure—and not a useless one, Congressman."

To Yslan's surprise, Congressman Villianne smiled. The feral look had returned to the man's face, and his 'Thank you, Ms. Hicks' made the hairs on the back of her neck stand up.

The rest of the questioning was not so pointed, but everyone made it clear that she would have to seriously justify her budget before the committee met again in three months.

Two hours, and an unpleasant phone call to her boss, Leonard Harrison, later, Yslan found herself eyeing the bottle of Tennessee mash on the mirrored shelf on the other side of a Georgetown bar. Then Emerson Remi's shadow crossed the liquor bottle and she lost all interest in having a drink.

"Hicksy, a bit early for you if I remember correctly."

"You do—and you know you do, Emerson."

"Mind if I take a seat?" he asked as he sat on the bar stool beside her. "So what are the doofs over at NSA doing sticking you with this loser of an assignment?"

She smiled and turned to him. "That's classified information, Emerson, and, as a reporter, you should know that." But her smile had faded before she finished speaking. Why did it always feel like she was wearing the wrong clothes when she was with him? Because he was the best-looking thing in almost any room—like Alec Baldwin before he got fat and thought he was funny.

"Bourbon—got Woodbridge?" he said in the bartender's direction. As the bartender poured him the silky brown liquid, a waitress came by and put a plate of chicken fingers in front of Yslan. For a moment Yslan was going to claim that she hadn't ordered this but thought, fuck that, and said to the waitress, "Ketchup please." Then she smiled at Emerson—or did her best to smile.

"I could watch you eat chicken fingers forever."

"What do you want, Emerson?"

"Synaesthetes. Tell me all about you and the NSA and synaesthetes."

The waitress brought over a small cup of ketchup and put it down beside Yslan. "Bring the bottle, will ya?" The waitress gave a sigh and retreated to wherever waitresses retreat.

"How's your drink, Emerson?"

"Good. Woodbridge is very good. And your chicken fingers now that you have catsup?"

"I love that you say catsup and not ketchup."

"Ketchup is the brand name; the product name is catsup. Like Kleenex and tissue."

"Like fuck yourself and leave me alone?"

"Not exactly like that."

Yslan thought, *I can't wait until he gets old, puffy and bald.*

"A penny for your thoughts?"

"Oh, Emerson, you should know that a good southern girl's thoughts are worth well more than a penny."

The bottle of ketchup arrived—the waitress departed. Yslan tilted the bottle over her chicken fingers but nothing came out. She shook it—no ketchup. She then held it in her left hand, aimed carefully, and thumped the bottom with her right palm. A large glop spat from the bottle and landed on Emerson's white linen shirt—right over his nipple.

She laughed.

He didn't.

He finished his drink and said, "I'll be watching you, Hicksy, you and your freaky, geek friends. Because I can smell a story— and you and those weirdos stink of one." He turned and waved— he may have said ta-ta, but Yslan didn't hear it.

## 6

# DECKER TAKES A JOB, OR TWO OR THREE

DECKER TRIED TO RESIST BUT COULDN'T. HE HOPPED UP onto the sidewalk just south of the Junction, took out his touch-screen iPod and opened the Safari browser. The morning sun momentarily made the screen difficult to read. Then his fingers raced across the tiny keyboard as if they had a will of their own. The website came up quickly. Decker thought of it as his "sin" site—sin as in that which is punished, not syn as in synaesthetes.

The outsiders' part of the synaesthetes' website had the usual dry, offhanded definitions of synaesthesia and a link to Daniel Tammet's BBC videos. All very cold—analytical—for outsiders. Without a prompt Decker punched in his access code—Seth-comehome. The screen went black and stayed that way for well over a minute. Then within the blackness a square of denser blackness appeared over a square of lesser blackness. Decker thought of it as a clear reference to Mark Rothko's paintings. Then slowly, as in the paintings, the squares began to pulse—and images began to appear. Then came the feared words:

**WELCOME FELLOW TRAVELER**

Again without prompting, Decker supplied his second password, and the welcome disappeared to be replaced by a menu—but one unlike any other computer menu. This one was purposefully without order, misspelled, misaligned and confusing. It reminded Decker of a small notice he had seen years ago on a

New York City lamppost: INTERNATIONAL ESP CONFERENCE—IF YOU HAVE IT, YOU'LL KNOW WHEN AND WHERE.

Decker entered the main chat room, but he chose to lurk rather than participate. He'd never participated. It scared the bejeezus out of him when he heard his distant cousins "participate"—because "speak" would be the wrong name for what appeared before him on the screen. He actually thought of it as below him—as in he was looking down on it from some considerable height.

The first "speaker" put up a corner of an early Jackson Pollock painting—upside down—with the screeched comment: *Why is this art!!!*

Decker leaned against the wall of a building and watched his tiny screen. He'd never seen synaesthetes get this close to something this important before.

A barrage of comments followed, attempting to explain that which they did not understand. The Pollock painting was a foreign language to them, but one that was of interest—like something just beyond the horizon. Decker knew that the greatest of the abstract expressionists like Rothko had gone beyond the horizon and come back with their unearthly visions of another world.

Another screamed comment: *Is this really art?*

Decker knew that the only logical response to the Jackson Pollock painting was a Paul Klee canvas. To which a Larry Rivers mural should then follow. But the participants in the chat room didn't have a way of knowing that. These folks knew—no, that's wrong—they sensed that there was something important, something quintessential out there but couldn't figure out exactly what that something was.

Decker didn't leave his perch as the chatters fumbled and bumbled and missed the point—blind men in a darkened room.

He suddenly felt as if he was being watched.

He looked up from the tiny screen and across Bloor Street he saw a scruffy, fat man/boy. He was standing on top of the manhole that was the most southerly exit of the underground steam tunnel system that used to connect many buildings in the

Junction—Decker's house being one—to the old coal plant up by the abandoned train depot. Decker thought he knew all the panhandlers on Bloor West, but maybe this guy was new. Decker hoped the guy was willing to fight for his place on the sidewalks out here.

He clicked off his iPod and entered the fruit store near Runnymede. The prices were always good at this Asian market, but the quality varied. So he chose carefully then got into the somewhat long line.

The Korean woman at the cash register was screaming. The black woman ahead of him, shocked, clutched her $3.99 Nicaraguan pineapple to her chest. *Painful,* Decker thought, but so very Toronto—black woman, from her together appearance and middle-class demeanor probably Grenadian or Trinidadian, holding a piece of Central American fruit, shocked to her very marrow that the Korean woman had raised her voice to a white man— just shocked! *Verklempt,* Decker thought—the Yiddish word for "choked up" coming from the ancient recesses of his brain's storage bins. His atheist/Jewish mother used few Yiddish words, but *verklempt*—that she'd used. Good word, he thought—appropriate word.

The white man, who was the object of the Korean cashier's wrath, began to argue his case. "Bruised. They were all bruised."

"All?" the Korean woman huffed. "All apples . . . whole bushel bruised? Not possible."

"Did my son return the whole bushel?" the white man demanded.

"Yes, yesterday . . ."

"Then they were all bruised—the whole bushel."

"No! No. No. Not bruised when I sold him the bushel. Not bruised."

"If my son brought them back, then they were bruised."

"Then he bruised them."

"Nonsense."

"He bruised them when he peeled them."

"No. The machine that peels the apples takes only one at a time . . ."

The Grenadian or Trinidadian woman dropped her pineapple. It hit the floor but did not bounce. The Korean cashier stared at her, commanding her to pick up the Nicaraguan delight and daring her to claim that now it was bruised too.

In the meantime the white man was in the middle of a complicated explanation as to the mechanics of the apple peeling machine he used to make his pastries.

Decker allowed himself to slip forward into his facial mask and slowed his breathing. He looked up at the white man—about forty-five, married, unhappy, two boys, Austrian.

He stayed beneath the jet stream for a moment, listening to its whoosh above him, then, although he knew he shouldn't, entered it. He closed his eyes—three parallel lines. The man was telling the truth about the peeling machine's workings. Decker turned toward the Korean woman—although now hefty and virtually without an identifiable waist he sensed the presence of a thin girl, a domineering father, a rapacious uncle, tears, envy of dancers in midnight studios—and she too was telling the truth about the bushel of apples being without blemish when she sold them to the white man's son.

The shabbily dressed man Decker had seen on the other side of Bloor Street entered the store, eating from one of the two pints of Californian strawberries he held in his dirty hands.

Decker felt the man's presence before he saw him.

Then the man was pointing at Decker—gesticulating wildly in his direction. Decker suddenly felt as if the earth had moved beneath his feet, and he reached out to support himself against one of the tables holding papayas. Fortunately it accepted his weight with only a slight groan.

Two strong store workers rushed at the man with the strawberries and hustled him out of the shop.

When Decker looked up the man was gone; his two green

cardboard pint baskets emptied of their strawberry goodness lay on the ground near the door.

Before Decker could think about the man, the Korean cashier demanded, "Bring in the boy!"

For a second Decker thought she was talking about the man with the strawberries, then he remembered the bruised apple argument.

"Why should I bring in my son?" the Austrian replied.

*Because there is a liar here,* Decker thought, *but it's neither of you two.* The black woman slipped her pineapple back onto the shelf and took another. The Austrian swore he would never shop in this fruit market again. The Korean cashier said, "Your pastries no good anyways, and too expensive, much."

Decker smiled. Better this mixed-race city than the all-white one he had grown up in—even if you couldn't leave your bicycle unlocked on the street.

"Next, next here." The Korean woman tabulated the cost of the fruit in Decker's basket, then asked for $10.27. He went to reach for his credit card then realized two things. One, that his Visa card didn't seem to work anymore, and two, that this store didn't take credit cards—no fruit market took credit cards.

"Ten twenty-seven," she repeated. He handed over twenty dollars and, as she gave him his change, she announced, "Have a good day."

It sounded just a wee bit more like a command than a recommendation, but then again the meaning could easily have been lost in translation—just another multicultural moment.

Decker stepped out onto Bloor West and his cell phone rang.

"Yeah." Decker wasn't much for cell phone courtesy. He pressed the device hard to his ear, almost gave up, then shouted into the thing, "Yeah!"

"It's me."

"Eddie, you sound like you're calling from Poland or something."

"Nope. They've got better cell phone service in Poland than here."

"Here as in Toronto?"

"Malaysia has better service, so does China—and India, off the charts. Buddy, I think even western Borneo . . ."

"Nice to know that, Eddie . . ."

"When it comes to cell phone service, Hogtown is in the pig shit. But hey—*tempus fugit.*"

"I think you mean *'Sic transit gloria mundi.' 'Tempus fugit'* means 'time flies.' *Sic transit,* et cetera, means 'so goes the world'—or in your terms, 'pig shit happens.'"

"Always nice to know that someone cares about the dead stuff."

"Okay, Eddie, I'm tired. I taught late last night."

"Yeah, well, *sic fugit gloria*—and her sister if she has one."

"Eddie!"

"Okay. Three requests came in last night while you were doing whatever it is that you were doing."

"I was—"

"Yeah—and I thought you could get the twenty thousand dollars that Seth needs in one, two, three."

The only news he ever received about his son, Seth, Decker got through Eddie. He knew that Seth was out in western Canada somewhere. Where exactly he didn't know—Seth never told him. But the boy was nineteen, made his own decisions, lived his own life, and this was the very first time he'd ever asked for money. Decker thought of asking Eddie where Seth was, what his phone number was—and why suddenly he needed twenty thousand dollars. But Decker knew that Seth didn't want him to know any of these things and he knew that Eddie would never betray Seth's trust—certainly not the way that Decker had. He hoped against hope that Seth wanted the money to go to college, but he doubted it. Seth was intensely bright but way too independent a thinker to have a successful university career.

"So who wants what?"

"An Orlando firm wants you to watch the final vetting of a new head of sales before they give him the job. Willing to pay fifteen thousand dollars."

"Okay—no sweat, done that before."

"Then there's something in Pittsburgh for eleven thousand two hundred and ninety dollars, and a third thing in Cleveland for ten thousand."

"Eleven thousand two hundred and ninety dollars? Where did that figure come from?"

"Just call me wild and crazy."

"Crazy, sure—you've always been crazy."

"Fine. So?"

"Okay—sounds good."

"Yeah?"

"Yeah what, Eddie—I hear a but."

"Two t's or one?"

"One."

"I'm just concerned about the timing."

"Did you check the—"

"Airlines? Yeah—you can make the first two in one day if you're willing to fly a puddle jumper to Dallas to make your connection to Pittsburgh. It's tight but doable. And there's a wild outside chance you could even get from Cleveland to Toronto that same night. But I doubt it. I'll book you a hotel in Cleveland and get you a reservation on that late flight just in case—but the timing is way too tight, you'll never catch that one."

"Oh boy, a night in Cleveland—and second prize is two nights in Cleveland."

"Rock and Roll Hall of Fame is there, river on fire, Dennis Kucinich—hey, good times."

"Yeah."

"So I'll book you a hotel."

"You said that already, and there's still a 'but' hanging on here."

There was a moment of silence on the phone. Decker could hear Crazy Eddie inhale deeply—a little early for that, but what the hell. Finally Eddie said, "You've never had three requests at once."

"So—is three a bad-luck number or something?"

"No. But it's odd—three at once is odd. I have a bad feeling about this."

"More of that 'what I'm doing is dangerous' stuff?"

"What you are doing *is* dangerous stuff, Decker."

Decker thought about that. "They pay enough to get Seth his money?"

"With some to spare."

"Then set it up, Eddie—I don't teach again for two days, so this fits perfectly."

"Too perfectly."

"What's that supposed to mean?"

"I don't know."

"Me neither. Set it up, Eddie—a night in Cleveland somehow seems appropriate punishment for someone like me."

"Is there a trash can around you, Decker?"

"Yeah, it's Bloor West—more trash cans than stores open after eight o'clock."

"Then toss your cell into it and walk away. The forty-eight-hour rule is still in effect."

Eddie didn't trust cell phones, so he had Decker buy a new one every forty-eight hours. "Too bad, I was getting to like this one."

"The things we own end up owning us," Eddie said without a hint of sarcasm.

"That's from *Fight Club,* isn't it?"

"Very good, you're not as stupid as you look."

"Thanks, I guess . . ."

"My pleasure. Now dump that phone."

"Okay. Set it up, Eddie," Decker said and clicked off. Then he tossed his phone into the recycle section of the trash can—and walked away.

Eddie hung up the phone and lay back on his bed, amazed that his damaged leg was shaking wildly in its brace—something it hadn't done for years.

## 7

## YSLAN AT THE NSA

YSLAN MADE A DETOUR BEFORE RETURNING TO HER OFFICE, to the only place on the planet she thought of as holy—the Vietnam Veterans Memorial—and the imprint of her father's name on the obsidian surface, Sergeant Lernon Hicks: the father she'd never met, but the relative who she felt closest to.

She ran her fingers quickly over his name, and then as she had done so many times before she told him how her week had gone—her petty successes and her doubts about her present assignment.

And she knew in her heart that he had listened. She felt lighter—less alone.

At the office she passed through security quickly, then mounted the back stairs and shut her door before Leonard Harrison could get to her. She flipped open her computer and called up the important files she kept encrypted there. She read the transcript of Decker's last acting class lecture. She quickly cross-referenced the voyaging stuff in his talk with rest of his lectures they'd recorded over the past three and a half years. There were many previous examples.

But she couldn't remember him ever broaching the subject of secret names before.

She flashed her assistant a request for the video of Decker's lecture, then did a quick search for the topic of secret names among the more than two thousand pages of transcribed lectures they had from his classes. There were no previous references.

She thought about that for a moment—then about the secret name she'd had for herself for so many years.

The loud knock on her door announced that Harrison wanted to speak to her. "It's open."

Harrison strode into her office. He was holding two folders. "We need to talk about you and that congressional committee."

"Why?"

He was careful not to look too closely at her. Once he did, he knew he would find it hard to take his eyes off her. "Because without their money we're up a creek."

Yslan made a face and stood. "That's not really what you want to talk about, is it."

"No." He put the files on her desk—facedown.

"Then what?"

"Did you get the sense that the committee knew what we are really up to?"

"You mean the 'special talents' we've been tracking?"

"Of course I mean that. Did they buy it that we were tracking what you like to call silly synaesthetes?"

She thought about that—ran certain sequences back in her head. Finally she said, "For now. But they're not as stupid as they look. They know we're up to something."

"Great. Just fucking great! Have any of our analysts figured out anything more about Decker Roberts or the others—anything that gives us a clue as to how the hell they do what they do?"

Yslan hesitated, then said, "No. Sorry, but . . ."

Harrison flipped over the two folders; both had Arabic names on the covers and were designated top secret. "I need your guy Decker's help with these. And I need it soon."

"Why, is there an imminent–?"

"Not your purview!" He saw the shock on her face and had a momentary impulse to let her in on all this, then decided against it. "All you need to know is that one of these two assholes is telling the truth—but I don't know which one." He let out a long sigh, then said, "Get this Decker Roberts to work for us or figure out how he works."

"He's a Canadian . . ."

"So?"

"Do you want me to kidnap him?"

"Or seduce him or corral him or just fucking get him to tell you how he does it so we don't need him." As hard as it was for him to take his eyes off her, he looked past her out the window—all those people out there going about their business, relying on people like him to keep them safe. He turned and picked up the two folders from Yslan's desk and left the office without saying another word.

Yslan turned back to her computer and hit F6 and up came the day's reports on the doings of the "special talents" she had been tracking—she thought of it as handling—for the NSA for the past five years.

## 8

# ORLANDO, FLORIDA

"SO?" THE BALDING EXEC AT DECKER'S SIDE ASKED FOR THE third time.

Decker ignored the man, wondered why Disney had picked Orlando, then turned up the volume on the overhead speaker and stepped closer to the one-way mirror. On the other side of the glass, the company's fiftyish head of human resources was interviewing a well-dressed younger man.

Decker had already surmised that they were trying to fill a vacancy in their Paris office that controlled their vast European sales force. He didn't bother learning more, since further information wasn't essential to the successful completion of his work and the subsequent pocketing of the giant company's $15,000.

Decker felt the small digital recorder taped to his right thigh. It calmed him. For a moment he had a visual of John Dean at the Watergate hearings saying, "Oh yes, everything said in the Oval Office is recorded." It was his favourite YouTube clip, even though it happened when he was only a kid. He played it over and over again, always astonished by the naïveté—or was it just the honesty—of the man.

It reminded him that there was a time when actors imitated the way real people acted, unlike today, when everyone you meet seems to be trying to imitate some performance they've seen on television. Cabbies act like the smart alecks they see on the tube—cops wouldn't know how to walk without *NYPD Blue*; doctors imitate versions of *ER*—all backward. All of it. So that

John Dean's naïveté seemed one of the last honest acts in a desperately dishonest world.

He put his fingertips on the thick glass. The two men on the other side continued their conversation. Decker slowed his breathing. Instantly he felt the cold approach, then the weight in his right hand. He closed his eyes, allowing the light to filter through his lashes—and watched. He tilted his head, and the clarity flew up his nostrils, hit his upper brain stem and played out on his retina screen. He saw—and he knew—beyond doubt. Beyond scientific certainty. Beyond all reason.

"So?" the bald exec demanded for the fourth time.

Decker felt the cold retreat, but it took longer this time. Every time he "went up," the cold was just a little more intense and lasted just a little longer—and his suspicion increased.

Decker stepped away from the glass, flexed his right hand and opened his eyes.

"You're supposed to be the expert—so tell me already!"

Decker reached up and turned off the overhead speaker, then picked up his coat. "Do you have my money?"

"Yes. In cash, as you asked."

"I should charge more now that our dollar is worth as much as yours."

"I have the agreed upon fifteen thousand dollars in U.S. currency. So tell me."

This one was simple—too simple? Decker dismissed the thought. He didn't care. This company made more money in a year than some third-world countries made in a decade. He held out his hand. The bald man passed over the money.

"Thanks," Decker said, pocketing the cash. "Your applicant isn't telling the truth. He's not an idiot, so he's trying to cleverly not tell the truth, but clearly he's not telling the truth. He could be lying, prevaricating, equivocating, paltering or just plain old fibbing. I really couldn't tell you which. What I know is when people tell the truth—and he isn't."

"How do you know that—something he did or the way he spoke or moved or what?"

Ah, that television stuff about fingers twitching and eye movements betraying a liar. Decker liked the actor on that show, Tim Roth. Thought he was an amazing talent. But the show was based on a bogus premise. Yes, a person can learn, with years and years of practice, to piece together the physical manifestations of those who might be lying, but it's far more art than science, and the margin of error even for those who are really good at it is way too high for it to be of any real use. Humans are just too damned varied in their response to any given stimulus. And the kinesics notion of establishing a baseline of behaviour simply has too many assumptions in it to be reliable. Kinesics is just good guessing, period. But the TV show was fun—voodoo hoodoo—but fun.

"My job's done here," Decker said as he headed toward the door. But at the door—for no particular reason; just a moment of ego burst—he stopped and said, "And so's your interviewer, by the way. Not telling the truth, that is."

Decker did what he thought of as "escaping" from the Orlando office tower by heading to the basement and exiting through a crash door. Outside he took the USB key from his digital recorder, put it in a preaddressed and stamped envelope and popped it into a U.S. Mail box. Then, as Eddie had instructed, he took three different cabs and just made his flight. It would get him to Dallas, where he'd grab his flight to Pittsburgh.

He'd directed plays in the regional theatres of the American South, and he was a fan of southern writers. The South seemed to be, in its own way, in touch with an "otherness" that Decker recognized, so he found himself anxious to watch the magic of the South just beyond the plexiglass window of this three-seat-across puddle jumper.

The engine roared as the plane bounced into flight, although it never bothered to break the cloud cover.

And the magic of the South did come into view—the land lost its green as the plane scudded westward and the white beaches of the Florida Panhandle painter-taped the coast. Industrial patches sprouted by the water—petroleum and its invariable partner, pharmaceuticals.

Then the mighty Mississippi River segued into hundreds of snakelets heading home—to the sea. A sudden mist along the Gulf obscured the division between land and sea and then, before the modern, haunted pall of Dallas, ancient myths loose their emanations and dragged you inland toward the Deep South. An old land in a new world, where corpses lie in shallow graves—and never get to tell their tales. Beyond it the new Industrial South beckoned—telling you to forget the old and embrace the new—but its argument is not convincing. The shining towers of the insurance industry only distract from the underworld, the real Deep South, where ancient, ivory-white bones poke through the ground in winter rains.

Decker watched, knowing there was something important here, something he needed to understand—to be able to understand himself.

As Decker settled back to watch the Mississippi, Henry-Clay Yolles tracked his every move. From what he thought of as his "big chair" he watched the replay of the interview on one screen and read Decker's response on another. He thought, *Very impressive, Mr. Decker Roberts, very impressive indeed.*

## 9

## THE FURTHER VOYAGE OF
## MICHAEL SHEDLOSKI

MIKE WASN'T SURE IT HAD BEEN DECKER IN THE FRUIT SHOP. Things were getting mixed up—off balance—in his head. Now he was standing on another manhole cover staring at a lamppost—or that's what it looked like to anyone who was passing by. Some sad misbegotten man, crying his eyes out under a lamppost on Annette Street in the Junction in West Toronto.

That's what it looked like from outside.

From inside Mike saw the boy struggling against the rope. Reaching up and trying to relieve the tension on his neck—to stop himself from strangling.

Then the boy turned toward him and held out his hand. Mike saw the fingernails—the boy's fingernails—the painted fingernails and his face.

He stepped back then he heard the gurgle. *Death really does have a rattle,* he thought. Then he looked around him. Across the way the old library. Beside it the Masonic Temple. Down the block the old Heintzman House, but here the lamppost from which a fourteen-year-old boy had hung by the neck until death.

There was always evil around the portals. Mike knew that. And churches nearby trying to fend it off. But the evil was winning— Mike could feel it. He needed to find Decker and warn him, or else he could be hung from a lamppost like that poor boy had been more than a hundred years ago.

# 10

## PITTSBURGH

DECKER SAT IN AN INTERNET CAFÉ—PLACES HE ALWAYS thought of as al-Qaeda cafés—just down the road from the Pittsburgh Public Theater, and tried to recall what play he had directed there; something by Christopher Durang or maybe it was Joe Orton, he couldn't remember. Back then he was directing six or seven plays a year—often reading the script for the first time on the plane the day before rehearsals started.

Decker always liked Pittsburgh. He admired the people who had toughed it out after the big steel mills closed down. Those who remained loved their hometown and the surrounding countryside. And they'd made themselves a clean, smart little city.

He checked his watch; he still had more than half an hour to kill before his second of three truth-telling sessions.

He looked up—nothing but potential terrorist operatives and teenagers playing games their folks wouldn't let them play at home. Fine.

His fingers opened the synaesthetes web site as if they were leading and Decker was just along for the ride. He entered the chat room—and lurked. For a moment the screen was blank then a video popped up. A young monk stood, back to the camera, in a perfectly cylindrical, domed building. The young man tilted his head back and sang a pure note up into the dome. Nothing happened for a second, then a cascading ring of echoes one after the other came down toward him. Before the first reached him he sang a second note, this one a third higher than the first, followed quickly by a third note a fifth higher than the first. Then he opened his arms and whole chords of music—in echo—wrapped around him.

Decker stood, amazed, because he thought, just for a moment, that the young monk, bathed in the chords of the oddly familiar liturgical music, rose off the floor and floated in midair.

Decker looked around. One strange creature had turned toward him, then shrugged and returned to his screen.

Decker sat and punched in his tertiary code, which led him to what he thought of as a small side room off the main chat room, what Eddie called their "blocked" room. He signed in again and sent the electronic tone that would summon his friend.

In under a minute Eddie's unique script bibbled across the bottom of the blank page: *If you're asking why your son needs the money, don't! I've already told you that Seth swore me to secrecy. And I won't betray that trust and you know I won't, so don't ask me to. How was Orlando?*

Decker was tempted to walk away but typed: *Fine.*

*Pittsburgh, Cleveland then home—piece of a cakewalk.*

Decker could sense Eddie smiling as he unapologetically mixed metaphors. *Yeah,* he wrote.

*You're not using your own computer. Why?*

*Cause.*

*With all you have to say you should write a blog.*

*True,* Decker typed, then hit the disconnect button, paid for his time and left the café.

His second truth-telling session was in a nondescript office tower downtown. He scouted the back of the building and found a side exit through the ground floor's janitorial station. Then he established that there were U.S. Mail slots on every fourth floor.

He took the elevator up to the forty-second floor, identified himself as David Rose to the attractive older woman there. She handed him a file and indicated that he should follow her.

They entered a small room with an industrial table, a monitor and a set of headphones.

"I need to be able to see," he said.

She parted the curtain on the wall and there was a clear glass pane.

"One-way mirror?"

"Yes."

"Russian?" he asked her.

"Kazakhstani, but my Russian is very good—I'll translate for you if it's necessary."

Soon the light in the next room came on, and a young pale-faced man entered and took a seat at a long table. He fidgeted.

"Sergei Lomotov. He plays for the Penguins," the woman beside him said.

Okay, Decker thought. Russian hockey player, a left-winger if his memory served him. He looked to her. "What's your name?" Decker asked.

"Luska."

"Okay. Luska, who else is—" But before he could finish his question the door of the other room opened and two men in grey suits entered. They were followed by a guy Decker recognized as the Pittsburgh Penguins general manager—a classic Canadian prairie-hardened man. Then in came an older man who sat beside the hockey player and patted his hand. European, Decker thought. "His translator?" he asked Luska.

She nodded.

"And them?" Decker asked indicating the two guys in grey suits.

"Investigators."

Okay, Decker thought.

The opening set of questions to the young Russian hockey player were just basic data: place of birth, schooling, early hockey experience, and his time with Moscow Dynamo. He answered all of them truthfully.

Luska's fingers flew across her computer keyboard, transcribing the dialogue word for word.

Decker looked out the window to clear his head. Below them

was the confluence of the Allegheny, Monongahela, and Ohio rivers. Three Rivers Stadium used to be there—now there's PNC Park. What's a PNC anyways?

Then one of the investigators asked if the kid knew a man named Boris Barionofky.

The young player dodged. He was truthful but circumspect.

Suddenly the interrogators' questions began to come more quickly, often not waiting for the translator to complete his response. Without any segue, the nature of the questions changed.

Way more accusatory.

"How many times have you met Boris Barionofky?"

"When was the last time you met him?"

"Who else was in the room with you two?"

"What exactly was discussed?"

"Has he contacted you since you came to America?"

"When was that?"

"Did you meet or speak on the phone?"

The translator pleaded with them to give Sergei a chance to answer the questions. The head investigator turned on him. "Keep your fucking mouth shut. Sergei understands English well enough to answer our damned questions. Don't you, Sergei?"

The boy looked around wildly, clearly trying to find a place of safety in this cage of lions.

Then the interrogator tossed three photographs onto the table.

Luska reached into a folder and handed copies of the same three pictures to Decker.

Each clearly showed the young hockey player with a barrel-chested middle-aged man.

The hockey player suddenly stood and shouted something in Russian.

Decker turned to Luska, "My sister is . . ."

"Sick. He said, 'My sister is sick and needs help.'"

Then there was a moment of silence in the room.

The general manager swore softly. The interrogators looked at each other, then left the room.

Decker turned to Luska. "Give me your transcription." She did. "Come back in ten minutes."

She got up and left the room. Decker quickly read through the transcript and underlined the truths. The others he noted were some sort of lies. Probably just equivocations he thought, but it wasn't his job to decide.

He opened the door and called for Luska. He handed her the transcription and explained what his notations meant. She thanked him and handed him a thick envelope—$11,290.

Decker stuffed the envelope with the money into his shoulder bag and headed toward the elevator, but when Luska turned away from him he ducked down the escape stairway, went through the crash door on the thirty-sixth floor and was about to deposit his self-addressed envelope with the USB key for this interview into the U.S. Mail slot there when he thought better of it and pocketed the thing. He raced down the remaining thirty-six flights. After switching cabs three times he got to the Pittsburgh International Airport in beautiful downtown Coraopolis, PA.

Henry-Clay wanted to clap his fat little hands, but he thought the better of it. He clicked off the images on the flat-screen TVs mounted on his office wall and said to the air, "Even when he doesn't speak the language. Even then he knows a truth from a lie." Henry-Clay flicked off the video player and threw his copy of Decker's annotated transcript toward the circular wastebasket against the wall. It hit the far side and rimmed out. He rolled his office chair over, grabbed the transcript, dunked it, raised his arms, and announced, "Three-pointer!"

Then Henry-Clay punched a button on his console. "When's he getting to Cleveland?"

## 11

## CLEVELAND, OHIO

AFTER A HALF-HOUR FLIGHT HIS PLANE TOUCHED DOWN, and twenty minutes after that, Decker entered the main offices of the *Cleveland Plain Dealer* and approached the front desk. "You have a package for David Gerts."

The security guard asked for ID.

Decker showed him his fake David Gerts driving license and took the package.

"Room two oh seven, down the hall and up the stairs." Decker nodded. "Welcome to the *Plain Dealer,* Cleveland's finest daily newspaper."

Decker suspected two things. One, that the guy hated having to say that to everyone he served, and two, that the *Cleveland Plain Dealer* was very likely Cleveland's only daily newspaper. As he made his way up the stairs to room 207 he wondered if a plain dealer was a forthright merchant or perhaps a guy who sells farmland or a very boring seller of used cars. At room 207 he clicked on his tiny digital tape recorder and opened the door to yet another office.

A secretary nodded a greeting and led him to a boardroom.

Two *Plain Dealer* staff writers were interviewing a man Decker recognized as the Republican senatorial candidate.

Decker was introduced as a researcher sent from the head office—better than when he used to be flown in as a play doctor and spent his time in the light booth putting together notes for the show's producers who didn't have the balls to tell the director that Decker was there to replace him.

The interview proceeded. Decker took notes and closed his eyes over and over again. And when he did the room unaccountably got cold, and for a moment his wife's stricken face shrouded in veil upon veil of ALS came alive in his mind—only her eyes able to move, staring at him, accusing him, imploring him to answer the last question she had ever been able to ask him: "What have you done, Decker? What have you done?"

"I'm sorry if I bore you," the politician said.

Decker opened his eyes and realized the man's comment was to him.

"You don't, sir. I have an eye infection that requires I close my eyes periodically to keep them lubricated." Decker thought, *Lie better.* So he added, "Doctor's orders." And thought, Shit—*I really am a lousy liar.*

The senatorial candidate shot Decker a look, then continued his pontification on subjects ranging from *Roe v. Wade* to the Iranian nuclear threat.

After the interview finally ended a secretary plunked down almost thirty pages of transcript in front of Decker. It took him only a minute to underline the two untruths.

He stepped out of the room and gave the transcript to the secretary. She gave him a thick envelope with the name David Gerts on the outside—and $10,000 in cash inside.

He made his way out of a side door and checked his watch.

It was tight, but he really didn't want to spend the night in Cleveland. He hailed a cab and threw fifty dollars on the front seat. "Get me to the airport—fast."

He ignored Crazy Eddie's three-cab rule and, with his fast cab and the flight's forty-minute delay in departure, he just made the flight to begin his voyage first to Detroit and from there on the eleven o'clock flight to Toronto—and his home in the west end of the city, the Junction.

●  ●  ●

Henry-Clay watched the videotape of the interview and checked it against a copy of Decker's notes. The entire transcript was marked as truthful except for two statements. The first was, "Young men, I have a wholehearted and spiritually backed commitment to the values that made this country great—family values."

"Yeah, Senator, family *über alles,*" Henry-Clay muttered, then added, "and what about those hookers in Huff you were taped with?" No great surprise that was a lie. Seventeen pages later Decker had marked his second and final statement as an untruth when the would-be senator stated his "one hundred and five percent opposition to the sale of Internet drugs from Canada into these here United States." There were twenty-six more pages of claims and boasts, but none were marked as lies.

"Very good, Mr. Roberts—very, very good. So you can pick out a single lie buried in hundreds of truths, half truths, and opinions—like finding a kernel of corn in a barrel of cow shit. I do believe we can do business, Mr. Roberts."

Henry-Clay stood. He'd made up his mind. He turned to the window and eyed the Treloar Building on the other side of the Ohio River. The tall building was bathed in golden light by the setting late autumn sun.

He caught his reflection in the window and said to it, "He's our new one—I can feel it."

The light on the squawk box on his desk blinked. Henry-Clay liked the look of old technology; it made him feel that he was the direct descendant of all the other great capitalists going all the way back to the robber barons. He pushed a button on the old thing.

"Yeah?"

"Mr. MacMillan is on the line, sir."

He checked his watch. Right on time, as usual.

"Good. Patch him through." He loved saying that.

Henry-Clay quickly gave MacMillan Decker Roberts' flight

details. "I know you had men on him, but I want you to follow him personally, Mr. MacMillan. This is our new boy, Mr. MacMillan, and I want to know everything, and I mean *everything,* about him."

Henry-Clay smiled. He felt like he was steering a great ship—he liked steering the ship. It had always been his experience that motion was better than stillness. Motion solved problems. Motion made money.

# 12

## *MAC*

MAC TOOK NO CHANCES. HE'D BEEN WAITING AT THE CLEVE-land airport just in case Roberts made the last connection to Toronto.

When Decker entered the departure lounge, Mac turned on his tiny video camera. He lifted his copy of *USA Today* to cover his face, although he thought it unlikely that Decker Roberts had any idea that he was being followed—and had been followed by Mac's men from the moment that Henry-Clay Yolles had told him of Decker Roberts' existence.

# 13

## *MIKE AT DECKER'S HOUSE*

SO MANY CHURCHES AND RIGHT AROUND THE CORNER from Decker's house. They must have known—they must have felt the evil a long time ago. Mike could feel it. So many churches and other religious buildings on Annette, Runnymede, and Dundas. He'd memorized the names, and as he prepared to spend his third night waiting for Decker he recited them—as if he were saying the rosary: Keele Street Christian Church, St. Cecilia's Catholic Church, High Park Korean United Church, Vida Abundante Igreja Pentecostal Portuguesa, Czechoslovak Baptist Church, Church of the Nazarene, the Sharing Place, Gracia de Dios Iglesia Cristiana del Nazareno, Runnymede Presbyterian Church, St. James Catholic Church. Then again and again as darkness took the city and Mike wondered if he was strong enough to withstand another night out in the cold. But he had to. He had to be there when Decker got back from wherever he was. He had to warn Decker.

Warn him that he was going to be used by the Enemy—as he had been used.

The Enemy had found us and now was using us.

He looked around, worried that he had spoken out loud. And there were a lot of dogs on Decker's street. He liked dogs—all dogs—but some dogs didn't like him. Then there was Decker's motion-sensitive porch light. He had to avoid that. He had to remember that light.

He curled up behind the recycle bin in the alley at the side of Decker's house. There was a steam pipe there that gave off some heat. He got as close to it as he could. Then he began to recite his rosary again: Keele Street Christian Church, St. Cecilia's Catholic Church, High Park Korean United Church, Vida Abundante Igreja Pentecostal Portuguesa, Czechoslovak Baptist Church, Church of the Nazarene, the Sharing Place, Gracia de Dios Iglesia Cristiana del Nazareno, Runnymede Presbyterian Church, St. James Catholic Church and on and on into the night.

Just past one in the morning Decker walked from his cab toward his turn-of-the century house in the Junction. Twenty seconds later Mac parked his car and put a stub of a cigar in the corner of his mouth. He settled in to watch. Mac was good at watching.

Mike heard first one car, then another pull up in front of Decker's house. He hunched back into the shadows and prayed that it was Decker. He was so cold and things were getting mixed up in his head. He saw a man get out of a cab and start up the slanted driveway toward the front door. It must be Decker. It had to be Decker. And Mike was cold—so cold. He recited his rosary one more time quickly, then bolted from his hiding place—forgetting about the motion-sensor porch light.

Decker saw the porch light snap on, a blur of movement cross it, and a large shadowy thing was right up in his face, grabbing his coat and shouting at him. "He's got the ratio!"

Decker felt instantly nauseous—as if he were falling down a cavernous well.

Mac saw the shouting shadow at the same time Decker did. But he wasn't nauseous—he was astounded.

Mike stepped aside, and the porch light struck Decker's face. For a moment Mike couldn't speak—it was the same face, but an older version, of the boy hung from the lamppost. Finally he managed to shout, "He's using us. The Enemy's got the ratio, my ratio, the ratio—and my master ratio—no, my master password. He's found you. Don't you see! Secret ratio, secret password. Secret, secret, secret. Oh, no. Oh, no. Oh, no. Don't you see? Ratio. Don't you? Password. How many times do I have to tell you?

How many times! I gave it to him. Both. I betrayed us. Betrayed us all. Don't you see?"

Decker saw the flabby lips moving but was so overwhelmed by nausea that all he heard was the word "ratio." He was about to be sick—fuck, he was going to throw up.

Mac reached for the handgun and the bowie knife beneath the seat. This was not happening. Not happening on his watch. He threw open the car door.

The light from inside the car drew Mike's eye.

For an instant, Decker saw the fat man's face. Then he heard a car door slam and the light blinked out.

The Enemy's assassin! And then Mike was running, crashing through fences, running and running and reciting his rosary.

Decker found himself on the cold interlocking bricks of his driveway and suddenly felt better. He looked around and saw the taillights of a sedan speeding down the street, and the fat thing, whatever it was, was gone. He got to his feet and scanned the street, and all was as it had always been—the old, stodgy Junction. He thought of calling the police, then let it go. He wasn't hurt, hadn't been robbed. Some poor, crazed thing had . . . he didn't know what it had done. As he climbed the steps to his house he said aloud, "Using a ratio? What the fuck!" He looked around again to make sure that "the thing" wasn't there, then he opened the door—and was home.

# 14

## HENRY-CLAY'S DECISION

"AND YOU'RE SURE IT WAS RATIO-MAN?" HENRY-CLAY DE-manded.

Mac pulled the BlackBerry away from his ear—his boss was shouting, no, screaming. "Yeah, it was him. I told you we should have dealt with him, not just fired him."

Henry-Clay took a deep breath—then a few more. He had to calm himself. He had to think. "Mr. MacMillan—what exactly did you hear him tell Roberts?"

Mac repeated it pretty much as Mike had said it—using us, told him the ratio, etc.

Henry-Clay thought about that. Then about the ratio. Then about the potential lawsuits, nightly ads on television encouraging liars to join a class action against Yolles Pharmaceuticals, years of litigation—fucking lawyers up his nose, down his throat, inside his head—massive stock losses—and he's right on the edge of a gold mine, an antidepressant-inspired gold mine—looking into a pure vein of money! He thought about all that . . . then about murder. "Mr. MacMillan, Ratio-Man knows too much."

"Granted, but what about what Decker Roberts just heard?"

Henry-Clay paused. Decker Roberts could be a valuable asset, and he was loath to let go of an asset.

Mac pressed, "He knows, Mr. Yolles—and unlike Ratio-Man he's not a nut, so people might take what he has to say seriously."

Henry-Clay nodded in his darkened office but didn't reply.

"He knows too much to live, Mr. Yolles."

Henry-Clay let out a long breath. Killing Ratio-Man was more like putting a dog down, but killing Decker Roberts would be crossing a new frontier for the owner of Yolles Pharmaceuticals.

"Is it really necessary, Mr. MacMillan?"

"It's prudent, Mr. Yolles. Prudent."

"And there's no other way?"

"To be sure that this Roberts guy doesn't talk? Not that I know. Just his bad luck, Mr. Yolles, just Mr. Roberts' bad luck."

Henry-Clay thought about that, tried to weigh the risks against each other—killing versus his bottom line—and made up his mind. He felt better—Decisions R Us. "Your report on the Junction says there's been a lot of fires, Mr. MacMillan."

"Seems there's a firebug in those parts."

"Good, that'll cover our tracks. Burn him down, Mr. MacMillan— he lives in an old house, doesn't he?"

"Yeah."

"Well, old houses have fire problems, don't they?"

"They do indeed. When?"

"Can it be done tonight?"

"For the right amount of money, anything can be done. Tonight or any night."

"Tonight. Decker Roberts does not see the dawn—got it, Mr. MacMillan?"

Henry-Clay slammed down the phone, stood and made himself think it all through carefully one more time. Mac would take care of Decker up there, then come down here and take care of Ratio-Man, but there was a loose end. How the hell had Ratio-Man found out that he was scouting Decker? Henry-Clay allowed his mind to retrace his steps from seeing Mikey on the Discovery Channel while drunk in Puerto Rico to tracking him down—to setting up the fake job interview.

It had taken Henry-Clay less than twenty minutes to get Ratio-Man to address the issue of placebo ratios—in fact, the guy was happy if anyone listened to him. And oh, yes, Henry-Clay Yolles was listening closely.

"Well, there has to be a ratio. Everything in nature has a ratio."

"Placebos as well?"

"Surely."

"And would you be able to establish that exact ratio, Mr. Shedloski?"

"Sure. It'd be fun."

Henry-Clay had offered him a job then and there. Mike had beamed—he'd found a friend.

And within a few weeks of examining Yolles Pharma's research and Henry-Clay's MA thesis on "The Use of Placebos in Pharmaceutical Pricing," Michael Shedloski had entered Henry-Clay Yolles' office and pronounced an astonishing figure—a ratio of placebo pills to real pills well in excess of four times the accepted, although never used, figure. It posed a potential savings of almost 40 percent on every package of pills—risk free to the client, and more important without costing Yolles Pharma almost anything.

"And you're sure of this?" Henry-Clay had demanded. "Sure as your life—you're sure of this ratio?"

"Absolutely. People like me know this sort of thing."

Henry-Clay remembered pausing for a moment and rolling around the idea of "people like me" and asked as calmly as he could manage, "And there are more people like you out there?"

Mike stuck out his chest and proudly announced, "I meet them every day on the website I set up for us, in the chat rooms." He almost giggled, then added, "And, I installed a program that saves the e-mail and IP addresses of everyone who's ever accessed the site. I'm not supposed to, but I did and I have them—everyone, broken down by time of day and frequency. Why shouldn't I? After all, it's our website, for people like me." Then Ratio-Man had put his hand to his mouth just like he was a kid who'd just sworn in front of his parents.

"I didn't know you were a computer genius too."

Henry-Clay saw the man retreat. "I'm not. I don't know anything about computers. Oh, my goodness, I shouldn't have told you that. Promise me you'll keep it a secret. Promise me, please." The poor man seemed ready to pee his pleated corduroys.

And Henry-Clay had given Ratio-Man the five-hundred-dollar bonus he'd promised for the ratio and told him what a fine fellow he was and metaphorically scratched his scruffy tummy, then said, "Here are the keys to my condo. Why not spend the night there—as a present from me. A way of saying thanks."

Mike took the keys and stuttered something to the effect that "it's really, very, you know, nice of you . . ."

But before Ratio-Man could finish whatever it was he was trying to say, Henry-Clay added, "And there'll be a present there—just waiting for you to unwrap."

Mikey loved presents—really loved them. So with more attempts at thanks and twice almost forgetting the keys to the condo, he finally got to the office door and said, "But you won't tell about that website thing, will you?"

Henry-Clay made a lip-zipping mime and a throwing-away-the-key gesture—and Mike smiled and left the office.

Without a pause Henry-Clay dialed the nastiest hooker he'd ever met and asked her if she'd like to make an easy $1,500.

"Nothin's easy with you, darlin'."

"I'm not the client. I'm the bank account but not the client."

"So who's the client?"

He told her, then informed her that he wanted her to wear an ocular implant and a mini camera attached to her choker.

"That's kinky even for you."

"Yeah—so?"

"Sure. Where and when?"

When Michael Shedloski opened the door to Henry-Clay's condo the first thing he saw was a partially clad Nasty Natasha—née, Linda Lee Feldman. Henry-Clay had sat back in his big chair and watched the view from a hooker's vantage point. He found it instructive—and exciting. But it was the cochlear microphone that allowed him to feed the hooker lines; that really thrilled him.

When Ratio-Man's pants were down around his knees and his none-too-clean jockeys bulging appropriately he whispered to Natasha, "Tell him if he touches himself you're leaving."

She did and he whimpered that he wouldn't touch himself.

"Good," Henry-Clay said, and Natasha repeated that.

"Ask him if he'd like you to touch him."

She did—and he certainly did.

"Fine. Now tell him that he has something that you want. And until you get it you won't touch him now or ever."

Henry-Clay was enjoying this. He told himself that he was accessing his feminine side—then laughed at the very idea that he had a feminine side.

"What? What do I have that you want?" Ratio-Man pleaded.

"The access codes to the synaesthetes website and his master password," Henry-Clay said.

Mike resisted for a few moments, but Linda Lee Feldman was hard to resist, and Henry-Clay carefully jotted down the complex algorithmic codes that allowed him to take control of the website—and allowed Mike a sexual experience that was going to have to last him for quite some time.

The first thing Henry-Clay did on the website was use the algorithm to change the master passwords so Ratio-Man couldn't access the site.

Once in control of the website Henry-Clay explored for other people like Mike. First in the chat rooms—then in the captured e-mail and IP addresses. And he'd found some weird-assed wackos but no one of any value—until he followed a hunch. There was a frequent user from Canada who never entered the chat rooms but spent a lot of time on the site. Where was he on the site? Lurking, sure, but lurking that long? He accessed the map of the site and noticed a surprisingly blank area. He waited for the next time the Canadian signed in and followed him—tracked him—to a blocked side room on the website's empty space. There he found his Canadian user—Decker Roberts.

Henry-Clay approached his office window. Across the river the Treloar Building was bathed in floodlights. He pulled his eyes away from the building and returned to the problem at hand.

Somehow Ratio-Man had found that he had made contact with Roberts. How? Was it possible that wimp hadn't given Nasty Nat the only access codes to the site? No, he'd have given his left nut—maybe did. So it had to be something else.

He thought about the first time he saw Ratio-Man on TV, standing beside his incredible balancing statues. Totally symmetrical, he thought—and just like that he had it. Of course: Ratio-Man was also Balance-Man, and he wouldn't create a website without another in perfect balance with it—a mirror site!

Sure, Ratio-Man would have an equal and opposite site. A balance. Fuck. That's how he must have found out about Henry-Clay's plan for one Decker Roberts.

Henry-Clay quickly went up online and in less than five minutes found the mirror site. He cursed his foolishness and was tempted to throw the computer through the plate glass window.

But no. Decker dies in the fire tonight. Then fat Mike ends his days and the threat is over. Henry-Clay put his right hand up to the cold windowpane then drew it away. As he lifted his palm, the frosted imprint of his hand remained, then slid mistlike into oblivion, another place—no, *the* other place. Now it was only a fleeting memory of a hand on a glass pane. A flicker of life gone forever.

*A death,* Henry-Clay thought. Then he corrected himself. *Two deaths.*

It was getting cold out there—in more ways than one.

Back in the Junction, Mac flipped open his Zippo and lit his stump of a cigar, which was still in the side of his mouth. He watched the end of the cigar accept the flame then breathed out a dense fragrant fog of smoke against the frosted windshield as he told himself, *Tonight's a fine night for a wee conflagration.*

## 15

# NIGHTMARES

DECKER KNEW HE WAS DREAMING, DREAMING OF SHANGHAI in the early 1990s before many Chinese spoke English—before they entered the capitalist race to oblivion. He knew what the dream was, but he couldn't make it stop.

A Caucasian face loomed up, filling the entirety of his dreamscape screen. "Don't take anything but ten U.S. dollars. No wallet. No wristwatch. No jewelry."

Decker felt the cold, then something in his hand and looked down—blood. He knew it was part of the price for his gift. Then there was an address on Nanjing Lu.

He watched helplessly as he left his wedding ring, watch, and wallet in his room, waited for the dark to take the great city, then stuffed a single American ten-dollar bill in a front pocket of his jeans and headed toward the Bund.

Suddenly he felt something smooth between his lips and tasted the divine mix of opium tar and human saliva. He breathed the smoke in deeply. Time began to slip—and elongate—and he knew he was dreaming in his dream—and he felt the presence of the other.

Then he was out on the street. The damp Shanghai night air knifed through his clothing. He stumbled to the curb and hailed a taxi from the waiting line of vehicles. The lead cab pulled up to him and the window slid down. He reached into his pocket for the card given to him by the theatre to explain where he lived—but it wasn't there. His wallet wasn't there either. He remembered! He'd left the wallet with the card and all his money back in his room. He stepped away from the taxi. The driver screamed something at him. He turned and ran. His feet flying along the cracked pavement, then suddenly he was at the river—at the river? How had he gotten to the Huangpu River? He turned to his left and headed in the other direction.

The tile-roofed buildings of the old city seemed to loom forward, crowding the street. He felt hundreds of eyes, angry eyes, watching him. A man held his daughter's hand as she lifted her skirts and peed on the sidewalk. Then he shouted. Had he been staring? Where the hell was he? He headed back uptown—made a sharp left and there was the river again! The river?

How late was it? He looked to his wrist. No watch of course. Lost—utterly lost in Shanghai, in the middle of the night, without money, without identification, without even knowing what the time was—adrift in a vast foreign sea and the opium snake still alive and now very, very angry in his veins.

A sharp female voice stopped him. He turned. The tiny peasant woman dressed in filthy rags stepped out of the blackness of the alley as she always did. She held a baby so dirty that it looked like it was made of mud. Her left hand was outstretched toward him, clearly begging for money. He stepped back, his heel hit the curb, and he found himself on the ground.

Then the mud baby was on his chest.

He looked up and the woman was speaking, and despite his extremely limited Mandarin he understood every word. "This child is you. Has always been you. And will always be waiting here for you. You will return to the filth that you came from. If you refuse to do what must be done, you will be abandoned by your friends and family—lost in a dark room that has no windows and no doors. And you will search—endlessly—for a way out. But you will never find the way out. Everything you fear will happen to you—as it has happened to this child."

He suddenly realized that he was seeing the woman from an odd angle. This was fucking new! With a cold shock he knew that he was seeing the peasant from the baby's eyes. Then those eyes turned, and there he was—crazed, banging his head over and over and over against a wall. Tears staining his cheeks—a scream in his throat. Then an older voice—his older voice—pleaded, "I couldn't do it! But please don't forget me, please don't forget me here." And he held up his left hand and there was blood—and he shivered from the cold.

And he knew it was a dream, and he knew the dream was part of the burden of his gift, and he knew that one night he would dream the dream and never awaken from the nightmare.

Then he smelled the smoke. There was no smoke in his dream, but he smelled smoke. Then he felt intense heat rising through the floor of his second-story bedroom floor.

Decker threw aside his bedcovers. The tendrils of smoke coming through the bedroom walls immediately shocked him into the present.

He flipped the light switch—nothing. But in the orange glow of the growing fire on his balcony he could see billows of smoke swirling into his bedroom from under the door. When he stood the floor was warm—fuck, it was hot. He reached for the door handle to the balcony and it burnt his hand. He stepped back as the glass shattered and the window frame burst into flame.

He grabbed his shoulder bag, pulled on his shirt and pants and made himself take a slow shallow breath and think. The balcony was of no use to him; flames were everywhere out there. The smoke from under the door to his bedroom was increasing by the second, and the floor was so hot that it scalded his feet. "Heat rises, heat rises," he repeated to himself. So the way out is down. If he couldn't get out the front door, he'd try to get to the basement and escape through the steam tunnel that used to connect the older houses of the Junction to the generating plant up by the now-abandoned train station. He knew he'd have to open the bedroom door and that he might be engulfed by smoke when he did. If the fire had started down there, it could be working its way up the stairway—but the stairway was the only way down.

He threw open the door—instantly smoke filled his lungs and

blurred his vision. He fell to the floor and crawled to the bathroom, hoping the window there would allow him a way out. But the wall with the window was consumed in fire, and the molded plastic bathtub and shower were beginning to melt. He grabbed two towels and shoved them into the sink and was genuinely grateful when the water came on. He soaked the towels and then turned the faucet toward his jeans and shirt. With one wet towel over his mouth and head and the other over his shoulders he raced to the flaming stairway. Some of the steps were on fire, others smoldering, but the carved hardwood banister was still in place. He reached for it and it accepted his weight as he half walked, half slid down. Six steps from the bottom a spindle broke and he crashed to the floor below. To his right the front of the house was a wall of fire. Behind him the kitchen and back room were ablaze. He scrambled to his feet and threw open the door to the basement. He took one step and crashed through the stairway to the cement floor some seven feet below. He'd have broken a leg for sure, but he glanced off his exercise ball, slightly cushioning his fall.

He looked to the basement exit but it had already cracked under the assault of the fire. Above him flames licked their way along the joists. He scrambled into the laundry room and yanked against the drier with all his strength. It slowly ground forward, revealing the hole to the Junction's steam tunnels that he'd found when he first bought the house.

He literally fell into the tunnel and then pulled himself along until he got to the main shaft. He sat back, sweat and the smell of burnt hair—his burnt hair—momentarily overwhelming him.

He pulled his shoulder bag to him and tried to catch his breath. As he did he heard approaching sirens, then the heart-wrenching grinding and twisting and tearing of his house as it was eaten by the great fire monster.

"I can barely hear you, Mr. MacMillan."

"It's the fire trucks and the police."

"Yeah, yeah, yeah. So talk to me," Henry-Clay demanded.

"He's toast," Mac replied. There was not a hint of a smile in his voice.

"Are you sure? How can you be sure, Mr. MacMillan?"

"I have eyeballs on the back of his house and no one's come out that way and I'm watching the front and not a soul made it out that way either."

"And the thing's on fire?"

"It's a fireball. Completely consumed. Crossbeams should be coming down any moment now."

"And he's in there. You sure he was in there?"

"Saw him sleeping myself before I set the devices. He's toast—as I said."

Henry-Clay felt the sweat from his armpits dripping down his torso, but his breathing was stabilizing. He realized he'd dodged a bullet—a big fucking bullet. "I want you home now, Mr. MacMillan."

"To finish Ratio-Man?"

"Yes, it's definitely time to tie up that loose end. Come home, now."

"How do you know he'll come back to Cincinnati?"

"'Cause I know our Ratio-Man, Mr. MacMillan—I know him."

Twenty-five minutes later Decker pushed open the manhole cover and hauled himself out of the steam tunnel system near the corner of Keele and Dundas. Shortly after that he was on the sidewalk across the road from his house.

Flames leapt from the third-story dormer window. Decker pushed past the crowd that had already gathered to watch the show. Everything was a damned entertainment! Then a support beam cracked, sending the second floor tilting then crashing to the ground, pulling the west wall inward at a sickening angle.

Firemen rushed to the south side of the house, trying to prevent the fire from spreading down the street. The house to the north of his home had been abandoned for years and was already ablaze.

Decker stood there—just stood there—wondering, *What the fuck do I do?* Finally he turned to a police officer and said, "That's my house!"

The officer led him down the street to a patrol car. A senior officer was entering something into the police computer. He turned off the monitor and eyed Decker the way a diner looks at an unopened clam on his plate then said, "Get in."

After the preliminaries—name, etc.—the police officer closed his flip pad and asked, "So where were you when your house caught fire?"

"Where was I?"

"Yeah, where were you?"

"Asleep, where do you think I was?"

"And before that?" He added an odd hand movement to accent something or other. Decker took a deep breath—another person who learned how he should behave by watching bad acting on TV. Decker let out his breath slowly then said, "You mean earlier in the day?"

"Yeah. Where were you then?"

"Why does that matter?"

"Where . . . were . . . you?"

"I was in the States." For a moment Decker thought of the $36,290 he had in his shoulder bag.

"Just got back?"

"Yeah, around one."

"Ah, I see, around one," the officer repeated as if that were important somehow. "Where were you?"

"In the States. I told you. Now what's going on with my house?"

The officer coughed or laughed—Decker couldn't tell which. "Going on? Not much. It's on fire—you may have noticed. How did you manage to get out?"

"Through the steam tunnel in the basement."

"Really?"

"Yeah, really." Decker took a deep breath and asked, "So, what am I supposed to do now?"

The officer looked at Decker as if he wanted to poke him with a stick. "What do you mean by that?"

"Well, shit, I've never had my house burn down—what do I do?"

"You got a friend? Call. Get a place to sleep. Then tomorrow you contact your insurance company," he said dismissively and switched on the computer monitor on his dashboard. Then he added, in case Decker didn't get the message, "Do you mind?"

Fuck, he even delivered that line like a cheap actor. Art was supposed to imitate life, not vice versa.

Decker got out of the car and looked up just as the roof of his house erupted in flame. He turned and walked down the street, toward the only real friend he had in the world—Crazy Eddie.

# 16

## *CRAZY EDDIE*

CRAZY EDDIE OPENED THE DOOR BEFORE DECKER RANG THE bell. Decker was suddenly exhausted. He sagged against the doorframe.

"What the . . ."

"My house burned down."

Eddie grabbed Decker by the arm and guided him into his house, past a spare bedroom door that was usually open but was now shut, to the kitchen at the back of the house.

"Sit. I'll make you some tea." Eddie did his strange hop/hobble to the stove.

Crazy Eddie had begun his voyage to profound craziness on a sunny Sunday afternoon on the playing field of Ledbury Park Junior High School twenty-five years ago. For reasons that few, if any, of the participants could articulate, Decker and a batch of his high school buddies would meet most Sundays in the fall before the Bills game. And before Joe Ferguson and Fred Smerlas took the field to demolish the Freeman McNeil–led New York Jets, Decker and his friends would play middle-class, tackle football—without pads or helmets or protection of any sort.

On that particular Sunday Eddie led a successful blitz that sacked Marty "the Chunker" Steinberg—but despite the crunching of the Chunker, no one had been hurt. Three downs later, he felt something pop and then retract up into his left calf like an over-extended elastic band that suddenly snaps. Nothing happened in the play that tore Eddie's Achilles tendon; just Eddie falling to the ground, screaming in pain, after which he was never able to run again except in his pot-induced dreams, wherein he always ran, then cried.

Decker had known Eddie for years, and although there was a passing respect—as only bright high school boys can have for each other—there was no real connection between the two until both young men found themselves streamed to be doctors. Fourteen hundred students at Bathurst Heights Secondary School, and only thirteen of them—all male—were deemed likely to enter premed programs and hence forced to take four years of physics, four years of chemistry, four years of biology, four years of Latin for some reason, two of trig, two of calculus and a year of German.

Of the thirteen, only Decker and Eddie had absolutely no desire to ever see the interior of a hospital, but both found themselves ten days from graduation and about to fail a course because they had not finished the requirement to complete an original piece of research in physics.

So the fates—in the guise of the board of education—shoved the two young men together. And, necessity, fueled by some very good blond hash, allowed them to complete, in a mere three hours, the world's only definitive research into the effects of both speed and acceleration—on taste.

Decker drove his mother's convertible Mustang while Eddie licked a chocolate ice cream cone. At ten miles an hour Decker turned to Eddie and demanded, "Flavour?" Eddie responded, "Still chocolate," and noted on a graph that chocolate—at ten miles an hour—maintained its intrinsic chocolateness. The same occurred at fifteen miles per hour, twenty miles per hour, twenty-five miles an hour and thirty miles an hour. But at thirty-five miles an hour Eddie noted the slightest movement in the taste towards vanilla— away from strawberry. However, this deviation was not evident at any of the upper speeds. Their speed versus taste chart looked this way:

Taste vs Speed

STRAWBERRY

CHOCOLATE

VANILLA

10 mph   20 mph   30 mph   40 mph   50 mph   60 mph   70 mph   80 mph

They named the anomaly at thirty-five miles per hour the Aviday/Eddylay variation and postulated that this deviation from chocolateness was part of the same series of godly incongruities that gave the world the missing link and the Bermuda Triangle— and possibly Communism.

The physics teacher, Mr. Gallanders, grudgingly accepted their project, probably because he was anxious to get Eddie's anarchic spirit out of his classroom.

So they both graduated.

In late August, Eddie's grandfather died and left him an annuity that amounted to about fifty dollars a month. Two weeks later, Decker went to university on a scholarship. Eddie went to Afghanistan.

For two years Decker heard nothing from Eddie—then a postcard arrived. It had only ten words on it. YOU'VE NEVER BEEN STONED TILL YOU'VE BEEN STONED IN KABUL. No signature. No need for one.

While Decker was breaking into the theatre and trying to find as many soul mates as possible, Eddie was in active pursuit of his god—or gods.

Years later, the pursuit led him to San Francisco and a daughter who was taken from him in a vicious custody dispute in which his common-law wife claimed he had sexually molested the child—an untrue accusation that Eddie did not have the funds to fight.

All of which tilted both men toward a cold January afternoon on Yonge Street just north of Sam the Record Man, where Decker heard from the sidewalk, "Hey, cheapskate, slow down before the chocolate tastes like vanilla."

It was the winter of 2003 and Decker had just returned from twelve years in New York City, two failed Broadway shows, a son and a desperately ill wife—and an interesting sideline in a business he called "truth telling."

"You have a place to stay, Eddie?"

Decker repeated his question.

Eddie brushed some snow off the brace on his left leg, pointed at the sidewalk, and said, "Nothing wrong with this place."

"A bit chilly."

"You get used to it."

"We have an extra room; you're welcome to it."

"Maybe you should check with your significant other before you make that kind of offer."

"She won't object." Before Eddie could question that statement, Decker added, "She hasn't objected to anything or moved from her bed for over a year."

Eddie's left eyebrow lifted slightly.

"ALS," Decker said, "Lou Gehrig's disease. I've been told we're almost at the end."

"Long road?"

Decker nodded.

"Just another path," Eddie said.

Decker checked for a note of sarcasm. There was none. Eddie reached into his cavernous coat pocket and tossed a baby football at Decker. Decker caught it. "Consider it my rent," Eddie said.

Eddie moved in that night and proved himself to be as conscientious and kind a caregiver as there was on this earthly plane.

Decker's wife died in Eddie's arms, more in love with Crazy

Eddie than she had ever been with Decker—and all three of them knew it.

Three months after the funeral, Crazy Eddie waited up for Decker after one of his increasingly popular acting classes and said, "Lend me five thousand dollars."

Decker was genuinely shocked by the request. "Why?"

"I want to go back to school. I never really went to school."

"And you want to go now?"

"Yeah, I'm thirty-seven, mechanically inclined and digitally ignorant."

"You want to study your digits?"

"Ha, ha, ha—Luddite! Lend me the money and I'll devise a system that will keep you safe. You think you're so clever with this "pay me only in cash and no drives to the airport." Any fool who hired you could find you, Decker. I'm not sure what it is that you do when you disappear for a day or two every other month, but I know you come back with a stack of cash, and people who can afford to pay that kind of money—well, they can certainly afford to track you down if they want to, and they could be dangerous."

"Wealthy people are dangerous?"

"Think about it, Decker."

Decker did—and understood that Eddie was right. More important, he understood how much he needed this crazy man in his life. "I'll transfer five thousand dollars to your bank account."

"No you won't. I don't have a bank account. I don't trust white people with my money."

Decker stared at him—Eddie was definitely a Caucasian.

Again Decker nodded, then headed toward the basement. Eddie followed and watched as Decker opened the small floor safe and counted out five thousand dollars.

Eddie took the proffered cash and said, "And we're moving. Too many people already know how to find you here."

"We're moving?"

"Yes, you've—well I have, in your name, put a bid in on a house out in the Junction."

"Is that in the city?"

"Town extends west of Christie, Decker. Not your usual stompin' grounds, but still in this city. Time to expand your horizons, Kemo Sabe."

Decker was, as usual, impressed by Eddie's effortless mixing of metaphors and almost complete bypassing of the rules of spoken English. "Fine. But where is the Junction?"

"Where Dundas Avenue is north of Bloor Street."

"Dundas Avenue is south of Bloor Street."

"Not out in the Junction, it ain't. You'll love it out there. Slaughterhouses up the road; hotdog Tuesday is really somethin'; used appliance shops and no liquor. It's a dry part of town—very good pizza, though, and great used bookshops. And oh yeah, a twenty-four-hour taxidermy shop."

"Just in case I need something stuffed in the middle of the night?"

"Precisely. You never know when you'll need their services."

"Are there schools out there for Seth?"

Eddie looked away. Seth was Decker's almost constantly silent son. Decker had done his best to get Seth as much care as he could, but the boy took his mother's death so hard that what little chatter had come from him before ceased almost entirely after her passing. "Yeah, there are schools, and one or two of them even teach in English."

"They're mostly French immersion schools?"

"French? Are you kidding? Ukrainians and Poles don't spend much time speaking French. Shit, few of them really speak English. Not like the Estonians."

"What's an Estonian?"

"Remember the Hanseatic League?"

"Didn't they win last year's all-star game?"

"More ha-ha-ha. The ignoramus is so funny."

"So what about Estonians?"

"They're tall and very blond. Your type, as I recall. And they speak a very refined English."

Decker took a step away. "Sarah hasn't been . . ."

Eddie interrupted, his voice hard. "For you she died the minute she was diagnosed with ALS—at least be honest about that."

Decker nodded. It was a difficult thing for him to admit, even to himself. A truth as solid as a horizon line. And her death hadn't changed that. She had been sick for so long that he assumed that when she finally died he would feel some kind of relief, a burden set down, but he found himself constantly migrating to his son's bedroom and watching the boy sleep.

He remembered nights when Seth, as a child, had sat bolt upright and pointed at his feet, screaming, "Buggy bite my foot!" Decker would calm him, then watch as he lay back—eyes wide open—fast asleep. After Sarah's death he knew no way to comfort Seth—and the boy still slept with his eyes wide open.

Once the perfunctory funeral was over he took Seth as far away as he could manage; Kruger Park in South Africa is pretty damned far away. But not far enough. Seth's silence intensified, and moments of real violence erupted out of that silence, so that much of the trip was conducted in a steely, resolute fury, which the boy expressed in a series of unfortunate ways and places.

At the amazingly expensive Djuma private game reserve, Seth slipped out of their cabin one night, crept into the open-air bar and smashed every bottle and glass he could find. Decker had awoken in the night and not finding Seth immediately had called the main lodge. Two trackers arrived at his door with rifles at the ready. It was dangerous to be out at night, as the camp was in the midst of an area rife with lions and Cape buffalo. They finally found Seth asleep in one of the bar's wicker chairs, his hands blooded with shards of broken glass. When Decker later asked the boy about it, Seth denied breaking anything, despite the fact that it was obvious that he had. Because Decker cared about him, he couldn't definitively tell if the boy was telling the truth—it was one of the absolute limitations of his gift.

When they got back home Eddie stepped in and was as good with Seth as he had been with Sarah, and Decker tentatively reentered the single world.

It surprised him how many of his ex-students suddenly found their way back to his class. Susan and Samantha from Vancouver; Kristin from Victoria; Catherine and Maureen from the city. All in their late thirties, unattached and seemingly anxious to take class—then hang out afterward.

But he sidestepped their advances and committed himself to expanding his acting studio and his lucrative sideline in truth telling. But he kept his worlds separate—no one from one world knew the people in the other. Decker liked it that way. No—it was the way it had to be.

Decker looked up as Eddie placed a mug of steaming tea in front of him. An old doll was lying on the counter across from him. "You collecting?"

Eddie looked back and said, "They're the next big thing. Baseball cards, Beanie Babies, bobbleheads and now old dolls." He picked up the "well loved" thing. Decker was too tired to notice how carefully Eddie handled the doll as he put it on the counter. "How was Cleveland?"

"What? Oh, yeah." Decker reached in his shoulder bag and tossed twenty thousand dollars in loose bills on the table. "That's the money for Seth—you'll make sure . . ."

"It gets to him—yeah. Of that you can be sure. So how was Cleveland?"

There was something odd about the way Eddie posed the question, as if it was an evasion: "look there—don't look here." But Decker couldn't be sure. "Fine. Orlando was taking candy from a baby. Cleveland was revolting."

"And Pittsburgh?"

*Dangerous,* Decker thought and made a mental note to hide the USB key he still had in his pocket.

"Pittsburgh, Decker?"

Decker just shrugged. "Okay."

"Good," Eddie said, then without a segue asked, "So what happened to your house?"

"It burned down."

"To the ground?"

"Isn't that where things usually burn down to?"

"Good point."

Decker pushed the tea aside. He never liked tea. "Eddie, I want to get hold of Seth." Eddie looked away and took a small stoppered test tube from a cookie jar beside the stovetop. Decker assumed it was a fine Vancouver Island grass bud. "Eddie, I know you know how to get in touch with Seth. You're the only one here he gives a damn about."

Eddie smoothed out a rolling paper as he said, "He doesn't want to talk to you, Decker."

"I know that. But I need to talk to him now."

"Why? The fire?"

"With the house gone, how will he get in touch with me?"

"When's the last time he tried to get in touch with you?"

"It's been some time now."

"Could you be any more vague, Decker? He's your son and you don't even remember when you heard from him last. That's sick, man, sick." Eddie expertly adhered two rolling papers together, shook the bud out of the test tube, then crumpled the top of it onto the rolling papers.

Decker understood that with Eddie's valiant, but failed battle to get access to his daughter, his own distance from Seth must appear incomprehensible. All he could say was, "He hates me, Eddie."

"Ain't that the truth."

Decker thought about that. A truth: my son hates me.

"Look—if you can get in touch with him, tell him I'd love to hear from him."

"Get an untraceable cell phone, give me the number, I'll get it to Seth."

Decker gently closed his eyes. Nothing—no lines, no squares, nothing. He couldn't tell whether Eddie was telling him the truth or not. Never had been able to—he cared about Eddie. No, more than that. He needed Eddie to keep him centred—maybe even to keep him safe. Certainly to give him some perspective on how he was living his life.

"Look, Decker, if he wants to talk to you, he'll call. He's nineteen; he makes his own decisions. He'll be the only one with the number, so if that phone rings, it'll be him."

"Wouldn't it be easier if you just gave me his phone number?"

Eddie took a deep drag, stood and crossed to the doll on the counter. He pushed back its bristly hair and said, "It would, but then I'd have betrayed your son's trust—and I'm a lot of things, Decker, but I'm not a betrayer."

Decker had never heard anyone, outside of an acting exercise, use that word in a sentence before. He nodded and pulled on his coat.

"Where are you going?" Eddie asked.

Decker almost said, "Home," but stopped himself and said, "I don't know."

Eddie said, "Use my bedroom tonight. I'll sleep in the guest room."

Decker nodded. He was on the sick edge of overtired. He dropped his coat to the floor and headed toward Eddie's room—his feet seemingly heavier than the six-inch-wide old floorboards upon which they trod.

"Hey!"

Decker turned back to Eddie just in time to catch the football Eddie lobbed at him.

"Tomorrow's another day."

For a moment Decker tried to figure out if Eddie was quoting the musical *Annie* or Scarlett O'Hara from *Gone with the Wind*. Then he didn't care.

He didn't remember the rest of his short walk to Eddie's room or crawling beneath the comforter—or where the hell the football had gotten to.

The tears—for his failures with his son—those he remembered.

# 17

## *THE DAY AFTER A FIRE*

WHEN DECKER AWOKE, HE DIDN'T KNOW WHERE HE WAS. Then he heard Eddie humming in the kitchen. A lullaby of some sort. He put on some clothes Eddie had left out for him, had a cup of coffee and was at the bank on Bloor West a half hour after it opened.

After an appropriate amount of folderol he opened his safe-deposit box. He was about to put the remaining $16,290 into it, then decided against it. He extracted his house insurance policy and returned the safe-deposit box to the diffident, evidently put-upon teller.

Back at Eddie's he refused to let himself dwell on the fire. He was going to deal with this just as he dealt with other problems he'd encountered: he'd put it into his past as quickly as possible and commit himself to work—if not to forget, at least to move on. He placed a call to his insurance company.

As he listened to a mutilation of a Van Morrison classic his head filled up with junk. "Beneath the spreading chestnut tree . . ." bits of doggerel, moments of slanting light that blinked him toward perception then vanished as he turned toward them. A one-legged young black man, toque topped, on crutches crosses a bridge; a Zambian Irish man in Swaziland, cattle meandering the marketplace, gas pumps and a toilet with a key. Brother Malcolm at Chartres asking, "So, Decker, are you staying?" A small bricked-in doorway at the side of the apse that took his breath from him. Single trees on the topmost edge of mountains. And rocks daring a climber to mount their heights—to what? Hope—like the one-legged man—walking toward hope.

He was about to hang up, thinking he was so scattered that he couldn't deal with this, when someone picked up.

"Can I help you?" The voice on the phone could have cut cheddar at forty paces.

Decker told the receptionist about his house. *So coldly,* he thought. As if he were talking about someone else's home.

He was put on hold for just under five minutes and finally an agent picked up. She took his information—the second time this phone call he'd offered up this data—and told him that an assessor would arrive within the week. Then she added, "I'm sorry for your loss."

Decker said, "Excuse me?"

"I said, sir, that I am sorry for your loss."

The words didn't make sense to him. Decker understood that she was offering condolences, but houses don't die. They burn or are sold or fall apart. People die. Feelings die. Suddenly he ached to talk to his son. If only he knew where he was. Somewhere out west. As far away from here as he could get and still stay in Canada.

"Sir? Are you all right?"

Decker wondered about that. He knew he was probably in some sort of shock or post-traumatic something or other, but he said, "Yes. Yes I am. I just don't know what I'm supposed to do."

"Do?"

"Until the assessor arrives. What do I do?"

"See if there's anything that can be retrieved from the fire. Then continue your life—that's my suggestion."

And that's what Decker tried to do.

It had begun to rain—predictably, it would. As he walked west toward what used to be his home the rain pelted the few remaining leaves from the trees. Fall was ending and the ugly season was approaching. He felt it more than saw it.

There's something skulking about the Junction in the rain. Something hunched, hidden. The proliferation of Protestant and Catholic churches along the short stretch of Annette Street along with the half-dozen storefront Pentecostal holy-roller outlets a mere hundred yards north on Dundas bespeak a truth that Decker had always believed: that there was something complicated that needed to be kept in check out here.

It was what gave him the idea for a Ken Burns–style documentary that he'd sold to Trish Spence's production company. The working title was *At the Junction*.

He'd begun to research the idea by attending a meeting of the Masonic Temple on Annette beside the old library—business attire please. Instantly a queasiness came over him as these well-dressed old Torontonians turned back the clock to the good old days when there were no Caribbeans or South Asians or Jews in their city.

Across Jane Street—known throughout the metropolitan area as a "bad" street, bad meaning Jamaican—is yet another secret of the Junction: Baby Point. A wealthy enclave that if you didn't know it was there, you would never find it. In the midst of the multimillion-dollar older homes is a private park with four tennis courts and a lawn bowling green. Like so many wealthy people, they had managed a private club on public land—ah, so very old Toronto that.

Up on Dundas the remains of an American film shoot still have a block of storefronts painted to look like Brooklyn. They even had a three-sided subway entrance put on the small park at the corner of St. John's Road to complete the look.

But there were other secrets here. One of the local high schools is the most highly rated secondary school in the region. Another school, just a few blocks away, is absolutely at the bottom of that list. The highly rated school is almost entirely white and Asian—the low ranking, almost entirely black. How do they manage this? Well, the highly ranked school made freshman year so hard and so math intensive that . . . well, you can fill in the rest.

Determined to "get on with his life" he found a pay phone on Bloor Street and called Trish Spence's number. After a half ring he was promptly put on hold. While he waited for Trish to pick up he decided he needed to replace the computer he'd lost in the fire. He organized his life on his two Gmail accounts, and he couldn't imagine not being able to access the synaesthetes website. Eddie was a computer genius, but Decker only needed a simple machine that Eddie could soup up, password it to safety, then encrypt it to within an inch of the edge of the digital world.

"Trish Spence here, sorry for making you wait." The voice on the other end of the phone hadn't changed much over the years.

"Hey Trish, it's me."

"Decker! What's shakin'?"

He loved that. From fuck-you black-business-suit woman to California beach bikini girl in two lines. He could almost hear her smack her lips. She had to be in her early forties now, but when she spoke it was like talking to a young Joni Mitchell—California, I'm comin' home. He liked it. He liked her, he always had. "I need a meeting," he said.

"Got new material for *At the Junction*? Or you just anxious to see me again?"

"Always. Can your company lend me a computer?"

"What happened to . . ."

"My house burnt down." It startled him how easy it was to say that.

"What?"

"Yeah. Can I borrow a notebook for a few weeks until my insurance claim gets settled?"

"Sure. Just come by."

"When?"

"Five o'clock at Rancho Relaxo on College by Spadina—evil mojitos."

"I teach tonight."

"Oh, be that way. My place in two hours. You okay, Decker?"

Decker didn't answer her question. He didn't know the answer to her question.

Decker ducked under the police tape and stood in what remained of the front hall of his home.

The sleet had turned to snow. The first snow of the year drifted through the charred roof beams.

After a divorce or a death—or a fire—you get to see everything anew. As if a light that had always been off was suddenly turned on. It removes the shadows, throwing a sodium-harsh light on the emptiness.

Fire doesn't annihilate a house—it eviscerates it. It leaves the biggest of the bones while immolating the vital organs within. It reminded Decker of all the apartments in New York City he had left—how after he had moved out all the furniture but had to stay the last night to return the phone to Ma Bell. How sleeping on an air mattress those final nights he always was amazed how small the apartment felt without the furniture—and its occupants.

How small a house is after a fire.

Something glinted in the fading light, and Decker knelt to get a better look. A silver picture frame—charred and twisted. Despite his best efforts he couldn't remember what photograph had filled the now empty frame.

He stood, brushed the ashes from his knees, and left the property. It was surprisingly easy to do. It shocked him. Like a three-legged dog, he thought. When a dog loses a leg it doesn't pine for its missing limb. It simply becomes a three-legged dog. Decker knew he should move forward—out of his old burnt house—into whatever future awaited him. But unlike a three-legged dog, Decker knew that he could never really free himself from his past—a past that had two failed Broadway shows, the awful death of his wife and a fourteen-month memory gap in it.

He crossed the street to where his '99 Passat was parked. He was lucky that he'd had no garage and that his three-year battle with city hall to allow him to park on his own property had failed. Otherwise his car would have gone the way of his house.

He opened the trunk and the CD changer there. In 1999, CD player theft was evidently quite popular, so Volkswagen had installed a CD changer in the trunk. Ever so convenient if you're driving and you want to change to a selection you didn't happen to load into the changer. He scanned the numerous disks he had borrowed from the city's fabulous—truly fabulous—library system.

Decker flipped through the jewel cases. T. S. Eliot reading his own poems, sounding a wee bit like Monty Python's impersonation of an Etonian snot-nosed silly walker—too bad. Decker loved the words—just not, in this case, the speaker. Besides, ol' T.S. was from St. Louis, Missouri—what was he doing talking like that? There were also CDs of Elliott Gould reading Raymond Chandler's *Lady in the Lake* and Tim Robbins reading F. Scott Fitzgerald's *Great Gatsby*. He popped in the latter, got back in the car and as Fitzgerald's revolutionary cadences began he allowed the car to dictate his course.

Much to his surprise he ended up less than a mile away at George Bell Arena, where he had taught Seth how to skate, and where he had watched his talented son play dozens and dozens of hockey games. For a moment he remembered Seth's open face and huge smile after scoring a winning goal.

He entered the cold arena.

Like all cinder-block buildings, it echoed. In this case, with the thud of pucks smashing against wooden rink boards. Decker pulled his coat tightly around himself to fend off the dank cold of the place and climbed the steps to the seating area.

On the rink a pickup game was in progress. Most of the players were men in their mid to late thirties. One of them clearly knew what he was doing out there. He probably had managed a brief career in the national game and just as likely had fallen prey to injury—inevitable in a game played literally at breakneck speed.

Decker sat and watched the fluid carving and movement on the rink.

The arena echoed but he felt private there—safe—like he had as a kid inside the snow-pile igloo he'd built. He'd slowly carved away the ceiling so that he could see light outside but no one could see in—to his privacy.

A shout from the rink brought him crashing back to the present as a puck sailed past his left shoulder and rattled on the seat two rows behind him.

With a shock he realized that he had slipped back into layers of his past without consciously intending to. He knew it was not a good sign. Maybe a result of the lingering shock from the fire, he hoped. But he knew he had to be careful of such behaviour. Unless he wanted to be like those others—incapable of being part of the world; freaks with strange abilities but nothing really more than embarrassments; kids who peed their pants when they stood to answer questions in class.

He calmed himself as he had done so many times in the past by reciting a simple mantra—"You are from them, but not of them."

He picked up the puck and tossed it back to the ice. The talented player he had spotted earlier batted it from the air and in one graceful motion headed back up ice. The game continued. Decker smiled. Sure it does; the game continues.

Metro fire captain Hugh Highlander was thinking about the Bantam girl's hockey team he coached. How they really needed a scorer. Girl's hockey, even at the high rep level at which he coached, seldom had more than four or five goals a game. And he was tired of losing 2–0, 2–1, 1–0—he needed a scorer.

"Over here, Captain," the young fire department tech called from behind a charred upright.

"Coming," Hugh called as he hoisted a leg over a fallen beam and moved deeper into the charred wreck of Decker's house. He'd seen way too many of these old houses—now so prized— go up in flames. They were never built with any thought to fire, or even comfort. On the whole, what this city referred to as century houses were built for workers by their employers. They were made cheaply and not intended to last. But yuppies or yippies or Generation Xers fancied them and gussied them up—but seldom did they go deeply enough into the intrinsic problems of the houses' design to solve any real issues. Like so much renovation, their efforts just plastered over troubles. Especially when it came to fire. And these old things burned hot and fast—and often. But then again he knew that there had been suspicious fires in this very neighbourhood in the past sixteen months. As Hugh maneuvered his now growing bulk deeper into the wreck he took a deep breath and attempted to sharpen his focus. Arson was a serious crime, he reminded himself. If it was arson.

The young fire tech pointed at a V scorch mark on the remaining standing wall. When an object catches fire it leaves such a mark—the bottom of the V pointing to the source of the fire. The young tech pointed out three more V marks. They were none too subtle. Each blocked a potential exit.

Hugh's expression darkened, but he made himself speak slowly. "The kitchen was there?" The fire tech brought out the house blueprints and nodded. "We dealing with a gas fireplace?"

"No sir. Gas for the drier in the basement, but that's it."

"And the gas line is . . ."

"Nowhere near those," the young firefighter said, pointing at the V scorch marks.

Hugh turned from the tech and within five minutes found the telltale pour patterns that arson specialists called puddles on the cement stoops outside both the front and back doors. A flammable liquid when poured on a floor will cause fire to concentrate in these puddles. Hugh took a deep breath and looked for the final signifier of arson. He found it in the back of the house where one of the few remaining windows had a spiderweb pattern of cracks, 'crazed glass.' He turned to the men around him and shouted, "Watch where you put your feet. I want pictures of everything. This is now a crime scene."

# 18

## *ARSON*

IT WAS AN ORDINARY SUNDAY AT THE THIRTY-SEVENTH PRE-cinct in the city's west end. A robbery at a convenience store around Keele and Eglinton. A disturbance near one of the box stores on St. Clair. A noise complaint from the rich folks of Baby Point—they just didn't want the kids playing street hockey in front of their homes. What country did these people think they lived in? And, as it had been for the past five months, the boom-ing *thump thump thump* as the commuter train system rammed new pilons deep into the soggy ground up at the old depot. And just for a bit of added multicultural spice Tamil protesters were sitting on the expressway that joined the city west to east along the waterfront, blocking traffic for three miles in either direction.

Garreth McLean—twelve-year veteran of the Metropolitan To-ronto Police Service—had drawn Sunday duty. Since his divorce he often volunteered for Sunday stints to allow the married guys time with their kids. As he did his paperwork he kept his police radio turned up to full volume, just to keep in touch. He overheard radio chatter from the riot-geared cops who were monitoring the protest on the expressway. The demonstrators had just unfurled a Tamil Tigers banner and draped it across the roadway. The Tigers pen-chant for using suicide bombers to press their claims for a home-land hadn't gone over well with the citizenry, despite the large Tamil population in the city, the largest outside of Sri Lanka proper. The Tigers had been named a terrorist organization by the federal government more than a decade ago, and few people—except those currently blocking traffic—disagreed with that assessment.

Garreth was pleased when he heard a commanding officer order his men, "Take down that rag. Now!" The television on the other side of the room was carrying a live feed as the riot police forced their way through the crowd and ripped down the banner. The protestors howled. *Such is life in the Big Smoke,* he thought.

Garreth smiled and returned to the files on his desk. The first was an arson report from Fire Captain Hugh Highlander. Garreth wondered how Hugh was health-wise. Then he stopped wondering as he began to read the report on the most recent blaze—just a few blocks from the station. The phrase "definitely not an electrical or gas-related fire" leapt out at him.

He marked down the owner's name and got the crime site report from his computer. Something about the name Decker Roberts sounded familiar, but he couldn't place it. He ran it through the data banks—nothing. He put the file to one side and drew a large question mark on the front.

At one o'clock he took his lunch break and made his way up to Dundas. Now that the street finally allowed alcohol in its restaurants, there were more interesting places to grab a bite. And now that he wasn't burdened with a potential mortgage or potential kids' education costs—having neither house nor children—he had the money to indulge.

*Children,* he thought, and the memory of Decker Roberts bloomed full in his brain. He swore aloud. Decker Roberts. His father had a case almost forty years ago with a Decker Roberts. Garreth knew it because it drove his father to drink—literally.

Garreth remembered finding his strong bull of a father thrashing around in their basement. Swearing at the walls—at the bottle of single-malt scotch—at the world as a whole. Swearing at a person—no, a kid—named Decker Roberts.

Back then—it was another world—back when his father had been a decorated and honoured homicide detective.

Mike giggled as his bus pulled into the Cincinnati Greyhound station.

He'd done it. Gotten away from the Assassin and gotten back to Cincinnati. He couldn't wait to get some General Tso's take-out and some chips, and lock his door, and forget all that stuff he'd seen in the Junction. Awful stuff. That boy on the lamppost. Awful.

He flagged a cab and hopped in.

The voices had been wrong. He'd done it. He'd delivered his message to Decker. He'd done it. Himself. Done it himself. He wasn't too fat. He wasn't.

Maybe Natasha would like him better now.

Now it was up to Decker.

For a moment Mike considered the possibility that Decker hadn't understood what he had said to him about the ratio. Then he reran the tape in his head. No, he'd told Decker everything he'd have to know. Now it was up to Decker. It was Decker's turn.

"Stop here," he said to the cabbie. Then he balanced two Canadian two-dollar pieces end on end in his palm and showed them to the startled taxicab driver.

"It's all just a matter of finding the right ratio," he said. "Just the right ratio."

"Well that may be," the cabbie said, "but that ain't real money. I need twelve American dollars—plus tip, naturally."

Decker still had time to kill before he taught, so he drove north and east, zigzagging his way to Bathurst and Lawrence—the homeland—and Leena's restaurant.

Once there, Decker ordered a pastrami sandwich. Not Schwartz's on the Main in Montreal—but good—and from his past. His atheist/Jewish mother would have approved. She had been primarily a culinary Jew.

As he took a second bite it occurred to him that this deli could make a fortune if there was a cardiac clinic next door. Pastrami and heart exam—today's lunch special. More practical than the "Souper Lunch Special"—which this day featured lentil soup.

The waitress hustled him into buying a diet ginger ale ("Schweppes, don't ya know?") and a full dill that he didn't actually want. But hey, deli once every six months—have a pickle and splurge.

Around him snippets of dialogue knifed through the somewhat steamy air. "Thin you've got thin—That booth's open, yeah, but booths are for three or more—*kineahora,* so many choices; hard to choose, don't you think, Moishe?"

Over to one side Decker noticed a man with liver-spotted hands trying to make an event out of his lunch—perhaps the only event in his long day. The man's loneliness reached across the restaurant and touched Decker. A younger woman came in and ordered takeout. She turned and eyed the older men in the restaurant, her thoughts clearly etched across her face; *Will my guy become one of these old geezers?*

Poofy-haired women talked loudly of kids and grandkids and a world gone nuts—*meshuga.*

Decker took in the scene around him—the mise-en-scène. As with the synaesthetes, he was like these people but not of these people. Like a wisp of smoke within a fog—he could hide here, be taken for one of them. But it wasn't true—he was not one of anything . . . anything.

"Care to share, Decker?"

He looked up. Leena's kindly face looked down at him. A sad smile dominated her once-beautiful features—features that had been beautiful until Decker had gone back to using his gift.

It happened when he went with Leena to buy a used car. They were both sixteen and had been an item for a while. As the salesman pitched cars to Leena, Decker closed his eyes over and over again and told Leena when the salesman was telling the truth and when he was not.

She had been impressed, and showed her appreciation in a new way later that evening. Driving back from Leena's place that night, Decker considered using his gift more often—until the police arrived late that night to ask him when he had last seen Leena.

It turned out that she had been in a serious car accident. The beauty of her features had not survived the three operations she'd needed to reconstruct her facial bones.

As he spent time at her hospital bedside he began to feel that his showing off—his use of his gift—had caused this to happen to Leena. He also saw a question deep in her blackened eyes that he would only understand years later. It was the same question his ALS wife would demand an answer to: "What have you done, Decker? What have you done?"

"Care to share, Decker?" she asked again.

Decker noticed the deepening sadness in her. It had been that way since her husband died four or five years before. He couldn't remember exactly.

"Of course you don't—want to share, that is. Private Decker's never been into sharing." Leena sat and put the condiments back against the wall, slid Decker's plate in front of him, and rear-ranged the cutlery the way it was before Decker fiddled with it. "Still moving stuff around on tables, eh? That doesn't change either? So what are you doing here, if you don't mind me asking?"

"Just having a bite."

Leena laughed a short chortle. "Is it good?"

"It's reliable."

"I'll tell the cook. I'm sure he'll be thrilled."

"Sorry."

"Don't be. So what's up, Decker? You never come here unless something's happened to you."

"Really?"

"You're reliable for that."

He knew without closing his eyes that he could not tell if she was telling the truth or not—in a profound way he still cared about her.

He told her about his house burning down. He almost told her about the insurance company's "sorry for your loss" but thank-fully stopped before he got there.

"You have a place to stay?"

Decker nodded.

"You look thin. Anyone looking after you?"

High school was a long time ago; here they were into their forties . . .

"No one special."

Leena did that sad smile thing again, stood, then put his bill on
the table and said, "You remember my number?" Without waiting
for an answer she wrote it on the bill. "Call. I'm often home."

Clearly a truth.

Mac watched from the shadows down the hall as Mike fumbled in
his backpack for his apartment keys. He wondered what kind of
grown-up wears a backpack like some dumb college kid.

But then again, Mr. Shedloski was a great deal like a college
kid. An overaged, undersexed, way-too-old college kid—the kind
of college kid who didn't get invited to the parties. The kind
of kid who, when he was young—some twenty years ago—no
doubt not only read *Science Today* but actually did the experiments. He probably followed the directions in the back that
showed its avid readers "How to Build an X-Ray Machine from
Old Television Tubes." The magazine neglected to inform the
geeks that if they did build their jerry-rigged X-ray machine, they
could sterilize the entire neighbourhood if they failed to line the
walls of the room with lead.

Mac smiled as he patted the bowie knife at his side and
reached for his garrote. A few steps, a twist—and the world is
one mathematic weirdo less. *No great loss,* he thought.

Then Michael Shedloski turned. The two men locked eyes. Neither expressed fear. Michael quickly calculated the odds of his sur-
vival—and was not happy with the ratio—so he charged. Spinning
with surprising balance he was just about to land a heel to Mac's
throat when the Assassin's knife cut deep into the soft flesh of his
thigh—then twisted and slashed through the large artery there.

Mac grabbed the keys and opened the door. Michael Shedloski
was bleeding out fast. By the time he'd dragged the body into the

apartment, Ratio-Man was even whiter than usual—and he wasn't moving.

Mac quickly searched the man's backpack but couldn't find his computer. Then he turned to the apartment.

Against one wall was a stack of signs. The topmost was the damned thing the weirdo used to carry as he marched up and down in front of Yolles Pharmaceuticals after he'd been fired: "Who's Jumping Now?" In the front room there was one of the freak's weird balancing-act statues. A second tiny one sat by the front window.

He threw open the door to the bedroom and was greeted by a bizarre statue of Ratio-Man done in stacked computer peripherals with three printers as the guy's chest. The likeness was amazing.

Something caught his eye. Something about the statue was wrong. Something was off balance.

It was then that he heard the sound of dogs—large dogs— barking, and their master's, "Okay, we're going to Mikey's. I promised my dears and that's where we're going."

Mac swore under his breath, took a quick look around, then, without Mike's computer, crashed out of Ratio-Man's apartment and raced down the stairs so quickly that when the police later interviewed the dog owner all he could say was that the guy was big and white.

Decker arrived at Trish's apartment on College above Bar Italia just a few minutes before five. She greeted him with a kiss that was a bit too friendly, tossed the network's notes on the table, and retreated to her bathroom. Over her shoulder she said, "I don't think I know anyone whose house has burnt down."

"Well you do now."

She stuck her head out of the bathroom and asked, "You weren't inside it when . . . ?"

The lie came easily to Decker, "No. Absolutely not."

"Thanks to the gods for that," she said and shut the bathroom door.

Decker knew that she meant it. He could still tell when she was being truthful. He liked her but had never committed himself to caring about her.

Decker picked up the network's notes, cleared a mess of old magazines from a chair, sat and took a look around.

Trish's professional life, as an independent TV producer, was ordered to the point of being anal. But Decker knew her personal life was anything but ordered. Still, Decker was surprised by the new appearance of piles of newspapers in the corners of her living room and the dishes stacked to overflowing in the kitchen sink. He had a pang of conscience. Had her contact with him done this to her? At least there were no cats. *Yet,* Decker thought. *No cats yet.*

Decker had first met Trish seven years ago when he was summoned to the set of a prime-time TV show whose young female lead was having a meltdown. Decker often got the call in such situations.

This actress's breakdown was costing significant cash. Decker's assistance would cost considerable cash as well, but less than having an entire crew doing nothing but eating the free food.

Decker knew the show peripherally. Some of his best students played guest leads, but the producer, in true dumb producer fashion, had decided he wanted two untrained actors to play the leads—one of whom was now puking her guts out as Decker entered her trailer.

Behind him a tall, blond associate producer, Trish Spence, said, "Clara, this is Decker Roberts."

The actress looked up from her kneeling position. Decker took a good look at her. Twenty-two, maybe twenty-four tops. Single, from the country—he'd bet Newfoundland—close to her mom but very, very frightened just now. He turned to Trish. "How much time do I have?"

"We're burning just over five thousand dollars an hour."

"Yeah, but that doesn't answer my question."

"An hour, Mr. Roberts. Please, no more than an hour."

Decker liked what happened to Trish's face when she said

please. All the bullshit hard-assed crap fell away and an interesting woman emerged. A woman caught between the beauty she had been as a teen and the handsomeness she now possessed in her mid-thirties but didn't know if she liked. And alone—whoa— huge alone.

He smiled at her.

She caught his smile and smiled back. Both felt the connection—his aloneness and hers.

"Give me half an hour, Ms. Spence."

"Trish. Call me Trish."

"A half hour, Trish. Got an extra walkie-talkie?"

Trish took a spare from her belt and handed it to Decker.

"Good."

Trish left the dressing room and the actress stood up to face Decker.

He read her quickly and made a decision. Hard—not soft. "So Clara, you have exactly five fucking minutes to tell me what the fucking problem is. Five and no more than five."

Clara cried a little, yelled a lot, threw something that Decker caught like a football aimed at his head and finally said, "The second AD."

"What about him?"

"The way he looks at me . . ." She began to cry again, then repeated, "The way he looks at me."

Decker pressed the talk button on the walkie-talkie.

"Trish here."

"You sleeping with the second AD?"

"God no."

"Good. Fire him. Do it now. Right now." Decker clicked off and tentatively put a hand on Clara's shoulder. She looked into his eyes. "Clara, he's history. Trust me, he's got about ten more minutes on this set." She came close to smiling.

"I feel bad about . . ."

"Don't. Now what else?"

"The director . . ."

"He stays, Clara—I agree he's an idiot, but he stays. Show me your script."

She did.

He turned to the end and found her final line in the screenplay. *"You see—there—that's the way, come on, please—let's go."*

Decker circled it then asked, "Do you know how to chart?"

She shook her head slowly—tears filling her eyes.

"Not the time to cry, Clara—time to work. So you see your final line?"

She nodded.

"That's where your journey in the film leads. Toward you showing the male lead the path—the way. Right?"

"I never thought about it like that—but yeah."

"It's called a super objective, but that's not important. What's important is how each scene either gets you closer to succeeding at your objective or farther away from it. Nobody shoots in sequence anymore, so an actor has to know where along the journey line each scene is. Yes?"

She nodded. Her beauty was returning, and her brightness was asserting itself. *Good,* Decker thought, *very good.* He liked Newfoundland actors, had trained several; two were on their way to stardom.

Twenty-five minutes later he opened the door for Clara and nodded toward Trish.

"Is she . . ."

"Ready to work? I think so. Is the second AD gone?"

"Left the set twenty minutes ago."

"Good. You can always replace a second AD, but you can't replace your lead."

Trish nodded.

"If the director leaves her alone she should be fine. I gave her a phone number; she's to call if she gets lost—no, when she gets lost. Okay?"

Trish smiled. "You know . . ."

"What?"

"I wasn't going to call you."

"Yeah, there are those in this town who aren't fond of me."

"Me too. That people are not fond of—not . . ."

"Got it."

"Good. By the by, I always hated that stupid fuck."

"Which one?"

Trish laughed—brayed, actually. Decker liked her for that too.

The shoot went fine. Trish called on Decker's services several times thereafter, and when she began to produce her own projects she approached Decker about joining her production company. Decker declined the offer but on her suggestion began to bring her projects. The latest was *At the Junction.*

Trish came out of the bathroom and grabbed her winter coat. "That laptop on the table's for you. Two weeks Decker—two weeks tops."

"Thanks."

"Read the network's notes?"

"Yeah . . ."

"They're right, Decker, these first four are okay but it needs a better mystery to continue."

"And better writing," Decker said.

"I'm afraid I agree, but he's the network's guy."

"Why can't they hire real writers?"

"After we answer that we can work on world peace, okay?"

"Got it."

"Good. Now find me a mystery to drive episodes five through eight. And look, my offer to you to do the voiceover—at least at the top of each episode—is still on the table."

"I'm thinking about it."

"Okay—but think about the mystery to drive episodes five through eight first."

"It's out there, Trish. Trust me. The Junction has secrets—big, complicated secrets."

"Good, find them, 'cause we need them. Look, I gotta go."

"Heavy date?"

"I'll tell you later. Lock up for me. And keep the keys." She tossed them to him, her smile delightfully malicious. Then she was gone. Decker thought about doing the voiceover for the show, then forgot about it, but he didn't forget to take the computer or keep her keys.

## 19

## THE END OF A LONG DAY

LEONARD HARRISON REREAD TODAY'S TESTIMONY OF THE terrorist suspect being held in Dubai, then tried to cross-reference it with the other jihadi's interrogation from Pakistan. They still didn't jibe. One of them was telling the truth—but which one? They had a week to figure that out. Two new suspects had been taken in for interrogation. With any luck, one of them would confirm which of the two threats was real.

And now this Decker Roberts fire in Toronto.

His National Security Agency had spent too much time and effort on Decker Roberts for this all to go south now. And there were still too fuckin' many things they didn't understand about the whole world of synaesthetes—especially about their inner circle—important things that the NSA needed to understand before they became of interest to other . . . interests. Enemy interests.

Leonard Harrison pulled the file on an early test run he'd made on Decker using a North Carolina law firm and an insurance deposition. The guy had nailed it—called a truth a truth.

He put the file next to the two terrorists' testimonies, thought for a moment, then called in Yslan Hicks.

Her file on synaesthetes was still considered by many a joke just as the Mad Mullah file had been the brunt of many a joke until nineteen men and four airliners changed the world.

After an abrupt knock, Yslan entered his office.

Harrison pointed at a plane ticket and a sealed letter on his desk.

She picked them up.

"You're going back to Leavenworth. The letter's a reintroduction—it's required to see our friend there." He noticed her hand tremble a little. "It's time to go see him again. That's first."

"Why?"

"Because we're missing pieces—whole hunks of basic knowledge. And our time's running out."

A wave of darkness crossed her beautiful features, "Is the clock ticking on one of those interrogations?"

"Again, Agent Hicks, that's not your purview. Decker Roberts is your concern, and he might soon be on the move."

"He travels at least four times a year without fail. And he just got home, so he won't be leaving for a while."

"May not be true this time."

"Why?"

"His house burnt to the ground last night."

"What?"

"The police claim it's arson."

"Someone tried to kill Roberts?"

"I think so."

"But he escaped?"

"Through the steam tunnel in his basement."

Yslan thought about that. So whoever set the fire didn't know about the steam tunnels. They must have been new to the Junction. "Any idea who, sir?"

"No. And when they find that Roberts is still alive they may try again."

Yslan threw her hands up in the air. "All this work and now this?"

"Is it possible that someone on the oversight committee knows about our special synaesthetes?"

Yslan hesitated.

"Well, there better not be!"

"I said before I don't think they know."

"Well, fucking find out." He indicated the plane ticket in her hand. "Go."

"And if they try to kill Decker Roberts again?"

"You won't let that happen, will you, Special Agent Hicks? I'll authorize as many men as you need to keep him safe. How many do you want?"

"We have four up there already. He's not a pro, so I assume four will be enough."

"Take six—and you makes seven. Keep him safe, Yslan. The NSA needs his services."

He pointed to the airline ticket and said, "That first. We need to know more—we need to understand how there can be synaesthetes like Roberts out there. If he even is a synaesthete." He threw his arms up in the air as if he wanted to pull something down to him and turned away from her.

"We're in the dark about way too much of this whole thing. We need to know how guys like Roberts work." He turned back to her. "Set your guys on Roberts."

She waited for a moment longer to see if there were more orders forthcoming. Evidently there weren't, so she turned on her heel and headed toward the door, offering Leonard another enticing view. At the door she turned back to him, almost catching his eyes watching her backside. "I'll report from Leavenworth."

"You sure as hell will."

She closed his office door. Harrison turned to his window and stared at his view of Capitol Hill and thought of the approaching danger and his need of the services of a man like Decker Roberts.


Decker turned his head in profile to the class and pointed a slender finger to the side of his head, "There is a part of the brain stem attached to your nose. It is the storage depot of memory. Everything that's ever happened to you or you did to someone else is catalogued there. Every thought, every feeling, every smell, taste, touch and everything you've ever seen or heard—music itself—is there. It's the brain's flight recorder—its black box. It is, in a very real sense, you." He listened to himself as he introduced the fundamental methods of how to recall memories, but as so many times before he was thinking of a fourteen-month span in his own life from which he had no memories whatsoever except the feeling of something metal in his right hand and a coldness surrounding him.

He completed his explanation of keying—his own method for accessing a specific memory from the black box. "Acting is about selecting, not pretending. Everything you need to act is stored in that black box. Your job is to figure out how to access your memory centre—accurately—then be able to repeat that mental voyage with ever-increasing speed so that your acting partner says her line and you instantly respond with your line fully backed with the emotional reality of your memory. It's like playing a Chopin piece. No one jumps in and just plays that complicated music. You go at the hard parts slowly, working out the fingering. Then gradually you increase the speed until the notes blend and become music. It's the same with acting. You slowly work out the synapsal links to the exact memory that you need for the emotion of the scene, and then you increase the speed of access until it simply becomes you feeling what you need to feel when the text requires that you feel it."

He turned once again in profile to the class and pointed at the upper part of his brain stem. And even as he repeated the salient points of his method he knew that anatomically what he said was not strictly true—that a memory is most likely a reformulation drawn from many different aspects of the event or place or person being recalled. He knew that anatomically there wasn't a single place in the brain in which memories are stored. Memories recalled are not replications of time and place, etc. but are strands of responses to the remembered thing. But these facts—these truths—don't help actors. Despite the fact that Decker's black box simile was false, it still worked for actors in accessing past memories. *False but it works,* he thought. *An untruth leading to a truth. A lie leading to something valid. A sugar pill that cures a fatal disease.*

For a moment he thought he had been speaking aloud, but when he looked at the class it became clear that he had just paused—and they were still waiting for his next idea. "Good," he said, "let's give it a try." He sensed them pulling back in their seats. He smiled. He'd been here many times with many different groups of actors. "Write on a fresh page the most difficult thing you've ever had to say to someone, then on the flip side write the most joyous thing that has ever been said to you. These lines are called drone notes. Every scene has one. It's the moment of most intense pleasure or pain that you as a character experience. You have to use your heads to find them, then use your hearts and keying to open them up so that they come to life inside you and reinforce your sense of being present. Drone notes. Big-time actor tool—professionals only, please."

He looked at the attentive faces and said, "Scot, you start."

Scot had studied with Decker for just over two years, and his work was extraordinary. This was talent that walked and talked—and the industry had discovered this gift of the gods.

The exercise took the better part of two hours. At the end of it he turned on the cameras and called for the first scene.

Eleven scenes and four and a half hours later Decker assigned the scenes for the next class and closed up shop.

Once the actors were gone it occurred to him that this was his only home now. Could be worse, much worse.

He stood in front of the large window facing Adelaide Street. The rain/sleet continued its pit-pat rhythm. He reached out and touched the cold pane. *Home,* he thought—*my home.*

He heard the notes of a piano sonata from across the street. He'd never heard anyone playing before, but then again he was seldom in the studio this late at night. A phrase popped unbidden into his head: "If I sense the trees, I enter the forest."

Years ago he'd stumbled upon a fabulous singer/songwriter named Paul Scheel in a tacky piano bar on the Lower East Side. The first time he heard Paul play the song he called "Ordinary

Day"—about a man who completes his normal day, goes home, and then ends his life—Decker knew he was in the presence of something special. He tracked Mr. Scheel from club to club, from Far Rockaway to Queens to New Jersey and back to Manhattan. Some nights Paul would play "Ordinary Day"—many nights he didn't. Finally after a midnight set Decker approached Paul as he was packing up. "Oh, my one and only real fan," Paul said before Decker could speak. "Are you stalking me or something?" Then Paul laughed. Up close Mr. Scheel was more impressive aurally than visually. "You want an autograph?"

"No. But thanks." Decker suddenly felt a wee bit nauseous.

"Then what?"

"Can I ask you a question?"

"You just did."

"Yeah, but that's not my question."

"So what's your question?"

"Some nights you play "Ordinary Day" and some nights you don't."

"That's a statement, not a question."

"Why? That's my question. Why do you play it some nights and not others?"

Paul lit a cigarette and looked at Decker.

"You like that song?"

"I wouldn't say like is the right word."

"So what do you want to know about it?"

"I told you, I want to know why you play it some nights and not others."

Paul put his hands on the piano keys. For the first time Decker noticed his fingers were badly crippled. "I have four songs whose endings have a chord progression that could lead me easily to 'Ordinary Day.'" He played the simple progression. Then he played it again. "So I play that progression at the end of each of those four songs, and if I can sense the trees, I enter the forest."

"And the forest is where 'Ordinary Day' lives?"

"Like a black mamba in a tree—ready to fall on me once I enter the woods."

For an instant Decker saw deep red welts on Mr. Scheel's crippled hands—what he now knew was the price—then they were gone and Paul Scheel was heading toward the door of the bar. He turned back and said, "I see your forest and you see mine—but that's it. I'm not hidden from you or you from me. So now I have to move on. Never really liked New York anyways."

"Where will you go?"

"Someplace where you can't find me. Your forest will infect mine, or mine yours. Only one of us can live in the same place—don't you know that?"

Decker sat over that last thought. Across the way a truck was backing up to a loading dock. Decker wondered what was being shipped at this hour of the night. Then he heard a loud knocking on the studio door.

It was clearly not a student wanting to deliver an application for class. This was a demand to open. Then came a clearer demand; "Mr. Roberts, open the door, police."

Decker felt the beard on his face. The cell phone was on the couch. He pocketed it and went to the door. He didn't know exactly why the police would be at his studio, but he assumed it was about the fire. After all, he had made no effort to hide his identity as the owner of the house in the Junction and as the artistic director of the Professional Actors Lab. His secret identity was reserved for his truth-telling business.

He opened the door. Garreth presented his ID and Decker stepped aside to let him into the studio.

"Nice," Garreth said.

"It's open—way better than teaching in a church basement."

Garreth made a sound that could have been affirmative or negative—it was hard to tell which.

"Can I help you, Officer? I assume this is about my house."

"Why would you assume that?"

Decker did his best not to roll his eyes. "My house burned down yesterday."

"And where were you before that happened?"

"I've already answered . . ."

"Indulge me."

"In the States."

"Doing what?"

"Business."

"Can you prove that?"

"Why should I have to prove anything?"

"You have your ticket handy?"

Decker stepped back. "Should I get a lawyer?"

"Why would you need a lawyer?"

"Because it sounds like you're accusing me of something."

"Is there something I should accuse you of, Mr. Roberts?"

Decker let out a long breath. "No! My fucking house burned down. If I'm anything I'm a victim here."

"Of what? A victim of what?"

"Of bad wiring or I don't know what—whatever burns down houses. I'm a victim of that."

"Of arson."

"What?"

"Arson. Your house was torched, Mr. Roberts."

"What?"

"Torched. This wasn't an electrical fire. Or a gas leak that found a spark. It wasn't a carbonated beverage shorting out a wall socket."

"That can cause a fire?"

"In an old house with copper wiring, yes."

"It wasn't any of that, so what was it?"

"Incendiary devices set inside your front and back doorways, Mr. Roberts."

Decker took a few steps back into his studio. Incendiary devices! Fuck—bombs!

"How did you manage to get out, Mr. Roberts?"

"I wrapped myself in wet towels and ran down the stairs, then out through the steam tunnel exit in the basement."

Garreth looked at him.

"What?"

"You didn't increase the value on your insurance lately, did you? Remember, we can check."

"No." Then it dawned on Decker what this man thought. "You've been watching too many movies, Officer. No one in their right mind would set fire to their house while they're still in it. It's like that crap in novels where the least likely person is the one who did it." Decker put on a bit of a swagger and said, "Hey, it's got to be the blind, Alzheimer quadriplegic whose wife beats him on a daily basis—hey, it's got to be him. Wake up, Officer. I almost burned to death in my own house."

Garreth ignored Decker's rant. "Have you got a passport, Mr. Roberts?"

"Yes, but . . ."

"Is it here with you? Because it's not in your safety-deposit box."

"How did you . . . ?"

"Banks like police officers. Now where is your passport?"

"It was in my house."

"Really? Did you use it to cross into the United States? Officer Randall at the scene of the crime reported that you said you'd just returned from the States—as you reiterated to me just now. And as you are no doubt aware, our American neighbours don't allow anyone into their fine country without a passport—something about terrorists, I believe."

"Okay. That's enough. I don't have to answer any of these stupid questions. Now get out of my face."

"Mr. Roberts . . ."

"Am I under arrest?"

"No but . . ."

"Then I don't think you have any right in my place of work, which is now my home as well. And yes, to save you the trouble,

Stafford Street is zoned for work/living spaces. This isn't the nineteen-sixties; we have rights now."

"Indeed we do."

"Get out."

"Here's my card." He almost added "Don't think of leaving
town," then stopped himself and asked instead, "Have we met
before?"

"No."

"Have you ever been in trouble with the law, Mr. Roberts?"

Decker closed the door in Garreth's face then shouted, "No!"

Decker did his best to wash in the bathroom sink, then un-
folded the couch and stretched out. He heard the hum of the city
all around him. He placed the cell phone beside him in case Seth
called in the night—much of Western Canada was three hours
behind Toronto time. His last thought before falling asleep was to
charge the phone in the morning.

# 20

## *HENRY-CLAY*

HENRY-CLAY WATCHED MR. MACMILLAN'S VIDEO OF DECKer's house collapse then glanced at the small newspaper photo on page twenty-two of the very dead Ratio-Man. He nodded and tossed the paper aside.

Henry-Clay smiled. He knew that he was never special. He had no secret talent, he wasn't blessed with particularly good looks or a powerful physique, he wasn't even, if truth be known, all that bright—he just fucking worked harder than anyone else around him. He thought of films like *Wall Street* and *Boiler Room* as instructional videos.

He hated comic book heroes. He thought it unfair that superheroes won because they had superpowers. The bad guys just used their brains and worked hard—like him. They, as far as he could see, were emblematic of the American work ethic. They were rightly American heroes making something from nothing using only their brains and willpower. The superheroes might have represented the values of Jupiter or Neptune or something but certainly not of this earthly plane.

Henry-Clay had spent his undergraduate years at all-fun Tulane in pre-Katrina New Orleans, where he made the first of his great business decisions and quite a name for himself on campus—in his mind the daily double. He kept book for the Green Wave's basketball team. As a natural adjunct to his bookmaking he also arranged for point shaving in the games. As a short guy it was his only access to the basketball court. He also thought of it as one of the few things at Tulane that the black and white students did together—fix basketball games, that is. When—after Tulane inexplicably blew a ten-point lead in the final minute and a half of a game against Ole Miss—it became obvious to anyone with eyes that something was up, Henry-Clay exiled himself to Europe, where he completed his degree and latched on to an idea he knew would eventually have to take hold in America—the morning-after pill.

Then he spotted an obvious business opportunity in the good ol' religious U.S. of A. So upon his return to this side of the pond he set up the first of what would quickly become twenty-seven abortion clinics in the Midwest.

The returns were good, and he was about to double his empire when some nut shot one of his doctors. Then another, and Henry-Clay decided to return to a safer line of work—pharmaceuticals. A pill for every problem—and new problems to unearth for which pills would be needed.

He knew he'd have to get a graduate degree to bust into the pill racket, but he had no real aptitude for math or sciences. He returned to his alma mater and bulled his way through math and physics, but chemistry actually required some finesse—which Henry-Clay knew he lacked. But he kept at it and eventually at age thirty-two he earned an MS in chemistry from the University of Chicago, although writing and publishing his thesis almost killed him. But his real work at that fine institution of higher learning was recruiting. All around him were some of the brightest young scientists in the world, and few if any had twenty dollars to their name or any business savvy—of which he had an abundance.

Two failed marriages and several millions of dollars over the dam and with the help of the Ratio-Man he found himself sitting on a gold mine. Until Ratio-Man found his way to the Junction and told Decker about the drug ratio—that left him no choice but to have both dealt with.

No choice. Fuckin' no choice.

It made him feel helpless—like a damned kid. Infantilized.

That's what the idiot shrink he saw exactly one time called him.

"You've been infantilized, Mr. Yolles," he'd said.

"Explain that to me, Doc."

"It's one of the few conditions that are passed down from one generation to the next."

"What are you talking about? Down syndrome and dozens of other dysfunctions are passed from one generation to the next."

"Yes, but those are genetic."

"And this infantilizing is passed down from one generation to the next how, if not by genetics?"

"By behaviour. It's passed down by behaviour."

"What? My parents taught me to be this infantilized person?"

"No doubt without meaning to, but, yes, they taught you. What did your father do? Was he in business?"

"No. He didn't do much of anything to the best of my knowledge. He got up each morning and went for a swim in the university pool, but I don't ever recall him working."

"And he's dead now?"

"A long time back."

"How did he die?"

"Just sort of—of old age."

"How old was he when he died of old age?"

"Not that old."

"How old, Mr. Yolles?"

"In his forties."

"Too young to die of old age, wouldn't you say?"

"Yeah, yeah, yeah, I get that."

"Do you remember much of him?"

Henry-Clay looked away.

The shrink tried another tack. "Did he ever share his memories of his youth?"

"Yeah. As a young kid he remembered going to New York and catching the boat to Europe for the opera season. He talked about that a lot, and opera—he loved opera."

"And what did his father do?"

"He was a builder. Owned the biggest building in this city."

"Owned—as in past tense?"

"Yeah, he lost it."

"How did he do that?"

"The market crash in twenty-nine—you may recall the stock market had a wee bit of a problem that year."

"Yes, but most people didn't lose their buildings in the crash."

Henry-Clay took a deep breath. "My grandfather was one of five brothers. They all invested together. When the market crashed in twenty-nine my grandfather and his youngest brother convinced the other three brothers that now was the time to get seriously into the market and make a killing. They all mortgaged everything they owned—their homes and their buildings—and put it all into the market. They lost it—everything. Everything." Henry-Clay stood up suddenly and walked to the window of the psychiatrist's office. "See that building across the Ohio River?"

The psychiatrist nodded. "The Treloar Building?"

"Didn't used to be called that when my grandfather and his brothers owned it. The day after they lost everything my grandfather held hands with his youngest brother and they jumped off that building. Apparently that was the family agreement. Their insurance money was split evenly between the five families, but—and here's an interesting but—the families of the brothers who didn't jump never talked to the families of the two brothers who did. Never talked to my father. I never even met my cousins except in passing, and even then the tension was so great we had nothing to say to one another."

"So you see?"

"Their suicide infantilized my father, who then infantilized me? Is that what you're saying?" Henry-Clay turned and picked up his coat. "Thanks for the advice, Doc, but by the by—I'm the richest of all the progeny of those five morons and I could buy that building back if I wanted to, and the rest of the buildings on that street."

"Then why don't you?"

"Because I've been infantilized—don't ya know?"

Henry-Clay banished the memory then turned to his computer—time to find a new freak. Using the algorithm that Ratio-Man had given Nasty Natasha and yesterday's date he entered his web master codes for the synaesthetes website and got a shock. Decker Roberts was lurking in the chat room.

## 21

## A VISIT TO LEAVENWORTH

LEAVENWORTH FEDERAL PENITENTIARY LOOKS LIKE A TURN-of-the-century high school gone crazy on steroids. Its front capitals and portals are formal and could have been those of a post office in a large city, but they weren't—they were the gates to a world of pain and suffering.

Yslan had only been in a federal penitentiary once before, and had promised herself that she wouldn't return, but here she was at Harrison's request—showing her letter of introduction and her ID to a fully armed guard who sat behind a bulletproof plexiglass screen.

The guard shoved a metal tray through the hole in the glass and Yslan deposited her wallet, ID, cell phone, her dad's ring and her watch. Then she emptied her pockets of change and added those to the rest. She walked through a metal detector and the thing buzzed. She held up her arms and the guard took his time establishing that her metal belt buckle was the culprit.

Forty-five minutes later she was sitting in an interview room that smelled vaguely of fear and vomit covered by antibacterial soap, waiting for Martin Armistaad, a convicted fraudster and mathematical genius who had predicted too many market highs and lows for it to be an accident.

Before his arrest he was number one on her NSA special synaesthetes file. Now he was an aging, balding man with a greying beard.

"Thank you for seeing me, Mr. Armistaad," Yslan began.

The man scratched a red patch on his flabby left forearm and nodded.

"I know you didn't have to agree to this meeting, sir." That last made her feel queasy—more Clarice Starling crap. She reminded herself that Hannibal Lecter was a fiction, then stopped herself from such sophistry. The man sitting in front of her was as other-worldly as Thomas Harris' nightmare creation—not a cannibal but someone with uncanny abilities. And both she and Mr. Armistaad knew it.

For a moment Yslan wished that she'd never been introduced to the idea, let alone the reality of synaesthetes—that the ground beneath her feet was the solid terra firma that she thought it was before she met the likes of Martin Armistaad. That the world was a real place with real rules. Not the shifting miasma of Martin Armistaad—and Decker Roberts.

She looked up and felt as if the creep somehow read her thoughts. "How's the food in this joint?" she said, unable to stop herself from poking out at the man across from her.

"The dining lounge leaves something to want but if you're bad enough you get room service, so . . ." He allowed his voice to trail off as he raised his eyes to hers. *Pretty eyes,* he thought, then he corrected himself; *Hider's eyes.* It almost made him laugh.

"You don't know, do you, Special Agent Hicks?"

"Know what, Mr. Armistaad?"

He winked at her then said, "Nothing that I could tell you. Something you'll just have to figure out for yourself." Before she could respond he added, "So what do you say we start again. You pretend that I didn't have to agree to this meeting—I believe we were on that lie, weren't we."

Yslan took a breath and spat out, "Thanks for taking this meeting, Mr. Armistaad."

He opened his arms and then laced his fingers behind his head, shimmied down in his chair so that his pelvis was aimed more directly at her face. "What can I tell you, Ms. Hicks? My social calendar is very full but I was able to sneak it in—as I did the last time we met." He smiled, the antecedent for his "it" obvious to both of them. He was missing a front tooth.

"Thank you for seeing me again."

"Not a problem." More scratching.

"In your early essays you state that all your thinking is purely mathematical. That there are natural cycles in the world and that they relate to the figure eight point six, which is generated from the mathematical reality of pi."

He stared at her. No more scratching.

"Do you still believe that, sir?" Still too much Clarice fucking Starling!

"Yes . . . and no, Ms. Hicks. I think I believe, as you are learning, that there is something else at work in the universe. Something that Hamlet sensed when he saw the ghost of his murdered father, something that great artists see—something other."

"I see."

"Not yet you don't." He smiled again then added, "Do you?"

"No. Not personally. No I don't see 'something other.'"

"That's why you are here, isn't it, Ms. Hicks. You could read my writing online—everything I've written is in the public domain. You see, I'm not allowed to charge for anything I write in here—am I?"

"I guess not."

"I'm not." This last was very hard. Angry. "So I ask again, Ms. Hicks, be honest with yourself and answer my question: why exactly are you here?"

"To understand what I can about how you worked."

His surprisingly thin tongue licked his lips, leaving a glistening sheen as he whispered, "Liar."

"Tell me how it works, Mr. Armistaad."

"Fine," he said. Then just as she thought he wasn't going to speak again he added, "I closed my eyes, Ms. Hicks, and the world aligned—the other world."

The rest of the interview was unhelpful. He tinkered with her—enticed her—then threw cold water on any idea that she thought she'd understood. But he had confirmed something that she and Harrison needed confirmed—that there might well be an "other" out there.

And Yslan was convinced that somehow her special synaes-thetes were the access—the path—to that "other."

## 22

## A NOOSE TIGHTENS

DECKER EXITED THE SUBWAY AND HEADED TO THE BANK OF pay phones. He knew where almost every remaining pay phone in the city was located because Eddie preferred that he used them whenever possible.

He called Visa for the third time to see if they had finally figured out what the problem was with his card.

Six prompts later he was informed by an electronic voice that his account at the RBC had been emptied of all its funds and as a result his last payment check had bounced so his card had been cancelled.

After swearing at the electronic voice and trying in vain to find a real person to talk to he flashed his Metropass and got back on the subway and headed first north then west—to Eddie's place.

The city was doing its rain/sleet dance. No doubt the local news would try to pacify the public by mentioning that although our weather was bad, Buffalo was getting slammed. But who cared? He pulled up the collar on his coat and bent into the wind. The city was quickly being transformed from its usual overpractical unhandsomeness to just plain old ugly—and fast.

"But Eddie, you said they were secure."

"Did I say that? Doesn't sound like me." Eddie moved the old doll from its perch on the counter to the table.

"Eddie!"

"Well, it's simply not possible to make anything one hundred percent safe any longer."

"So someone could hack into my bank account?"

"With ease, I'm afraid. The only thing that keeps any individual bank account safe is how many individual bank accounts there are. But if the hacker has you personally in his sights—then forget it. He's got you—game *finito*—kill *la musica*."

"Then there's nothing you can do to keep your money secure?"

"Not a damned thing."

"Then how's all that razzle-dazzle with blind websites and digital drop boxes and closed chat rooms keeping my identity safe— or secure, for that matter. You were the one who said I needed all that stuff."

"You do need all that 'stuff'—your truth-telling business could get dangerous, which is why I bounce your data through fifty different servers in thirty-five different countries and of late I've looked into using quantum cryptography." Seeing Decker's quizzical look he explained, "It uses photons on dedicated dark fiber remains of laid cable."

"Is that supposed to mean something to me, Eddie?"

"Soon it will be in every home—but not yet."

"Would that keep information safe?"

Eddie thought for a moment then said, "Not for long. Any lock one human being can invent another can pick. It's just a natural process."

"So there's no real way to keep my identity safe?"

"Well there is—sort of."

"How?"

"By balancing things."

"What?"

"I keep your identity safe by balancing things."

"Balancing things between what and what?"

"Between simple and complicated, Decker. Your identity is digitally kept safe by being too simple for the smart guys to consider but too complicated for the uninitiated to figure out— balance."

Decker looked at him. Something was different about Eddie, or was it about this conversation? He didn't know. Finally he said, "So balance keeps my identity private and secure?"

"And safe."

"Unlike the money in my bank account, which is neither and hence is gone."

"Like dust under the bridge," Eddie said, then added, "You'll just have to use the money in your other bank accounts and the cash in your safe. Come on, Decker—we should all have such problems." Eddie stood and hobbled over to the sink. He plunked a bit of dishwashing liquid on his hands and scrubbed.

Decker watched Eddie's back for a moment, then grabbed his coat, felt for his car keys, and left.

Decker sat in his Passat across the street from the remains of his house and watched as two heavyset men secured floodlights to the tops of several metal stands. They were evidently preparing to continue their work through the night. Decker counted two cars, two trucks, and half a dozen police techs—most of whom were dressed in white protective coveralls. He knew they would shortly be going over every charred beam and fragment of what had been his life.

An hour later, from the pay phone at the corner of Bloor and Runnymede, he called into the answering service that Eddie had set up for him. He punched in his thirteen-digit PIN number—s-e-t-h-m-y-o-n-l-y-s-o-n. There was a single new message.

A tense male voice identified himself as representing the TD Bank, and that "as of this moment the bank is canceling your line of credit and calling in your two-hundred-thousand-dollar loan. Any failure on your part to respond to this phone call within twenty-four hours could result in criminal proceedings." He then went on to list a series of numbers for Decker to call.

Decker stepped out of the glass phone enclosure.

"You all right?"

Decker turned. The drunk who stood outside the liquor store

and usually banged a tambourine as he massacred "Yes Sir, That's My Baby" had just asked him if he was all right.

*I must look as awful as I feel,* Decker thought as he put coins into the man's battered ball cap on the sidewalk between his feet.

"Any requests?" the man asked.

Decker resisted saying, Can you sing "Far, Far Away," thought of Seth and instead asked, "Do you know anything from *Tea for the Tillerman?*"

"Ain't he a terrorist now?"

*A believer,* Decker thought, *not a terrorist,* but he said nothing.


"Don't do that."

Decker quickly put the stack of books back on the floor. "Sorry, Theo."

"I like the mess here exactly the way it is, so don't move things, don't try to impose your sense of order on my things, Decker."

"Okay, I'm—"

"Sorry, yeah, you said that—always moving stuff around. What is that, anyway?"

"I won't do it again."

The dingy little gay man was the owner of the Junction's best used-book shop and the area's foremost amateur historian—and Decker's friend and coresearcher on the documentary.

They went down the aisles narrowed by thousands of used books, some on shelves, many simply stacked on the floor, passed rotting cardboard boxes of old cassettes from which Decker had first heard John le Carré read his novels, then racks of yesteryear's porn rags with the genteel appellation of gentlemen's magazines—as if women's magazines had pictures of naked men flaunting their parts. Then down a steep set of stairs made narrow by six-foot-high stacks of books on either side.

"Trish thinks we need more mystery for episodes five through eight."

"Okay."

"Okay? As in you have something mysterious?"

"Yep. I found a real oddity in the amalgamation between the Junction and the city. A fact that doesn't align."

"Meaning what?"

"One of the police cases in the Junction didn't make it onto the police blotters of the amalgamated city police force."

"Clerical error?"

"It's possible, but it was the only pending police investigation in the Junction that didn't survive the amalgamation."

"What kind of—"

"A public lynching."

Decker looked at him sharply.

"Of a boy."

"In the Junction?"

"At the corner of Annette and Mavety—just around the corner."

"And there's no mention of the crime on the city's records after the merger?"

"I've checked and rechecked and there's no mention of it—anywhere. The crime just went away. Just like that." Theo snapped his fingers. They made no sound.

"Things do get misplaced in a merger," Decker said.

"Or mergers are arranged so things can get misplaced. We always wondered why the Junction bothered to join the big bad city."

That sat like something hot and heavy between the two men.

"No mention of suspects in the Junction's records, I assume?"

"None."

"Details of the victim?"

"Not much. He was a fourteen-year-old male—no distinguishing marks, nothing except that his fingernails were long and painted."

"A gay kid?"

"They didn't call us gay back then."

Decker thought about that. Theo seldom talked about his sexual orientation.

Then Theo asked, "What reaction would a fine upstanding

Junction family have if one of their own was smitten by one of mine?"

"It would have to be a powerful family to have bought all that silence for all these years so that all that remains of a boy's entire life is one sentence in a police file."

"I agree."

Theo took a long wheezing breath and coughed up something whose colour hadn't yet been named. The coughing suddenly increased in intensity, grabbed hold of him, shook him like a hard wind does a loose canvas sail.

"Damn it, Theo, take a pill."

"They only work sometimes," he huffed out between spasms.

"Well maybe they'll work now."

Decker reached into Theo's shirt pocket and took out the bottle of pills, shook one out and handed it to the older man, who swallowed it dry. Theo's breathing shallowed and slowly his cough eased.

"See, Theo, it worked," Decker said. "Take your damned pills, will ya."

Theo muttered, "Yeah, that pill—that particular pill worked. I'm telling you they don't all work anymore. It's like new razor blades. When they come out with a new product they're great—actually cut the whiskers off your face. Then once people begin to buy them, they lower the quality."

"So you think your pills . . ."

"Who the fuck knows. Who the fuck knows what's actually in any fuckin' pill . . ." Theo dried his mouth with his sleeve.

"You okay?"

"For now."

"So someone lynched a gay teenaged boy just before amalgamation."

"Yep."

"And because the case didn't get to the city's police blotter you assume a powerful Junction family was behind this?"

"Yep."

"Write it up and get it to Trish." He turned to go.

"Where're you going?"

Decker didn't hear the question. He was thinking about powerful families—people powerful enough to burn down his house, get his credit card cancelled and have his loan called. Powerful people he was a threat to. He and Eddie had been careful to cover his tracks, but clearly someone had found him.

"Earth to Decker."

Decker stared at Theo.

"Where—are—you—going?"

Decker smiled, then said, "Out." ·

Theo smiled back, "Mit whom?"

"Friends."

"Unt, when you comink back?"

"Later."

Decker put out his hand. Theo shook it—they held each other's hands just long enough for neither of them to know what to do next. Finally Theo withdrew his hand and said, "Safe voyage." Then he pointed to the back door.

Decker nodded. *Polonius saying good-bye to Laertes,* he thought.

Decker used his key and entered the side door. Eddie's house was quiet. Decker passed by the kitchen. The doll sat on the table as if it owned the place. He went to Eddie's room where he collected the $16,290 he'd kept from his recent earnings then headed back out the side door. He thought about leaving Eddie a note, but decided against it.

A half hour later he handed over four packages with U.S. addresses to the Chinese man who ran a post office from the back of his convenience store then headed over to Stafford Street and his studio. He went to open the door of the old building but his key wouldn't turn the tumblers. He stepped back. It was then he saw the city notice: THIS BUILDING IS CONDEMNED.

"And one more makes four," he muttered as he circled around

the back and accessed the rear fire escape from the top of the Dumpster. Once in the lab he bolted the door behind him and went into the small kitchen. Beneath the sink at the bottom of a stack of prop dishes, pots and pans he pulled out a plastic cutlery tray. He flipped it over. In the indented slots he'd secreted USB keys. He carefully pried them out. Each held a recording of a truth-telling session. He recorded every session, but these he had kept hidden. Eddie had warned him long ago that overhearing some information could be dangerous, and each of the sessions on these USB keys had struck him as exactly that—dangerous.

He assumed that one of them would tell him who was behind all this.

Holding the USB keys in his palm he added the Pittsburgh key from his pocket and reentered the studio. He set up Trish's computer on a simple IKEA table, then slid in the first key, marked "Stanstead." He plugged in his earphones, hit enter, listened to the voices from the past and began his search—his voyage.

# 23

## STANSTEAD

HUNKERED INTO A BORDER DIVOT OF QUEBEC'S EASTERN Townships exists a strange little community called Stanstead, Quebec. In fact, the community is so close to the U.S. border that in its only bowling alley a bowler bowls from the True North Strong and Free and hits pins in the Land of the Free and the Home of the Brave. The community has several other odd quirks. The first is that is has a bunch of different names—Stanstead, Rock Island and Beebe Plain. It also has a private school that stands in stark contrast to the pronounced poverty of the area. In the summer an exclusive girl's hockey camp takes over the campus.

Rich girls from Toronto and Montreal and Boston and New York City descend on this little town whose one attraction outside the hockey rink is an ice cream store. Oh yes, there is another attraction for the rich girls—the local boys. Poor boys from working (when there is work) class families with whom several of the girls develop an across-the-tracks summer dalliance. But on occasion it gets to be more than that.

The first time Decker went to the small town he had been hired by a New York City law firm to interview a Stanstead cop. It seemed that a local boy's love for a rich New York City girl was evidently returned by said girl, who had ended up pregnant. The girl refused to tell her father who had impregnated her, so Decker had been hired to see if the police knew which boy had done the nasty deed.

"Stanstead's a small town," Decker had said.

In response Officer Matthews had grunted—or sort of grunted. What was it with cops and grunting? But at least this fat cop was his own man. No modeling his behaviour after some bad TV actor here.

"Is it the kind of place where everyone knows everyone else's business?" Decker pressed on, following the script the lawyer in New York City had given him.

Officer Matthews shifted his considerable bulk in his wooden chair behind the cluttered desk. The chair creaked. He took a chipped coffee cup and perched it on the top of his protuberant stomach. "Nah. That's a big city myth about us small-town folks."

Decker quickly shut his eyes. Random lines and swirls crossed his retina—the man was not telling the truth. "Okay." Decker nodded. "Maybe not everyone knows everything. But a budding romance might draw a few eyes, don't you think?"

"Okay. I'll buy that."

Decker closed his eyes—a simple, perfect square. "Did you know Carrie Kimmel, one of the girls at the hockey camp?"

"Yep. A cute girl."

"Was she dating one of the town's boys?"

"It wouldn't surprise me. She struck me as a pretty wild filly."

Decker had been given three names. Boys' names. Local boys. "Was it Lawrence Allen?"

"No."

Decker closed his eyes. A parallelogram. "Peter Ethan?"

"No."

Two perfect triangles. "Robert Irwin?"

"Nope."

Squiggly lines—Officer Matthews was not telling the truth.

"What kind of boy is Robert Irwin?"

After a lengthy pause Officer Matthews said, "The Irwins aren't rich. Not many folks in Stanstead are rich, but the Irwins are good people and he's a good boy."

Decker had named Robert Irwin as the probable father in his report and been paid his fee. He had put it behind him and gotten on with his life, but then, three months later, the New York City law firm contacted him again.

Apparently the boy, Robert Irwin, disappeared—only to be found in the icy river behind the hockey rink several months later. There was a suicide note but a lot of doubt about the actual cause of death. The local police were stretched. The girls were all back in their respective cities and safe wealthy homes. The girl who was the object of the boy's desire was somewhere in Europe—on an extended semester abroad.

They prepared a second script for Decker. It seemed vague. "What's the point?" Decker asked the lawyer.

"Do you want this job or not?" the lawyer had demanded.

Decker told them that he wasn't comfortable working this way, but when they doubled his normal fee—well, he agreed. It was the two-year anniversary of his wife's death and he silently promised to give the money to the ALS Association.

The second interview of Officer Matthews was completely different than the first.

Decker had little more than said hello than Officer Matthews tossed a photo onto the desk and turned it to face Decker. Instantly Decker's gorge rose and he had to fight the urge to push the thing away. Just barely contained by the colour eight by ten was a teenage boy lying on his back, eyes wide, his chest bare, his mouth filled with silent horror, encased in the ice of the shallow stream behind the hockey rink.

"Robert Irwin?" Decker managed to get out.

"Who else?" the heavyset cop said as he inserted a hunk of chewing tobacco into his cheek and flipped on a Hank Williams CD. "Rich people never pay for their crimes."

Decker was stunned by his candor and completely forgot the script the lawyers had given him. "Do you mean that this wasn't a suicide?"

"No suicide here. One of theirs murdered one of ours. Simple as that."

• • •

Back in his studio Decker hit the pause icon on his computer. He stared out the window at the winter sky. He clearly recalled closing his eyes—two squares, side by side. Officer Matthews was telling the truth—at least the truth as he knew it. He double-clicked on the play icon.

"No suicide here. One of theirs murdered one of ours. Simple as that."

The unabashed class anger had been something new to Decker, but before he could comment the jowly cop had continued. "That rich Jew girl loved Bobby. Wanted to leave her rich school and come live with him. Here. In Stanstead."

Decker allowed the Jew part of this to slide. He'd heard a lot of griping about Jews in his life that should have been aimed against rich people, not specifically Jews. He remembered being in High Park watching a kid's baseball game. Beside him two men were bitching loudly about how expensive it was to have their kids play rep hockey. Fair enough. It was outrageously expensive. But then one said, "You know, I was at Forest Hill to watch a game and these fuckin' Jews had their kids in fuckin' five-hundred-dollar skates. Kids in five-hundred-dollar skates. More than I make in a week for fuckin' skates and these . . ."

Decker couldn't resist saying, "Hey, if you went to wealthy WASP areas of the city like Leaside or Humber Valley you'd see the same thing." For a moment a light seemed to dawn in one of the guy's eyes, then it went out and the two walked away. It was just easier for them to blame Jews than see it as clearly as this cop saw it—rich versus poor.

"Her family objected to the relationship?" Decker suggested.

The cop made a dry mirthless sound that could have been a laugh. His substantial belly rose a little, challenging the strength of the buttons on his plaid shirt. "Yeah, you could call it that. They objected to their precious little cutie marrying a white-trash boy from bum-fuck Quebec."

Decker didn't know what to say. Finally he blurted out, "Proof. Do you have proof?"

The cop looked at him the way that experts always looked at dilettantes. He went to spit then decided against it. "Girl was pregnant with Bobby's kid."

"Are you—"

"Local drugstore remembers selling Carrie Kimmel a pregnancy kit. Remembers it because the girl came back for two more—and bought the only expensive one it had."

"But you don't know—"

"What the results of the test were? No, I don't know that. I do know this, though." He reached into his desk and pulled out an evidence bag. He smoothed the transparent surface and turned it toward Decker.

It took Decker only a moment to realize that this was a teenage girl's love letter. The words "Bobby, I can't wait to have your baby" stood out like a line of blood on pale skin.

Matthews reached across the desk and took back the evidence bag.

"And you can't get the American police to help with this?" Decker asked.

"Not much love lost across this border. A lot of history still playing itself out here. During the Revolution, British supporters left the United States and many settled here. It's why this town speaks English, not French."

"Yes, but United Empire Loyalists came here a long time ago."

"Yeah, but this is more about class than anything else. Bobby was made from cheap tin—our little hockey princess from platinum and jade."

The words of an old song flew into Decker's head: "And Billie Joe McAllister threw something off the Tallahatchie Bridge."

"So which rich New York City law firm sent you to see me, son?"

Decker made up a name.

"You're a bad liar—don't make it part of your profession."

For a moment Decker thought Officer Matthews was going to ask exactly what the fuck his profession was, but he didn't bother pursuing that line of questioning. He lurched to his feet, hitched up his pants, turned up Hank Williams, then pointed to the office door and said, "Use it."

Eight hours later Decker faxed his report to his New York City employers. "Officer Matthews clearly believes that Bobby Irwin was murdered and that Carrie Kimmel was carrying his baby."

A package arrived at Decker's P.O. drop box the next day, containing thirty thousand dollars in U.S. funds. Decker forwarded it anonymously to the ALS Association.

Decker listened to the end of the recording a second time, then removed the earphones. He had intended to listen to all of the recordings and then make up his mind where to begin. But he shelved that idea as, in his mind, he heard Officer Matthews repeat, "One of theirs murdered one of ours. Simple as that."

Decker finally understood that he might be an accessory to a murder. First he'd identified the boy, then found out how much the Stanstead police knew about the boy's death. He closed the laptop, slipped the other USB keys into his pocket, silently bid the safety and security of his studio good-bye and left by the interior freight elevator.

## 24

## CHARLES CLEAREYES

AROUND THE CORNER, AT POLITICA, HE DROPPED FIFTY cents into the pay phone.

The First Nations actor, Charles Cleareyes, picked up on the first ring.

"Sorry for calling so late."

"Decker?"

"Yeah, Charles, I need a favour."

"Sure. I owe you." Charles had been an extremely popular actor for several years. Then, on a whim, he cut off his waist-length black hair, and before you could say "The Lone Ranger's a racist," the work dried up. Charles came to Decker—a wife, two asthmatic kids, and no career. They had, carefully, together over time reinvigorated the actor who had been ignored by the business. A business that for years had cast his hair and ignored his talent. And once again, Charles Cleareyes was a popular and much-used actor.

Decker had charged him very little. He seldom charged needy actors very much since his truth-telling business was supplying all the money he needed.

"How're the kids?"

"Growing like weeds."

"And Joan?"

"Her Little Princess Dance Studio is a huge hit with the girls way out here in nine oh five land. Suburbia can't get enough of her."

Decker understood why. Joan had a real gift with kids and kids' dreams. He envied her that.

"So what can I do for you, Decker?"

"Do you know your way around Akwesasne?" Decker heard Charles take a deep breath. Akwesasne was the Mohawk reservation that straddled the Canadian-American border south of Montreal.

"Yeah, but the politics on that reservation are dangerous as hell. What is it that you want, Decker?"

Now it was Decker who took a deep breath. "I need you to get me across the U.S. border."

"Without the Americans knowing, I assume?"

"You assume correctly. Don't ask me why because I won't tell you."

Charles laughed.

"What?"

"I thought you were going to ask for something difficult. Like horseback riding or something."

Now Decker laughed. Charles Cleareyes was the only First Nations person that Decker knew who was violently allergic to horses. So much so that in film after film Charles appears on horseback—bare chested, beautiful, and regal—and Benadrylled out of his mind to stop himself from sneezing throughout the take.

An hour and twenty minutes later Decker was on the late night bus to Montreal. Early the next morning he transferred to an Eastern Township bus line—and as the cold noon sun finally broke through a low hanging bank of clouds, Decker, for the third time in his life, walked into Officer Matthew's office.

The intervening years hadn't reduced the officer's waistline, although they had added a brilliant red sunburst of broken capillaries across his left cheek and forehead. Hank Williams had been replaced by early Neil Young, but essentially the man had not changed. He was as immutable as the granite that was quarried just north of his town.

Officer Matthews didn't offer Decker a seat or a smile or say a word of any sort.

So Decker launched in. "I believe that Carrie Kimmel was carrying Bobby Irwin's child. I assume she had it aborted before the boy was murdered by—if not directly, then indirectly—the girl's father or someone else in that family. And I believe that a law firm in New York City has been paid to get information about the matter."

Officer Matthews spat a thick line of tobacco juice just past his outstretched left cowboy boot and expertly into the circular trash can upon whose rim the heel of his boot rested. "That's a whole lot of believing you got there."

"So?" Decker asked, not knowing exactly what the "what" was in the "so what" question he had posed.

"So, I think you have a lot of it right."

"But not all of it?"

"Nope. You got the law firm part wrong."

"They weren't representing the girl's family?"

"Nope."

"Nope?"

"Nope." He spat a second time—another swish. "The girl used her mother's maiden name for when she played hockey—don't ask me why. The girl's real last name is Charendoff. Carrie Charendoff."

Just for an instant Decker closed his eyes, felt the cold approaching, and saw perfect parallel lines cross his retina. When he opened his eyes Officer Matthews was reaching for a much-used cardigan sweater.

"Cold all of a sudden," he said as he dug into his desk drawer and pulled out a business card. He put it on the desk, stood, and left the room.

Decker picked up the card: Singer, Rubin and Charendoff, Attorneys-at-Law, Patchin Place, New York City—the very firm that first employed him. But Ira Charendoff was not representing Carrie Kimmel's family—he was her father.

Six hours later Charles Cleareyes walked Decker across the Canada-U.S. border inside the Akwesasne Reserve and helped him into the trunk of the car of a First Nations friend heading to Albany. Once they were past what the Mohawks referred to as the "last spying place," the car stopped and Decker joined his host in the front seat.

From Albany he took a bus to New York City. Seven hours later he stood outside the entrance to Patchin Place off Sixth Avenue at Tenth Street as he had almost four years ago when he was first prepared by a lawyer named Ira Charendoff for his interview with Officer Matthews of Stanstead, P.Q.

The phone rang on Yslan's kitchen table. She picked it up before the first ring had completed its cycle. "Yes. Good. Where?" She listened for a moment. "I'll be there in three hours—don't lose him."

## *RETURN TO MANHATTAN*

"WHERE TO?" THE CABBIE ASKED—WELL, DEMANDED. IT WAS New York after all.

Decker wasn't ready to deal with Charendoff. The U.S. Mail wouldn't have delivered his four packages yet. He'd have to give it a few more days to be sure that they arrived. He yelled over the roar of the traffic, "Columbus and Sixty-ninth." To himself he whispered, "The old homestead," then he pulled out his key ring and examined the old keys there.

As Decker's directing career had heated up, the modest Upper West Side had become complicated for him. Over and over again he had bottles of beer slammed down on the bar in front of him—actors who tended bar remembered directors who didn't cast them much better than directors remembered actors whom they had not cast.

And when a store opened on Columbus selling antiques and cheese, Decker knew it was time to move.

Through his wife's brother they found a rent-controlled apartment on Fifty-eighth Street beside a ramp to the Fifty-ninth Street Bridge. Real people lived on the East Side—people with nine-to-five (well, in New York, eight-to-seven) jobs and families. And he and his wife started theirs with a boy—Seth by name.

Seth sat on Decker's lap many an evening on the stoop of the building. Together they saw Hulk Hogan when he first came to visit Cyndi Lauper in the building beside them. The boy took a special joy in learning the names of fancy cars as they disgorged their rich drivers in front of the private dining club nearer the river as well as the names of the more mysterious vehicles parked in front of the high-end whorehouse near Second Avenue.

Decker directed in Philadelphia and Pittsburgh and Chicago and Cincinnati and Seattle and Williamstown and on occasion in New York, and Seth grew, and his wife got unaccountably thinner and frailer until the day that Seth held his hand as the doctor pronounced the death sentence of ALS. And the web that would eventually encase his wife wrapped the first of its slender but adamantine threads around her thin shoulders, and she began the voyage inward that would ultimately end her life.

Sitting across Columbus Avenue from their old place Decker watched the parade of Manhattanites as he ate his Cuban rice and beans and allowed himself once more to be amazed by the energy and life that was New York City—one of the crowning achievements of the West. An achievement wrought from guts and hard, hard work and belief.

The waiter brought the bill, the price of which tempered Decker's approval of Manhattan. He resisted the impulse to lick the remains of his rice and beans from his plate, paid for the meal and, after satisfying himself that his keys still worked, began the journey first to the East Side then downtown—back to Patchin Place.

The law office of Singer, Rubin and Charendoff was located in the secluded mews below Eleventh Street off Sixth Avenue, Patchin Place. It was an address one didn't soon forget—Eugene O'Neill wrote *The Hairy Ape* in one of the houses in this exclusive enclave, and eccentric Djuna Barnes bemoaned her lack of fame as Theodore Dreiser and E. E. Cummings tapped away at their typewriters across the way. Now Patchin Place was a principal address for therapists. Decker couldn't help feeling that going from great writers to tillers of the fields of the mind was a move in the wrong direction.

But as Decker walked the cobbled stones of the mews he sensed history rise from the ground all around him. Although he had lived in a turn-of-the-century house in the Junction, history was both deeper and more profound in New York. More souls had both trod these stones and, more important, left their indelible marks here than in the city of his birth. At times he thought it was a matter of focus and New York's active looking for the next big thing. After all, he had taken a show that he opened as a simple song cycle in a bar on Tenth Avenue—when Tenth Avenue was somewhere that you avoided—and two years later had a $2 million Broadway musical. But even more important, New York mythologized itself; writers wrote about it, composers put it into song, painters endlessly portrayed it. Decker couldn't imagine what a song about the Don Valley Parkway would sound like, or who the hell would paint the vista down Dupont Avenue. Yet here, streets and bridges and buildings had entered the ethos—become a part of being in the West. Of the achievement of the West.

Decker passed by the front door of Singer, Rubin and Charendoff, then took a position across from the white door and opened his copy of the *Times* and waited. Shortly a burly man, clearly a lawyer, and what was just as clearly his secretary—not his admin assistant, a secretary—stepped out. "It's fuckin' cold!" the man announced. In the manner of a great many New York City lawyers he spoke loud enough so that people within a half-mile radius could hear and understand how very important he was. The secretary read something off a notepad and the lawyer responded, "What do you mean no one down there will accept a collect phone call? We represent their damned country. Peru is our client. So they have to accept a fuckin' collect call." A black limo edged its way down the narrow roadway and pulled up. The lawyer and his secretary hopped in. The lawyer's final words to her seemed to float on the cold air: "Call the lying cunt, she'll have to wait to cash the last alimony check, call her and . . ."

Decker was grateful that he couldn't hear the end of the command. But, then he didn't care. This guy wasn't the one who'd sent him to Stanstead.

Decker contemplated what to do next. In fact, he hadn't thought much past getting to Manhattan.

He needed information. Better still, he needed someone with access to information.

Decker was not a cop or a detective or an investigator of any sort. He had a powerful talent but it was limited. If he cared about the person his gift didn't work at all. Recordings often caused him to make mistakes. He needed to hear the person speak—and it helped if he could also see the person as he spoke. Somehow he had to arrange to overhear a conversation in real time with this Charendoff guy. Not so simple with a high-profile lawyer. Especially one who had already seen Decker twice and would be understandably suspicious if Decker were just to show up at his door asking questions.

So he needed a surrogate—no, an ally. Decker wasn't good at such things—he remembered the "doesn't play well with others" statements on his grade-school report cards. It was hard for him to trust. He trusted Eddie. He trusted Leena. But in neither case did he trust them with everything about himself.

But he couldn't do this on his own. He needed a partner. Decker had done important service for dozens of people who now lived in New York City. He preferred a partnership based on trading service to one based on any notion of personal duty or responsibility. It was cleaner—more predictable. Besides, free was often the most expensive. He allowed his mind to roam over his New York contacts. The producer who lived in Chelsea whom he had helped twice in the past with actors who were resistant to their directors but had big contracts and couldn't be fired; his old lighting designer, whom he had set up with a job in academe; the four actors who had leads in shows whom he prepped for big episodes.

He ran the names of the actors in his head and envisioned each. All four liked him—no, that's not necessarily true, they used him when they needed to. All four were on the rise, but only one was a real star. And only a star could get a big-shot lawyer to take his call and then get him to attend a meeting at the place of his choosing.

Lawyers and stars—yeah, that fit. He opened his small phone

directory and turned to the J page—he always listed actors by their first names.

He walked back out to Sixth Avenue and approached a bank of phones. Much to his surprise one of the three was actually in working order and not occupied by a bearded creature calling on Jesus for a loan or some other sort of favour. He pumped the thing with coins, dialed and waited through the inevitable generic message. When the beep finally arrived Decker said, "Hey, are you too big a star to pick up the damned phone?"

There was a pause. Decker considered hanging up but he knew that he needed help if he was ever going to get close to the lawyer who had sent him up to Stanstead. Then he heard the still remarkably youthful voice of Josh Near—star of the NBC series *The Extraordinaries*. Now in its fourth season, the show was really a phenomenon. Huge ratings despite the fact that it was in the gritty territory into which usually only HBO dared venture. Decker really liked the show, partially for its acting and writing but even more so because it seemed to show the New York City that Decker knew—the New York City before Disney had made it safe for Midwesterners. Shit, they have the rest of the country— why did they need New York as well?

Decker remembered sitting down beside Josh at a showing of *Heaven* at the Toronto Film Festival—in the years before it became so tony that he couldn't bear sitting with those folks to watch a movie. Decker had spotted the young actor and took the seat beside him. As he did, a woman came down the aisle in a backless summer dress—she had one of the six or seven great female backs in the Northern Hemisphere. Both of them had noticed, and despite their age difference they had seemingly bonded over that. When Josh headed south across the border, he had kept in touch with Decker, who prepared him for a great many of his important auditions.

Decker had also prepped Josh for his four biggest episodes in *The Extraordinaries*' first season that launched both him and the show into the stratosphere—TV talk-wise.

"Decker?"

"Yeah."

"How are you, I haven't heard from you . . ."

". . . in quite a while. Look, I need a favour."

"Sure, you need a place to stay in New York?"

"Maybe, but that's not the favour."

"Okay, so what can I do ya?"

Decker resisted saying "That LA talk doesn't suit a good Canadian boy" but chose to say, "Invite me over—I haven't had lunch yet."

"Sure. You know where I live?"

"Oh, yeah, a little hard to forget your address."

One Fifth Avenue was as fancy as its address suggested. Josh lived in a corner apartment with a view of Washington Square. Not the one that Henry James wrote about, since it was now filled with NYU students and tourists and Haitians and Zimbabwean refugees hawking designer goods with misspelled names such as Goochie and Pravda.

"You look good," Josh said.

"Thanks. And you look obscenely young for someone your age."

"Thanks back at you for that."

"How goes the show?"

"I'm doing my best not to let it become just work."

"A good idea." In fact a very good idea, because when acting becomes just work—an art descending into a repetitive craft—then there really is no point in doing it at all.

"Coffee, beer, wine?"

"A beer would be good."

"Lager, ale, dark, light—"

"Just a fuckin' beer, Josh. Jeez, we may have to pull you out of this town before you become one of them."

"Truth? I like being one of them. Or at least being taken for one of them."

Decker understood this idea in his bones, but it was something you only admitted to a fellow Canadian living south of the forty-ninth.

"So you wanted a favour, Decker?"

Decker hesitated. How well did he really know Josh Near? He knew him as an actor, as a student—as a fellow admirer of female backs. "Yeah," Decker said, accepting the proffered bottle of French beer. He took a sip. It tasted of something that should not be put into beer. "I need you to play a role for me."

Josh's thin blond eyebrows rose to form a perfect inverted V. "You have a film to direct, Decker? I thought that—"

"No. It's not a film. It's a slice of life."

"Oh? And who do I have to play?"

"Yourself. Josh Near, TV star."

"I think I can handle that. When's showtime?"

"Tomorrow at Bob's Big Ol' BBQ on Twenty-third, if you can arrange it."

"Consider it done."


Less than an hour after Decker left the posh apartment with a commitment from the young actor, Josh found himself staring out at Washington Square Park and thinking about the obligations of friendship—and the nature of betrayal. He liked Decker. In some very real ways he owed Decker for a lot of his success. Decker had supplied advice and prep time as Josh negotiated the complex waters leading up to his big chance at NBC. But there was a problem. A cocaine problem. A pending charge in Toronto that despite huge sums of money he'd already paid his attorney just wouldn't go away. Josh tapped out a smallish mound of coke on the mirrorlike black slate countertop then cut it into lines with an Amex Platinum Card and thought about Decker's odd request to call a lawyer in Patchin Place then interview him in a restaurant with a script that Decker would provide. It all sounded a little—no a lot—fishy.

He cut then snorted a thick line. When his head cleared he

looked out the floor-to-ceiling window. The view of Washington Square wasn't great, but it was New York—and the chicks dug it. Dug him! Or was it just his access to so much coke? He didn't bother working his way through that. He had more important matters to deal with.

He picked up the phone and punched 4 on the speed dialer. It annoyed him that his lawyer's number in Toronto had reached number 4 on the list. The phone was answered on the first ring and a voice that he had become all too familiar with said, "To what do I owe this surprise phone call?"

Josh eyed the second line of cocaine on the kitchen counter. "Hold on a sec." He put the phone down and with a dexterity born of much practice snorted the line. It flashed bright colours in his head—then the clarity—and the bravery returned. "Sorry."

"Sure, Josh."

Josh told his lawyer about Decker's strange request.

"Let me run this past a few people up here. Maybe someone in law enforcement will salute the flag."

Josh hated it when lawyers tried to be cool. "Could this help my situation?"

"Hard to say. So tell me everything you know about Decker Roberts." Josh realized this was the last chance he'd have to back out. To not betray his friend and mentor. He licked a finger and ran it along the counter with the coke remains, then rubbed them into his gums—and told his lawyer everything he knew about Decker Roberts.

## 26

DECKER DROPPED INTO THE STAPLES ON THIRD AVENUE AND bought a Cambridge writing tablet and a new pen. Hard things he liked to work out longhand. Then he hopped the bus up Third Avenue and walked over to the park that faced the East River. The one where Woody Allen talked the night away with Diane Keaton in *Manhattan*—the one to which Decker had taken Seth when his wife's anguish had been too great for either of them to bear. The one where he'd lied to Seth—telling him that everything was going to be okay. That his mother was going to be just fine. The one where he first sensed that although he couldn't tell when Seth was being dishonest, the boy could spot every untruth his father ever told him.

The cold in New York could be as cold as anywhere else, but the day was clear and the sun warmed things enough for Decker to sit outside. The Silvercup Bakery—now studio—was across the river. The great bridge, which once crossed, according to F. Scott Fitzgerald, anything could happen "even Gatsby could happen," was to his left—and the empty page on his lap. He allowed himself to envision Josh, then he put words in his mouth.

Garreth knew that he had overstepped his authority when he went to Decker's studio, but something about that guy . . . So when the word came down the line that Josh Near was "shopping" Decker from New York City, Garreth went directly to the Crown Attorney's office and made a pitch to trade Josh's coke charge for the whereabouts of Decker Roberts, who he said was a suspect in an arson or perhaps a string of arsons, one of which had caused the death of an elderly night watchman.

It took a bit of doing, but by eight o'clock the deal was done, and by nine o'clock Josh had his assurance that his coke charge would be dropped if he gave up Decker Roberts—and Garreth thought of his father's rage at a young boy of that same name: Decker Roberts.

Yslan hit the return key on her iPhone and the name Josh Near came up, followed by his basic data. She scanned it quickly and assumed that he was one of Decker's students from Toronto. Decker's movements in New York had at times made sense—at others were indecipherable. She understood him visiting the two places where he had lived with his wife and son, but what was he doing in Patchin Place and why the meeting with Josh Near? But more important was Josh's phone call to his lawyer in Toronto that they had intercepted. What was that about?

She hit her speed dialer. Her boss, Harrison, came on the phone, "Yeah."

"I think we've got trouble here in good ol' River City."

"Do you have enough men to look after it?"

"If you keep the local cops out of it."

"I'll try. They're not all that fond of us up there. How soon do you think this is going down?"

"I don't know—I'll get back to you."

## 27

## A LITTLE ACTING

"YOU'RE NOT GOING TO TELL ME WHAT THIS IS ABOUT, ARE you, Decker?"

"It's about truth . . ."

". . . justice, and the American way—I saw that one too."

Decker looked out the window of Josh's apartment. In Washington Square Park two inline skaters were making magic with their movements. *Reaching into the jet stream,* Decker thought, *and they don't even know it.* He had a strong impulse to retreat to the Museum of Modern Art, surrounding himself with those who had put their heads up in the jet stream—voyaged—and come back to us with their visions of another world: de Kooning, Klee, Jackson Pollock, especially Mark Rothko, whose chapel in Houston was Decker's North American Chartres.

"So what is it you want me to do?" Josh asked.

"A little bit of acting, playacting if you wish."

"With a lawyer?"

What was that strange edge to the word "lawyer"? For the umpteenth time Decker asked himself if he trusted this young man. But what choice did he have? Charendoff had seen him twice when he had sent him to do his dirty work up in Stanstead, so he needed someone like Josh Near to get access to him. Finally he responded, "Yeah, with a lawyer—think of it as playing a scene and the lawyer's your acting partner."

"What's my action, Decker? If I had the right to write the end of the scene, what would the lawyer do?"

"I taught you that."

"And a bunch of other stuff, but answer my question, Teach."

That edge again. "Are you all right, Josh?"

"I'm fine, Decker."

Decker couldn't resist. He flicked his eyes shut. Squiggled lines—then flattening into trapezoids. At least partially a truth. But then again what answer to the question "Are you all right?" doesn't have some 'squiggle' to it?

"In fact, I'm getting better and better," Josh added apropos of nothing in particular.

Perfect rectangles—a truth.

"Don't do that!" Josh snapped.

"What?"

"That eye-closing thing."

Decker didn't realize it was so obvious, but then again Josh was a superb actor—and a great actor sees and hears like the narrator in a major Russian novel. "Sorry."

"Do I bore you, Decker?"

Decker was about to say "Hardly" but pulled out his notebook and turned it to face Josh. "Look. Just go through it with me like we'd go through a film scene or an audition. Okay?"

"We going to chart?"

"I don't think it's necessary—this is all done in one take."

"Drone notes?"

"They'll be obvious when you hit them."

Josh shrugged.

"So look, I've written out the lines I need you to say in capitals. The lawyer's probable answers are underlined." He looked up and Josh was all concentration—good. The guy had incredible focus when he wanted to use it. "So you begin with a greeting of some sort—any way you like—to which he then responds something like: 'I represent lots of performers.'"

"Actors," Josh said sharply. "I'm an actor not a performer. Circus guys are performers."

"Right. Actors. So he says he represents lots of actors. And you respond to that with: 'I need someone who can help me with things on both sides of the border—I'm a Canadian. You knew that, right?' To which he answers, 'Sure, absolutely.' Although I'm sure he didn't have a clue about that. But you continue: 'So I have business dealings on both sides of the border. And in Quebec as well. Can you handle things in Quebec? It's Napoleonic Code law there.' He probably hadn't heard of Napoleonic code law since law school—and even then only in passing—but I'm sure he'll say something like: 'We have loads of resources in the firm.' Then he'll probably mention Louisiana since it has Napoleonic Code law."

"How do you know shit like that, Decker?"

"I just do. Then I need you to ask him: 'Have you ever been to Quebec?' I have no idea what his answer will be to that, but whatever it is, positive or negative, you continue: 'I like the eastern townships south of Montreal a lot. I'm thinking of setting up a business near the border.' If he asks you what kind of business, hedge as if you're hiding a great prospect and say: 'Not sure but I think there are real opportunities up there.' Then you be sure to say this exactly: 'You or your firm ever done any business up there?' Let him answer that. Then ask: 'Ever been up there yourself?' Let him answer that too then say: 'I met the Irwin family there a while back. Do you know them by chance?' Let him answer that, then cut him short, claim you have a meeting and that you'll get back to him. Once you get the answer I want you to cut off all conversation."

"Who are the Irwins, Decker?"

For a moment Decker really wanted to share his knowledge of the potential murder, then he stopped himself. "Just a name drawn from a hat."

"You're a lousy liar, Decker."

Decker was really tired of hearing that.

"Don't try acting, Decker, it's beyond your reach."

Decker didn't reply, glad to have moved past the "who are the Irwins" question.

• • •

It took Josh only one phone call. "Okay, my people have set the meeting for two tomorrow afternoon at that restaurant."

"Did they reserve you a table?"

"Of course."

"Get them to tell you which one."

"Sure."

"Good." Decker was about to leave when he said, "Bring your cell phone. I'll call you before you enter the restaurant, then leave your phone on, on the table and connected to me."

Bob's Big Ol' BBQ was on Twenty-second around the corner from the Chelsea Hotel where Leonard Cohen, another fine Canadian boy, made it with Janis Joplin and then wrote a song about it. A sort of kiss and sing thing. The restaurant was a New York City chic diner—pulled pork on a white bun for $17.95. Decker arrived a few minutes early and walked carefully past Charendoff as the man perused the menu. An expensive leather briefcase was at the lawyer's side. As Decker had assumed, Charendoff arrived first and took the side of the booth facing the door—the power position. Decker had reserved the booth behind them and sat back to back.

Decker ordered a ludicrously overpriced glass of red wine. Then another.

Josh was late. Even for a star he was pushing the acceptable limit.

Decker cursed him quietly and ordered dinner.

A commotion at the front of the restaurant signaled Josh's arrival. Decker sighed and swallowed the second glass of wine. It hurt going down. He flicked the toggle on his miniature digital recorder and checked the position of the polished soup spoon to his left at the table's edge. He adjusted it slightly so that he had an image of the lawyer in the concave of the spoon—three-quarters turned away and upside down, but an image nonetheless. Then he cupped his hand over his cell phone's tiny earpiece in his left ear.

Josh finished signing autographs and posing with young women for photographs. Decker always wondered about boy-friends' willingness to take pictures of their ladies draped around stars. Didn't they know that their girlfriends would be fantasizing about the star the next time the two of them were mid coital thrust?

Josh approached the booth. He held the script folded vertically in his hand. Decker smiled to himself—first audition, hold the script. It lowers expectations and gives you something do with your right hand, but never look at it.

Josh, without referring to the script, went right to the first beat. "Thanks for meeting me on such short notice, I really appreciate it."

"Sure, my pleasure."

"So look, I'm in the market for a new kind of representation. I want a nonentertainment lawyer—someone smart that I can deal with in confidence—for a second opinion, if you understand me."

Then he put his cell phone on the table.

Nicely done—smooth, Josh.

Charendoff said that was a wise thing then added, "It's always my pleasure to meet people of real talent."

Decker smiled. It seemed that Charendoff was on the right track to get to "So what can I do for you" when Decker heard the sound of a zipper opening followed by a dull thunk on the table behind him. He glanced at his strategically placed soup spoon—a leather-bound stack of paper was on the tabletop.

"Mr. Near. Do you mind if I call you Josh? From your work I almost feel like I know you personally. So is it okay if I did that—call you Josh, I mean?"

"No, sure, Josh is fine."

"Well Josh, I hope you don't mind but I've taken the liberty of bringing you a copy of my latest screenplay. I think it's something special—and there's really a fine cameo in it for you."

Sound of the thing being pushed across the tabletop.

Decker winced.

"I actually only do this lawyer thing so I can have the freedom to write. Well, you know how it is."

Decker heard Josh stutter then mumble something—a sure sign he didn't know what to do next. Then he heard the scuffling of running feet and felt a strong hand grab him by his forearm and yank him to his feet. Then a woman's face was so close to his that he could smell the perfume at the base of her neck. Then in a whisper he heard her southern accent say, "Mr. Roberts, you are in danger, come with us quickly." Then she kissed him full and hard on the mouth. "Whoa there, big boy," she said loudly, "come on, honey, not here in front of all these fine folks." Then two sets of hands propelled him toward the front door with a flurry of "Hey, bro, you've had too much to drinks" and before he knew it he was in the back of a black tinted-windowed SUV roaring toward the Holland Tunnel.

Through the circular window in the swinging kitchen door of the restaurant Emerson Remi watched the action too—a Dubonnet on the rocks in one hand, a brisket on rye in the other. Being a reporter for the *Times* allowed you to know the cooks in places like this. He saw everything from his perch: Charendoff's early arrival, then Decker's, finally Josh's ostentatious entrance. He noted the vertically folded pages in Josh's hand. Earlier he had picked out the two undercover cops near the front door of the restaurant. They hovered—watchers shouldn't hover. Then there was the Scottish-looking thug at the bar. The whole thing appeared to Emerson as a set piece—with too many performers—sort of a *MAD* magazine Spy vs. Spy times two or three. Then he saw Josh approach Charendoff's booth and the two undercover cops tense. Josh sat opposite the lawyer and Decker tilted his soup spoon as he slid an earplug from a cell phone into his left ear. He saw Josh put his cell phone on the table. The lawyer brought out a thick sheaf of bound papers, then all of a sudden there was motion all around. From the side of his eye he saw the two undercover cops being badged by guys in grey suits, while Yslan, looking very pretty, kissed Decker and exited with him in a flurry along with two other men. As they did Emerson saw Josh slip out the side door of the restaurant. Then all was as it was before except Charendoff sat alone in his booth with his stack of bound papers and scowled. It was as if nothing had happened: the waiters waited, the patrons . . . patroned, although the Scottish guy had slipped out somehow.

Then he noticed what no one else seemed to have noticed—Josh had left his cell phone on the table.

Emerson entered the restaurant, sauntered over, reached down, and picked up the cell phone—and wondered if this could somehow get him to Yslan and her synaesthetes.

He was pretty sure it could.

# 28

## *GARDEN STATE*

THE WOMAN WHO HAD A FEW MINUTES BEFORE PLANTED A big one on him turned from the front seat and faced him. For the first time Decker noticed the extraordinary colour of her almost translucent eyes.

"I think you've got the wrong . . ."

"You're a very bad liar, Mr. Roberts."

Again with the bad liar!

"I would suggest that you shut up until we get to where we're going."

"And where would that be?"

"Somewhere safe," she said then added, "truthfully—somewhere safe."

Decker looked past her as they roared into the tunnel and was astonished to see the Holland Tunnel at four o'clock on a Wednesday afternoon—completely empty. He sat back. The wall tiles whipped by him so fast he thought they were flying—and in some ways they were. Decker clutched his laptop to his chest and reached for a seat belt.

"Is there a seat belt law in New Jersey?" the woman with the translucent eyes asked.

"I'm not dying in New Jersey. It would just be too stupid." He buckled up. And they sped on. He wanted them to talk or spit or do something. They didn't. The beautiful girl looked straight ahead. The two men who had hustled him into the SUV—one beside him, the other driving—didn't remove their wraparound sunglasses or move a muscle. The one in the backseat was a cleaned-up version of Mr. T. The one who drove had immaculately coiffed grey hair—Ted Knight from the old *Mary Tyler Moore Show.* Finally Decker said, "So, aren't you going to put a blindfold on me or something?"

"Why, Mr. Roberts, do you like being blindfolded?" the woman said as she turned toward him.

"Not particularly. So if you're not going to blindfold me, you won't mind telling me where we're going."

"Deeper into New Jersey," she said. A smile creased her wide, expressive mouth.

"So you don't mind me seeing where we're going?"

"With some people I'd mind—a lot. Not with you. You use buildings as markers to find your way home, Mr. Roberts. When your usual subway entrance is closed and you have to use another exit, you haven't got a clue where you are. You set records for a lack of sense of direction, so I don't mind you seeing where we are going because you haven't got a chance in hell of finding the place again—do you?"

Decker glanced at Mr. T out of the side of his eye. He was tempted to ask how she knew that stuff about him but thought better of it when Mr. T momentarily turned his gaze toward him.

"No questions."

*That was pretty straightforward,* Decker thought. A large green sign announced that they were entering the outskirts of Newark—New Jersey's toilet.

The woman turned to face him. "Why not get in touch with Eddie?"

"Excuse me?"

"You heard me, Mr. Roberts. Get in touch with him—he'll want to know where you are. This car's wired and you're welcome to use our Wi-Fi for free—not like at Starbucks. Or you could meet him in the synaesthetes chat room."

Decker wanted desperately to talk to Eddie, but he hesitated. Why? He didn't know, but he knew he shouldn't call Eddie. Couldn't let Eddie know where he was? Was that it? He didn't know. He just wasn't sure anymore—not sure. He turned away.

"Or you could call Trish. Sure. Let's do that." She dialed then handed him the cell phone she'd taken from him in the restaurant and put her BlackBerry to her ear.

The phone was already ringing. "Don't worry, the caller ID is blocked and I can hear every word either of you say. It's called conferencing. Welcome to the twenty-first century."

Trish picked up on the third ring, "Okay, you have exactly twenty seconds to identify yourself. This blocked caller ID is bush league, whoever you are."

"It's Decker," Decker said warily.

"Hey. I love the stuff Theo gave me."

"Good."

"Yeah. Lynchings are good. Fuck; they're great."

"Yeah."

"Decker, you okay?"

Decker looked at the woman in the front seat, her face an open challenge—"Go ahead, tell her and see what happens."

"Yeah. I'm fine."

"Good. The network put the rushes of the first episode in front of a group of people—a trial audience. What do you call it when they do that?"

"Stupidity and cowardice."

"Yeah. That too and funny. Show could use more funny, Decker. And I still want you to do the opening voiceover."

"Me too," Decker said, never taking his eyes off the woman in the front seat.

"Really?"

"Yeah."

"That's great. So when can you come in and record the pilot voiceover?"

Decker looked at the woman and raised his shoulders. She hit a button and the connection went dead. Then she reached for Decker's cell phone.

"I need it or my son can't call me."

"He hasn't called you for a long time."

"How do you know about that?"

"We know lots about you, Mr. Roberts."

"Did you ever find out what happened to Leena that night after she bought the car? Awful, that. Such a pretty girl then."

So this woman knew about that too.

"What is it exactly that you want from me?"

"Recognize this picture?" She handed him a photograph. It showed him getting out of the trunk of the car on the American side of the Akwesasne Reserve.

"No, I'm afraid I don't."

"Lie better, Decker. Lie much better, because illegal crossing into the United States is a federal offence. Heard of Leavenworth? Not a place you'd enjoy very much."

"Okay, I recognize the photo."

"Good."

"How's about this one?" She showed him a photograph on her BlackBerry from the restaurant where Josh had met Charendoff. It showed a square-faced Scot in his mid-forties or early fifties. In good shape. Fine grey hair that no doubt had at one time been blond. Piercing blue eyes.

Mac had always taken a good picture.

Decker didn't recognize the man in the photo and told the woman as much. She said, "Take another look."

"I don't know who he is."

She put the photograph aside then said, "The problem you have is that neither do we."

## 29

## MAC AND HENRY-CLAY

MAC SAT IN HIS CHEAP HOTEL ROOM AT 107TH AND AMSTER-dam. He'd just got off the phone with Henry-Clay, who was not pleased that he'd lost Decker—not pleased even a bit.

Mac knew that it must have been feds at work—efficient, organized, clinical and grey suits equals feds. He'd told Henry-Clay as much, and the man had simply said, "Find Decker Roberts, Mr. MacMillan—find him fast."

Mac sat with the pages of the script Decker had written for Josh opened on the Formica tabletop—beside a large glass of scotch.

"Feds," he mumbled. He had a cop cousin in Montreal who told him an interesting story about American feds. It may have just been a rumour the guy was repeating, but it had the ring of truth to it. The cousin claimed that the RCMP had been tracking Ahmed Ressam—the Millennium Bomber—from the time he left his apartment in Montreal as he made his way across Canada. The RCMP didn't want to arrest him on the Canadian side of the border because of the lax refuge claimant process north of the forty-ninth parallel that could very well have seen Mr. Ressam back on the streets in less than a week as he awaited the often four-year-long claim review. So the RCMP had simply followed him at a distance, and when he headed to the American border they informed the FBI—who decided that a female customs officer should make the bust. Nice touch that. But when later the U.S. president claimed that terrorists came from Canada—well, the RCMP and almost every Canadian police officer who knew the story were not pleased.

Mac thought about that. Then he finished his drink, flipped open his cell phone and began to round up the troops—on both sides of the border.

Henry-Clay threw his crystal glass against the far wall and it shattered with a surprising crackle and pop. It left a fine stain on the wildly expensive silk wall covering, but truth be told, he couldn't care less. Although his dates seemed impressed by crap like that.

He reminded himself that Mr. MacMillan had never failed him, and they'd been together for quite a while.

He'd first met the man in his Tulane years. A roughneck Scot from the Ninth Ward who talked as if he were raised in the depths of Brooklyn. Later Henry-Clay learned the reason for this: the same families that ran the docks in Brooklyn ran the docks in New Orleans. So Stanley Kowalski actually did talk like Brando in the movie—a New Yorker, not a southerner.

They'd met in a bar on Tchoupitoulas. Henry-Clay was buying a round for the table when this scruff monster half bull half man moseyed over to the table and sat down with him and his friends. Before Henry-Clay or any of the others could say anything, MacMillan said, "Get the fuck out." Then to Henry-Clay he said, "Except you."

The others gladly skittered away leaving Henry-Clay to his fate. "Can I buy you a drink?" Henry-Clay asked.

"Why would you want to do that? I'm not one of your pussy friends."

"As you will."

"What? Is that some faggot thing or other?"

"No, it's not. It's nothing."

"So why'd you say it?"

"I have no idea why I said that—I apologize."

"Good. So what's the point spread on Tuesday night's game?"

Henry-Clay brightened—a new client. "Tulane by five and a half."

MacMillan shook his large head. His almost white curls fell across the wide expanse of his forehead. "Nope. Got that one wrong."

"Really?"

"Trust me—Rice by three."

"That's an eight-point swing in two days. Can't be done."

"If Rice doesn't win by three points you're in serious shit, little man. Maybe you should consider getting out of this game. It's too tough for a soft guy like you. I'd get out and get out fast or things could get very rough here for you."

Henry-Clay looked at the man across the table from him. Most assuredly the guy could take his head off and toss it in the garbage can if that's what he wanted. But Henry-Clay saw that something else was at work here.

This man was as much an outsider as he was. So he pushed his drink across the table to the man and said, "Come work for me."

MacMillan laughed a short chortle. "I don't work for kids."

"I'm not a kid. I'm the most successful bookmaker in Orleans Parish and you know it and I can give you what you really want."

"And what is it that I really want?"

"Respect. It's not about money or pussy for you—although both of those are important to you. What's more important and will in fact lead to the other two is respect."

Henry-Clay noticed the man slowly uncoil.

"What's your name?"

"MacMillan. Some call me Mac."

"Not me. I'll call you Mr. MacMillan like you deserve. Now tell me how much they were going to pay you for this."

And MacMillan did.

And Henry-Clay doubled MacMillan's take—and Henry-Clay had his henchman. Like every businessman he needed a little muscle now and then—not too often, but sometimes people needed to be persuaded to change their minds. And Mr. MacMillan was more than capable of doing that.

That was a lifetime ago—well before he knew the real ratio of the placebo effect, a ratio that allowed him to pocket a full 28.25 percent more on every pill Yolles Pharmaceuticals sold. And well before he told Mac about Decker Roberts's son way out west on Vancouver Island.

THE SAFE HOUSE OR WHATEVER IT WAS WAS DEEP IN THE suburbs on a cul-de-sac at the end of a long road. It had an open field behind it and substantial distance between it and the houses on either side. It was surprisingly old—1910 or 1912, Decker thought.

They drove the SUV into a garage, the door of which closed quickly behind them. After Ted Knight and the woman inspected the house Decker was ushered into a back room. Mr. T pulled the window cord and the blinds flew up. The windows were bricked in with cinder block. "Nice view."

"For your protection," the woman said as she gently pushed him farther into the room.

"Is there room service? I could use a Coke."

"Get some rest. We start in an hour."

"Start what?" The woman didn't answer. Mr. T nodded and left. "Fine. Good answer. And how long will this thing, whatever it is, go on?"

"Until it's finished."

"That makes sense."

"I have to tell you that I am completely unimpressed by snappy retorts."

"Too bad, here I thought we'd been getting on so well that I was sure we'd have a second date."

"If I were you, Mr. Roberts, I'd rest."

Suddenly Decker didn't feel so smart. "What do you want from me?"

"The truth, Mr. Roberts. Just the truth."

"Sure."

She held up a hand to stop him from continuing. "In an hour—actually in fifty-eight minutes."

"Okay. Fine. I don't suppose I get a phone call."

"You had a phone call. You called your producer, Trish."

Decker sighed. "Yes I did."

"If it was me, I'd have used my phone call to ask for some legal representation—but you chose to talk about your TV show. What's it called?"

*"At the Junction."*

"Sounds dull. Get some rest."

Decker looked toward the small cot in the corner of the room. "What's your name?"

"You haven't earned the right to know my name yet, Mr. Roberts. See you in fifty-seven minutes," she said as she closed the solid oak door. Old houses have solid doors.

Decker heard the dead bolt slide to, then lay down on the bed—and much to his surprise fell into a sound and dreamless sleep.


Emerson Remi had friends. Princeton was good for that sort of thing—especially if you were bright and had solid Princetonian bloodlines. Emerson was and had. His little black book had the numbers of every member of his secret-society dining club and all their important contacts. He quickly looked up a number in San Jose and dialed. Three minutes later the brains behind the global GPS system was on the line, and five minutes after that Emerson was following the man's instructions on how to trace the final number dialed on the cell phone he had found in the restaurant—Decker's number. Then how to triangulate its position when that phone was next used.

Emerson sat in the bar of the lobby of the Algonquin Hotel in Midtown and waited. As he did he wondered if Dorothy Parker had sat on the very stool upon which he now sat. "If every girl at Smith and Bennington were laid end to end, I wouldn't be the least bit surprised." Well, he'd done his part in that.

Yslan used the fifty-seven minutes to contact Harrison in D.C. and get updates on Charendoff, Josh, how the New York cops reacted to being taken off the case and most important who the older man was who sat in the restaurant hiding behind the copy of the *Daily News*. The guy was a player—it was written all over his rugged face. The Roman legions had been defeated only twice in their entire history. Once by the fanatical Parthians, the other time by the Scots—no doubt led into battle by men like this guy. Then she asked what was foremost on her mind: "How much time do I have?"

"It's hard to say."

"No more corroboration on either of the terrorist's testimony?"

"Not yet—but we have leads, Special Agent. Let me deal with that—you deal with Decker Roberts." Then he hung up.

A curse rose in her throat but she swallowed it down and concentrated on the new information as it came to her BlackBerry. None of it was all that helpful. She demanded updates on what she thought of as Decker's four Junction contacts—Theo, Eddie, Leena and Trish—then she asked for and got copies of the cancellation orders for Decker's credit cards, the arson report on his house, the calling of his loan at the TD Bank and finally on the condemning of his studio.

Mr. T stuck his large head into the room. "Coffee?"

She nodded. "And I want anything that comes in while I'm with him brought directly to me." Mr. T left and was immediately replaced in the door by Ted Knight. "You let Mr. Roberts keep those USB keys."

"Yeah."

"Can I ask why? It's against procedure."

"So's kidnapping," she snapped. Then she shrugged. "I want him to give me those USB keys voluntarily. And the digital tape recorder in his pants pocket."

"Sort of a test?"

"More a QED." In answer to Ted's questioning look she said, "*Quod erat demonstrandum*—thus it is proved. You northerners didn't have the quality education we had in the South."

"True," Ted said. "The few of you who can read down there can read quite well."

She smiled. She knew he'd gone to Cornell, was a smart guy, but unlike her he'd been educated outside the syntactical realities of the King James Version of the Bible—certainly outside its precepts.

"Shall I wake him?" Ted asked.

Yslan recalled some nonsense in the film *Usual Suspects* where a cop claimed that the one who falls asleep is always the guilty party. Idiocy. Some sleep, some cry, some jerk off—what they do doesn't mean anything.

She stared at the grey-haired man for a moment. What did she really know about him? Then she said, "Sure. Wake him up. It wouldn't be right for a fine southern lady to wake a sleeping gentleman."

Mac's man watched the surfers on their boards riding the swell off the west shore of Vancouver Island. He knew that one of them was the man he'd been sent to follow, so he stepped back into the tree line and watched as the first snowflakes of the season fell into the vastness of the Pacific Ocean.

# 31

## *DECKER AND YSLAN*

ROUGH, STRONG HANDS BROUGHT DECKER BACK FROM A darkness within the darkness of sleep. He saw that a sturdy table had been set up at the foot of the bed—and sitting on the far side of the table was the woman with the translucent blue eyes. A gooseneck lamp on the table was the only light source in the room. She signaled him to sit at the foot of the bed. He did. Then she waved Ted Knight and Mr. T out of the room. There was a long pause. Decker looked at the woman. Thirty-two—maybe thirty-four—thirty-six tops. Closer to her mom than her dad. Brothers—tons of brothers. He glanced at her left hand—no wedding ring, nor band of lighter skin—but he didn't need that reassurance. He knew she was single. No kids. Her left index finger lay, partially curled, against her fully extended middle finger—so she had been a smoker. No nicotine stains—so past tense.

"What's the smile for?" she asked.

"Not Marlboros or you've come a long way baby or Kents, but something in a soft pack, filterless—Pall Malls?"

"Nope. I was a Luckies girl."

"Like your grandfather?"

"That one's too easy, Mr. Roberts. All the GIs smoked Luckies in World War Two. But the rest was impressive. However . . ." She hesitated, then said, "That's not your only parlour trick, is it?"

Decker looked at her, then glanced at the door. It wasn't closed. "Am I under arrest?"

"No."

"Then I can go?"

"No."

"Then I'm under arrest, dammit."

"If you want it that way—sure. You illegally entered the United States of America. We can arrest you for that. If that's what you want. Or you can stay here in protective custody until we figure out who tried to kill you."

"Nobody tried to kill me."

"Your house burnt down."

"It was a complete fluke that I got back to town that night. I was supposed to stay over in Cleveland but I lucked into a late flight that had been delayed. They probably thought the place was empty."

"Who did?"

"The arsonist who's been torching places in the Junction for months."

"And the calling of your loan and the cancellation of your credit card and the condemning of your studio—those were all mistakes, just accidents as well? Who do you figure did that to you?"

"I don't know."

"Neither do I, but someone's making your life a misery." She pulled out the BlackBerry with Mac's photograph a second time and turned it to Decker. "Who's this guy?"

"I told you I don't know."

"Why were you in Orlando?"

"Business."

"And Pittsburgh?"

"More business."

"And Cleveland?"

"Your turn to guess."

"More business?"

"Good guess."

"You've never done three business trips back to back."

"Is that so?"

"Yeah. It's so."

"If you insist."

"Fine. Why did you contact Josh Near?"

"He's a friend—a former student."

"And why did you have him meet with the lawyer—that Char-endoff gentleman? And don't deny that you did. You were sitting in the booth directly behind them." She leaned forward. "Did you know that Mr. Near has a pending cocaine charge in Toronto? And that less than ten minutes after you left his apartment on Saturday he was on the phone with his lawyer in Toronto asking if he turned you in if it would help with his little drug misunderstanding? Did you know that?"

Decker rapidly went over his conversation with Josh. He'd needed Josh, so he never really tested him for truthfulness.

"Would you like me to repeat my question, Mr. Roberts?"

"No," Decker said. His voice was suddenly hoarse.

"Josh shopped you, Mr. Roberts. Do you know that term?"

"No, but I can guess its meaning."

"Good. That's what the two flatfoots were doing at the door of the restaurant. Did you notice them?"

"No."

"Well, they were both New York City undercover cops."

"And you? What are you, you people?"

"Not cops, Mr. Roberts." Yslan let out a long breath and withdrew her eyes from him. "I'm concerned for your safety, Mr. Roberts. And for the safety of your kind," she added.

"What does that mean—your kind?"

"You know what it means. I'm not sure how much time we have, and there's a lot more going on here than even you can imagine, so I'd really prefer not to play games. Someone tried to kill you—okay, burned your house to the ground. Someone—I assume the same person—cancelled your credit cards, called your two-hundred-thousand-dollar loan and condemned your studio. So whoever this is, they've got a ton of resources and are pretty damned serious about warning you, don't you think?"

"Warning me?"

"Think for a second. If, as you think, they weren't trying to kill you—they could have, Mr. Roberts. In many ways it makes more sense than sending such an elaborate message."

"A message about what?"

"I don't know about what, but I'm willing to start with the who, as in who have you pissed off of late? Because whoever it is, is evidently anxious to show you what damage he can do to you if you fuck with him."

Decker touched the USB keys in his pocket and felt the once, comforting feel of the digital tape recorder beside them. "What concern is all this to you—this is my problem, not yours. I don't even know who the hell you are or what the hell you're doing here with me."

"Okay. I work for the NSA," she said as she put her elaborate ID cards on the table for him to see. Then she laid out Ted Knight's and Mr. T's. She handed him a phone number and his cell phone. "Call. They can verify who I am."

Decker took the phone but didn't call.

"I have responsibility for the synaesthetes file at the NSA. It's my job to keep you and yours safe."

"Why?"

"Don't play at this. Surely it's clear that a person with your particular talent could be a great asset to the NSA—to the safety of this country."

Decker looked at his hands—he had a momentary flash of Seth's hand in his as they left the cemetery. "What's your name?"

"As it says on my ID, Special Agent Yslan Hicks."

Decker nodded.

"What, Mr. Roberts?"

"And you've decided to help me?"

"No."

"No?"

"No. It's my job to help you, Mr. Roberts."

• • •

"So you thought that you could catch Mr. Charendoff lying about knowing the Irwin family and then you'd know that he had the boy in Stanstead killed?"

"Or he killed him himself."

Yslan shook her head.

"What?"

"Rich people hire out."

Decker nodded.

"And you think he did it because the kid impregnated his daughter?"

"No, because his daughter loved that boy . . ."

". . . and was contemplating throwing away all the advantages her father had worked so hard to give her, yeah, yeah, yeah."

"Well, yes."

"Mr. Roberts, the girl's getting married in Paris in six weeks." She checked her watch, "Five weeks and four days, and if there was a baby, it is no more."

"And Robert Irwin's death in Stanstead?"

"Could have been murder. Could have been suicide. Tough call."

"That's not how the local cop saw it."

"Ah, the fabulous Officer Matthews."

"You met him?"

"Don't you get it—we've met everyone you've met. Every-where you've gone, we've gone. You've cost us a fortune fol-lowing you all over the country." Seeing Decker's stunned look she added, "Hopping in and out of cabs and using basement exits isn't exactly the sophisticated way to throw off a tail—and you'd better believe that we have the best tails in the world working for us."

Decker seemed to get his composure back and said, "Yes, but Officer Matthews was certain—"

"I'm sure he was. But he's a local cop. He sees the world through his eyes—local eyes. Girls from rich families invade his town every summer, sometimes have romances with his young men. He was certainly telling the truth from his point of view—but it's not necessarily *the* truth."

"How much did Charendoff know about this?"

"He's had investigators up there, so he knew that what evidence existed wasn't very compelling. Look, he's a lawyer, Mr. Roberts, if he did it he's not going to compound his problem by going after you."

"But I knew things. I was privy to—"

"Privy to? Let's be honest. You guessed, but guessing doesn't count. You don't know enough to make yourself a target, although that little stunt with Josh Near at the restaurant could well have gotten you into Mr. Charendoff's sights."

"So you don't know that Charendoff didn't have Robert Irwin killed?"

"It's impossible to prove a negative. But my guess—I guess sometimes too, and I'm pretty good at guessing—is that he did what rich people who get into trouble always do."

"And what's that?"

"They buy their way out, Mr. Roberts. A Paris abortion. A Paris boyfriend. A Paris wedding—not cheap."

"But effective in getting a rich girl to forget about a poor boy in Stanstead, Quebec?"

"You can answer that question yourself."

"So it's not Charendoff who's after me?"

"I don't think so." A long pause settled between the two of them. Decker filed it away under To Be Understood. There was something about Charendoff and Stanstead and the dead boy encased in ice in the river that was important to all this—but he couldn't figure out exactly what.

"So how did someone like Charendoff find you?"

"I'm an urban legend."

"Like alligators in the sewers?"

"There are alligators in the sewers."

"And men who can tell when other people are telling the truth?"

"No."

"No?"

"No. Not men, man—me."

"So you're gifted?"

Decker wanted to say "And burdened," but kept his mouth shut until finally he said, "Charendoff contacted me through this." Decker flipped her a card: www.whatthefucksthetruth.com.

"Catchy."

Decker shrugged.

"They contact you, you get back to them if you want?"

Decker nodded.

"A dead-letter drop."

"Nope."

Yslan looked at him.

"An electronic dead-letter drop. This is the twenty-first century, isn't it, Ms. Hicks?"

## 32

*SETH*

SETH STRIPPED THE PLASTIC FROM THE CATHETER AS HE glanced at the BCG medication on the table. Bacille Calmette-Guérin vaccine, originally developed to prevent tuberculosis, was the only thing keeping his cancer at bay.

His chemotherapy treatments had gone reasonably well this time round, but he knew there was a limit to the miracles that the pharmaceutical industry could offer. But he was grateful for those miracles.

As the nurse practitioner entered the small room he inserted the catheter, slowing just briefly as it passed his prostate.

"You prefer to do that yourself?" she asked.

"I do," he said.

She opened the opaque brown wrapper and removed the delicate vial containing the even more delicate BCG. She inserted the 50 ml of live vaccine into the open catheter valve and pushed the plunger.

It didn't feel like much of anything, but Seth had to keep his corrosively active imagination in check. When he first contracted bladder cancer he'd made the mistake of going to a cancer site on the Net. The first thing to catch his eye was the word "stoma." The word entered his mind and grew there—like a cancer. The only way to deal with it was to rearrange the letters to form other things. So the terrifying "stoma" first became "atoms," then "stoma" became "stomach," then "stomach" became "stew pot," then "stew pot" became "Studebaker." And him sitting on his father's knee naming cars as they drove by. And him pointing, then yelling, "Studebaker, Daddy, a Studebaker." And it had been. The only one they ever saw. A pleasant memory—so much better than a harbinger that life as he knew it was over.

"You can take it out now," the nurse said as she handed him two sanitized wipes.

He took a breath, and as he had done so many times before pinched the neck then removed the lengthy rubber tube in one swift motion.

Leaving the urology clinic Seth didn't bother looking at the other men sitting in the waiting room or listening to the *Sesame Street* puppets sing "One of These Things is Not Like the Others" on the wall-mounted monitor. If he had he would have been surprised that there was a man there who was as out of place in this old man's world as he was. He would also have been surprised that the man walked up to the front counter and, when the receptionist was busy explaining to a patient the procedure to remove a stent, had reached over and taken Seth's medical chart.

The rest of the day after a BCG treatment was always a crap shoot. Some days he had no reaction, others fever, chills and so little energy that he couldn't write. He guided his beat-up Volvo out of town and headed toward the ocean—and a quiet place to sit it out. He sensed the nausea would be coming up soon; it was going to be one of those days.

It was not hard for the man who stole Seth's chart to follow the Volvo despite the fact that on Canada's west coast there were a lot of beat-up old Volvos. But the young man drove slowly and soon it became clear that he was headed toward the same beach as before.

Seth stood well back and watched three surfers squiggle into their almost inch-thick wet suits, pull on their hoods, and head into the always-cold Pacific water.

Surfing was his refuge—the rhythm of the ocean beneath his

board brought him far away from his illness and his "talent" that he was, over the years, more and more sure was related to his cancer. The sun pierced the almost omnipresent cloud cover—a rarity but much appreciated. This wasn't California after all—this was Vancouver Island.

Seth took out a writing pad and leaned against a naked maple tree that bent toward the ocean. He liked the strength of the thing. No leaves but its roots held onto the rocks refusing to fall. Refusing to give up its life. He often came to this spot, and wrote leaning against what he thought of as "my bent tree." He opened his notebook and allowed his dreams to the page. This day the dreams were filled with rage—nineteen and already so sick that he could sense the approach of the end.

For a moment he had a chilling vision of his mother—cobwebs pinning her arms to the side of her wheelchair, tent caterpillars enmeshing her head, growing out of her mouth. And heard her final words to his father: "What have you done, Decker? What have you done?"

His cell phone chirped at his side. He looked at the number on the scratched screen—he just couldn't keep his electronic stuff in good working order. It was Eddie. The only one from home he cared about. But he looked at the surfers a second time and wondered if he was up to hearing from his past. He took a deep breath and, keeping his eyes firmly on the ocean's horizon, said, "Hey Eddie."

"Wassup, Seth?"

Seth didn't answer—he never answered open-ended questions.

"Right. Okay. You figured out how to store a number on that phone of yours yet?"

"Yes," Seth lied—he'd never figured out anything about the cell phone except how to receive a call and make one. "Whose number?"

"Your dad's."

Seth took the phone from his ear. Not a good time for this. He wasn't feeling strong—and he needed to be strong to deal with anything from or about his father. He walked down to the waterline, the hard dark sand chilling his feet. He heard a muffled squawk from the phone and put it to his ear.

"You still there?"

"Yes, Eddie. Shoot."

Eddie gave him the number of Decker's new cell phone, and Seth wrote it with his toe in the sand. "Got it."

There was a pause. Seth asked, "Any progress on the legal front with your daughter?"

"Some."

Seth didn't need to see Eddie or close his eyes—a lie.

"You need anything, Seth?"

*Just a bit more life,* he thought, but he said, "No. I'm good. Look after yourself, Eddie." And before Eddie could respond Seth hung up the phone and stuffed it into his backpack. He constantly forgot to recharge the thing so he was surprised that it actually worked this time.

The call wasn't long but long enough for Mac's man to get a fix on the caller—Eddie. The man quickly BlackBerried that information and what he'd learned from Seth's chart to Mac. Then he lit a cigarette and watched.

Seth went back to his bending tree and leaned against its reassuring strength. He tore out the page of his ranting then started a story about a cell phone that only worked when trouble was approaching. Halfway through the BCG kicked in seriously, and he moved quickly into the brush and relieved his stomach of its contents. Then, for the hundredth time, he cursed the gift he'd inherited from his dad.

Returning to his perch he saw a young surfer take a wave and reach her head up into the clear jet stream—and in her own way fly. And as she did, a wave that started its life all the way in Japan roared ashore and erased the phone number Seth had etched with his big toe in the sand.

## 33

## HENRY-CLAY

HENRY-CLAY ALMOST CLAPPED HIS CHUBBY LITTLE HANDS. *A gift from the gods,* he thought. Decker has a son. Mac's guy finds the boy. The kid has bladder cancer and his lifeline is BCG—that happens to be a drug with no profit margin whatsoever.

It took Henry-Clay three phone calls and less than two hours to secure the exclusive Western Hemisphere rights to both make and distribute the thing. The company he bought it from was so grateful to get out of the racket that they almost gave it away for free—almost.

*BCG,* he thought. *Insurance.* Henry-Clay believed in insurance as most people believed in motherhood and apple pie.

"The ropes that bind," he said aloud as he looked out his office window.

The phone on his desk rang. It was his private line—for emergencies only. "What?"

"Sorry boss, thought you'd like to hear—we just got approval for the new antidepressant."

Henry-Clay smiled—five years and eleven months, record time—money well spent to speed up the process. "How long until we can go into production?"

There was a pause on the other end.

"What?" Henry-Clay demanded.

"You put us into production almost two years ago, after we got the second of the preliminary approvals."

Now Henry-Clay's smile grew to radiance. Of course he had.

Despite all the warnings against doing so he'd taken the proverbial bull by the proverbial horns, and now they were way ahead
of the curve. Way ahead. "So how long until we can market it?"

"Almost immediately."

"And the price?"

"Acceptable. A full thirty-five percent less than we thought."

*Actually 36.25 percent,* Henry-Clay thought—the ratio Ratio-
Man had given him—over three times, over three fucking times,
the accepted placebo ratio used commonly in the profession.
Over three times the savings. A miracle. A fucking miracle. And
all it had cost him was six weeks of minimum wage, a $500
bonus and Nasty Natasha's $1,500. And for that he got not only
the ratio but also the algorithm to control the freaks' website.
The only better deal ever swung was by the Dutch for Manhattan
and the feds for the Louisiana Purchase. But those were governments—he was an individual, what this country is about!

The new drug was going to make him a fortune—as long as
he could silence this Decker Roberts. If Mr. Truth showed his face
in his hometown they'd arrest him for arson—so now he was on
the run. Okay. Dead would have been better, but on the run is
good, and if by some wild chance he figured out the connection
to Yolles Pharmaceuticals he now had the means to keep Roberts'
mouth shut. A son's death warrant is a powerful sword to hold
over a father's head. Insurance. Ah, insurance.

It had been risky testing Roberts in the first place, but Henry-
Clay was confident that Roberts couldn't trace the three requests
back to him. Besides, he'd needed to know exactly the extent of
the talent this truth guy really had. Clearly it was powerful.

Finally he said, "Thanks for the call—I want a meeting tomorrow on our promotion package and daily updates on sales thereafter. I want every evening newscast on the big four to have our
product front and centre. Do you think we could get Katie Couric
to take a dose on air? Just kidding. But wouldn't that be something? Look, I want people to think that they are the only ones
*not* taking—what are we calling it, anyway?"

"We usually wait for you for names."

He thought for a moment—dammit, he wished that Miltown hadn't already come and gone. How brilliant was that choice? Miltown 2? Miltown redux? Nah. Maybe a gerund—Streaming? Rafting? No too—just too, too. Happinex? Too on the nose. Contentrex? No, but ending in "ex" is always good. "I'll get back to you with a name. In the meantime book the spots and get our creative guys in this office first thing tomorrow morning. I want America a happy place in six months."

He hung up and thought about that. About happiness. He knew it was the only product to sell in America. After all, it's in the Declaration of Independence under "pursuit of." Something makes you thin—and you happy. Something makes your teeth sparkle—and you happy. Something makes your hair shine—and you happy. Something makes your skin perfect—and you happy. But with this new drug, no preliminary step is required—it goes right to "makes you happy."

He picked up the phone with the scrambled line and added a final small piece of insurance—just in case something went wrong with the drug. "Yes, it's Henry-Clay Yolles, I'd like to speak to Congressman Villianne."

## WHAT'S A LIE

DECKER WAS EXHAUSTED, BUT THE WOMAN ACROSS THE table from him looked fresh—attentive. In his acting class he would have called her fully present. And somehow more beautiful after all these hours of grilling. How could that be? Didn't she ever get tired? They'd been at it for he didn't know how many hours. There was no exterior light in the room, so he had no idea if it was day or night—and of course they'd taken his watch. It gave him eerie memories of a night in Shanghai.

After finally dismissing Charendoff as a suspect he handed over a USB key and said, "Then there's this."

*Good,* Yslan thought, *very good.* "So tell me about it."

"Why not just listen to it?"

"I'll listen later. Now I want you to tell me about it."

Decker looked at her for a moment then started, "Well, there was the thing with the Penguins just a few days back."

"You had a thing with penguins?"

"The Pittsburgh Penguins."

"Ah, those Penguins. You Canadians and your ice hockey."

"Hockey."

"What?"

"It's hockey—not ice hockey."

"Yeah, who cares? So, tell me about these Penguins."

"It was one of the hardest for me to get right."

"To tell if he was lying?"

Decker looked away.

Yslan pressed on, "Why was that, Mr. Roberts?"

" 'Cause he was a young Russian defenseman."

"Was his youth, his nationality, or his position the problem?"

"Ha, ha, ha. His English was spotty and his translator seemed to be taking liberties with his translation. The questions—all of which came in rapid, uncompromising English—were all about the young Russian's 'business' connections back in Moscow. A team of investigators grilled the kid while the Penguins' manager watched. I viewed the whole thing through a one-way mirror they had installed especially for this interview, but they'd skimped on the sound equipment so I had to keep adjusting my earphones to make sure that the treble and bass were balanced."

"Why is that important?"

"Standard speech is in a very limited range. If it's artificially changed it can cause confusion for me."

"In detecting if the guy is lying?"

"No. In detecting if the guy is telling the truth."

"Right. Of course, you know when someone is telling the truth."

Decker stared at her. "That's the point of all this, isn't it?" Yslan nodded noncommittally. "Look, if you don't believe I can do that then what the fuck am I doing here?"

Now it was Yslan's turn to stare. Decker couldn't hold her eyes. "I don't believe in the supernatural, Mr. Roberts. I don't believe in extraterrestrial life. I don't believe that there are angels or guardian spirits or whatever it's fashionable to call them. But I do believe that there are mistakes that happen in human anatomy—genetic errors or simple physical trauma that can lead to some unusual abilities. I believe you have such an unusual ability. That good enough?"

"Sure," Decker said. He found that he was having trouble keeping his voice steady.

"So, the Pittsburgh Penguins?"

Decker considered his options then decided to continue. "Well, the opening questions to the young Russian were pretty basic. Then one of the investigators demanded to know if the kid knew a man named Boris Barionofky."

Suddenly Yslan was on her feet. "Spell the last name."

Decker took a guess. She opened the door and spoke quickly to Ted Knight, who nodded then disappeared. Yslan turned back to Decker. "Go ahead."

"What was . . ."

"None of your damned business. Go on."

"Well I assumed this guy, Barionofky, was somehow associated with the oligarchs who took over Russia when the Soviets disappeared."

There was a sharp knock on the door. Ted Knight handed Yslan some papers. Her face darkened. "Your assumption is correct, Mr. Roberts." She flipped to the second page and whistled through her teeth. "This Boris guy is a superstar asshole businessman." She handed the papers back to Ted Knight, who now took up a position in the corner of the room. "So how did the Russian kid answer the questions about this Boris character?"

"He ducked and dodged."

Decker allowed his mind to drift back to the small office in Pittsburgh.

"Surely there was more than ducking and dodging," Yslan demanded.

"Yeah, there was sweating."

"There was what?"

"The young Russian began to sweat shortly after the first question about Boris."

"Well, surely that's a sign."

"Sure it is—oh, yeah, it's a sign. It's a sign that he's nervous, that he's hot, that he's annoyed, that he ate something that disagreed with him, that he doesn't like being asked questions, that someone's cologne bugs him—sweating only means shit on TV. In real life physical signs can mean anything. Anything. It's why no court accepts the results of a polygraph test." Decker glanced at the old wall socket then asked, "Could I get a glass of water? Evian if you've got it." Yslan nodded, and Ted Knight quickly produced a bottle of Evian. "Thanks." He took a deep swig. "Then the questions began to come more quickly with the interrogators often not waiting for the translator to complete his response. The young Russian suddenly stood and said *'Moya sistra balna y nuzhdaetca v pomoschti.'*

"My sister is . . ."

"Sick, Ms. Hicks. He said, 'My sister is sick and needs help.'" There was a moment of silence in the room.

"Was his sister sick?"

"Without a doubt."

"And you were sure of that?"

"I was sure that he believed his sister was sick. I assumed that the sister's illness made the young player vulnerable to the approach of powerful, dangerous men from his homeland. He could be asked to throw a game in return for better care for his sister or the like. No doubt that was the Penguins' concern. But it wasn't mine. I got my money and got the hell out of there." He pointed to the USB key and said, "You can hear the whole thing for yourself on that."

"I told you I'd do that later."

"So what do you think about this Boris as behind all this crap that's been thrown at me?"

Yslan looked to Ted Knight then said, "Doesn't strike me as likely."

"Why?" Decker demanded.

"The kid played last night for the Penguins. Isn't having much of a season—awful plus minus. Few minutes per game, but he still plays."

"So what does that prove?"

"Not much except that they renewed his contract for three years. You should read the sports section more often."

"I guess."

"So if there was a problem with this Boris it must have been solved."

"And this Boris guy couldn't come after me?"

"He certainly could. He's no doubt more dangerous than ol' Boris and Natasha from *Rocky and Bullwinkle*—wasn't she the sexiest thing in cartoons?"

"That's a bit weird to say."

"Be that as it may, I don't think ol' Boris is behind all this. Betting on hockey is penny-ante. Boris has probably moved on—at least that's what our data suggests. Oil and gas is easier than hockey players with severely schizophrenic sisters."

Decker was suddenly on his feet. "What the fuck is this? You already knew all this?"

"Yep. I told you we've been following you for a long time and we have better resources than you do."

"Then why make me repeat it?"

"To see if you'd lie to me. You're not the only one interested in truth, Mr. Roberts."

Decker allowed his eyelids to shut gently—straight lines.

"So is that eye-closing thing part of how you do it?"

Yslan nodded toward Ted Knight. The man left the room without being asked. Yslan tilted her head and said, "So, you going to tell me how all this works?"

"Why should I?"

Yslan took a deep breath. "Look, Mr. Roberts, you still don't get what's going on here."

"This Boris guy could be a real danger to me and that creep Charendoff may have orchestrated a killing and he definitely used me to confirm information, which makes me an accessory, doesn't it?"

"That's a legal call."

"But the guy planned and executed a murder!"

"In all likelihood, yes. But that's not the NSA's concern."

"What the fuck is?"

"You. Mr. Roberts. Your safety is the NSA's concern. And there are some people who clearly want to do you harm—maybe many different people."

Decker saw her rub her left index finger against her middle finger. She wanted a smoke. Finally she said, "Do you know who Alan Turing was?"

"The British World War Two cipher guy?"

"The guy who cracked the German's Enigma machine, allowing the Allies to know virtually everything the Nazis were going to do."

"Yeah, so what about him?"

"During the war the British spent a fortune keeping him safe because he was a valuable, irreplaceable asset."

After a long pause Decker said, "Like me."

Yslan nodded. "You're a valuable and valued asset, Mr. Roberts. That's why the NSA is interested in you—and why you're here in this safe house. And, I might add, costing the American taxpayer a pretty penny."

"And did he—Turing—live a long and happy life?"

Yslan looked away.

Decker knew that once Alan Turing's usefulness had ended for the British they literally fed him to the dogs. He was prosecuted as a homosexual then chemically castrated. Shortly thereafter Mr. Turing had had enough of this life—and ended his in a cold water garret, alone and no doubt crazed—and probably looking for a way out of room in which there were no doors.

Yslan turned back to face Decker. After a brief pause she said, "So, are you going to tell me how this trick of yours works?"

"It's not a trick."

"Fine. How does it work?"

Decker thought for a second, then attacked. "How much do you know about telling the truth?"

"A lot I think."

"I doubt that. So tell me, Ms. Hicks, what's a lie?"

"A lie?"

"Are you suddenly deaf? What's a lie exactly?"

"Exactly?"

"Don't do that echoing thing. If you don't know just say you don't know."

"So, I guess I don't know exactly what a lie is."

"Few people do. They assume it's simple but it's not. A lie is a complicated thing. For example consensus is kind of lie—it means that some folks have been convinced to say yes when in fact they mean no. Sharing is a kind of lie—as one young girl said to her father when he explained what it meant to share, 'You mean I get less.' And yes, that's what sharing means—it's a kind of lie. So's a placebo—it's a sugar pill parading as the real drug. Despite the fact that it does the same work as the real drug, it's not the real drug—it's a fake, a lie. When first-world people travel to the third world and they manage not to see the poverty—it's a lie. Ballet is a lie—no one actually moves like that. Opera is a big-time lie—no one sings like that, and the old fat guy couldn't possibly be Romeo. The word 'self-taping' is a lie. The actor is either doing the taping or the acting, but surely not both. The old Soviets were famous for lies; the People's Republic of this or that—which people? The U.S. missile called the Peacekeeper was a swell lie. News reports showing dead bodies always at a forty-five-degree angle makes death seem like sleep. I can assure you that death is not like sleep at all. So those news reports are intrinsically lies. Weather forecasting, economic forecasting, any forecasting—all lies. Doctors' diagnoses—good guesses at best, lies at worst. Then you get to the easy ones—fortune cookies, the reading of entrails, astrology, religion. All easily recognizable as just forms of lying—or hoping. But then again, hope is the only universal liar who never loses his reputation for veracity."

"Who said that—that's not yours."

"Right. How did you—?"

"I've studied your speeches for almost three years. Memorized some of your better opening addresses to your acting classes, and 'veracity' isn't a word that shows up even once. So who said it?"

"Robert Green Ingersoll, a U.S. lawyer in the late eighteen hundreds. Don't ask me how I know that—I just know."

"Like you just know when someone's telling the truth?"

Decker didn't answer. Knowing the authorship of a quotation

was just a fluke of memory—knowing when someone was telling the truth was a gift that came with a heavy burden.

"Okay. So you're not going to tell me how it works, are you?"

Decker returned her stare.

"All right, when did you first know, Mr. Roberts?"

"A long time ago."

She opened the door and called to Mr. T. The large man appeared at the door. She looked back at Decker. "You like Chinese, we know that—how spicy?"

"Spicy."

She gave Mr. T a few bills and ordered hot and sour soup, potstickers, crispy beef, dried green beans with pork, and two steamed buns, then closed the door on Mr. T and turned to Decker. "Dinnertime."

"Is it really?"

She smiled slowly. "It's dinnertime somewhere in the world."

Decker nodded. "You see, your statement that it's dinnertime is both a truth and a falsehood. Pure truths are rarer than you think."

"Okay. I get that. So how did it start—this ability to tell when someone's telling the truth?"

"Could I get a Tsingtao with dinner?"

"No."

"A refill for my Evian; it's losing its bubbles."

"Sure. I think that's within our budget. So, how did this thing of yours start?"

"If I don't tell you I don't get dinner?" he asked.

"Yep—and then I waterboard you just for the heck of it."

"That's not so funny."

"How did it start, Mr. Roberts?"

"Well, my father was a doctor."

"Born in 1920, died on Good Friday a few years back."

"And like so many doctors," he continued, "he felt he was equipped to handle any kind of business deal. He was rich, he was smart—he was a perfect mark just waiting for the arrival of the right con man. And sure enough one arrived, bearing, of all things, a curling rink. Well, not the rink itself, but building plans for the rink and a business plan that promised a doubling of the investor's money in three years, max. Curling was going to be big, explode on the scene. Well, it exploded all right, and every penny of my father's investment was lost when the building never materialized."

"What does that have to do with—"

"My father had the guy over for dinner before the deal. When the meal was over I told my father that I thought the guy wasn't telling the truth. My father laughed at me—but after he lost his money he didn't laugh and he began to look at me funny, funnier than he usually did. Two years later when I was eleven my father asked me to caddy a round of golf. It was fine with me, I'd never caddied before but I assumed my father was going through one of his periodic cheap phases, so I agreed.

"Between the 'No, that's a pitching wedge, not a sand wedge' and 'Where in the dickens did that ball get to?' my father indicated his golf partner and said, 'Listen to my conversation with this man.' 'Why?' I asked, but my father just said, 'No reason, just take a close listen.'

"So I did. I overheard what sounded like some kind of business pitch—a slew of facts and figures that came so fast I felt my head literally tilt back."

But he wasn't about to tell Ms. Yslan Hicks about sensing a stream of cool, clear air above him. About how he breathed deeply, then sensed something heavy in his right hand and a coldness surround him—and a name, a girl's name.

"Later that day I told my father that his golf partner was not telling the truth.

"'You're sure he was lying?' my father asked.

"'Not telling the truth,' I corrected him.

"'About all of it?' he pressed.

"'No. He gave you some truths.' I enumerated them for my father—they were few and far between.

"'And the rest were lies? All of it?'

"'Well they weren't truths,' I told him. A week later my father burst into my bedroom, almost catching me—well, doing something I wasn't supposed to be doing."

He noticed Yslan smile at that. "I had brothers," she said as explanation.

"Well he came into my bedroom and told me that I was right. Right about it all. Then of course he asked the natural question: 'How did you know?'

"I told him, 'I just knew.' It's funny; when I think about that moment, do you know what I remember?"

"No. Tell me."

"I remember the four framed pictures of clown jugglers hanging on the walls that my father had brought home after a meeting with a pharmaceutical detail man—they grinned down at me. Scared the shit out of me for years. At any rate, then he did something stupid. He said, 'I wasn't at the hospital last night, that wasn't why I came home late.' He stared at me and I stared back. Then he did a typical science thing by asking me, 'So, am I lying about that?'

"I told him I didn't know.

"He demanded, 'Why not?'

"I told him, 'It doesn't work on people I care about or family.'"

Decker had thought at the time about telling his father about the lines in his head—how they aligned when he heard a truth—then decided against it, as he decided against telling the southern girl across the table from him.

"My father's eyes widened then he said, 'I want you downstairs next Thursday night.'

"I protested, 'But you and your friends are way better pool players than—'

"'I know,' he said.

"'But I'm not good enough to play with—'

"'No you aren't, but come down and play that lying trick of yours.'

"I really didn't want to do it, but I did. After their game ended and the men left, my father asked me what statements made by his friends were truthful. I identified the very few truths spoken that night, then added, 'And Mr. Walsh pocketed a twenty that belonged to you.'

"'You saw that too?'

"'Yes.'

"My father nodded slowly. 'This is pretty interesting, don't you think?' he said.

"But I didn't really find it interesting. I found it scary and isolating. And I didn't like the way my father looked at me—like I had confirmed in his mind that I really was a freak. So I stopped using it."

He didn't bother mentioning that he kept feeling the cold and the metal thing in his hand—and the blood.

"Fine. When did you decide to use your—"

"When I was sixteen with my girlfriend."

"Leena."

He shook his head. "Yeah, Leena."

"And how . . ."

"I'm not going into details, but it scared me enough that I didn't use it again until my second Broadway show went bust and I found myself without employment—with a very sick wife and young boy who hadn't talked nearly as much as a three-year-old should have, living in New York City—not the easiest place to survive such circumstances.

"I put in a call to a guy I used to know when he directed plays who had left the theatre racket, gone to business school, and now worked for Lehman Brothers.

"We met later that week at a bar whose astronomical prices for drinks made me literally weak in the knees. The guy, Barry Manson, was gloating. He knew perfectly well that I could hardly afford to breathe in bars like that, let alone drink, then eat, then drink some more. But many theatre people who leave the business enjoy seeing those who hold on fail.

"And my last show had definitely failed. The show criticized newspapers and was promptly murdered by said newspapers when it came to reviews. How we couldn't see that coming during the months of rehearsal and the one hundred and twenty out-of-town performances was just one of those mysteries that happen when artists lock the door to the outside world while they work.

"Well, Barry was drinking—really enjoying himself—having an expensive, swell time.

"Finally I asked, 'Could you make use of someone who could tell beyond all doubt whether a person was telling the truth?'

"Barry gave me an odd look. 'I don't know,' he said.

"'That's not true.'

"'Hey! I made seven figures last year.'

"'Maybe six, maybe five—definitely not seven,' I said.

"'What about eight figures?'

"'Come on, Barry, if you'd made eight figures you would have told me long ago—fuck, you'd have hired a skywriter, taken out a full page in the *Times*.'

"'True enough.'

"'Yes, true enough.'

"One hundred and ninety dollars' worth of drink later, Barry postulated a plan to use my 'gift' to review business presentations.

"The first two 'vettings,' as Barry liked to call them, were basically successful. I actually sat in as they did the interviews. I caught one job applicant in a nontruth and confirmed the statements of the second. Barry managed to get tidbits of payment for me, but neither he nor I was thrilled with the arrangement. Something about the third vetting, of an attractive Puerto Rican woman, was fishy from start to finish. At the end of the interview I was outside smoking—yeah, I used to smoke too—and the woman approached me. 'Confusing, huh?'

"'Excuse me?' I was surprised that Barry was nowhere to be seen.

"'You were confused as to whether I was lying or not.'

"I nodded slowly. 'Yes, I'd have to agree with that.'

"'Do you know why I confused you?'

"'No. No, I don't.'

"'Because I was telling the truth—but not my truth. Every answer I gave applied directly to my older sister.'

"'Every one?'

"'Even my name. I'm not Ellen Rios, I'm Susan Rios.'

"Yes you are, I thought.

"'I'm thirty years old.'

"'No you're not, and neither is your sister.'

"Ms. Rios nodded. 'Impressive. I'm a journalist.'

"'A nontruth.' I said flatly.

"'Okay, I was a journalist. I used to work in your hometown.'

"'That's true. Probably with the *Globe and Mail*. And you probably quote P.G. Wodehouse to the other fake Brits over there.'

"'Well, P.G. was important . . . '

"'If you went to girls' private school, wore tartan skirts that didn't cover your knees and you had a thing for Jewish boys then, black boys now.'

"'Even more impressive. I'm interested.'

"'That's true, but interested in what?'

"'Making you some real money.'

"'And why would you be interested in doing that?'

"'Because I'd split the proceeds.'

"'How?'

"'Seventy-five, twenty-five.'

"'Need I ask which end is mine?'

"'No need. I have the contacts you need—you don't.'

"'I have the talent.'

"'But without contacts you have no way of converting that talent into cash. You can stay with your Mr. Manson and do parlour tricks—or move up to the big time.'

"I jettisoned Barry as easily as clipping a fingernail and for six months pocketed five thousand dollars almost every other month, at which point it occurred to me that I had enough contacts of my own. My name was out there in the business ether. But, while I was making some money, Ms. Rios was getting rich—so over drinks one night I told her of our imminent divorce.

"'Well, I knew it would come sooner or later,' she'd said."

Decker didn't bother telling Yslan the rest. But he had said, "An untruth." A real look of disappointment had crossed Ms. Rios' handsome face. "What?"

"I was hoping . . . forget it."

But Decker knew that she was hoping that he had come to care about her, which would have stopped his ability to see whether she was telling the truth or not. He shook hands, gave the waitress a fifty and set out on his own.

He said, "And my gamble paid off. Word of my ability spread through the New York business community, which inevitably got it to Chicago, then to Cincinnati, Wichita and throughout the American heartland—where money was thrown about for expertise with as much abandon as a baboon throwing its shit at a passing car on Chapman's Peak. Know where that is?"

"Nope."

"Cape Town."

"Never been."

"It's pretty special. At any rate, I left her. The world pursued me, and thus my fee of up to fifteen thousand dollars in small bills was born."

"Okay. Good," Yslan said. "What about this whole acting thing. How'd that start?"

"I had a pretty female neighbor . . ."

". . . on Strathallan Boulevard in Toronto—Karen, wasn't it?"

"If you know, what the hell are you asking me for?"

"Because I only know the facts. You followed her to an arts summer camp. She was a drama kid so you became one. Then you acted in high school and won a few awards from Sampsons."

"Simpsons. Simpsons Drama Festival."

"Best actor one year, best director the next. Then you were off to Rochester to work in a summer stock theatre. Did you have legal working papers?"

"I was a kid."

"You crossed the border without papers just a few days ago. Is this a thing with you?"

"Where's this going?"

"And you directed professionally at that summer stock for the first time. *Of Mice and Men,* as I remember."

"Be accurate, Special Agent Hicks. You don't remember—you remember your notes."

"Right. Then off to the Yale School of Drama."

"After an undergraduate degree."

"Yeah, after that. And then from there to New York and the regional theatres."

"Well, you've got my résumé down pat. But I don't hear a question."

"Sure, Mr. Roberts. Here's the question: did you use your gift in any of that—before you were with this Barry guy?"

"No," he said. "My professional directing eye had gotten keen enough that I didn't need it in my work." He knew that his "keen eye" was a subset of the gift, but he wasn't about to share that.

"So when did you begin to use it again—exactly when?"

He was going to tell her about his Broadway contract but decided against it. That was his sin. His private sin—which he felt led to his wife's illness.

He said, "When I sat at my wife's side as her doctor told her that 'your feelings of weakness and lack of balance are probably just temporary. Your body will right things soon.'"

Decker had closed his eyes and would never forget the lines swirling in random patterns across his retinal screen. When the meeting was over he had asked his wife to wait for him outside. She'd looked at him funny but he'd said, "Do you really want to see how much this little consultation cost?" She'd smiled that wan smile of hers and slowly left the office. Once the door was closed, Decker turned on the doctor. "You're not telling the truth."

"I am, Mr. Roberts; the body can right itself."

"Yeah, I get that, but what's wrong with my wife?"

The doctor signaled Decker to sit and pulled out a stack of test results. Although none were conclusive, all pointed toward a diagnosis of ALS.

"Then why not tell her that?"

"Because people who are told they *may* have a deadly illness too often succumb to the illness well before they have to. The brain is a more powerful determinant of health than the body."

Decker had nodded; with that he agreed. "But you believe she has ALS?"

"I believe she will shortly begin to exhibit the opening symptoms of ALS, yes."

Decker had closed his eyes—four parallel lines, and tears.

"Do you need a moment, Mr. Roberts?" the doctor asked, pushing a tissue box across the desk.

*No,* Decker thought, *I need a way out of dark room that has no door, that's what I need—what my wife needs.*

Decker looked up—Special Agent Yslan Hicks was staring at him.

"Now it's your turn to answer a few questions," Decker said.

Yslan pulled her eyes away from his and said, "Okay, what do you want to know about me?"

The door opened and Mr. T stuck his large head in. Yslan turned to him; "Not now." The door shut. Decker sensed something odd in this too—but what?

"What do you want to know?" Yslan prompted.

"I'm going to write down three statements, and I want you to read them to me in such a way that I will believe you're telling me the truth."

"Okay," she said and slid a piece of paper and a pen across the table.

He pulled the goosenecked lamp to him. The plug almost

came out of the old wall socket. He wrote quickly on the paper and slid it back across the table to her. "Would you say that each of those three statements are truths?"

She read the three statements.

"Are they all truths?"

"Absolutely."

"Fine. Then read me those three statements and make me believe they're truths." Decker gently closed his eyes and leaned back.

Yslan suddenly felt self-conscious and quickly realized that if she tried to make him—force him—to believe her, that she would sound false even if she were telling the truth. Suddenly a line that she had read over and over again in the transcripts that she had of Decker's acting class lectures came into her head; "Think the thought, swallow the thought—say the stupid words."

And she did. "My name is Yslan Hicks and I work for the National Security Agency of the United States."

Three perfectly straight, parallel lines moved across Decker's retinal screen.

Decker nodded, "Next."

Yslan took a breath and said, "My job at the NSA is to keep synaesthetes safe."

A square within a square. Decker nodded.

Yslan looked at the third statement, thought the thought, swallowed the thought, and said the stupid words: "I believe Decker Roberts is a synaesthete like the man who can recite pi out to 22,500 digits is a synaesthete."

For a long moment there were no figures at all on his retinal screen, then he felt a moment of bitter cold and something metal in his right hand, then squiggles from all four directions entered his screen. Special Agent Yslan Hicks was lying to him.

## HAS ANYONE SEEN MIKE?

"I'M NOT SAYING ANOTHER WORD UNTIL I CAN MAKE A phone call."

Yslan looked at him. She realized that something had changed. She handed him his phone and left the room.

Decker quickly dialed Eddie's number. Eddie's voice mail picked up on the first ring, and Decker hit the agreed-upon code. Eddie plugged his phone into his computer and watched the sine wave on the screen. It stabilized and he picked up. "Where are you?"

"Somewhere in New Jersey."

"The Garden State?"

"So they claim."

"Good movie, great sound track."

"Yeah. Eddie, I need you to check something for me."

"Shoot."

"Yslan Hicks. Y-S-L-A-N. And Hicks as in *Beverly Hillbillies* kind of hicks. Claims she works for the National Security Agency."

"Okay. So what do you want to know?" he asked, glancing at the sine wave on the computer screen.

"Does she? And what is that agency about, and what's her story?" Decker heard a curse from Eddie's end of the line. "What?"

"Hang up. Hang up now." Eddie slammed down his phone and shouted, "Fuck me with a crowbar!" as he stared at the sine wave on the screen: it was going nuts.

Emerson Remi smiled as he clicked his handheld shut. New Jersey? Not usually classy enough for Ms. Yslan Hicks, but hell, close enough to drive. He finished his glass of sherry—he'd come to like sherry lately—and flipped his doorman a ten-dollar bill to get his car from the garage. He'd drive out—surprise her—in New Jersey.

Decker knocked on the door to his room. Yslan said, "It's not locked." Decker pushed open the door and saw Yslan and Mr. T at a small breakfast table. There was a bag of Chinese takeout on the counter and a plate of muffins beside a jar of organic peanut butter on the table. Mr. T had evidently just smothered a choco-late chip muffin in peanut butter. Even Guy Fieri wouldn't eat that.

"You've finished your phone call? That was quick."

"Yeah," Decker said. "I need my computer."

"Why?"

"Because I do."

Mr. T wiped his mouth. Yslan nodded and the large man stood from the table with a surprising grace and went into the next room. Decker noticed Yslan watching Mr. T closely—as one would a pet tiger. Moments later he came back with the com-puter.

Decker took it and returned to the bedroom. He looked at the door; the light beneath the door was unbroken by the shadows of feet.

His fingers raced across the keyboard as he called up the syn-aesthetes website. The outsiders' part of the site came up with the usual dry and offhanded stuff. Decker punched in his access code—Sethcomehome. The painted black squares came up and began to pulse. Then:

WELCOME FELLOW TRAVELER

Decker supplied his second password and waited. The worm-hole entrance to the chat room appeared. He didn't enter—he went to the blocked room where Eddie's message waited for him.

He scanned it quickly. There was a small story about Yslan in front of a congressional committee defending her budget for tracking synaesthetes, her educational credentials, a confirmation of her place at the NSA, a quick bio of her more than modest southern roots, then a down and dirty bulleted list of the above-ground work and covert activities of the NSA.

Decker read it a second time, then committed it to the abyss. So she was who she claimed she was. Southerners interested Decker. They had secrets; he had secrets.

He closed the blocked room and couldn't resist entering the chat room—where he lurked.

Images in rapid succession filled the screen, the visual equivalents of screaming. Bloody medieval crucifixions followed and seemed to scorch across the monitor. Then written responses—some in grammatically ludicrous English, others in preposterous versions of other languages—then more wild images and screeds of colours and weird mathematical shapes.

If there was an *uma* of synaesthetes—and Decker thought there might well be—the *uma* was in distress. Could it be from what was happening to him? He had no clue.

Suddenly a sound so piercing came from the speakers that Decker had to turn off the sound on his computer.

Here were people locked in a dark room with no way out.

In his head he heard his own voice, now aged: "Don't forget me. Please don't forget me here."

Then an image materialized on the monitor of hundreds and hundreds of pieces of random junk—bottles—somehow balanced to form an extraordinary tree. A flash. Another angle of the amazing thing. Then a photo flashed on for an instant. It looked like the pear-shaped man he'd seen on Bloor West. The man on the monitor was on a street corner beside the spectacularly balanced tree thing carrying a hand-painted sign that read "What's Your Ratio!"

The image vanished as quickly as it appeared.

Decker felt a tingle deep inside him. He tried to get the image back but couldn't.

Fuck! Was that the guy he'd seen? Then he remembered the

sign—"What's Your Ratio!" Wasn't "ratio" the word that the guy who attacked him in front of his house had screamed at him?

Another image came up on the monitor. This time the man was facing away from the camera but he was carrying two signs and his head was tilted back as if he was shouting. The signs read "I worked here" and "Who's Jumping Now?"

Decker nabbed the image before it could disappear and pasted it to his desktop.

Then in simple plain English, the phrase HAS ANYONE SEEN MIKE? scrolled across the bottom of the screen.

The door to his room opened and Yslan stepped in. "So, did I pass the test?"

Henry-Clay was up on the synaesthetes site waiting for Decker. He snapped his computer off and called Mac. "Got him. Meet me in my office in an hour, Mr. MacMillan." Then he hit the button on his desk's squawk box and said, "Send in Congressman Villianne."

## 36

## MOVEMENTS TOWARD NEW JERSEY

EMERSON APPEARED TO THE CASUAL WATCHER AS AN EF-fete fool, but he was nothing of the sort. He hid within the guise of the overindulged, trust-funded elite. He hid and made connections to powerful friends—and admirers—at the *New York Times* and NBC.

So once he located the source of Decker's cell phone transmission he contacted his editor and NBC and organized a flotilla that formed up—and headed for deepest, darkest New Jersey.

In Cincinnati, Henry-Clay listened to Congressman Villianne's pitch for further support. "A fellow graduate of Tulane, a protector of the dream state of Louisiana, a staunch Republican bulwark against the marauding of out-of-control Democrats"—blah, blah, blah, blah. Henry-Clay was watching the congressman's mouth move up and down, but he was thinking about Decker Roberts. The danger posed by Decker Roberts. The congressman's undeniably succulent lips stopped flapping; he'd evidently completed his pitch. Henry-Clay checked a second time to make sure that the man had finished, then launched in with his description of the new antidepressant that he was bringing to market. About its undeniably good test results and its efficacy. For good measure he reminded the congressman of the extensive investment his company had made in helping the very few children afflicted with that dreadful disease—the name of which had already escaped him—"and at no profit whatsoever to my company," he added. Then as a clincher he asked, "How much did my corporation donate to your last campaign?" Henry-Clay knew exactly how much they had donated, and more to the point, how he and his IT expert had expunged any mention of Congressman Villianne spending time with that KKK douche bag Darryl Marmalukes. Not an easy or cheap trick. The only others ever able to accomplish this—remove an entire history from all available sources—as far as Henry-Clay's expert told him were the diamond giant De Beers and the powerful Soong family in China. But he had managed it for the congressman—and now he wanted this popinjay to do his part in return.

"I see," the congressman was saying.

"I want you on the drug oversight committee."

"I'm not senior enough."

"Who stands in your way?"

The congressman named two men and a woman. Henry-Clay made as if to jot down their names. He knew their names—had for some time. Two he knew personally. The third, the woman congressman from Maine, was a liberal Republican and rumoured to be untouchable. He'd see about that. Everyone was touchable.

"So, if these three all have to step down due to other commitments or family concerns, you'd be next in line?"

The congressman nodded, then gave a smile that Henry-Clay had known all his life. It was the smile the Nevada senator gave Michael Corleone in the privacy of the Don's office before Michael arranged for the hooker to die in the senator's arms. It was the smile of old America. Of the privileged. It made Henry-Clay feel short and fat—and greasy—just as it was intended to do.

"How much?" Henry-Clay asked.

The congressman acted as if his mother had been called a blow-job expert.

"Oh, cut the crap. You're down here with the rest of us, squirreling for pennies." Henry-Clay reached into his pocket and threw a handful of change on the floor. "For every cent you pick up I'll donate fifteen thousand dollars to your campaign coffers—through your Nassau connections, naturally."

The congressman stood and buttoned his linen jacket. He headed toward the door.

"Fine," Henry-Clay said. "But there is exactly six dollars and sixty-seven cents on the floor. Multiply that by fifteen thousand dollars a cent, and you are looking at five thousand dollars more than a million dollars. A lot of money to leave on the table—or in this case, on the floor."

The congressman stopped—turned—and got down on his knees.

*Good,* Henry-Clay thought—*more insurance.*

MacMillan stooped and picked up a penny from the floor. He pocketed it without a moment's hesitation or any embarrassment that he had expended so much energy for a single penny. Henry-Clay almost laughed—the congressman had left a hefty sum on the floor, but MacMillan didn't. The man looked almost the same as he always looked, but Henry-Clay sensed an additional weight on the Scot's broad shoulders.

MacMillan tossed a photo on Henry-Clay's desk.

Ratio-Man was on his back, his hands reaching toward the lens, white from loss of blood, a towel shoved deep into his throat to stop him from screaming.

Although it wasn't necessary to present proof, Mr. MacMillan did, and Henry-Clay appreciated that.

"Got a lighter?" Henry-Clay asked.

MacMillan tossed him a Zippo.

Henry-Clay lit the photo on one corner as he held it by another—then he dropped the remains of the photograph into the large crystal ashtray on his desk and watched the final bits of Ratio-Man blacken and disappear. He felt the slightest shiver. It was something new for him, his very first murder.

He needed Decker Roberts to be his second.

"There may be a problem," MacMillan said.

"What?"

"I couldn't find the freak's computer."

Henry-Clay considered sending MacMillan back to get the damned thing, then thought the better of it. Ratio-Man's apartment would be a crime scene. Instead, he reached into his desk and took out the file on Decker Roberts and handed it to MacMillan. For the slightest moment they touched, Henry-Clay's soft hands and MacMillan's stonelike fists. "His last access to the website was from this address in New Jersey. Find him, Mr. MacMillan. Find him quickly."

*Now this was fun,* Emerson thought as he drove at the head of a flotilla of cars packed with journalists and trucks ready to broadcast the news to the world. He wished the car he sat in was a convertible so he could stand up as he led his troops. Like George C. Scott in *Patton*—yeah, he was the Patton of newsmen—leading his troops into the dangerous wilds of New Jersey.

## 37

## INSURANCE

"SO WHAT ELSE YA GOT, MR. ROBERTS?"

Decker didn't say anything.

There was a knock at the bedroom door. Ted Knight leaned in and whispered into Yslan's ear. She turned to Decker. "I'm tired of playing defense. Give me the rest."

He reached in his pocket and took out the final USB key.

She took the thing and plugged it in. "Good."

"Aren't you going to ask me if I have any more?"

"You don't have any more, Mr. Roberts. You had the three USB keys and that digital recorder—we've known that from the beginning."

"Then why didn't you just take them from me?"

"Because, as much as you don't believe it, I'm on your side. I wanted to earn them from you. Okay?"

Decker didn't know what to say to that.

"It's password protected. I can get our guys to find out what the password is but it could take a half an hour that I'm not sure we ought to waste on crap like that. So what's the password?"

He gave her the password. "It was a deposition for a class-action lawsuit against an insurance company that a huge law firm wanted me to watch. I kept this recording for what I think are pretty obvious reasons."

"Where was this?"

"In Chapel Hill."

"Dean Smith basketball, the pat of butter in the sea of grits, where fucking Sherman housed his horses in the theatre—that Chapel Hill?"

"None other."

She hit play.

"The first guy speaking is the lawyer who hired me."

*Lawyer: Why is there no central registry for insurance policies?*

*Another Man: It would cost a lot of money.*

Yslan hit pause. "That's the insurance guy?" Decker nodded. She hit play.

*Lawyer: Actually it wouldn't.*

A long silence followed. Then a third voice said, *"He's answered your question, move on."*

"The insurance guy's lawyer?" Yslan asked. Decker nodded again. Yslan hit play again.

*Lawyer: How many times has your insurance company been sold in the past decade?*

*Insurance Man: Four I think . . .*

*Lawyer: Actually it's six, and a seventh is pending. And your company is sold less often than most. Why are insurance companies sold so often?*

*Insurance Man: It's a business. When someone wants to buy and the price is right you sell. Simple.*

*Lawyer: Simple. Really? Are clients of the insurance company informed of the sale of the company?*

*Insurance Man: By letter.*

*Lawyer: Is there any marking on the envelope of this letter to inform the client that there is something of importance inside—that this isn't just another piece of junk you get from your insurance company trying to sell you yet more worthless crap?*

*Insurance Man's Lawyer: Which question do you want answered—the importance one or the crap one?*

*Lawyer: Is the envelope marked important?*

*Insurance Man: No, every communication from an insurance company is important. Why should this be any different?*

*Lawyer: Because the policy numbers change, the contact changes, everything changes except for the demand for payment that always stays the same.*

*Insurance Man: Just good business practice.*

*Insurance Man's Lawyer: Done with the envelope? Good. Let's move on.*

*Lawyer: So Mr. Cyril missed his final payment on his annuity?*

*Insurance Man: So the record says. It's a shame.*

*Lawyer: Yeah.* (long silence while papers are shuffled) *Is this sort of thing a common occurrence?*

*Insurance Man: I really don't know; I'd have to check.*

*Lawyer: Actually, you don't. Our forensic accountants have done the checking* for you.

*Insurance Man:* (sound of a chair scraping) *Hey, are you sandbagging me? Can he do that?* (this last evidently to his lawyer)

*Insurance Man's Lawyer: This is just a deposition. Answer his questions. We get to rebut this nonsense in court.*

*Lawyer: Well, it will be interesting to watch him refute figures generated by three different forensic accounting firms that clearly show that part of the actuarial model for this kind of annuity assumes a six percent failure on the part of the client to make final payments.*

*Insurance Man: If you don't pay, you don't get the capital back. That's clearly in the contract that your Mr., Mr. What's His Name signed.*

*Lawyer: Mr. Cyril. Do you know the specifics of Mr. Cyril's policy?* (sound of rustling papers) *Don't bother telling me that you have thousands of clients and how would you know the specifics of Mr. Cyril's policy. It's only Mr. Cyril's policy that is at the centre of this class action. So do you know the specifics of his policy?*

*Insurance Man: Yes.*

*Lawyer: Well, just for the record, here's how it was. He purchased an annuity in 1986 from you.*

*Insurance Man: Let's be accurate. From us and a co-insurer.*

*Lawyer: Yeah, the ever reliable co-insurer as the guilty party— how very convenient. At any rate, Mr. Cyril purchased an annuity in 1986 for one hundred thousand dollars. The policy paid out six thousand dollars a year, while Mr. Cyril had to pay fifteen hundred dollars a year on top of the hundred thousand.*

*Insurance Man: His yearly payments—all policies have yearly payments.*

*Lawyer: They certainly do. Do you know how many years Mr. Cyril paid his yearly payment?*

*Insurance Man: I'm sure you'll enlighten me.*

*Lawyer: He paid every payment from 1986 until 2008. Twenty-two years of payments—every one on time.*

*Insurance Man: But he missed his last payment.*

*Lawyer: Because he was in the advanced stages of Alzheimer's disease.*

*Insurance Man: As sad as that is . . .*

*Lawyer: Yes, I can see that really breaks you up. He pays one hundred thousand dollars up front then an additional thirty-three thousand dollars—twenty-two years times fifteen hundred dollars a year. He misses one fifteen-hundred-dollar payment in all that time and your contract with him is broken.*

*Insurance Man: He got his annuity every year.*

*Lawyer: Yes, but the point of an annuity is that the purchaser gets his annuity and upon his death the principal—the one hundred thousand dollars—returns to his estate.*

*Insurance Man: Yeah, if—and you can underline that if—if he pays the payments.*

*Lawyer: And how exactly does an Alzheimer's patient make those payments?*

*Insurance Man: Again, as sad as Mr. Cyril's case is, this is not our problem. We held up our end of the bargain. He got his annuity faithfully from the company.*

*Lawyer: Sure while you got to play with his hundred thousand dollars for twenty-two years for well below the market rates. The return on bank CDs in the eighties was well over ten percent. You got his money for four and a half percent.*

*Insurance Man: He got his annuity.*

*Lawyer: Yes. But the annuity only makes financial sense— taking a four and a half percent return when a ten plus percent return was available—IF you can get your principal back upon your death. Underline that IF.*

*Insurance Man: And this guy would have got his principal back IF he had paid his premium as stipulated in the contract. As was requested from the letter we sent him when he was thirty days in arrears* (sound of a piece of paper being pulled out of a file).

*Lawyer: Interesting that you have a copy of the letter you sent to him but absolutely no recollection of the details of the account. Interesting, don't you think?*

*Insurance Man's Lawyer: Interesting or not it's not against the law.*

*Lawyer: Yeah, but putting together a scheme where the math only works if six percent of the clients are too infirm, too senile, too shut away to make final payments just might be.*

*Insurance Man: Just sound business practice. Not illegal.*

*Lawyer: You define illegal too narrowly. Have you heard of* Rae Ellen B. v. the State of North Carolina? *No of course not, why should you? Well you should because it forges into this area of what's illegal. Briefly the case worked this way. A man in Winston-Salem, North Carolina, rounded up all the drunks off the street and put them in a house that he owned. The town was happy to have the drunks off the street. The state was happy that they didn't have to supply housing. Everyone was happy—except that there was a catch. The drunks all had to sign life insurance policies with the house owner as the beneficiary. The house owner, naturally enough, wanted to keep his guests happy, so he supplied them with as much cheap alcohol as they wanted. The fact that it just hustled these folks to their graves was "just sound business practice." Or so everyone thought until* Rae Ellen B. v. the State of North Carolina—*when the court ruled that the drunks were not responsible enough to sign their insurance policies AND that supplying alcoholics with cheap liquor was at very least manslaughter if not murder two, AND—and here's the one*

*for you folks to think about—and here I quote the court
"any enterprise whose basic business model is founded upon
the death or infirmity of another has both transgressed the
laws of God and man." And the decision was upheld all the
way through the Supreme Court. Your business model was
based on the actuarial reality that at very least six percent of
your annuity clients would miss their final payments due to
illness. You have transgressed the laws of God and man.*

Decker was on his feet, unable to hide his agitation.

Yslan hit the pause button. "What?" she asked.

"Play that last speech again."

Yslan did.

Decker closed his eyes and it was like shooting stars—completely random patterns. The guy who hired him might not be telling the truth. Hard for him to be sure from a tape. "Could you get your friends to check that legal citation?"

Yslan stepped outside. The moment she did Decker began to shake. Clearly the insurance guy was lying—that's what he told the lawyer who hired him—but only now did he realize that the lawyer who hired him might be lying too. So when Yslan returned and told him that there was no *Rae Ellen B. v. the State of North Carolina* and that most annuities do not include the return of principal upon death, it did not surprise him.

Yslan asked, "Why did they need you there at all?"

"It puzzled me then, it's why I saved the tape—"

"And the law firm hired you?"

"I think so. The guy who paid me certainly made out that he was from a law firm."

"But he could have been from the insurance company parading as the law firm?" *Or,* Yslan thought, *this could have been one of Harrison's little tests that it sure would have been nice if he had shared with her.*

"I guess he could have been from the insurance company. I really don't know."

"Why would they do that?"

"I said I don't know." But Decker was thinking back to a small room in Orlando, Florida, with a one-way mirror and a bald exec at his side, where both the person being interviewed and the interviewer were lying—both lying.

"Do you often not know who hires you?"

"It's not my concern. They pay, I provide a service—simple as that."

"Telling them if someone's telling the truth?"

"Yeah. That's what I get paid for."

"But what service did you render here?"

That's precisely what Decker was wondering. Like in Orlando where both parties were lying. What service was he providing? Why the fuck were they paying him anything, unless—unless they were trying him out, auditioning him.

Auditioning him? To see if they wanted to use him?

Then a line flew into his mind: "He's using us."

And suddenly Decker was sure the balance guy was the man he'd seen on Bloor Street, then in the fruit market, and it was this Mike person who had attacked him on his driveway and screamed, "He's using us." But there was something else he'd said. Something about a ratio—a ratio? "What's Your Ratio!" his sign said. Then there were the other signs: "I worked here" and "Who's Jumping Now!"

Suddenly there was the sound of a doorbell. An ordinary doorbell. It startled Decker that something so normal could happen in this place. Then a voice—a somewhat high, effete American voice was calling out, "Hicksy, oh Hicksy, I know you're in there."

# 38

## ESCAPE

THAT VOICE GOT LOUDER AND LOUDER.

Yslan said, "Stay!" turned, and ran toward the front door.

Decker heard a sound he knew really well—the sound of generators, generators that supported camera crews. "Hicksy! Hicksy!"

Decker looked out of the room. Yslan was in conference with Mr. T and Ted Knight. The knocking at the door was getting louder and the glare of the camera lights could be seen beneath the door and around the jam. The men nodded and Yslan threw open the door.

A tall preppy-dressed man smiled benignly as six full camera crews turned their undivided—at least until a better story came along—attention towards Special Agent Yslan Hicks, who stood in the door doing her best to be just Ms. Ordinary Citizen.

Decker looked at Yslan's tense back then turned to his room. He opened the bottle of Evian, and putting his finger over the top shook it hard, then he aimed it at the old wall socket. He hoped the information he'd gleaned from the cop back in his studio about what could cause a fire in an old house was right.

Nothing happened for a moment, then all the lights in the house went out and the sound of sizzling came from the walls.

Decker took a deep breath. When flames came from the wall socket, he grabbed his computer, checked that his cell phone was in his pocket and charged toward the front door, yelling as loudly as he could. Lights and cameras panned to him as Mr. T reached toward him. In the lights' glare the large black man backed off and Decker pushed past Yslan into the front yard.

Immediately cameras and microphones swung toward him. Decker stared straight at Yslan and her two goons and said, "Good evening."

"Your name sir?" demanded a reporter.

"Martinelli, Joshua L. Martinelli."

There was a pause—Decker knew full well he didn't look like someone named Martinelli—but it was in fact the pause he had counted on. He grabbed the mic from the startled interviewer and shoved it under Yslan's chin. The cameras and lights turned to take in the moment.

"So Ms. Hicks, do you work for the NSA?"

"No, I don't," she hissed between clenched teeth.

Decker covered the microphone with his hand and said, "Don't grind your teeth. Not good for the jaw and it looks bad on camera. Like a guilty person with something to hide."

She whispered back, "Don't do this."

He looked at Mr. T.

"I'm just not sure, Ms. Hicks, whether we were really meant for each other, you know what I mean?"

A glimmer of a snarl creased her beautiful lips, then disappeared.

Shouts from behind him of "take your hand off the mic" and "speak up" prompted him to shove the mic back beneath Yslan's chin.

"You don't work for the National Security Agency?"

"No."

"And you wouldn't be involved in kidnapping, would you?"

The word "kidnapping" rippled through the crowd of newsmen. One stepped forward and demanded, "Are Mr. Martinelli's claims true?"

Others crowded in and Decker cautiously stepped back. The windowpane to his right cracked and smoke poured out—and all hell broke loose.

Decker bulled his way through the reporters but was surprised to be stopped, facing the tall preppy-dressed man.

"Emerson Remi," the man said in a low voice with his hand out. "Hicksy's friend."

Decker didn't take the proffered palm—almost couldn't with his growing vertigo.

"Fine. But all I need do is raise my voice and you're not going anywhere. Nice fire, by the way."

"What do you want, Mr. Remi? Your story's over there," Decker managed to say.

"Yeah there's a story, but it's not my story—the one that tells what is really going on here. This has to do with synaesthetes, doesn't it?"

Decker tried desperately to concentrate—was he going to faint? "And if I give you that?"

"I'll help you get away from here. The black guy is still by Hicksy's side, but I don't know where the white-haired gentleman got to—no doubt he's looking for you . . . Mr. Martinelli."

"Yeah," Decker said and stepped back. For some reason that lessened his disorientation.

"Here's the keys to my car. My number's on this card. Call me, I'll make it worth your while." Suddenly he stuck his cell phone in Decker's face and shot five quick shots, each accompanied by an eye-popping flash. "These pics go to every news agency and police force in the country if you don't call. I'm sensitive that way." He paused. "Canada? Right. That accent—no *ehs*—but that nasty upward inflection and the *oots* and *aboots* gives you away, brother."

The word "brother" made Decker pause before he said, "Fine."

"Oh . . ."

"What?"

"You have that reporter's microphone—I'm sure he'd like it back."

Decker stared at the thing in his hand then gave back the mic, turned, and began to run—with every step away he felt oddly better. Over his shoulder he heard Emerson's mocking voice, "Go, Leaves, Go."

He was tempted to turn back and say "Leafs! Not Leaves, you moron" but didn't.

As Decker moved away Emerson looked down at his cell phone. He pressed a menu button and a code, and a small dot came up on a map. The map was of the local area. The dot was Decker Roberts in motion, sent from a tiny transponder stuck on Emerson's business card. He said a silent thank you to his Princeton dining club fellow who now ran the world from San Jose, California.

Emerson looked at the dot on the map and smiled. "I'm right. I'm not alone. There's not just a me—there's an us."

Forty-five minutes and three wrong turns later—once going through the same tollbooth on the Jersey Turnpike twice before he finally got it right—Decker got to the Newark Liberty International Airport. He parked the car illegally, wanting it to be found, then ran to the terminal. Using his one remaining credit card he bought a ticket to Atlanta then headed toward the rail link that would bring him back to New York City. He assumed they would quickly find the car then the ticket to Atlanta. He also assumed they would know it was nothing but a bluff. But he had few more cards to play.

The train to New York disgorged him at Penn Station with hundreds of others. People were his best blind. He needed time to think. He believed that Mike—the balance guy—was his key to finding out who was behind all this. He just needed time to think, to find the order of things—maybe even to chart.

Suddenly he laughed. Chart your own life—yeah, but what's my final line?

*Final line, the last thing I ever say?* he thought. And suddenly he felt very cold, and knew for sure that the fire in his house in the Junction was not just arson—it was an attempt to get him to his very last line.

He shook it off. An odd idea popped into his head. It made him laugh.

The guy beside him gave him a funny look and said, "I could use a chuckle—what's ticklin' you?"

"A Monty Python sketch. You remember them?"

"English, right?"

"Yeah. Well they had a sketch about an old knighted actor. The director says to him, 'Well, Sir Riley they're all there now. Yes, all the words are there. Now let us try to get them in the right order.'" Decker chuckled again. He stopped chuckling when he looked at the man beside him.

The man was clearly unmoved. Finally he said, "I don't get it," turned, and left.

Decker realized that sketch had popped into his head because like the old actor he had all the facts—he just needed to put them in the right order. He fell into step with the hordes of people leaving Penn Station from the Thirty-fourth Street exit. There was an odd sense of order in their movement that he knew could only be understood from above. Decker knew that's what he needed to do, stand above the events of the past and see their order.

It was snowing and he thought of that and the notion of order. Lines from Chekhov's *Three Sisters* came to him. The older officer is pontificating that there was a meaning to everything that happens. A younger cynical officer turns to the window and notices that it's snowing outside and says, "It's snowing. What's the meaning of that?"

"It means it's cold, you asshole," Decker said aloud. It was New York City, everyone spoke to themselves here. He stuck his hands deep into his jacket pockets and turned into the wind.

## 39

# HIDING—A COLUMN OF SMOKE WITHIN A FOG

DECKER HAD ALWAYS KNOWN HOW TO HIDE. HOW TO FIND the place behind the furnace, the access to the dumbwaiter or the laundry chute. And now he found himself hiding—again. And it was no surprise. Even as a kid he'd known that one day he'd have to hide in earnest. Other kids practiced walking with their eyes shut or hopping on one leg. He'd practiced hiding because if he didn't hide really, really well they'd lock him away. After much practice he determined that the best place for a column of smoke to hide is in the midst of a fog. Smoke within a fog—that was him within the world of synaesthetes, not actually one of them, but enough like them that he could hide in their midst. He allowed himself to be seen as one of them so if someone had to categorize him they could. "What's he, Mommy?" "Oh, he's a synaesthete—look it up, it's in Mr. Webster's big red book." "Oh, that's why he's so weird, Mom?" "Sure—sure—sure it is—don't stare, it's not polite."

Decker leaned against a lamppost and listened to the steady din of the traffic on Seventh Avenue.

He was beginning to suspect that he was not the only column of smoke hiding in the fog. There might be other hiders—he wished he had a better name for them than that, but "hiders" would have to suffice for now. There were others who had gifts that would be best kept from the eyes of the world. Gifts that were best pawned off as madness or obsession or synaesthesia.

The hiders were blessed and cursed with the ability to put their heads up into the jet stream and access the pure air there.

He'd seen others do it—often subconsciously. Most athletes didn't have a clue where their genius comes from. Sometimes the surfers do—or the skateboarders. The young man who invented all the early skateboarding tricks was so terrified by his gift that he hid it in drugs—and now will serve the rest of his life behind bars in a Hawaiian prison. But it's more often the solitary artist or monk who has a glimmer, a sense that there is a somewhere else—that there really is a there out there but you have to imbibe a deep draught of the jet stream. And there's a whoosh—always a whoosh up there. The jet stream drags you back—it always drags you back . . . to where it all began.

He thought about the profound sense of nausea he'd felt near Emerson Remi, and the other times—with the strange Ratio guy in his driveway the night his house burned down and with the pianist, Paul Scheel. A phrase popped unbidden into his head—"If I sense the trees, I enter the forest." Then Mr. Scheel's comment, "Your forest will infect mine . . . don't you know that?" Well he knew it now.

He thought again of the nausea he'd felt when Mike approached him and when he was near Emerson Remi—their forests interfering with mine. Or were their forests surrounding his—his forest—his what? If they were a forest, what was he?

Three cop cars roared down Seventh Avenue, sirens blaring and lights flashing. Decker turned toward them. For a moment he felt the flush of their cherry tops cross and recross his face. Then they were past him.

As he watched them turn the corner on Twenty-sixth Street, he made up his mind.

He was going to find Mike. That would cost some scratch, but his remaining credit card was too dangerous to use. He was pleased that he'd followed his normal procedure and mailed money to himself for safety's sake. In Toronto he'd divided the $16,290 he'd had left over from his three quick trips into four parts. One he'd mailed to the post box he'd kept for years at the Kinko's on Ninety-second Street; another to the American Express office on Forty-third. Yes, you can still mail things care of American Express. It was long enough that the combined efforts of the U.S. Mail and Canada Post should have been able to deliver his packages.

He took the bus up Sixth Avenue then walked across Ninety-second Street—and right by the Kinko's. No one seemed to be loitering, looking for him. But then again Yslan's cohorts were more sophisticated than street cops, so he spent a full half hour watching the comings and goings before he was satisfied that it was safe to enter the store. As he stepped into the Kinko's he reminded himself that he'd had the post box there for almost eighteen years—paid for it faithfully each month.

The Kinko's was just marginally warmer than outside. The configuration of the store had changed—naturally enough. He asked at the front counter and was pointed toward a stairway that led to an entire basement wall of post office boxes.

Decker found number 221-S and inserted his key. The key slid in easily—but refused to turn the lock. Decker reminded himself that the damned thing hadn't been opened for years and applied pressure. As the lock resisted and the key bit into his fingers he remembered his wife holding that very key between her thumb and index finger and demanding, "What's this key to? What are you hiding, Decker?" Then she'd opened her mouth but chose not to speak. Decker was now pretty sure that what she was going to say was, "What have you done, Decker? What have you done?"

Decker pressed harder both to open the lock and banish the voice from his head. A sharp scrape of metal on metal—then the small door opened. Decker reached in and withdrew the envelope there. He put it down the front of his pants—four thousand dollars in bills is far too thick for a pocket.

The American Express office presented a more serious challenge. They may very well ask for ID. He'd only chanced using the American Express office because it was possible that whoever had set his house on fire, cancelled his credit card, had his loan called and condemned his studio had found out about his Kinko's post box. But he assumed that few people still knew about American Express' mail service.

He entered the large office and asked the young receptionist where he could retrieve his mail. The African-American woman pulled her eyes away from her computer screen long enough to give him a strange look, then pointed one large curved red fingernail down a corridor and returned her false-eye-lashed eyes to the monitor.

At the end of the corridor was a counter—not unlike a coat-check counter in a theatre. An ancient man sat on a stool on the far side. The man was so still that for a moment Decker thought he might be asleep. Then the man opened his eyes. "Bathroom's for patrons only," he said and closed his eyes.

"I'm here to pick up my mail."

The man's eyes not only opened, but they clearly brightened.

"Name?" the codger asked, a smile widening by the moment.

Decker supplied the false name he'd put on the envelope.

The old man disappeared through a door and in remarkably short order returned with the thick envelope. He held it out to Decker. "Thanks," the old guy said.

"What are you thanking me for?" Decker asked.

"Yours is the only letter this year. Without guys like you I'd be out of a job."

Decker hustled out of the office, grateful that he never had to supply any form of ID. Then he headed to Columbus Avenue and Sixty-ninth Street, where he picked up the money he'd mailed to that address, and then over to Fifty-eighth and First, where he had a shock—someone had opened the mailbox and taken the envelope. His $4,290.

So he had $12,000 to track down Mike—and his ratios. Whatever the hell those were.

## 40

## *YSLAN IN MOTION*

WHEN YSLAN FINALLY FIGURED OUT THAT DECKER HAD ES-caped in Emerson's car she considered several different ways of castrating Princeton's pride and joy, then simply pushed him aside with enough force for him to land hard on his tailbone. Then she called Washington.

Harrison was not pleased, to say the least, when he heard the news. "We need a serious talk when this is over—and it better be over soon."

"Can I ask about the two interrogations?"

"They are progressing. Three new people have been brought in. I'm a bit more hopeful we'll get some corroboration on which one of these thugs is telling the truth."

"Then you don't need Decker Roberts."

"Nonsense! We may not need him for this, but we'll need him in the future. He's your responsibility, Hicks. Find him—and fast." Harrison ordered the New York and New Jersey offices to join the search. "Now this Princeton snot, Emerson Remi, he's a former of yours, isn't he?"

"Yes, but—"

"Nothing's private here, Hicks. Nothing. Got it?"

"Yes, sir." She looked at Mr. T and Ted Knight and reaffirmed, "Yes, sir."

"So get this creep to bury the story. Promise him whatever you have to, do him against a tree if that's what he likes, but I don't want to see this on the evening news. Got it?"

Yslan did the best she could to hold her temper, then

organized her troops. Within the hour she received news of Decker's airplane ticket to Atlanta—and the whereabouts of Emerson's car.

When she summoned Emerson, he claimed that Decker had taken the car at gunpoint. "I wasn't going to die for a 2004 Benz. I mean, you know me better than that, I hope."

The image of doing something to Emerson against a tree that included two large spikes and a mouth gag entered her head, but she cast it aside and ordered Emerson to stay at hand.

"Sure, anything to help the constabulary."

Why Princeton guys imitated the very worst of the British was beyond Yslan.

She established that Decker never got on the plane to Atlanta.

In fact, the plane had been delayed when it was discovered that a ticket had been purchased but no one had taken the seat. Every bag had been off-loaded and each passenger had been forced to identify his or her luggage. When it was established that every bag had a passenger, the bags were reloaded and the flight took off—just short of three hours late.

Yslan didn't care about any of that. She wanted to find Decker Roberts. It was her job to find Decker Roberts. And after two days of debriefing him she was completely certain that she and Harrison were right: there was an entire world out there that they didn't understand, and Decker Roberts was part of and maybe their point of access to that other world.

She pulled Ted Knight and Mr. T back into the safe house's kitchen and quickly went through the list of things they'd found when they picked up Decker. The list included his three USB keys, his computer, his tiny digital recorder, his wallet, cell phone, and key ring—all of which Yslan had given back to Decker as evidence of good faith, back when she thought she understood him, believed they were on the same team. She threw aside the itemized list, then said, "Give me that again." She read through it quickly a second time and swore, "Fuck. Money."

"What?" Mr. T asked.

"How much money was in his wallet?"

"Just over a thousand dollars," Ted Knight said. "It's in there," he said, pointing at a kitchen utensil drawer.

Yslan's thoughts were miles away.

"He had two credit cards as well."

"The Visa was cancelled. What was the other card?" Yslan demanded.

"MNBA, MasterCard," Ted Knight said.

Yslan nodded. "That's how we found out about the airline ticket. I'm pretty sure he used it just to throw us off the scent. He won't use it for anything else." She turned away and said, "Money."

"What, boss?"

"Money. He must have a way of getting money."

"Bank accounts?"

"Only if he's stupid—and he's not stupid." Yslan picked up her notes.

"What are you looking for?"

"When he first got to New York, where'd he go?" Yslan demanded.

"Patchin Place, then the Upper West Side, then East Fifty-eighth Street, and then back to Patchin Place."

"Did we photograph his key ring?"

"Sure."

Yslan grabbed the photo and swore, "Fuck me rigid." Before either of the men could comment on her extraordinary statement, Yslan was punching Decker's previous New York City addresses into Google Earth. "Son of a bitch! We thought he was going to sightsee his old homes."

"He wasn't?"

"I don't think so," Yslan said, looking at the photo of the keys again. "Get us a car and tell our Manhattan guys to stake out both places and every post office box near either of Roberts' addresses. Then have them check if the front doors and the mail box keys have been changed at Decker's former apartments on West Sixty-ninth and East Fifty-eighth."

Before they were halfway to Manhattan, Yslan received the bad news. Neither the front doors or the mail box keys at either of Decker Roberts' New York City addresses had been changed for years. Yslan lowered her window and affixed a red flashing light to the car's roof. "Let's go, let's go, let's go!"

## 41

## A COLD DAY IN NEW YORK

DECKER TURNED UP THE COLLAR ON HIS COAT—LIKE BOB Dylan in that wonderful old album cover, he thought, except that there was no tousle-haired woman on his arm or song in his heart. Alone—again. Then he felt the cell phone in his pocket and tears came to his eyes and the word "lost" flew into his mind and gouged deep valleys there. He entered the Canal Street subway stop and went down to the third level where there are no trains—just a lot of bodies trying to find some warmth on a bitterly cold New York City night.

Decker awoke to a none too gentle kick from one of New York City's finest's boots. "Night's done, make like a bread truck and haul buns," the cop said.

Decker did his best to stretch. He'd slept on top of his laptop to keep it safe, and it had rewarded him by bruising the muscles of his side.

In line with the other men he made his way up to the surface. A cold wind greeted him. He knew he couldn't spend another night in the open—or in the bowels of the subway system. But hotels were out of the question. Since 9/11 you couldn't get a hotel room without presenting a passport. He couldn't figure out how to get around that, so he headed over to Tenth Avenue and began to walk south. Twenty blocks down he found what he was looking for. A TV show was doing a location shoot. The honey wagons were illegally parked on both sides of the street.

Decker hitched up his pants, tried to get the $12,000 comfortable in his shorts, and stepped into TV land. A place he knew very well. TV sets always had security guards, but no one wore ID, so there was no real way for the security guards to keep outsiders out. And if you knew your way around, and Decker did, there were lots of places to hide on a location shoot.

He realized with a shock that Don Turk was the show runner. Decker had worked for Don in the past—the distant past. The man was a genius. He was the guy who figured out how to shoot an hour-long prime time show in under a week—sometimes in less than six days. He'd saved the networks millions of dollars. They rewarded him by firing his ass—TV typical.

He'd changed the industry single-handed and inadvertently lined Decker's pockets. The demands of fast shooting put tremendous stress on actors to act without the input of directors—something that few people could teach actors. It was Decker's specialty. Actors raced to Decker's classes and to his home to get prepped for shooting.

Decker watched the comings and goings on Tenth Avenue—the relentless self-congratulatory attitude of everyone from the lowest gaffer to the leading actors—and it sickened him. Hubris was a real thing. These folks' overloud voices and swaggering walks tempted thunderbolts as far as Decker was concerned.

Decker passed by the hair and makeup trailer, thought about it, then moved on. He entered the snack wagon and watched a green-haired girl put out any number of sugary treats. Decker waited until the camera crew guys left, than approached the girl.

He awoke later that night in the green-haired girl's Queens apartment. She had been only too happy to stay at her partner's place in return for $500 and for another $200 had given him her passwords to her laptop.

That night he spent hours lurking at the syn website's chat room. Watching and listening, desperate to ask "Who's Mike?" but his desperation to know did not overcome his need for secrecy.

As he watched the interactions in the chat room he remembered the balancing man's weird signs: "I worked here" (wrong tense), "What's Your Ratio!" (wrong punctuation), "Who's Jumping Now?" (wrong everything).

Then the weird statement "He's using us!"

He contacted Eddie, who "met" him in the blocked-off room.

*Where are you?*

*Out.*

*Swell. How was New Jersey?*

*Fine.*

*More verbosity!*

Decker typed in the link he'd managed to find to the image of Mike holding the two signs "I worked here" and "Who's Jumping Now?" then typed, "Where is this, Eddie?"

*Give me a few hours.* Then Eddie was no more, and Decker felt as alone and as frightened as the day he found that Seth was gone.

# 42

## *EMERSON REMI*

EMERSON STARED AT THE MOVING DOT ON HIS BLACKBERRY screen and thought, *So, you do exist*. He quickly corrected himself. *No, we do exist. Not just me. Us!*

He remembered the touch of his *grandmère* that final night. He was six years old, a boy who seldom spoke. She'd called for him and shooed away his parents. Once the door had closed, leaving him alone with her, she reached for him. "Boy, give me your hand." He put out his left hand and she grabbed it with surprising force. She ran her rice-paper-dry palms over his. "Look," she said, pointing at the crazy quilt that kept the ebbing heat in her frail body. "Look at the pattern, the order." He did. "Don't try to see it. It's not there to be seen, boy. It's there to be sensed if you have the sense to sense it." She took a deep breath then barked, "Do it, boy!" He felt like she was going to call him Pip or something, but he knew that this was no Dickensian fantasy. This was the hidden world he'd sensed from the very beginning. The other place. The place where he belonged. A world that stretched back and back in time—a world of genetics itself. His *grandmère* was a mistress of the other world and she was testing him. Trial by crazy quilt.

"Find me in the quilt," she ordered. Her voice was firm. A duchess voice. An aristocrat of nature itself, crowned by the rising of the sun and the movement of the tides.

He stepped back a pace, away from the gentle reek of decay that was only slightly hidden beneath her rosewater perfume. He took in the literally thousands of odd-shaped and coloured pieces randomly sewn together generations ago—in the English backcountry with the standing stones in the far distance and the boulders in concentric circles radiating out from the farmhouse where old hands drew out pieces and made from nothing a history of their kind—able to be read only by their kind.

He allowed his lashes to gently close, then saw her face on his retina. But she was young and so beautiful that for a moment he thought his heart had stopped in his chest. He opened his eyes. He pointed to the foot of the quilt.

She nodded slowly and a smile took her face. With a single breath she released the tension from her body. And a calmness came into her voice. "Yes, boy, yes, boy . . ."

Later that night he stood by his *grandmère*'s side as the last of her light faded, then blinked out. She left this world proud, without a whimper or a cry. For an instant right after her passing, her image on the quilt shone like a sparkler on the Fourth of July, and then it receded back into the welter from which it had come. He took the quilt from her and pulled the sheet up over her head. He did not kiss her forehead or close her eyes. He felt her burden now heavy on his young shoulders.

He never explained to his parents what he had been doing in his *grandmère*'s room that night—and they had never asked. The most he ever heard about it was the odd whisper: "He's got the shine, like Ma"; "He's the witch's boy"; "He's something very old"—"But he's just a boy,"—"You ever see a boy with eyes that old?"

And so he had begun to hide. To find a blind in which he could function—Groton then Princeton were perfect. Within the effeteness he could pass as just another snot-nose. Another know-nothing trust-fund boy.

But he was hiding—another column of smoke within a fog—looking for his place in his *grandmère*'s quilt.

And he'd sensed from the beginning that Yslan was the means—the access—to some important end. She was not the end in and of itself, although he had enjoyed his time in her bed. But she was just a means to an end. So when he'd heard of her odd posting at the NSA he began to track her, and sure enough . . .

The dot on the screen began to move quickly. Emerson thought, *Run, Decker Roberts, run—but you and I have a date as surely as there is a sun in the sky.* Emerson felt strong. Felt the blood rushing in his veins. He wanted to stretch his neck back, open his jaws and howl like a wolf in the night. But he didn't— what would his fellow reporters think of such behaviour? And besides, Hollywood had made such a mockery of all that.

It was the thing that bothered him most. The easiest access to the jet stream was through sex. The pornographers accessed it without even understanding what they were doing. And people consumed it with the hunger of the starving. But this debased the jet stream. Made it common. The only other simple access to the jet stream was through faith. Twenty prostrations on the third Tuesday after the new moon and you get a gulp of the stream, but you don't even know what it is. You name it god, or angels, but it is neither. Like the pornographers, they denigrate the greatness, make it common, debase the truly sacred, the special, the real gift of the gods.

## 43

## SEMBLANT ORDER

DECKER SAT IN THE BAR ON AVENUE A THAT HAD A WI-FI HOT spot and waited for Eddie's response.

The evening news was on the surprisingly old TV over the bar. An item about a local politician caught cheating on his wife was finishing its tawdry reportage. The item finally ended and a commercial break followed. The first ad was for a new razor that had three hundred and seven blades or some such nonsense and made the usual wild claims. Decker thought of Theo's diatribe against new shaving products, then of the older man's rant about how some of his bronchitis pills worked while others didn't do a damned thing.

The ad finished with a swipe, naturally, then a dark screen held for a beat—an incredibly expensive moment of prime time nothingness. Sappy strings swelled. Decker feared that Celine Dion was going to warble but the music segued to a Keb' Mo'–like upbeat blues as a scene of a New England autumn filled the screen—in black and white. A sincere male voice announced the name of a new drug: Calatrex. "Calatrex is guaranteed to return colour to your life as surely as autumn brings colour to the trees of New England." Naturally the black and white scene turned to glorious gazillion-pixel colour. A happy young woman wandered through the scene, her smile glorious. A second voice-over followed, this one more matter-of-fact and lawyerly, announcing in staccato rapid-fire the potential side effects of Calatrex, which included such niceties as thoughts of suicide and rectal tears. Then a sultry female voice purred,

"Another fine product for a better life from your friends at Yolles Pharmaceuticals."

At the end of the newscast the business update included a story about the new drug.

*Calatrex, Yolles Pharmaceuticals' new antidepressant medication, made its appearance in American drugstores earlier today. Original information claiming that the cost of producing the drug was prohibitively expensive has proved incorrect, and the drug is now priced at a very competitive price point—and the shares of Yolles Pharmaceuticals were the big winners today on the New York Stock Exchange.*

Decker noticed the guy to his left staring at him. Decker picked up his drink and said, "Do you mind?" To which the drinker replied with a sneer, "No one ever brings anything small into a bar around here." Decker recognized the quote. It was from *It's a Wonderful Life*. The bartender says it to Jimmy Stewart in the dream sequence when Jimmy Stewart entered the other world. Decker thought it might also be from a Tom Waits song, but wasn't sure which one.

Decker took his drink and moved to a table, nearer the Wi-Fi hot spot. Once there he opened his computer. "I worked here—what's your ratio—who's jumping now—yeah, I'm thinking about that," he whispered as he waited for the computer to boot up. When it finally came online he quickly navigated to the syn site and then to the blocked room. No message yet from Eddie.

He was about to turn off the computer but found himself drawn to the chat room. Once at its entrance—its portal—he found that he was holding his breath. He'd never entered the room before—only lurked. He hit the command and entered the chat room, then watched as his fingers typed, "Who is Mike?"

That sat in the emptiness of cyberspace for less than five seconds, then image after image after image of impossible yet somehow beautiful examples of balanced junk filled the screen.

At the corner of his screen Eddie's icon—a naked cross-legged yogi with a huge erection smoking an equally huge joint—popped up.

Decker exited the chat room and reentered the blocked room. Eddie's message was clear and unambiguous. *You can just see over the top of one of his signs a logo on the top of a building. It took me a while to clarify it—but it's Yolles Pharmaceuticals in Cincinnati, Ohio. And your guy's name is Michael Shedloski—and hope you're sitting down Decker—follow this link.*

Decker hit the link to cincinnatipost.com/civiccrime and up came an image of Michael Shedloski, murdered in his apartment—no suspects.

Decker settled his breath and wrote down the address of Michael Shedloski's apartment, then thought about the man's sign: "I worked here." Where? At Yolles Pharmaceuticals? Then he thought of his warning—"He's using us!"—and the news item about Calatrex supposed to cost way more than it was eventually marketed for, then finally his lecture to Special Agent Yslan Hicks about what's a lie, specifically his reference to placebos being a lie that works.

He typed quickly: *Eddie can you find me a relationship between the phrase "What's Your Ratio" and Calatrex?*

In less than five minutes Eddie's response came back. *The initial estimates were that Calatrex would have to cost well in excess of $65 a pill. Hence unmarketable since the competition sells for $45 a pill. But Yolles Pharma is selling Calatrex for just under $40 a pill. Either they're trying to suck people into using the drug with a loss-leader price or they've found some way to lower the price, which is impossible, since the actual compounds used to make the drug have had a stable price for over twenty years—stable and expensive. The only thing that could really change the price is the placebo ratio.*

Decker was about to respond when his monitor went black. At the bottom of the screen he saw that the website was being hijacked from one server to another with incredible speed. He was about to shut down his system when an odd floating pattern filled the screen. Clearly this was a live webcam. The image slowly clarified itself—it was the back of an elaborately embroidered Chinese silk dressing gown. The robe began to ripple as the wearer turned slowly to the camera to reveal a grotesquely cartooned 3-D figure of a fat man, in all his exuberant, jiggly glory. The camera zoomed in on the behemoth's face—then his generous lips. "Welcome fellow travelers—and a big hello to you, Mr. Roberts."

Decker stabbed at the power button, then pulled the battery from the back of the laptop.

Back in Cincinnati, Henry-Clay howled with laughter as he took off the silk robe and turned off the cartoon-generator software attached to his webcam. "Got you, Mr. Roberts," he said aloud. He was just so pleased with himself—with the profound genius of Henry-Clay Yolles.

As Decker raced out of the bar he noticed that for some reason an episode of *Sesame Street* was on the TV—they were singing the "One of these things is not like the others, one of these things just . . ." ditty, which Decker had always hated.

The night was wet and fiercely cold.

*Cincinnati, Ohio, and Michael Shedloski's apartment are next on the agenda,* Decker thought.

He'd directed a play in Cincinnati; god, it had to be fifteen years ago, and there was that terrific kid there. What was his name? Yeah, Steven Bradshaw.

Decker assumed that Yslan had figured out that he was in New York City and would have the bus station and Grand Central covered, and LaGuardia and JFK were sure to be swarming with agents. But he needed to get to Cincinnati. As he walked across town, images of a New York City hockey girl and her love of the Stanstead boy leapt into his head. The image of the boy encased in ice almost made him retch. Decker felt a stabbing coldness in his bones. The boy was in the river—in the earthly version of the jet stream, locked in ice—just as Decker knew he would eventually be locked in a room without a way out. Then the phrases came like screams from the back of his head: "Can't wait to have your baby," "One of theirs murdered one of ours, simple as that," "Breaks the laws of God and man," "I worked here," "What's your ratio!" "Who's jumping now?"

Decker leaned against the wall of an old warehouse and tried to stop the world from spinning. If he'd been a real drinker he would have retreated to a bar and drunk away these fucking images. But he wasn't much of a drinker, so he stepped out on the avenue and flagged a cab.

The landlord at Decker's former Sixty-ninth Street address claimed he didn't know anything about "no letter sent here to a Roberts, Roberts who?" But at Decker's former East Side address, the response was a little different. Yslan had no sooner pulled out her NSA ID then the geezer who opened the door began to confess, "I didn't know what to do with it. I mean, I know it wasn't for me, but you know I didn't do anything wrong, did I? And even if I did it was a mistake—ya know?"

Yslan allowed the man to finish groveling then in her best fuck-you voice said, "Get it for me. Get it now."

The guy retreated into the apartment and she turned to Mr. T, a smile creasing her face. "Works better than showing a teenage boy a bra strap."

"I wouldn't know," Mr. T responded.

Yslan wondered if he didn't know because he'd never been a girl or because he'd never been a teenaged boy or maybe he'd never seen a bra strap—probably the last one.

The super returned with an envelope addressed to Decker Roberts and a further apology. Yslan dead-eyed him and said, "Never again. You got me, sir? Never again," then turned and moved down Sixty-ninth Street. As she did she opened the envelope and whistled through her teeth—$4,290 in hundreds,

twenties, and one ten was impressive—even to Special Agent
Yslan Hicks.

● ● ●

"Tenth Avenue," Decker said. As he did he thought, *Jeez, if Calatrex really worked, Charendoff could have put his girl on the
drug—made her happy without hurting the boy and saved everyone the bother.*

It would have saved Decker a whole heap of trouble too, because he knew in his heart that that whole thing was not over—
no matter what NSA Special Agent Yslan Hicks said. He knew he
would have to deal with Charendoff—and maybe sooner than
later.

On the small television in the back of the cab an ad for another drug was playing out its little morality play. The glare of a
sixteen-wheeler's lights scraped across his eyes. "Happy pills and
dead boys in icy streams," he whispered as he felt for the cell
phone in his pocket and begged it to ring.

Eddie's phone rang, and he saw that it was Seth. He plugged
his phone into the computer and watched the sine wave. When
Eddie finally answered it there was only a hum on the other end.
"Seth? Did you get the money order? You can cash it at any bank.
Seth?"

No answer.

"Seth? Everything's fine here—there?"

In Victoria, Seth stood in the rain, unable to tell if it was rain
or tears on his face, and wondered why he'd called Eddie—then
why Eddie sounded so very, very odd—and was clearly lying to
him.

Decker got out at Tenth Avenue, and sure enough, the shoot was
still going.

He was careful to avoid the trailer with the green-haired girl
and quickly spotted four guys smoking and gabbing. Bad skin,
heavy guts—certainly not actors. Drivers. If the drivers were

here, their cars had to be nearby, and so did the drive captain who controlled the keys. Twenty minutes later the drive captain stepped out for a piss and Decker slipped into the man's small cubby and stole three sets of keys. Ten minutes after that he was driving a late-model SUV toward Connecticut, and an hour and forty minutes later he parked the SUV in a large underground parking garage and walked the seven blocks to the Stamford Greyhound bus terminal.

Every bus going west from Stamford either went to Cleveland or Pittsburgh, and from there he could transfer to a Cincinnati-bound bus.

As Decker waited in the bus station cafeteria he began to play an old game. It was one of the two tangential gifts related to his truth telling. He thought of them as subsets of his gift. The first was his parlour game of being able to tell people's ages, their backgrounds, etc., which he used in his acting teaching. The second gift allowed him to find the pattern of events. It allowed him to help actors chart. He called the patterns "semblant order."

He took out a wad of paper from his pocket and smoothed it out on the damp table, then took a quick breath and began to chart. "I'm called out to do three truth-telling sessions in one day, I arrive home a day early, Mike the balance guy tries to tell me something in my driveway—He's using us, something about a ratio—my house burns down, one of my credit cards is cancelled, my bank loan is called, my studio is condemned, Josh, Josh's lawyer, Charendoff, Yslan Hicks, What is a lie, Mike Shedloski is found murdered in his apartment in Cincinnati, a boy is frozen in ice, one of theirs killed one of ours, simple as that, I worked here, what's your ratio, who's jumping now, Yolles Pharmaceuticals . . . Calatrex selling at a cheaper than rational price."

He put down his pen, folded the paper, put it in his shirt pocket, closed his eyes, and rolled these facts over and over in his head . . . looking for their semblant order. But he couldn't put them all together—not all of them.

For the slightest moment he closed his eyes again then opened them. He was breathing heavily—he could feel sweat on his fore-head, but his mind was clear. He repeated verbatim the definition of truth that he had given to Yslan Hicks in New Jersey, stopping at the point about placebos. Placebos—lies. Lies that work. Then he thought about Eddie's message about the price of Calatrex.

He shoved the battery back into the laptop and contacted Eddie: *Eddie, find me something stronger that connects "What's your Ratio!" and Yolles Pharmaceuticals.*

Eddie stared at the request on his monitor and then did a quick search, then a second, then a third. Finally he stopped and stared at the entry on his monitor. He tore his eyes from the screen and they found their way to the old doll on the newly made bed.

He stared at the doll for a long moment—then pressed the send key.

Decker followed the link Eddie had sent him, read the data there quickly, and knew his semblant order had led him in the right direction. Now he had a name—an enemy—the man who was trying to use him.

He typed: *Is there any way to know if this guy Yolles set up my jobs in Orlando, Pittsburgh, and Cleveland?*

Eddie's reply came back quickly: *Whoever ordered those jobs has as good security as I do—so it would only be a guess on my part. But I guess—Yes!*

Decker nodded. He didn't need Eddie's reassurance on this one. If this guy wanted to use him, he'd have wanted to test him first—to audition him.

Boarding for his bus was announced.

As he sat on the bus waiting for it to travel west he found the address for and e-mailed that terrific kid in Cincinnati—now no longer a kid, one Steven Bradshaw. From the excited e-mail response the man was surprised to hear from Decker but was willing to return a favour that Decker had done for him almost fifteen years earlier.

• • •

"Finally! Got the fucker!" Mr. T shouted at his computer screen.

"About goddamned time!" Yslan said.

"Sorry, but this guy Eddie's slippery. Clever and slippery."

"Yeah, yeah, yeah, what've you got?"

The man pulled up the entirety of the correspondence between Decker and Eddie. Yslan read it quickly.

Then he pulled up the entry off the link Eddie had sent Decker. He hesitated, then said, "You'd better read this, boss."

Yslan scanned the text. The article was entitled "The Economic Impact of Knowing Exactly the Placebo Ratio on the Pharmaceutical Industry." It was the kind of MS thesis that everyone had to publish to get their degree from the University of Chicago. The author was a much younger Henry-Clay Yolles.

# 44

## ON THE BUS

AS DECKER'S BUS PLUNGED WESTWARD THROUGH THE DARK-ness the motion lulled him. The last image in his head before sleep finally took him was that of a boy hanging from a lamp-post—his painted nails in motion at the end of his twitching fin-gers—in the Junction.

He dreamt that he was watching the cult classic *Pi* and he was the only one in the theatre who thought the film was not fiction—was actually a how *not* to documentary. And when the hero put the foot-long power drill into his own head, Decker woke with a scream on his lips.

He was panting and could smell his own sweat. Some people once up in the jet stream cannot come down—if your erection lasts longer than four hours see a doctor. If you put your head up in the jet stream and can't pull it out who do you call—a shaman? Ghostbusters? Decker took a deep breath. You call Brother Mal-colm is who you call—or your son.

The darkness on the bus was only broken by one or two read-ing lights. In the sallow tent of one of those lights he saw a tall blond-haired woman, curls atumble across her broad handsome forehead. *I have some real estate here in my bag,* he thought, then discarded the idea of approaching her because even as the bus sped west he knew that something in all this didn't fit. One of these things was not like the others, one of these things just doesn't belong, but one of what—of which?

At the midnight stop Decker picked up a copy of *USA Today*—the only available paper—and was startled by the lack of coverage of almost anything. Articles reduced to a subway ride's length—but this wasn't intended as subway reading. This paraded as real news and real commentary. And then there was the reporting about religion in everything from housing design to a school in Pennsylvania that played soccer for God—and succeeded well beyond expectation. Even the sports section had been reduced to simple sound bites.

He had a flash of a moment years earlier with Crazy Eddie. Roone Arledge was being interviewed on ABC. Eddie made the sign of the cross and pointed it at the television set. "Vampire, man. He's a vampire."

"Why's that?"

"Guy produced *Wide World of Sports,*" he said.

"The thrill of victory, the agony of defeat, that old sports show?"

"The first sports show, Decker, where they didn't bother showing you the whole game. They just cherry-picked the best moments and presented them. It removed any need to be really involved, to commit yourself and your time to a full game. Guy's a vampire, man, wish I had a silver bullet."

"Come on, Eddie. There's a place for shows like that."

"No there's not. It's like eating the icing off the cupcake and leaving the cake. Pretty soon they won't bother making the cake at all—just sell a slather of the sugary crap."

"So some folks like sugary crap."

"Human beings are not made to take shortcuts, Decker. Hasn't your wife's death shown you that—or how you treated Seth? You're to live your life, moment by moment. Your life isn't here to entertain you—it's to be lived. Fuck." He threw something at the screen—a plastic football, as Decker remembered.

Eddie was serious. He had profound doubts about the way we were all living our lives. Eddie's library was stuffed with religious texts—but not the easy how-tos. The King James version of the Bible and four massive commentaries, an Arabic/English Koran and Hadith, *The Tibetan Book of the Dead,* the Nag Hammadi library, the Apocrypha, *The Pagan Christ, The Dead Sea Scrolls Deception, Men Who Have Walked with God*, and Jack Miles' two brilliant books *God: A Biography* and *Christ: A Crisis in the Life of God*.

Seth had spent a lot of time in discussion with Eddie and read many of the books. When Decker first feared that Seth had left he went into the boy's room, hoping that he was just oversleeping. Seth's backpack was gone. A note was on his pillow: "I'll send back your books, Eddie, once I've finished understanding them."

The books came back one at a time—but there was never a return address on the packages.

Decker couldn't allow himself to think of that now. He turned on his overhead light and took out a writing pad. The first four episodes of *At the Junction* dealt with the rise and early success of the Junction. This fifth episode began with the city courting the Junction to join them.

Decker envisioned a meeting of powerful Orangemen—a secret meeting—out of which a young boy loses his life at the end of a rope.

Decker fleshed out the scenes over the next four hours.

In the morning the bus inexplicably stopped opposite a small grade school. Children were arriving for class. Some were running in circles. Some were making snowballs and tossing them when the teacher wasn't looking. Others were trying to perfectly balance each other on the teeter-totter. *Balance,* Decker thought. *Lots of this is somehow about balance.*

He flipped open his computer and in less than five minutes wrote the voiceover as newspaper headlines of the day to begin the pilot episode of *At the Junction*. He reread it quickly; much to his surprise, it didn't need a single edit. He saved it to a USB key that he would use to e-mail Trish from an al-Qaeda café once he got to Cincinnati.

"Weapon number one," he murmured.

The guy beside him said, "What?"

Decker replied, "Nothing, sorry to bother you," but he hoped that that voiceover was not nothing, since it started: " 'Mountebanks Invade the City.' Beware of fakery. New drugs in the marketplace have proved to be nothing more than sugar pills. Beware of door-to-door hucksters and charlatans selling happiness pills."

## 45

# A COLD NIGHT IN TORONTO

## TRISH

Trish finished her mojito at Rancho Relaxo and looked toward the men's room. He'd be coming out soon. Young men drank too quickly and always had to pee. She tilted her glass and watched the light refract through the liquid, casting momentary rainbows on the slate-topped table. She put an index finger into the cold liquid and stirred it.

Yet another young man, a frat-boy type, was eyeing her from the bar. She wondered if she'd had enough of young men. There was much to like about them. She and her girlfriend, who played the lead on CBC's only hit show, *Then and Now,* agreed that young men were fun to play with, but not so much fun to talk to or wake up beside. And Trish was on the wrong side of forty for all this. Maybe she should cut her hair—after all, who has long hair after she turns forty?

She looked out the window and saw the snow whipping by in almost horizontal sheets.

Her new young man made his reentrance from the washroom. She watched him self-consciously strut toward her—pride of conquest in every step as he passed by the frat boy at the bar. She liked his energy—that was for sure—but . . .

The door opened and a cold rush of air drew her attention. Two heavyset Scotsmen entered and nodded to her. She wondered if she knew these guys. Their piercing blue eyes should be hard to forget. But she couldn't place them.

One of the Scots raised his glass and winked at her. Then turned to the bar and stared at her in the mirror.

Trish felt for the pepper spray in her purse. She knew how to look after herself. For a moment she thought of Decker; she hoped he knew how to look after himself. He's a bit old, she thought, but interesting in a way that the young man, who just turned his chair around and straddled it, was not.

## THEO

Theo tried to control the coughing fit but found that he was on his knees, his pills scattered about the dust-ridden floor like tiny coloured rabbit turds. It was getting worse and he knew it. He braced himself for the inevitable second wave and it came even quicker than he thought. He rolled onto his back and, through the stacks of books, saw the snow swirling in squalls across the window.

He tried to recite Auden's poem "Stop All the Clocks" to distract himself. He knew that only time would end the fit and his greatest enemy was panic. The damned pills sure didn't help! Well actually, the one he took in the middle of the night stopped the cough just like that—like magic. But the two he had just taken didn't do squat.

His head slammed back against the floor as a new and more powerful wave of coughing forced the air from his lungs.

If Decker had been there, he would have picked up the pills and forced Theo to take more of them, but Decker wasn't there. Who the hell knew where Decker was.

He curled into a ball and waited for the beating to end, but these were not kicks from outside—these were boots with steel toes launched with incredible force from inside. He got to his knees, grabbed the edge of a bookshelf and tried to stand. The entire shelf of paperbacks tumbled down onto him.

On the floor again he saw that the book he'd been searching for about the Junction before the amalgamation had fallen in front of his face. He pulled it to him. As he did he cleared the way to two of his pills. He scooped them up and shoved them into his mouth.

They dissolved quickly, and much to Theo's surprise, he could feel them working. His cough softened and then disappeared.

## EDDIE

Eddie rolled out the new rug in the guest room, then stood back to see if it matched the recently painted walls. It did. He pulled a small table near to the bed and turned on the new lamp there. Too harsh. He replaced the bulb with a 50 watt diffused lightbulb. Turned it on and turned off the overhead.

The old doll sat on the bed with the new coverlet—and watched closely.

Eddie carefully removed the brace from his leg and lay on the bed and thought of the future he'd paid so dearly for—a future where his daughter would lie on this bed in this room in this house and they would be a family again.

## LEENA

Leena shook the snow from her down coat as she entered her apartment on Montrose. She liked her place—it was in the student ghetto and there was life on the street until pretty late. She liked that. She wasn't very good with silence.

She'd just been to the cemetery. It was sad that hers was the only rock on her husband's gravestone. She felt older than her years—much older. But that's how she felt, and she no longer fought it. She heated some soup and wondered what she was going to do with the rest of her evening. She didn't sleep much anymore. So she began to clean. When she came upon the shoebox in the back of her closet she stopped.

She poured herself a glass of red wine and took the shoebox to the small table in the bay window—and as the snow built up on the windowsill she read Decker's love letters from almost twenty-five years ago.

## GARRETH SR.

Garreth Sr. had had enough of hints and innuendos from his son. He was not a cop anymore, but he had been for almost forty years. And retirement gave him lots of time to think. And if this Decker Roberts was who he thought he was—the boy who had sent his life and career to hell—well, he'd sure as shit be waiting for him when he got back to town—and Toronto boys always came back to ol' T.O., like bad pennies.

So he sat in his rental car and tilted his hip flask, allowing the warming glow of good scotch into his mouth, while across the way through the falling snow he watched the house on Strathallan Wood in the North York section of the city where he had first met Decker Roberts. It had been cold that day too—very cold. And there had been a dead little girl, whose image never left Garreth's mind unless he drank her away.

## 46

## CINCINNATI, OHIO

AS SOON AS DECKER GOT TO CINCINNATI HE E-MAILED THE voiceover dialogue to Trish, then headed to Mike Shedloski's address. He needed more ammunition before he confronted the head of Yolles Pharmaceuticals.

Decker was not a good actor—had never been a good actor. But he understood acting and actors—how it and they worked. Just as he had never been a good musician but he understood what made music, music and not noise.

He knew how actors transformed. He knew that self-definition was at the core of the process—as long as the actor's centre was still and deep, images could be dropped into the pond of the self, like a pebble dropped into a mountain lake, and the person would change. If Decker thought of himself as Seth's father the pond would change and others would see him as older. If he thought of himself as Dr. Roberts' son he would be perceived as his youngest. So as soon as he'd left the bus he'd summoned his deep knowledge of himself then dropped the idea of himself as Dr. Roberts' son into the still waters and sensed the concentric circles move outward. The change in Decker was subtle. It wouldn't fool a photograph, but when someone showed people a picture of him a confused look might cross the viewer's face. Yes, it looked like Decker, but it didn't match their perception of the person they had met. It would not buy Decker much—but every bit of confusion could help.

• • •

Henry-Clay had stood silhouetted against the tall building on the other side of the Ohio River with his back to Yslan since she'd come into his office—like some dumb shot from *The Fountainhead*, Yslan thought. Then it occurred to her that this guy's personal motto could well be I will never work so another man may eat. Then she amended it to an appropriate gravestone for this creep: He never worked so another man could eat.

Henry-Clay saw the slender NSA agent's image in the glass beside his. He was tempted to move so his reflection crept on top of hers. He felt a familiar stirring in his loins, then turned slowly—much as he had on the website with Decker—to find the woman had extraordinary translucent blue eyes. Something odd in the genes, he assumed.

He was shorter than she thought he'd be and there was something rubbery about his lips and hands and eyelids, but his eyes never wavered and they betrayed, if not intelligence, at least a quickness—a fire.

Henry-Clay was surprised how much better looking she was in person than in the reflection in the windowpane or in the images Senator Villianne had sent him. He was pleased that the rest of the information the good senator had sent matched up perfectly with the woman standing on the far side of his desk.

"I'm sorry I had to make you wait, Special Agent Hicks."

She knew he wasn't the least bit sorry to make her wait, but said, "Be that as it may; Decker Roberts."

His lips formed an almost perfect O, and Yslan thought he might blow a bubble.

"Who?"

Damned close to Disney's Cheshire cat.

"Decker Roberts," she repeated.

"What an odd name. Shouldn't it be Roberts Decker, like the actor Roberts Blossom?"

*Home Alone*—another film that grew on you like mildew.

"No, it's Decker Roberts. Tell me everything you know about Decker Roberts."

"Nothing."

"Nothing?"

"Do you enjoy a late-night dinner, Special Agent Hicks?"

"Decker Roberts."

"Would he enjoy one?"

"Okay, Mr. Yolles. I'm a federal agent and I can have you arrested."

"For asking you out to dinner?"

"For withholding evidence, impeding a federal investigation—"

"Enough, Special Agent Hicks. If you don't want to go out with me, just say as much."

It was his lips. Yes, it was his lips. Like a tropical fish's. No. It wasn't just that. His mouth was way too small for his big head, but his lips were too big . . .

Then he puckered and blew her a kiss.


Decker first persuaded the Realtor to show him the place despite the fact that it was a mess, then asked to be left alone in the apartment—Mike's apartment.

He knew that this place—because of Mike—was important. Exactly why he couldn't say, but at least it was somewhere to start.

The apartment was surprisingly spare; no, not spare, Decker realized—balanced. Volumes, colours, shapes—all in a pleasing balance. It reminded Decker of some of the colonial buildings he'd been in. A perfect human ratio of height to width to length—the same ratios that da Vinci illustrated in his famous drawing of the Vitruvian man.

The only unbalanced part of Mike's apartment was the interior of his refrigerator, where junk food reigned supreme. Opened bags of potato chips of various kinds, flavours, and shapes—dill pickle was evidently his favourite—were scattered higgledy-piggledy with half-eaten cans of different types of ravioli—evidently cheese was his favourite—and takeout Chinese containers—General Tso's chicken took pride of place.

The smell was none too pleasant.

Decker closed the refrigerator, embarrassed that he had invaded Mike's privacy—as if he'd found a stack of girlie mags. He passed by the beautifully balanced pile of junk that formed a Celtic cross in the living room and entered Mike's bedroom. Surrounding the surprisingly small bed were several of Mike's balancing-act statues. Decker looked from one to the next. His eyes stopped at the statue that vaguely looked like Mike himself. Something was wrong with it. There was one, and only one, piece out of symmetry—a slender black laptop was squeezed between the speakers that formed the statue's left arm and the three printers that made up his chest.

Decker carefully removed Mike's computer.

He fired it up and contacted Eddie. Within five minutes Eddie had the computer's codes and full control of the machine. Ten minutes later Eddie found Mike's research for Yolles Pharmaceuticals, entitled "The Reality of Placebo Ratios—The Oddest Balance."

*8.6 again,* Eddie wrote to Decker

*8.6?* Decker wrote back.

*It's the same pi factor that Martin Armistaad based his market predictions on.*

*Martin Armistaad?*

*A fraudster, now in Leavenworth Penitentiary, but he accurately predicted, among other things, the exact day in the eighties that the market crashed.*

*I don't see how that helps us, Eddie.*

*Just saying, your guy's not alone.*

Decker pulled his fingers away from the keys. He wanted to be sure that he didn't write what was in his head: "no kidding." He was going to ask Eddie another question, then decided against it and typed, *"Thanks"* and without waiting for a response shut off the machine. He didn't know why, but he felt that the next important thing he needed to confront Yolles he'd have to find on his own. He thought about that for a moment—did he have to find it on his own, or did he want to find on his own without

Eddie's help? Or it was safer to find it on his own? He didn't know the answer to his own questions.

He closed the bedroom door and stepped into the living room. The sun was setting, throwing long lines of refracted light across the floor. Decker glanced down and then to the windowsill to see what was causing the rainbows on the floor. There on the sill was a miniature version of an office building. The tiny thing was made of match and Popsicle sticks and bits of glass through which the light was refracting.

Decker knelt to get a better look, and as he went to touch the miracle of both miniaturization and balance a building six blocks across town came into his line of vision—and to his amazement he saw that the tiny statue was a perfect replication of the building across the way.

Decker found himself holding his breath. Then he remembered Mike's sign: "Who's Jumping Now?"

Decker sat back on his butt on Mike's floor, opened the man's computer, and searched for the building on Google Earth. He found it, then quickly found its history—and the fact that Henry-Clay Yolles' paternal grandfather had jumped to his death from the building after the crash in twenty-nine.

Decker stared at the building and nodded. This could be of use—something personal. The more he knew about Henry-Clay Yolles, the better chance he had of forcing him to back off. Stage-trained actors always wanted to find textual support for behaviour. But Decker knew that the fucked-up hard-wiring of the human heart is much more important and powerful. Iago gives his reasons for hating Othello—"I hate the Moor: And it is thought abroad, that 'twixt my sheets he has done my office," and that Othello passed over him and awarded someone else a promotion. But neither is the reason for his hatred—his hatred is hard-wired and totally irrational. Decker hoped it was the same with Henry-Clay Yolles and the Treloar Building.

Decker tucked the laptop under his arm, then realized it was exactly where the computer had been on the statue. He stepped back, just brushing the balancing Celtic cross statue behind him—it fell to the floor. Decker stared at the dozens and dozens of pieces on the carpet. Pieces of nothing that Mike's genius had balanced into something of beauty, meaning. Tears sprung to Decker's eyes, and he felt the world spin on its axis. Then he was on the floor desperately trying to resurrect Mike's creation, but all the king's horses and all the king's men . . .

Decker stepped out into the hallway. The Realtor looked up from his BlackBerry and said, "Great place, no?"

Decker didn't answer—he was thinking about "Who's Jumping Now?" Decker sensed the pieces coming together, like the events of a script he was charting—they were all about there. Shortly it would be up to him to direct them like a stage play. No; for a man like Henry-Clay Yolles, a picture was worth a gazillion words. So not a play—a multimedia event. A multimedia event guided by a semblant order.

Decker left Mike's place and walked along Plum Street. Without thinking why he tossed Mike's computer into the first Dumpster he saw. Down the road he stopped in front of a bizarre minaret-topped building, which, surprisingly enough, was a synagogue. Farther down the street he saw a large Catholic cathedral. He nodded—a smile creasing his face, "Good, yes, very good."

Cincinnati presented the classic Midwestern anomaly. Overtly friendly people, deeply divided along racial and class lines—a profound belief that they were good people and a cliquiness that often went all the way back to high school. But in a pinch give me a Midwesterner. On a desert island he'll figure out how to read the stars, make a raft and get outta there. Their sense of their own goodness has been played upon by both pulpit and senate chamber over and over again. They were about the only white boys who fought in Vietnam—and they were believers, often marines, often signing up for second tours of duty even after honorable discharges and serious wounds.

If there's a fire, a flood, a hurricane or just a neighbour who needs help—give me a Midwesterner . . . but there can be also a sub-rosa Midwestern small-mindedness and violence.

Left out of the mainstream of Midwestern thought altogether, African Americans forged their own culture. As blacks escaped the South they followed the great rivers north and brought their music with them, so that jazz sprung up in unlikely places along the shores of the Mississippi, Ohio and Missouri rivers. When Decker used to work in the regional theatres in Pittsburgh and St. Louis and Cleveland and Cincinnati, he always did his best to befriend black stagehands—there were few black actors hired at the time—so they could walk him into the jazz clubs. Without a black man to vouch for you, no Caucasian ever got into the inner sanctum of black culture—the smoke-filled, liquor-saturated jazz clubs.

It'd been many years since Decker directed in Cincinnati's Playhouse in the Park, and he didn't even know who ran that lonely artistic outpost now. But he did remember a young black apprentice to whom he'd given his first role on the main stage—Steven Bradshaw. Steven had taken him to see Etta James.

Half an hour after leaving Mike's apartment, a broad-smiling, gap-toothed Steven Bradshaw was shaking his hand and saying, "Got your e-mail. What brings you back to Cincy?"

"You up for a little acting, Steve?"

The man's smile outshone the sun.

"I'll be back in half an hour. I need you in a sports jacket and open-collar shirt. And I need you against a neutral background with enough light—natural light—to pick up the proper colour and contours of your face. Okay?"

"Sure. What kind of pants?"

"Any or none; we're not going to see them in the shot."

"I'm just kidding, but at last I'm in front of the camera—good godamn!"

At the electronics superstore, Decker paid cash for a handheld digital camera and ignored the pitch to sell him the warranty. He bought an extra memory card and was about to leave when he saw a gigantic plasma screen TV on the far wall. "Can I rent one of those?" he asked.

They quoted him an astronomical price.

Decker thought of the unusual minaret-topped synagogue on Plum Street and asked, "How's about if I rent three of them?"

"Three times the price," the salesman said.

"Logical," Decker muttered, and he paid cash for the rental of three of the huge screens. "You'll deliver them?"

"For a price."

"Naturally. And they're wireless?"

"Everything's wireless now. Just plug 'em in and use the remote." He reached behind the counter and handed Decker two remotes. "They come with the package. No charge but you have to leave a hundred dollars apiece as a deposit. You return the remotes—you get back your money. Fair?"

Decker nodded, "Sure, that's fair."

The sales clerk clearly didn't know what the word "sardonic" meant. Much of the Midwest seemed to have missed the concept, so Decker repeated, "Sure, that's fair." Then unable to resist he asked, "How about throwing in a portable DVD player?"

The salesman looked at him like he'd grown a second head.

He paid for the DVD player in cash as well and headed back to Steve's.

Steve had set up a wooden desk against a soft white background. Decker reoriented the table so that the light from the kitchen window slanted across Steve's lovely blue-black skin, then told him basically what he wanted him to say. Steve took it in and gave it a shot. It was quite good—centred and smart. "Okay," Decker said, "let's get a sound level then put one down."

Yslan Hicks pulled out her cell phone. "The little prick claims he's never seen or heard of Roberts."

"Swell," Harrison said from his Washington office.

"If Christ had turned this guy's piss to wine he'd claim he did it himself."

Harrison stared at the wall of his office. It was covered with data about Henry-Clay Yolles. "Do you want to bring him in and sweat him, Yslan?"

"I'd prefer to crush his nuts and throw him out that big window in his boardroom."

"He come on to you, Yslan?"

"Does the pope wear a dress?"

"To the best of my understanding he does. So how do you want to play this?"

"I think Yolles is behind what happened to Decker."

"Did you tell him so?"

"No."

"And you've had no sightings of Roberts?"

"No."

"Roberts has to approach Yolles somehow. So use Yolles as the bait."

"That's what I'm doing," she said, glancing at her two guys. "Did you get anything on that guy at the bar back in the New York restaurant?"

"No."

"I don't like it, sir. There are too many loose ends." She didn't bother mentioning that some of the actions against Roberts didn't align. She didn't bother mentioning this since she wasn't sure how they didn't align or even exactly what she meant by things not aligning. It wasn't her way of thinking—and she was more than a little puzzled that that word came to her. She realized with a start that she'd been thinking differently since she'd kidnapped Decker Roberts.

"Can I ask about—?"

"No. Just find Roberts, Yslan. We need him."

"Because of the—?"

He hung up the phone. The immediate danger from the Pakistani jihadi had been dealt with. Two other witnesses clarified which one of these bastards had been telling the truth and which had been lying. But the danger had only been pushed into the future. He took out a folder that had now grown to a substantial width. There were dozens of other terrorist suspects that he was anxious to have Decker Roberts listen to—and then tell him which of their statements were true.

"It's good Steve. Really good."

"Thanks. It was fun. What're you going to do with it?"

"Use it, Steve." *To get Henry-Clay Yolles to back off,* Decker thought. "So here's some cash for your time." Decker handed him five hundred dollars. The young man looked genuinely hurt. For a second Decker thought he had not offered enough money, then he realized that Steve had done the work as a favour—a thank-you—and wanted no payment. "Sorry," Decker mumbled. "How 'bout this then—I'll take you out for dinner or whatever you like?"

Steve smiled that smile again and said, "For guys like you who liked Etta, I got just the place."

Yslan sat with her team at their makeshift command headquarters. Down the way she could see the Byzantine Isaac M. Wise Temple with its peculiar minarets. Farther down was the historic St. Peter in Chains Cathedral. *Lots of churches,* she thought. For a moment she flashed on a report of the area that Decker Roberts lived in, the Junction—lots of churches there too. *Why have houses of worship of different denominations and faiths side by side by side—all in the same area?* she asked herself. Then an answer surfaced from a silent place in her heart—to contain the evil here. She knew that Cincinnati was the sight of many of the most vicious riots in the history of the United States. Several before and right after the Civil War—with Kentucky just across the river many people in Cincinnati were torn in their loyalties to the Union. Several times blacks had been attacked by anti-abolitionists and large riots had followed. But the worst riot had been eighteen years after the end of the Civil War, in 1883. It was famous in law-enforcement circles. Months earlier two men had been convicted of the murder of their boss but only one had been hung. The second was confined to jail, and the city rose as one angry thing in protest. Two deputies died protecting the jail—a statue of one, Captain John Desmond, stands proudly in the courthouse lobby. All told over forty Cincinnatians were killed and many score in-jured—but it was the remnants of the rioters' rage that continued to scar the city. Yslan could still sense it.

With a shock she realized that she had never before felt or thought like this. Had it been her time with Decker Roberts that had made her so sensitive?

She didn't know, but she no longer discarded it as a possibility.

So why all the churches? Go back to their nature. Of everything ask, what is its nature? What does it do?

Yslan flipped open her laptop and accessed her private NSA files. She had only a few synaesthetes in the entire country whom she considered to possibly have talents that could aid the NSA; one of them was serving time in Leavenworth Penitentiary. But she had a much longer list of silly synaesthetes—those with a gift that was quirky but not intrinsically useful. She quickly scanned the list and to her surprise found that one of those silly synaes-thetes lived in Cincinnati and had been murdered three days ago.

"Let's go," she said, grabbing her coat.

The angry black slam poet was finishing his set as Decker and Steve entered the club. A trio of musicians graciously completed the young man's unfinished thoughts with a fine discordant flour-ish that segued into the profound opening chords of Coltrane's "Blue Train."

Decker and Steve took a seat at a side table. Steve ordered a pitcher of malt liquor. As offhandedly as he could manage, Decker asked, "You got any friends in the newspaper business, Steve?"

"I work for a local TV station—so sure."

Decker smiled and handed him a folded piece of paper. "Could you get this to them? They might be interested in it."

"Mind if I ask what it is?"

"It's a real estate item."

"Sure. I got favours owed me all over this town," Steve said, pocketing the paper.

"All over?" Decker asked.

"All over, Mr. Roberts," Steve said with a smile.

Outside the unmarked club, in a rented Escalade, Emerson Remi watched the dot on his BlackBerry settle and remain still. A group of young black men sauntered past the Escalade and were about to cause a ruckus when Emerson turned his head toward them. The young men, seeing Emerson's eyes, decided there was easier prey than the weird white guy in the dumb car.

Henry-Clay was on the phone to Congressman Villianne. "And I want more info on this Yslan Hicks, before the sun rises. Got it? Good—now go get it."

He slammed down the phone and called MacMillan. "Where are you?"

MacMillan responded.

"Mr. MacMillan, I need you—and some of your guys, post-haste." He hung up and looked out the window. The Treloar Building carved a tooth mark in the low-hanging winter moon.

The band was finishing its number as a pretty black woman, dressed à la the young Lena Horne, stepped up to the old-fashioned mic. She took the thing in her elegant fingers and a shiver ran through every man in the room. The drummer dumped his sticks and took out his brushes.

The girl's voice was little more than a purr of sound and stirred the hearts of everyone in the room.

"Like her?" Steven asked.

"What's not to like?" Decker responded.

"Good," Steve said. "She's my honey, Hialeah." Decker looked at him. "Her daddy liked the horses."

Decker noted that the room had suddenly filled and every eye was on Hialeah. He thought, *If this girl told them to jump over the moon, at least the men would give it a shot.* Decker nodded and whispered, "Thanks," for the good fortune to a god he didn't believe existed.

"For what?" Steve asked.

"For her," Decker said, but what he thought was, *Thanks for the final piece.*

Yslan showed the building manager the photos of Decker Roberts.

The man looked at the photos, then looked at Yslan.

"Have you seen this man, sir? It's very important."

"Well I think I have—but then again I think I haven't."

"What does that mean, sir?"

"Are these recent photos?"

"Very recent."

"Then I don't think I've seen him."

"Why do you say that?"

"Well I saw someone like that with the Realtor but I think he was younger—maybe this guy's younger brother. He have a younger brother?"

"When did you see him?"

"Earlier today. Came to look at the dead guy's apartment."

Twenty minutes later—and without a warrant—Mr. T stepped aside as Ted Knight opened the apartment door and Yslan stepped in. "Give me ten minutes." The men looked at each other—this was new, too.

Yslan stood alone in Mike's apartment. She looked at the pieces of the broken statue on the floor, then pushing open the bedroom door she saw the computer peripherals statue of Mike.

She felt surrounded by input—important input—that she couldn't sort into any meaningful order. She closed the bedroom door, then headed toward the exit—completely missing the miniature statue on the windowsill of the Treloar Building.

Later that night Decker sat with Steve and Hialeah and made a request.

"No one's going to get hurt?" Steven asked.

"No. It's only something for Yolles Pharmaceuticals to think about."

Steve turned to Hialeah and said, "Yolles Pharma has always rejected the idea that our community has health issues that need to be addressed—at least researched."

Decker looked at Hialeah but said nothing.

"It's just signs and stuff?" Steve asked Decker.

"Yes, Steve," Decker said, "but there have to be enough people to make a statement."

"You mean enough black people, don't you, Mr. Roberts?" Hialeah said, her voice tight, angry.

"Yes," Decker said, "black people to picket Yolles Pharmaceuticals."

Hialeah stared at her beautiful hands for a moment. Decker was sure she was going to tell him to get the fuck out of her life with this racial crap, but then she looked at Steve and said, "Do you really believe this could do our community some good?"

"It was you who brought up the problem with Yolles Pharma. It was years ago," Steve said.

"On the anniversary of our first date."

"Yeah, you complained a blue streak," Steve replied, his smile widening.

Hialeah turned to Decker and said, "And when would you like this little protest to take place?"

## 47

## CINCINNATI, OHIO, TWO

"HE'S A RANK AMATEUR BUT WE CAN'T FIND HIM, IS THAT what you're trying to tell me?" Yslan demanded.

Mr. T nodded and shrugged his enormous shoulders. Ted Knight said, "We've got people all over this town. We'll find him."

Yslan pushed her coffee away. "I prefer the hot black crap they call coffee in New York."

"This is Cincinnati, German coffee."

"It's shitty coffee is what it is." She got to her feet and stretched her back muscles. She was thinking, *What's Decker's nature? He's a special kind of synaesthete,* then she addressed the second part of Marcus Aurelius' famous question from *The Silence of the Lambs*—that damned film again! "What does he do?" She asked aloud.

The two men looked at each other, not knowing what she was asking.

"Look. He's not a cop or a PI with friends in a police department. He has to find support somewhere. Look what he's already managed. So who's helping him? So I repeat. What does Decker Roberts do?"

"He teaches acting," Ted Knight said.

"He works on documentaries," Mr. T added.

Yslan thought about that but it got her nowhere. Then she asked, "How did he manage to get things done in New York?"

"He contacted that actor Josh . . ."

"Near," Yslan said, but she wasn't looking at him.

"Yeah. Then he hid at that green-haired freak's place in Queens," added Mr. T.

"Yes, he did," said Yslan. "One an actor and one on a production crew of a TV shoot." Yslan turned back to the men. "What did he do before he was an acting teacher?"

"He directed theatre, didn't he?"

"Yes." Suddenly Yslan was in motion. "There's a professional theatre in Cincinnati, isn't there? That's got to be his connection here."

That evening's *Cincinnati Enquirer* carried a lead story in its real estate section—"Treloar Building Ready to be Sold to Mystery Buyer." Decker read the article in Steve's tiny kitchen and went to high-five him when the younger man put forward his fist—pound. No more high-fives—now we pound.

Steve smiled, and before Decker could ask how he managed to get the article in the paper so fast said, "The editor owes me a favour."

"Lots of people owe you favours, Steve?"

"You bet your white ass they do. So what else do we need to finish your business here, Mr. Roberts?"

Decker thought, *All the pieces are in place. Now I need somewhere to mount the event.* He said, "You know that weird building on Plum Street?"

"The synagogue?"

"Yeah, it looks more like a mosque."

"It's a synagogue in the old Byzantine style. That was the way they made them in the nineteenth century. Used to be hundreds of them in the world. Now the only one outside of Cincy is in New York City. The rest, Mr. Hitler took care of."

"Didn't care for the architecture?"

"Evidently hated it."

"How do you know so much . . ."

". . . about that synagogue?"

"Yeah."

"My cousin's the Shabbos goy over there."

Decker stared at Steve. "Is there anything in this town you don't know?"

"Nope," said Steve, completely without arrogance. "If a black man's going to prosper in a place like this, you have to know everything you can—and I know a lot."

"You do. So can your cousin, the Shabbos goy, get us into the synagogue?"

"Sure."

"And do you have somewhere else to live for a while?"

"Why?"

"This could get a bit dicey."

"Who all are looking for you, Mr. Roberts?"

"Folks."

Suddenly Steve was stern, "What folks, Mr. Roberts?"

"Feds," Decker said as simply as he could.

Steve suddenly smiled. "Whoosh—thought it was someone serious." He went to a cupboard and pulled down a suitcase, and for the first time spoke in full ghetto patois. "Black gent always gots a packed suitcase and cribs throughout the metro-poh-littan area."

A half hour later Yslan and Mr. T had the terrified artistic director of the Cincinnati Playhouse in the Park virtually on his knees with fear. After an initial and pathetically weak attempt to force Yslan to get a warrant, he handed over the theatre's records, which went back almost forty-five years and were—naturally enough, being from a theatre—all stacked in boxes and not yet computerized.

In a box marked 1993 they found what they were looking for—the program for a production of *The Dwarf* both adapted from the Swedish novel and directed by Decker Roberts.

"Great, and what do we do with that?" Mr. T demanded.

"We search out every name in the entire thing—everyone from usher to star."

•  •  •

Across town Henry-Clay held the Cincinnati *Enquirer* real estate section in one hand while he stared at the Treloar Building and shouted into the speakerphone. "Find out who the hell is going to buy the Treloar Building and offer him double what he's paying for it—and do it now."

That night at the club Hialeah sang three songs, then stopped. The quiet in the room was palpable. They waited, literally on the edge of their chairs, for her next words. She allowed a long slow breath into the mic then said, "There's a drug company in this town that needs to be taught a lesson."

As the sun rose, Yslan met with her team to compare notes. A startling percentage of the male actors from the production were dead. "AIDS," Yslan said. "Antivirals weren't around in any number then. What else do we have?"

"The rest of the actors, well, they're not actors anymore. Only one is even involved in the entertainment business."

"Who's that?"

"Guy named Steven Bradshaw. He works for a local TV station."

"And he lives in Cincinnati?"

"Yep."

"Where?"

Mr. T gave the address and Yslan ordered immediate surveillance.

"Anyone else?"

"Two of the ushers still work at the theatre. They're both pensioners now. One of the carpenters and one of the fly men on the show still live in Cincinnati."

"Find them and I want them interrogated. Take Roberts' picture."

Yslan looked down at the program. She quickly read the bios of the actors. Steven Bradshaw's bio claimed that this was his first

time on the main stage and he thanked Mr. Roberts for the opportunity.

She read the bio aloud.

"You want us to interrogate him?"

"Not yet. I don't want him scared away. But I want to know his
every—and I mean every—move."

At the table at the back of the copy shop Decker stared at his
handiwork. The deed for a commercial property in his name
looked a shitload like the real thing. The deed was for the Treloar
Building.

Decker put it on the small desk, then moved it to a corner. He
put his downloaded copy of Henry-Clay's MS thesis on the other
corner, then moved it to the left. Beside it he placed Mike's placebo research for Yolles Pharmaceuticals. He took his design for
the "Who's Jumping Now?" and put it dead centre—then flipped
open the portable DVD player and punched play. Steve's mock
newscast came up—Decker stepped back to see the mise-en-
scène. The flicker from the DVD brought his little stage to life. He
smiled at the semblant order there and said, "And now for a holy
place for an unholy act."

## 48

## GIVE DREADFUL NOTE OF PREPARATION

STEVE'S COUSIN, THE SYNAGOGUE'S SHABBOS GOY, A TERRI-
bly thin young black man, opened the back alley door to the synagogue and stepped aside for Decker to enter. Decker had always
hated the term "goy." It was as malicious as the slander "kike,"
and too many Jews thought it was okay to use the term because
they considered themselves victims—and victims always thought
they had the right to strike back at their oppressors. Yeah, but
how is the issue.

The Shabbos goy was an old tradition. Because Orthodox
Jews—and often Conservative and now even some Reform Jewish
Rabbis—will not do any work on the Sabbath, or Shabbos, they
needed someone not of the faith to open and shut the synagogue
and do basic things like turn on the lights. The relationship that
ensued between the often extremely literate (and sometimes very
wealthy) religious Jews and often semiliterate non-Jews who took
on the role of the Shabbos goy interested Decker. Did the famil-
iarity breed contempt or respect? Did Shabbos goys hide their
Jewish employers from the Nazis or aid the Germans in rounding
them up? What was the ratio of "good" Shabbos goys to "bad"
Shabbos goys, Decker wondered.

The old building, like any large interior space, was completely
unchanged by the arrival of three men. It simply included the
new additions. The building was the given—a visitor was an afterthought. The height of the place surprised Decker, as did the
two side galleries that looked more like they belonged in an Epis-
copalian house of worship. Then there was the ostentation. Even

when it was built in 1866 it invoked comments from the local press like, "Cincinnati never before had seen so much grandeur." Of course just down the street was Saint Peter in Chains Cathedral, which just proved that religions of various denominations seemed to enjoy showing off their financial prowess as if their gods loved the pretension of wealth.

Decker allowed himself to slowly walk the long centre aisle of the place and feel what he thought of as the heft of the space around him—just as he used to do when he walked into a theatre that he had never directed in before. Buildings have their own rhythm and sense of self. To put a piece of art into a building without understanding how the building worked was just folly—like throwing a Rothko randomly into a space, ignoring the ratio of its dimensions. It may have been what caused Rothko to fire three architects and finally contributed to his suicide before the chapel that bears his name was completed in Houston. For a moment, Decker wanted to head to the airport and go there—to just sit in the silence and commune.

He shook off the impulse and stepped up on the bimah—the altar. He stared at the tabernacle that held the Torah scrolls. Did he want this behind him or behind his adversary—or did he want to ignore it altogether?

The natural thing was to make Henry-Clay Yolles enter down the centre aisle so that he looked up at Decker on the bimah—like Princess Di's funeral. Did the Brits know how to stage a pageant in a cathedral or what! When the coffin came all the way down the centre aisle, then turned to the right and the huge doors opened to allow the light in and her coffin out—Decker remembered wanting to cheer.

But what Decker was planning was not a religious event. It was a worldly negotiation that he wanted played out against a religious setting. The sugar tasting sweeter because of the salt. He didn't need or want the backup of some folks' holy books—just the sense of sacred space to set off these most assuredly profane business dealings.

He climbed to the left gallery and looked across the way—and knew this was the right way to work. He in one gallery, his enemy in the other—with a yawning space between them.

Steve entered the old synagogue and stood at his skinny cousin's side, awaiting instruction. "So?"

"Perfect," Decker responded. "One here,' he pointed behind him. He then pointed across the way to the far wall of the other gallery and said, "One there and the last one by the front door below the rose window." A rose window in a synagogue? Very odd. He made a mental note to check that out.

Steve followed Decker's directions and jotted a few specifics on a small pad. "Can you find an outlet up there?" he asked.

Decker did.

"Good," Steve said, "and there's one by the front door. I'll check the other gallery."

"There're lots of outlets up there," Steve's cousin said.

"What about ways of hanging the screens?" Decker asked.

"No problem, we have lots of high-test cable to support huppahs and build sukkahs."

Decker stared at him.

"Hey man, I'm the Shabbos goy. I work here, I know the ins and outs of this Jewish thing," Steve's cousin said. He and Steve pounded fists.

"Good," Decker said, then added, "I'll be right down."

It took Yslan's guys only two runs with the metal battering ram to punch a hole in Steve's front door. And even less time to establish that he had packed up and run.

Decker sat in one of the side pews and looked at Steve. "I've gotten you in pretty deep. You can just walk away from all this. To this point you haven't done anything wrong or illegal."

Steve looked at Decker and said, "You changed my life the last time we met, and you're going to do it again."

Decker closed his eyes briefly—three straight lines across his retina. A truth—although an uncomfortable one for Decker. He didn't like the idea of having other people's lives on his conscience. "You brought your computer?"

"Here it is." Steve held it out to Decker.

Decker took it and handed over his wallet and all his remaining cash.

"Whoa—what's that for?"

"Expenses and to pay you for your computer and for safekeeping. You're going to have to pay the Super Store for the amount remaining for the screens when they arrive, and you'll need help, and I want you to pay for that help—and pay yourself. And pay your cousin. Maybe buy him some groceries. He looks like he needs some."

"Fine, but this is a lot of money."

"Four thousand two hundred and ninety short of what it ought to be."

"Wha—"

"Some guy on East Fifty-eighth owes me over four grand, and he better believe I'm going to collect."

Steve looked at Decker and was about to ask what that was all about then decided against it. Instead he asked, "Don't you need some cash in the meantime?"

"Sure. Give me a hundred. It's all I'll need."

Steve reluctantly took the money and pocketed the wallet—with Emerson Remi's card that had the electronic tracking dot on it. He headed out, but Decker called him back.

Decker showed him the two remote controls the store had given him. "Show me how these work."

Steve gave a smile and showed Decker the basic commands.

Steve said, "So, it's tomorrow?"

"Right. Let's say we're set by eleven o'clock. Eleven thirty is half hour—midnight is curtain."

"No problem. I'll get the screens delivered shortly after the evening service here is finished."

"When's that?"

"Shabbos goy said just past nine."

Decker was a little taken aback to hear the slander from Steve's lips but he managed, "Good."

"Where you going to be until then, Mr. Roberts?"

"Far away from you. I've made your life complicated enough without me endangering you by being close. Remember, don't go home until this is all, all over."

Steve nodded. "Cribs for me. Where you going to sleep tonight?"

Decker shook his head.

"Got it."

A sharp whistle from behind the bimah drew both of their eyes. Steve's cousin stepped forward. "Someone's coming."

"Good luck, Mr. Roberts."

"And back at you, Steve."

It was only hours later that Steve realized that he had pocketed one of the remotes—it would change his life in ways he never expected.

As Steve and his cousin left the synagogue, an Escalade slowly pulled out from a side street and Emerson watched the dot on his BlackBerry move slowly across the street map.

Yslan received word that Steve had left his house for places unknown. Twenty minutes later she was standing in his kitchen with Mr. T at her side. "Tear it apart. I want to know everything this guy knows."

"No computer," Ted Knight announced.

"Laptop, no doubt, and he took it with him."

"How do you know he has a computer at all?"

"Because this is 2009 and everyone has one."

The two men nodded.

"Find him. Find him fast." Then she noticed the picture in the side of the bathroom mirror—a pretty female singer, à la 1940. "And identify this girl."

• • •

Decker fired up Steve's computer, went to the synaesthetes website, and, staying far away from the chat room, contacted Eddie. The coffee shop was about to close, and the counter girl was giving him the evil eye—he'd sat over that one cup of coffee for almost an hour. *Arrange a meeting for me, Eddie.*

*With whom?*

*Henry-Clay Yolles of Yolles Pharmaceuticals.*

*Sure,* he typed. *What's the meeting about?*

*Tell Mr. Yolles that if he wants the Treloar Building he'd better take a meeting with me.*

*Okay. When and where?*

Decker gave him the time and the name of the synagogue.

*Odd time, odd place, Decker.*

*He's an odd guy—likes to burn down people's homes.* He didn't bother adding "And killing people like Mike Shedloski."

*Okay—consider it done.*

*And Eddie—*

*Yeah?*

*Get me this asshole's e-mail address.*

Eddie contacted Henry-Clay and told him who wanted to meet him and when and where and about what then shut his computer and grabbed for his dope stash. He rolled a bomber thicker than his thumb and dragged long and deep. Much later that night he awoke on the newly made bed and found the doll was on his chest and his damaged leg vibrating of its own accord in its brace. He couldn't stop its jackhammer action and it ached as it hadn't ached for many, many years.

Henry-Clay received the news from this Eddie person with equanimity. He'd faced many negotiations in his time. Yeah, the time and place were odd, but it was just a negotiation—and he liked negotiating. He took the hard copy of the e-mail he had from

Congressman Villianne and folded it carefully. He'd deal with this Yslan Hicks person later. Now he had to deal with this freak who could tell when someone was telling the truth.

In a way he admired Decker for having found him out—and then for taking the battle to him. He wondered for a moment if Decker had found out about Ratio-Man's demise, then he cast it aside. How could he? And even if he did—who cared? There was nothing there to link him to the murder.

He called for MacMillan and his men, then opened the safe in his room and took out the medical report he had received from Victoria, British Columbia, and the new agreement he'd signed concerning the bladder cancer treatment BCG.

He sat at his computer and typed a simple e-mail: *Track down the kid and be ready*. Then he pressed send—good. He was in motion again—it was always better to be in motion.

Decker was surprised how much a cheap room cost in Cincinnati—eighty dollars—and cheap hotels didn't bother with the charade that expensive hotels did. Expensive hotels wanted their customers to believe that they were the very first people ever to use the room, the toilet, the bed. Cheap hotels didn't bother with that.

Decker put Steve's computer on the table beside the lumpy bed and remembered to recharge the cell phone.

And dreamt of a filthy child in his arms—and cried in his sleep.

The morning dawned bright and clear—a cold December day in Cincinnati.

Hialeah made her final phone calls and prepared the signs for the march on Yolles Pharmaceuticals.

Steve's cousin rechecked the synagogue's schedule and informed Steve that all was clear for a nine o'clock delivery. He had six guys ready to help—for a price.

Steve relayed, verbatim, what Decker had told him to tell his cousin. "Set up the screens, pay the guys, leave the side entrance of the synagogue open and the lights on in the two galleries, then take the money and get yourself something to eat."

Steve's cousin laughed. "That Mr. Roberts concerned about my health?"

"He thinks you're way too thin."

Yslan flooded the black sections of Cincinnati and northern Kentucky with agents and copies of the young black woman's photograph. At 11:45 they got a solid hit. Four minutes later they had an address, and within the hour they had broken down the door to her apartment—and found nothing of value, although they came across several love letters from Steve.

Decker tried to sleep the day away. There was nothing more he could do. The protest was scheduled for sundown. The delivery was at nine o'clock—the meet at midnight—*Midnight in the garden of good and plenty,* he thought. Then the disturbing refrain "one of these things is not like the others, one of these things just doesn't belong" rose in his mind and like a king cobra, flared its hood and slowly turned its dead eyes to face Decker.

Emerson had had enough of what he thought of as "following the dot." Besides, Cincinnati bored him. Only Decker held some interest for him, and it had been days since he'd last caught a glimpse of him—and he was beginning to worry.

At five thirty Decker fired up Steve's computer and sent a quick message to Henry-Clay Yolles—*LOOK OUT YOUR WINDOW YOU CREEPY TURD!*

Henry-Clay did as instructed and was surprised to see a gathering of almost a hundred African-Americans, all of whom were carrying signs. He blanched—not from the numbers of people but from what was on their signs: "I worked here" and "What's Your Ratio!" and, most concerning, "Who's Jumping Now?"

• • •

At seven o'clock an unusual group of worshippers entered Isaac M. Wise Temple for evening prayers. Not your typical elderly mix of men. And the young rabbi who usually worked his way through the prayers mechanically found his eyes flitting from his text to the unusually rough, short-haired, blond Scottish-looking men who kept craning their heads in various directions as the service proceeded.

The young rabbi breathed a sigh of relief when they got up and left, or at least he assumed they'd left since they moved into the darkness near the entrance. He would have liked to have concluded that this was God's work, but he knew better than that.

Shortly after their supposed departure the service ended and the place emptied of its few congregants. Steve's cousin reported, "The delivery truck is going to be on time—they just phoned to confirm."

"And they have the screens?"

"Yes, cuz—be cool. We'll set them up like you wanted and then leave the side door open—just like you said."

"Thanks. I owe you."

"No you don't—you paid me just fine, cousin, but, Steve, you lock up when they're done. It's all got to be cleaned up before morning prayers, okay?"

"Got it."

"You going to be there?"

"Later. First I'm going to see my girl."

Yslan pulled the sign out of Hialeah's hand and said, "I need a word with you."

"Do you really?" Hialeah challenged as many strong and angry black eyes turned in her direction.

Yslan held her ground. "I just need to know if you know this man." She held up a photo of Steve.

• • •

Emerson was driving fast now. The dot was on the move—crazy fast—and jutting down alleyways and through garages. He followed and came out at what looked like a demonstration in front of Yolles Pharmaceuticals.

The crowd was moving in on Yslan, and despite the muscle she'd brought with her she knew she was in danger. Then she saw Emerson. Emerson! What the fuck was Emerson doing here? He was looking at his cell phone and turning his head. She followed his look—and there was Steve.

"Thanks very much, ma'am, for all your cooperation."

Yslan knifed her way through the crowd and got to Steve as Mr. T was hustling him away.

Emerson approached with a broad smile on his face.

"Arrest him."

Ted Knight pushed Emerson against the retaining wall and quickly frisked him. He threw Emerson's BlackBerry to Yslan, who scanned the map and surmised that there was a tracking device involved and the tracking device's signal was being generated from Steve Bradshaw.

Yslan turned on the young man but was surprised by the resistance she met. Even after they hustled him into a car he refused to offer up any information.

But when they searched him they found Decker's wallet and the remote control Steven had inadvertently pocketed.

"What's this for?"

"TV. I like TV."

"You're in a world of trouble and you don't even know it!" Mr. T shouted.

Yslan looked at the thing. Way more complicated than most—then she saw the high def key, and the one that controlled the number of pixels, and knew that this was for a very modern, probably huge-screen TV. Not the kind of thing that most people could afford to own. She flipped the thing open and saw the

Super Store's label on it. "It's a rental. Get them on the line; I want to know where the monitors were sent."

"Plural? Monitors?"

"The remote has an assign for up to four."

"And sent as in they were sent somewhere?"

"They're too big to carry, so they must have been 'sent' somewhere—I want to know where."

Henry-Clay listened to MacMillan's report from outside the synagogue. "We'll meet him—we'll all meet him. I've never been in that place—should be interesting."

"We might not all be able to get in there early without setting off alarms."

"The place has good security?"

"Reasonable. It's been a logical terrorist target for a long time."

"Okay. We'll go in when they let us in, and we'll all go in together at the appointed hour—except for you, Mr. MacMillan. Find a way to get in there, Mr. MacMillan, and report any doings there between now and our little meeting."

MacMillan closed his cell phone and looked around. He'd already figured out how to sneak back into the ornate building. Hiding in there would be easy—and he was good at hiding.

MacMillan didn't have to wait long for things to happen. A panel truck arrived and six black men took three huge monitors out of the truck and walked them into the synagogue.

MacMillan slipped into the synagogue during the confusion of moving the monitors and reported the arrival of the three huge screens to Henry-Clay, who said, "Okay—weird but okay." As an afterthought he said, "Get me details on the monitors."

Decker arrived shortly after the truck left. He watched the men efficiently set up the huge monitors then leave the building. Decker smiled at Steve's cousin and said, "Get something to eat."

Thinking himself alone in the synagogue, Decker went over his plan. He laid out his props and put Steve's computer, which he had loaded the night before, on a lectern on the west gallery. Then he pulled out his remote—and with a flourish hit the play button. Nothing. He pointed and clicked again. A profound nothing. He swore then calmed himself down and remembered Steve's instructions. He went through them—pressed—a profound, resolute, and uncompromising nothing.

He was tempted to throw the thing at the screen then he stopped himself and shook it—no rattle. He pried open the battery compartment—no fucking batteries! More than $7,500 to rent the damned screens and they wouldn't throw in damned batteries. He checked his watch. Enough time. He raced out into the night, passing so close to MacMillan's hiding figure that for a moment the Scotsman feared he'd been seen.

MacMillan checked to be sure that Decker had left the synagogue, then climbed to the monitor in the east gallery and reported to Henry-Clay.

"Give me the serial number of the thing."

MacMillan did. Henry-Clay hung up and called his IT guy. Within a half an hour Henry-Clay had his computer set up and an all-purpose remote. He was ready to do battle.

The Super Store manager played hardball with Yslan about giving her any information without a warrant.

"What is it with you Midwesterners!"

"We don't like terrorists from the Middle East or from D.C."

Yslan called Harrison, who after a colourful series of expletives about Midwesterners, put in a call.

Decker ran down yet another street trying to find a damned store that was open and finally found one attached to a gas station with an ancient-looking pump. For a moment Decker stopped and stared at the old thing—it had a crank on the side to bring up the gas from the reservoir. He turned toward the store. A greenish light came from it. "Am I in a Hopper painting?" Decker said aloud. And as soon as his words misted into the cold air, a car pulled up to the pump and the service area returned to its multi-use modern self.

The sudden time shifting terrified Decker. He knew it was a warning of some kind of sea change in his world, but he had no time to consider what it could possibly be.

He entered the convenience store, quickly found the batteries, and brought them to the all-night clerk who was idly leafing through a copy of *Player*—no doubt looking for the best articles. Without bothering to look at Decker he scanned the batteries then pointed to the figure on the cash register. Decker was taken aback by the price but reached into his pocket for his wallet. No wallet. The other pocket—a twenty-dollar bill. He handed it over. The clerk bagged the batteries without taking his eyes from his magazine and returned a single ten-dollar bill to Decker. "Sorry. Got no change," he said, clearly not the least bit sorry.

Decker took the single bill and stepped out into the cold night. Ideas were echoing in his head: a single U.S. ten-dollar bill, no wallet—at night. He looked around and he was not sure of the way back to the synagogue. Not sure where he was—with a single ten-dollar bill—suddenly the smell of the Huangpu River was to his left and the buildings all around him seemed to arch in. He was in the old city of Shanghai—and profoundly, utterly lost.

Mac opened the door and Henry-Clay entered the synagogue. Mac's men followed them. Henry-Clay looked around the building then assumed his place in the east gallery. He looked at the three hanging screens—and waited. He was good at that—as far as he was concerned this being forced to wait was just a negotiating tactic—one he'd used many times himself in the past so he took a seat in a pew and looked at what he thought of as "the rich Jew stuff."

Decker staggered down a roadway that had no street sign. He

clutched his coat around him. The night was getting incredibly cold. At least he had his watch. He looked down—the slight green light told him that it was already 11:25—and he didn't know where the fuck he was.

Then he saw the river. The Huangpu? How the hell did the Huangpu River get here? Fear wrapped itself around him like a sodden blanket, then whispered to him, "This is too big for you. Way too big." Decker felt himself nodding in agreement. He allowed himself to retreat to a cell without a door—a room with no way out. He pressed his back against a wall and found he could not move.

Mr. T had released Emerson with a stern warning to "keep your fucking nose out of our business," but Emerson wasn't going to take his marching orders from some has-been steroid freak. And besides, he had a sneaking suspicion that all this was leading back to that weird place on Plum Street. It made an odd kind of sense to him that it'd go there—the kind of sense his *grandmère* understood, and that he was beginning to understand. This whole thing had something to do with the sacred—the other.

Decker pressed his back against the alley wall and tried to stop his rising panic. Then at the far end of the alley he saw a figure— a figure with something in its arms. A baby! Then the figure was approaching, its free arm outstretched to Decker.

The scream that came to Decker's throat never hit the air. The figure came closer and closer its arm still extended.

Then it entered the glow of the streetlight.

Not a baby—a bag of groceries.

"Mr. Roberts?"

How did this thing know his name—and why wasn't it speaking Mandarin?

"Mr. Roberts, it's Chuck E."

Decker tried to retreat farther into the wall.

"Chuck E. The Shabbos goy? Everyone's waiting for you."

Then, over the Shabbos goy's shoulder he saw them.

## 49

## FIGHT IN A SYNAGOGUE

DECKER ENTERED THE SYNAGOGUE AND STOOD BENEATH the east gallery—where Henry-Clay was now waiting. Decker breathed deeply then took in the mise-en-scène. His lectern and computer awaited him on the west gallery. The three screens gave off their "I'm waiting" grey glow.

He reached into his pocket and took out his freshly batteried remote and pressed two keys. All three screens immediately came to life with the CBC logo he had downloaded from the Net, which was followed by the hackneyed CBC News theme song, then a title: "34.4 Percent of Calatrex Pills Are Fakes." A dissolve to Steve sitting at his kitchen table looking very newscasterly as he began: "Stunning new tests prove that thirty-four point four percent, more than one out of every three Calatrex tablets, are nothing more than sugar pills. At forty dollars apiece, that means that for a bottle of ten pills at least three and probably four are no more than white-painted candy and cost the consumer on average one hundred and forty dollars for nothing."

The newscast continued, and Decker crossed the darkness of the sanctuary floor and mounted the steps to the west gallery. Once he was at the lectern there, he clicked on a light and started up his computer.

Across the way he saw six men, one sitting on his own, who he assumed was Henry-Clay Yolles. He had a shopping bag of some sort at his side. The others were standing. All were backlit by the huge screen.

Decker hit the pause button—Steve's glorious smile filled all three screens. Decker leaned into the mic on his lectern and said, "This goes to air shortly unless we can come to some sort of agreement."

"About what, Mr. Roberts?"

Henry-Clay's voice surprised Decker. It was light—airy. Not whispered, but slightly sibilant.

"You burned down my fucking house."

"Did I?"

"Deny it?"

"I do deny it."

Out-of-sync spirals whizzed through Decker's head, then straightened into three parallel lines. For a moment Decker thought he had it all wrong. Henry-Clay's denial was true. Then he relaxed—wrong question elicits wrong answer. "Did you order the burning of my house?"

"No."

Random lines, no resolving into shapes—a nontruth. A damned lie. Then he felt the cold surround him and something metallic in his right hand. He had to use all his considerable willpower not to fall.

Henry-Clay took the universal remote from his pocket and aimed it at the screens. All three blinked out. "You're not showing that piece of rubbish, or I'll have so many lawyers up your ass that you'll think you're a law firm."

Straight lines. True. "Doesn't matter to me. The last thing you want is for this to go public, so bring on the lawyers."

A moment of silence from Henry-Clay. Then he said, "What do you want?"

"I want you to back off."

"Meaning what exactly?"

"Pay for my house."

"I had nothing to do with your house burning down."

Random lines—a nontruth.

"And have my credit cards reinstated."

"I had nothing to do with you and your credit cards."

Straight line! What?

"And get the bank to reissue my loan."

"What bank loan? I don't know anything about a bank loan."

Yet more straight lines.

"And you had nothing to do with getting my studio con-demned?"

"Not a damned thing."

A perfect cube—another truth. Decker faltered for a moment then thought, *One of these things is not like the others; one of these things just doesn't belong.* Then he thought, *No, dammit—three of these things are not like the other. Cancelling credit cards, calling loans, having a building condemned—legal things. Charendoff things. But arson—that's a Henry-Clay Yolles thing.* He smiled—one mystery solved.

"Are you really buying the Treloar Building?"

Decker hit F7 on his computer and a copy of the mock deed came up on the screens.

Henry-Clay turned to look at it carefully. Then he laughed. "You've been defeated by your own technology, Mr. Roberts. I doubt that I would have seen the imperfections in this fake if you'd put it on a table in front of me—but blown up to twice the size of God, in high-definition with a gazillion pixels, this is clearly a fake."

"True—actually, just a way to get you to see this." He pressed F8 on his computer and the newscast continued with a series of shots of the demonstration by African Americans outside Yolles Pharmaceuticals. "I thought you'd like that part—place and time and an ethnic group always helps a story have legs. This could be on every evening newscast by this time tomorrow. CNN has ex-pressed real interest. FOX is hesitating—but they haven't said no."

Decker looked at the gallery across the way—unless he was mistaken, there were two fewer men there now than before. He quickly moved to the access door to his gallery, and closed and locked it. He knew the old thing wouldn't hold for long, but it could give him a moment or two that could be crucial.

"So what do you say, Mr. Yolles—if I press shift F9 this thing wings its way to every major broadcaster in the country."

"They'll know it's a fake."

"Not after it appears on the Canadian Broadcasting Company— and there's already a copy of it up there."

"You have no proof of anything."

"Really." Decker hit F1 and the cover page of Mike's ratio document came up on the screen. Then he hit F2 and Henry-Clay's own University of Chicago MS thesis about placebo ratios came up. "From your silence I assume you see my evidence is compelling. Answer me this, Mr. Yolles. Why attack me?"

"Stupid question, Mr. Roberts. Because you know when something's the truth. A placebo by its nature is a lie, and you could expose Calatrex."

"I still might do that."

"I doubt it."

What did that mean? "You set up the interviews for me in Orlando, Pittsburgh, and Cleveland, didn't you?"

"Yep."

"To audition me?"

"I was just doing my due diligence. I needed to see if you lived up to your billing before bringing you onto the team."

"I'm not on your team. I'm not on any fucking team!"

"Sure, have it that way if you like. But as strange as it may sound coming from someone like me, we're all on some team."

Dylan's lyrics from "Gotta Serve Somebody" flipped into Decker's head.

"And you passed your 'audition'—got the role—and then Ratio-Man went and told you our little secret up there in the Juncture."

"The Junction."

"Who fuckin' cares! 'Cause now we're here." He aimed his universal remote at the screen and pressed a button. The screens went black. "Now it's time for my case. You ready, Mr. Roberts?"

Decker nodded—or at least he thought he nodded.

"Look at the screen, Mr. Roberts." He pressed a button and the agreement to hand over control of all BCG production to Yolles Pharmaceuticals in North America came up. "Let me summarize this little doc for you, Mr. Roberts. BCG is the accepted and only treatment for bladder cancer. It's a money loser so no one really wants to be saddled with producing the stuff. But after a bit of investigation I decided it was a good idea. *Comprendez?*"

Decker nodded.

"Speak up, Mr. Roberts—we don't want to misunderstand each other at this crucial 'juncture.' Do we?"

"No, we don't want to misunderstand each other—and yes, I understand what that document entitles Yolles Pharmaceuticals to do."

"Good. 'Cause here's another somewhat more personal document." He hit a button on his PowerPoint presentation and Seth's medical records that MacMillan's man had stolen from the Victoria hospital came up. "Note the name on the top, Mr. Roberts."

Decker stared at it, unable to speak.

Henry-Clay scrolled down through the document to DIAGNOSIS: BLADDER CANCER—then to TREATMENT: BCG.

Henry-Clay said, "And just in case you think this is fake shit . . ."

"Fake shit . . . what?"

"Wait for it, Mr. Roberts." Henry-Clay pressed the send button and a second later an order was received, and out on Vancouver Island a gun was held to Seth's head, and the phone in Decker's pocket rang.

For a moment Decker couldn't identify the sound—then he did and dug out the cell phone and flipped it open.

"Yes?"

"He told me I had to tell you."

"Seth . . ."

"Yeah."

"Tell me what?"

"I've been treated for bladder cancer for almost fourteen months. That's why I needed the money. Fuck. Why does he want me to tell you that?"

"I don't know," Decker lied.

"Don't lie to me. I always know when you're lying. I know when everyone's lying. Fuck this. I told you what he wanted me to tell you—now stay out of my life."

The phone went dead in Decker's hand. He found it was hard to breathe. He thought he saw the little man across the way laughing.

Decker thrust a finger at his computer. An image of Mike's statue of himself made in computer peripherals came up. Then his sign "Who's Jumping Now?"

A crashing sound behind Decker. "Call off your hounds, Yolles. That newscast goes to air unless I expressly tell them not to."

"I make one call and all BCG production and distribution stops. I can cut off your son's supply of the only thing that's keeping his cancer at bay." Henry-Clay reached over and took something from the shopping bag. It glittered in the light. "What do you think, fellow traveler?" he said as, in one quick motion, he put on the silk robe and turned slowly in the light. "What d'ya think?"

A long silence followed. The screens had returned to their muted grey waiting mode. The banging behind Decker had stopped. The yawning darkness between the two galleries seemed vast—a grand canyon of darkness.

Finally Decker said, "I'll trade."

"I thought you would," Henry-Clay said. "To be clear. If that newscast or any piece of it appears anywhere at any time for any reason, BCG production will cease on this continent. My understanding is that bladder cancer is painful—quite painful. Am I understood?"

"Yes. Did you have Mike Shedloski murdered?"

"No."

Broken lines—curves.

"Do you plan to have me killed?"

"That remains to be seen."

Suddenly the front door of the synagogue swung inward.

There was yelling and bright lights everywhere and dozens of federal agents swarmed into the place.

Decker sat back hard on the pew behind him and yanked at the wire Yslan had insisted that he wear. He reached for his cell phone, hit reply, and begged for Seth to pick up.

The phone rang as it flew through the cold Vancouver Island air and even rang as it hit the incoming wave.

Seth turned his back and walked toward his car thinking. *Shoot me, what the fuck's the difference.*

Mac's man didn't shoot him—his work was done here.

The phone rang and rang and rang until the cold Pacific salt water penetrated its casing—then it rang no more.

# 50

*AFTER*

"ARE YOU ALL RIGHT?" YSLAN ASKED.

Decker's face was stained with tears, he was freezing cold, and the dark space in front of him between the two synagogue galleries was begging him to jump and be done with the whole thing.

"Mr. Roberts? Decker?"

He felt the metal object heavy in his hand and the blood running through his fingers—and he was vomiting, his body throwing the adrenaline from itself in convulsive waves. His heart was racing.

Yslan was by his side, ignoring the bile and vomit and insisting, "Breathe Decker, breathe or you'll have a heart attack and die on me right here. Come on, Decker, surely this is the last place on earth you want to die."

Decker looked at her. What did she mean by that? How much does she really know?

Decker turned and saw Henry-Clay being read his rights by two burly feds while dozens of others rounded up the rest of Yolles' men. On the far side Decker saw Mr. T leading Steven in handcuffs. The young man was staggering, his eyes glazed, a light sheen of spittle at the sides of his mouth.

"What happened to—"

"We're not sure; he had a seizure or something. We'll get him to a hospital. We needed him to lead us to you."

"But—"

"We'll get him to a hospital, I told you that."

"Tell Ted Knight to do it now."

"Who?"

"White hair, prissy—Ted Knight."

"What?"

"Mary Tyler Moore—never mind."

"I'll google it and figure out what the hell you're talking about."

Steven suddenly fell to the ground. "Please get him to a hospital."

Yslan ordered it and Steven was carried out of the building.

Decker stood, reached beneath his shirt, and pulled off the wire Yslan had taped to his chest in the alley. He tried to clean his jacket, then he took the thing off and threw it over the balcony. A squawk from down below.

Yslan leaned over and commanded, "Shut it!"

And silence followed.

"Would Yolles . . ."

"Have murdered you? That's a possibility, but I wasn't going to let that happen."

"It's your job to keep me safe."

"Yeah, my job, Mr. Roberts. I'm you're guardian angel."

Images of a grotesque angel with a flaming sword at the gates filled Decker's head. "So what happens to him now?"

Yslan stood and Decker watched her.

"You suddenly deaf? What happens to him now?"

Yslan turned back to him. "We scare him—create as much bad publicity as we can, then cut him loose."

"What?"

"Think, Mr. Roberts. What exactly did he do that was against the law?"

"The placebos are a form of fraud."

"Accepted medical practice."

"But at that ratio? At eight percent sure, but not at almost thirty-five percent."

"It might be the right ratio—it's to be determined."

"He murdered Mike . . ."

"Did he? Who saw him do that?"

"Well he didn't do it himself, he had someone do it for him. He's rich . . ."

". . . and rich guys never get their hands dirty. In this case he covers his tracks. MacMillan probably did it, but he'd serve four life sentences before he ratted out his boss—he's Irish," she said the last with a smirk.

"Probably Scottish."

"Who cares?"

"Not fucking me." Decker was suddenly screaming. "He threatened me! He burned down my damned house . . ."

"Enough, Mr. Roberts. You threatened him too. You drew him here in the middle of the night. We'll hold him for as long as we can. Maybe we can get him a biker roommate for a few charming evenings, but I doubt it. He's already lawyered up. I doubt he'll even spend the night enjoying the hospitality of the city of Cincinnati."

"And my house?"

"Canada's problem."

"So he can come after me anytime he wants?"

Yslan thought about that and finally said, "Do you know the strategy of containment?"

"You mean the one that worked for forty years against the Soviets but that Bush didn't think was good enough to use against Saddam? That containment strategy?"

"Glad to see you haven't lost your caustic sense of humour."

"That one, Hicksy?"

"Don't call me that. But yes, that one."

"And how do I contain Henry-Clay Yolles?"

"With the threat of using your voiceover that opens each episode of your show to expose him."

Decker nodded, then his face darkened.

"What?" she asked.

"What happens if the show fails?"

"You mean it gets cancelled?"

"You know that's what I mean."

"Well, according to a brief study on my part, nothing at CBC has played for more than two seasons—except for that stupid dog show and the even stupider fisherman show—but those were back in the sixties. So I think you have Mr. Yolles under control for at most two years—assuming your show runs that long."

"I'll never use it because he'd cut off Seth's treatment. And he knows it."

"True. Well, it would have been nice if you'd shared that bit of information about your son with me."

"I didn't know it myself."

She looked at him closely. "What else haven't you told me, Mr. Roberts?"

He took a deep breath and looked away. There was a lot he hadn't told her—and a few things he didn't know enough about to tell her even if he'd wanted to.

"Listen, my job is to keep you safe."

"Yeah, yeah, yeah, so you've said."

"That's my job."

"And to use me."

"Have I used you yet?"

"Your 'yet' is duly . . ." but he didn't continue because Emerson Remi, accompanied by a full camera crew, bullied his way into the synagogue. Decker's mind raced back to his brief encounter with this man—the feeling of terrible disorientation when he was near Mr. Remi. Decker knew beyond knowing that Emerson Remi was like him—a hider, someone in the fog with access to the other world. But not necessarily a friend, let alone an ally. No doubt there were friends and foes in that other world just as there were in this one.

"What happens now?" he asked.

"We spotted a guy casing your old home in Toronto—the one you grew up in on Strathallan." She showed him the photo of Garreth Sr. "Do you know him?"

Decker shook his head.

"Come on, Mr. Roberts, who the fuck is this?"

"I don't know. I honestly don't know."

"Well, until we figure it out, you're with me—ball and chain."

"Can I go home?"

"And where exactly—exactly—would that be, Mr. Roberts?"

Their eyes locked. He knew—and she knew—that she wasn't asking about a physical place. Decker felt her gaze pierce his defenses and probe for an answer to that most invasive of questions. Finally he said, "Can I go back to the Junction?"

"Nope."

"What . . ."

"*You* can't go back to the Junction. *We* can go back to the Junction."

## 51

## *HOME?*

EIGHTEEN HOURS AND $435 LATER, DECKER AND YSLAN stepped off an Air Canada flight after a five-hour layover in Chicago—to a frigid Toronto evening.

Without bags they quickly got to Immigration, where Yslan momentarily disappeared, only to reappear on the other side of the counter, where she waited for Decker.

"Professional courtesy?" Decker asked.

"You could call it that."

"What would you call it?"

"Logical cooperation with a fellow law-enforcement officer."

"Our guys do that?"

"We share a border."

"Yeah, I know, the longest undefended . . ."

Yslan laughed.

"I said something funny?"

"That border's defended, boyo—you'd better believe that. Let's go, you're with me. I've got us hotel rooms."

"Something fancy?"

"Hardly. The U.S. government doesn't do fancy."

The old hotel on Lakeshore wasn't fancy. The constant din of the traffic rattled the walls—when trucks passed the lamp on Decker's small desk literally hopped up and down. Decker didn't sleep much that night.

The next morning Yslan entered his room without knocking and threw him the keys to his Passat. Before he could ask where the fuck she'd gotten those, she said, "We're everywhere you wanna be, Mr. Roberts. Oh yeah, I forgot."

She tossed him a thick envelope.

He caught it and recognized his own handwriting and the address on Fifty-eighth Street in New York City. He opened it and saw all the money.

"Four thousand two hundred and ninety dollars, Mr. Roberts, which I believe belongs to you. Go ahead and count it if you want."

"Thanks but I trust . . ."

". . . that all the money's there. Swell."

He put the envelope on the table between them. "I don't like being in your debt."

She pushed it back to him. "Tough. You owe me, Decker Roberts."

He didn't like the smile on her face. "And I assume you'll come knocking at my door to collect some day."

"Someday soon, Mr. Roberts, because in this world nothing is free. Be back here by four o'clock."

"Or else you'll send the Mounties?"

"The guys in the cute red suits and funny hats? Nah. I'll send someone you've never seen before—and you'll never know what hit you." She turned and was gone. Decker looked out the window—the snow was horizontal coming off the lake.

## LEENA

"You're not telling me everything," she sighed. "Of course you're not telling me everything—you don't tell anyone everything, do you, Decker?"

"Is the truth a defense?"

"Against what?" She sat at his table. "Tell me, Decker, tell me as much as you can."

And Decker did. How he didn't know where else to go. Who else to trust. How his house had been burnt to the ground. Trish and his TV show. Theo and their research. Eddie and his access to almost everything that was Decker.

She listened carefully as Decker's trembling hands rearranged the plates and cutlery on the table. Finally she reached across and grabbed his hand. "Don't do that!" Leena's voice was strong—it centred him. "Work from where you are now—sitting across from an old girlfriend. Work backward, Decker. Isn't that what you tell actors to do? Chart backward—isn't that the Roberts method?"

Decker's eyes looked wildly about him.

"You're sitting here talking to me, Decker. Now how the hell did you get here?"

## TRISH

Later that afternoon Decker slid into the booth at Rancho Relaxo beside Trish. He was happy to find her young man free—and she was strangely happy to see him.

"You okay? I was worried about you, Decker."

"Why worried?"

"You were gone a long time—no phone calls."

"One."

"Yeah, and that was fuckin' weird, even for you."

"Point taken."

She put the scripts for episodes five and six on the table. "Great stuff. That hanging—really great."

Decker riffled through the first script. His eyes quickly caught banal sentence after banal sentence. "We couldn't get real writers . . ."

"Once we're successful we can ditch the network's hacks and bring on novelists like you wanted."

He pushed the scripts aside.

"You okay, Decker?"

After a hesitation, he said, "I don't know."

"Can I help?"

"I don't know that either."

She shrugged her shoulders—strong, handsome shoulders. "I'm here for you. You know that, right?"

Decker didn't know what to do with that. He was used to being the one who helped, not the one who received assistance. So he just smiled.

"Drink with me, Decker."

He had one but declined a second. As he gently removed her hand from his and kissed her on the forehead she said, "I'm lonely."

He wanted to say "The world's lonely" but instead said, "Someone important will come along and see how very, very special you are, Trish." He got up. Put the keys to Trish's apartment that she had given him on the table.

"No," she said, flipping them back at him. "Keep them. Never know when you'll need them—or I'll need you to have them."

He pocketed the keys and waved good-bye as he headed toward the exit.


## THEO

When Decker entered the store, Theo was thumbing through some old copies of *Playboy*. "Changing your orientation, Theo?"

Theo pursed his lips and then stuck out his tongue. It was vaguely blue.

"Looking up a Gahan Wilson cartoon series."

"Which one?"

"Great farts of history. Here's number six in the series." He turned the magazine to face Decker. The cartoon took up a whole page. In it a large men's club reading room had dozens of sprawled figures of wealthy men clearly dead. Way over to one side a little old guy sat with a big smile on his face and a carton of takeout Chinese in his hand.

*Probably General Tso's chicken,* Decker thought as his mind ran back to Mike's apartment in Cincinnati.

Theo looked at his friend then snapped his fingers centimeters from Decker's nose. "Earth to Decker. Earth to Decker."

"Sorry, Theo."

"So has the traveler returned?"

"Yes. I'm back, Theo."

"Where were you?"

"In the States."

"Any news from the evangelical right you'd care to share?"

"Yeah the Tea Party guys want you down there right away— they need an old gay guy to rob a bank while assaulting choir-boys and advocating for socialized medicine."

"Ah, a modern-day Willie Horton. I'd make a great poster boy."

Both of them stopped. The shared image of the dead gay boy hung on the lamppost on Annette rose in both their minds—and killed any sense of bonhomie. It was their unique folie à deux.

Theo began to cough.

Decker offered a hand, but Theo pushed him aside and took out a small vial of pills. He popped one, closed his eyes—and the coughing stopped.

"Theo!"

"These are new. They work, but they turn my tongue blue and give me record-setting gas." He returned to his *Playboy* search, then he added, "For now. Now they work. Now that they are new, they work."

## YSLAN

"It's open," Yslan called out in response to Decker's knock on the door of her Lakeshore hotel room. It was just before four in the afternoon. She was fresh from a long run along Lake Ontario and just emerging from a shower, her thin frame flowing easily inside the hotel's white terry-cloth robe, a towel around her hair.

"It's not so pretty," she said, rubbing the towel against her scalp.

"What's not so pretty?"

"The lake."

"At least it's cleaner now."

"Toronto doesn't deal with its lake like Chicago does."

"To say the least."

"I mean, folks here know they're living on the shore of a big lake, don't they?"

"Yeah, but this is a mercantile city. It's always been that. The lake was good for business in the beginning—and easy to put roads next to."

"Yeah, but those easy roads cut the city off from the lake."

"I guess."

"Sorta dumb, don't you think?"

"Just practical."

"Explain Avenue Road."

"You lost me."

"There's a major street in this town called Avenue Road, isn't there?"

"Yeah, so?"

"Avenue Road? What kind of name is that for a street? Why not Boulevard Street or Lane Crescent?"

"I guess they didn't want to offend anyone."

"What?"

"This town's into that too—not offending. So maybe there was a battle over the name and they came up with the compromise."

"Avenue Road as a compromise?"

"Yeah—pretty inoffensive."

"Pretty ball-less if you ask me." Yslan removed the towel from her head and shook out her hair in Decker's direction. Misted drops—what Cape Towners call moth's breath—surrounded him.

Yslan turned away, then pointed to a brown envelope on the coffee table. "For you."

Decker opened it. A new Visa card fell out first, followed by a note from the TD Bank reinstating his loan, then a municipal order rescinding the condemning of the building housing his acting studio.

Decker looked up.

Yslan was in the bathroom. The door was ajar. She was three quarters back to him and had pulled down the top of the robe. He could the see the curve of one breast. He pulled his eyes away and said, "You do good work."

"Thanks," she said, pulling on a blouse then a fresh pair of sweatpants as she came out of the bathroom and walked up to him. For a second Decker thought she was going to put her arms around his neck. But she didn't. "So Yolles had MacMillan burn down your house."

"You mean try to kill me."

"Let's leave it at burn down your house."

"If we have to . . ."

"We do."

"So are they going to arrest him?"

"I doubt it. The evidence is circumstantial at best, and the NSA is not going to help you with this."

"Why?"

"Because we don't give a shit about your house."

"Yeah, yeah, yeah, you just care about me."

"Right, Mr. Roberts—just about you." Yslan turned from him and looked out the window at the dark lake across the six lanes of traffic. "But there's this too. We couldn't find any connection between Yolles and your credit card or loan problem—or the condemning of your building."

He nodded and mumbled the *Sesame Street* ditty.

"You can't keep a tune, but I think you're right."

"Yeah, but how do you explain all four happening at the same time?"

"Coincidence?"

"I wouldn't have thought that someone like you would believe in coincidence."

Yslan nodded slowly and poured two glasses of Chablis. "Normally I don't. But Yolles wasn't behind the credit cards or the loan or the building thing. We've got really good sources and Yolles is clean—about those three things. Clean."

"Yeah. I figured that."

"You did?"

"A wee bit redundant to try and kill someone *and* have his credit cards cancelled."

Yslan nodded. "The coincidence was the timing, not that two different people wanted to hurt you."

Decker thought, *Two people—Yolles and Charendoff.*

Yslan watched Decker closely. Finally she said, "Two people, but only Yolles is contained—at least for the moment."

Decker stared out the window for a long time. Finally he said, "Someone up here betrayed me, didn't they?" His voice was barely a whisper.

"You know the answer to that question. You've known that all along. You even know who it is—although you're not letting yourself see. You've known from the beginning." She took a small disc and handed it to him. Then she gave him his digital player.

He looked at her and she shrugged.

He turned from her and sat in the bay window seat and watched the snow swirl and swirl and swirl. It seemingly as unwilling to land as Decker was to face the obvious truth.

When he finally did, his heart broke.

## EMERSON REMI

Emerson liked the Royal York Hotel on Front Street across from the grand old Union Station. The Canadian Pacific Railway knew how to build spooky old hotels. Not as filled with quality ghosts as the Algonquin, but enough ghosts of interest to keep him happy—especially since this was Decker Roberts' hometown. His other-world compatriot's hometown.

He pulled on his raccoon coat—he hadn't had a chance to wear it since he left Princeton. Momentarily he regretted not buying a kilt, then stepped out into the frigid night air.

But he didn't feel the cold because the dreadful aloneness that he'd lived with—carried on his back was more like it—since the death of his *grandmère* was gone because he knew he was finally at home—no longer alone.

## GARRETH SR.

Garreth Sr. watched Decker's silhouette in the bay window of the Lakeshore hotel, room 218. He'd followed Decker all day.

He had no backup—only the knowledge he'd garnered almost forty years ago on a wintry day much colder than this.

## YSLAN AND DECKER

"Decker? Are you all right?"

Decker got up from the bay window seat but didn't look at her.

"I'm sorry, Decker, I really am. But it's him for sure."

Decker nodded.

She signaled him to approach the table. When he looked down there were photographs: a man outside, then inside Leena's restaurant. The same man two tables away from him and Trish at Rancho Relaxo.

"This is the same guy you showed me last night, the one who was watching the house I grew up in."

She nodded.

"Who is he?"

"That's what I want you to tell me."

"Well I can't, because I don't know who he is."

"Think Decker, think."

"I don't fucking know. I don't know him."

"Is that the truth, Decker? The truth?"

"Yes. Yes and yes. I don't know who that is."

"You're a lousy liar, Decker."

"Be that as it may, I don't know who the fuck that is. Got it?"

Yslan nodded.

"But you know who he is, don't you?" Decker demanded.

"No."

Squiggly lines. Special Agent Yslan Hicks had lied to him again. He headed toward the door.

"Where are you going?"

"I'm getting back to my life. I suppose it would be too much to expect you and your guys to leave me the fuck alone."

"Yeah. That would be too much to ask."

Straight lines—three of them. A solid truth.

# 52

## CRAZY EDDIE

THE PASSAT DROVE ITSELF TOWARD EDDIE'S HOUSE. UP WIN-
dermere, then right along the Queensway then swung up through
High Park. Halfway through the fabulous park Decker noticed
a large patch of light. Generator-supported portable lights were
shining on a stand of trees. Up in those trees were twenty or
thirty nice Canadian boys with hair driers blowing the snow off
the branches. He shook his head. Americans. They shoot up
here because of the cost advantages but they keep on forgetting
that we have a real winter in ol' Toronto. No doubt there's a film
shoot set for the first thing tomorrow morning in the park—a
summer scene perhaps. Can't have snow on the trees for a summer scene, so send those nice Canadian boys up those trees.

At Bloor he turned right and crossed Parkside, then headed
into what the locals call "the Indians": Indian Road. Indian Road
Crescent. Indian Grove, etc.

He parked the Passat across from Eddie's house and just sat in
the cold as his breath misted the windshield. His mind wandered
from image to image: Eddie licking the ice cream cone and announcing, "No change—still tastes like chocolate"; seeing Eddie
on the ground on Yonge Street, and first passing by him despite
recognizing him; Eddie's infinite kindness and patience with his
wife—and finding them together one night—and closing the door
before either of them could see him.

He felt the phone in his pocket and said aloud, "Call me, Seth.
Come on, call me and stop me from doing this."

But the phone did not ring, and before he knew it he had opened Eddie's front door and was standing in the hallway.

He could see Eddie back in the kitchen doing that peculiar hop thing he did with his bad leg when he wanted to cross space quickly. He heard Eddie singing and could smell something tomatoey. Odd. Eddie seldom cooked.

Decker saw Eddie do that funny hopping thing again as he recrossed the doorway to the kitchen—and Decker decided. He would get his stuff from Eddie's bedroom and disappear.

He closed the door behind him and headed toward Eddie's bedroom. He reached for the door handle.

"Don't."

He turned. Eddie's considerable bulk filled the door to the kitchen. "Don't open that door, Decker."

"Why?"

"'Cause you're either going to get your stuff and disappear forever, Decker, or you're going to move in permanently to my home—make it our home. Well? Which is it?"

Decker didn't respond.

"Well, I'll make it easy for you. Come out back." Decker almost didn't see the football as it came directly at his face. He blocked it just in time. The thing was hard. Would have broken his nose for sure. "Pick up the ball—meet me out back."

Decker did.

The snow in the backyard was almost a foot and a half deep. An arc light high on a telephone pole illuminated the considerable length of the yard.

Eddie appeared on the small stoop still wearing his apron. He signaled for Decker to throw him the ball.

Decker did.

Eddie whipped it back at Decker. In the cold—it hurt to catch.

"I don't get it, Decker."

"Get what?"

"Why you don't hop a damned plane to Victoria."

"And do what when I get there?" Decker threw the ball to Eddie.

"Track down Seth. What the fuck are you doing here when your son is way the hell out there? I'd do anything—I did everything to get my daughter back."

Decker heard the change of tense.

"Catch!"

Eddie lofted the football high in the air. Decker looked up, tracking the ball. He reached up for it just as Eddie's full weight struck him in the chest and he fell to the ground—tackled, a great *umph* of air coming from him. He looked up. Eddie was standing over him, breathing hard.

"Get up!" he shouted.

Decker struggled to his feet.

"Down and out," Eddie ordered. Eddie hopped back.

Decker raced six yards, then cut hard to the right. The ball almost took his head off as he made the turn. He tipped the ball in the air and caught it just as Eddie's body smashed into him a second time, driving him hard to the ground again.

"Get up. Get the fuck up!" Eddie screamed. "You want to live in my house? You at least try and find your son."

Decker got to his feet, feeling a pain in his side, and said, "I didn't do anything, Eddie. But what did you do? What?"

"What I had to, Decker. What I had to."

Then he understood—it was so obvious! Eddie had access to everything. He even put in the bid on the house in the Junction without asking. And, oh fuck, Eddie had been showing him over and over and over again what was going on but he hadn't allowed himself to see it. The guest room that Eddie slept in while Decker slept in Eddie's room! And the doll. The damned doll. "When's she coming home, Eddie? When's your daughter coming home?"

"Soon. Very soon, I hope."

"Is that what Charendoff promised you?"

Eddie didn't answer.

"Is it?" Decker demanded. Eddie couldn't meet his eye. "And what did you have to do for that asshole in return?"

"Warn you, Decker. Warn you not to fuck with him. Fuck, man it was only money. I gave Charendoff access to your passwords that allowed him to drain your bank account that got your credit card canned and sprung the call of your bank loan."

"And condemning my studio?"

"Yeah that was Charendoff—and me, too." Eddie took a deep breath then said, "Fuck, man, it was just money." For the first time Decker saw Eddie deflate—become a cripple. Then he mumbled, "Look what I had to do to try and get back my daughter, and she's still not here and I have no idea if she's ever going to be here. Look what I had to do—why don't you do a damned thing to get back your son?"

Decker didn't remember how he got to the airport or much about the flight to Victoria. He assumed the NSA was tracking him but he didn't care. He cared that when he arrived in Victoria it became obvious that somehow Seth knew he was coming and had erased almost all trace of himself in that city.

The only things Seth couldn't get rid of were the hospital records, which Decker managed to see as his next of kin. They were identical to the ones he'd seen on the three huge monitors in the Cincinnati synagogue.

Decker spoke to librarians and teachers, to street kids and hookers, to cops and preachers, to surfers and skateboarders, but no one claimed to have ever seen Seth.

Finally he found the beach where Seth surfed and shortly thereafter a hostel where surfers stayed. On a small bed in a back room he found Seth's old leather satchel. In it were three catheters, strong antinausea drugs, and a pad of paper. On the top sheet in Seth's messy handwriting was a note to him: "I saw your show. Hideous direction but clever script—although you really don't know dick about the people of the city or the Junction."

Decker picked up the pad, and an eight by ten colour photograph fell to the floor. It took his breath from him. It was of the boy encased in ice in the Stanstead stream, his mouth open, a hollow scream caught in the eternity of death. He turned the picture over. "This is what happens when you get close to people, Dad. Stay away from me."

On the afternoon of the winter solstice, when the sun barely cleared the horizon for five hours, Decker's heart was so heavy that he staggered to the Victoria airport and bought a ticket for the only place he could think of—the only place that he had any hope of finding relief. Houston, Texas—the home of the Rothko Chapel, a place that had healed him before. A place by, about, and for people like himself. A portal.

# 53

## *THE ROTHKO CHAPEL*

THE IRONY OF MARK ROTHKO'S CHAPEL BEING IN THE HEART of evangelical oil country; that it was initially intended for a Catholic college; that the artist killed himself before seeing the completion of his masterpiece was not lost on Decker as he entered the strangely hunching bomb-shelter-like structure.

He'd been in this ghost-filled chapel a thousand times—no, a thousand thousand times before, and never before, just as every time a person sees the ocean knows that he's been there before. Its pulsing waves a perfect match for the beating of his heart—its depths like the darkness of his mind.

And each time he'd been there he'd ignored the tall lamppost standing outside the entrance—like a gibbet waiting for a condemned man.

Inside, the massive black triptych on the north wall greeted Decker upon his entry—offset by two identically sized panels one to either side on slanted walls. The balance forced Decker's eyes to his left then his right. In both cases—east and west—to offset triptychs that pulled him toward them. Then around, to face the south wall, where a single massive black canvas hung—the only single canvas on a straight wall. It assaulted him, pushing him back to the centre of the room.

The very centre of the sacred space.

Then Decker sensed him more than saw him.

He heard the monk's pure voice sending single note after single note up to the ceiling and then heard the cascading chords of sound raining down upon him—releasing him from his earthly bounds—and him rising.

Decker didn't know if there were others in the chapel. He didn't care. They didn't stand between him and the greatness of the mad artist's work. The man had clearly drunk so deeply of the pure jet stream—been to the valley and returned with the images in these fourteen extraordinary panels and the building he designed to house his sacred vision.

Decker turned and faced the dark pulsing of the triptych on the north wall. Took a deep breath and felt the cold approach and something heavy and metal in his right hand. Then the pulse of the painting took control of his breathing, and his heartbeat slowed to match that pulse. He felt himself lifting his arms and turning in a slow spin. Rothko's panels passed by him in stately procession—slanted blackness, offset triptych, slanted blackness, massive blackness, slanted blackness, offset triptych, slanted blackness—then the perfectly proportioned triptych on the north wall seemed to open its darkness to him—and he knew, beyond knowing, that he was through the portal.

## 54

## DREAM HEALING

THE SUN BEAT DOWN ON DECKER'S SHOULDERS. HIS HAIR was matted to his forehead.

"This place is the temple of dream healing at Epidaurus. Now look about you," Brother Malcolm said. Decker did. "You have been seeking this place for a long time, Decker."

Decker looked up and read the motto above the temple gate: *Pure must be he who enters the fragrant temple.*

"Think nothing but holy thoughts," Brother Malcolm continued, "because you are badly out of balance. It is why you are here." Decker looked around him and sensed the timelessness of this place. "Christ will not walk the earth for another five hundred years. You have brought some gifts for Asclepius, the god of this place. After your long journey here you have eaten very little, avoiding the foods that will prevent dreaming—wine, meat, certain fish, and broad beans. Last night you bathed in the cold water of the fountains. This afternoon you saw the sacred plays in the theatre, listened to the birds sing in the perfumed groves and danced the sacred dances. Now step up to the statue."

Decker approached the giant statue of Asclepius. Incense filled his nostrils as the incantations of the priests floated on the still air. He took a wheat cake from his sack and offered it up to the god—and he felt lighter in his heart. And he was lighter in every way. There was a smile on his face. He turned—and gasped.

It was suddenly dusk.

He moved toward the temple, then stood—waiting. Somehow

he knew that he had to be invited to enter the sacred dream chamber.

"It is the hour of the consecrated lamps," Brother Malcolm said. "It is several days later. Your health has improved, but you are not yet in perfect harmony. You offer up money to the god for the sacrifice."

A wide slash of blood marked the ground in front of Decker, a ghastly crimson slur.

The priest had performed the rite on a sheep.

Brother Malcolm said, "It is time. You are invited into the dream chamber."

Decker found himself lying on one of the many raised ivory slabs, wrapped in the blood-flecked skin of the sacrificed sheep. He looked around him. There were many others wrapped in sheepskins on their ivory slabs. The person closest to him had obscured his features by drawing the animal skin over his face.

Decker turned and watched the movements of the yellow serpents on the floor below him. They were not poisonous, but there were so many and they were so large. He reminded himself that they were nourished by the god. The temple servants extinguished the torches. The air was heavy with incense. In the darkness Decker heard the famous anchorite Hildegard of Bingen's even more famous hymns sung by Paul Sheel's clear voice and the *swish swish swish* of the serpents against the rough floor.

"Sleep," Brother Malcolm said.

Then silence.

Then a pure boy's voice above the whispering of the snakes. "Sleep and dream your way out of your dream, Father."

Seth's voice in the dark.

Near him.

On the slab beside him with his head covered with the sheep's skin.

"Dream your way out—out of the room with no doors."

## 55

## THE JUNCTION—END, FULL STOP.

IT WAS SNOWING AGAIN—THIS WINTER WAS SETTING NEW records for the white stuff. Banks of it on the sides of the road were already chest high, and it wasn't even mid-January.

The snow drifted on the charred beams of what had one time been Decker's house. Standing across the street he watched as the flakes caught and held on the blackened skeletal remains. "What am I doing here?" he asked the chilled air.

His breath misted, then was blown back in his face.

He walked up to Dundas. Across from the Baker's Dozen, empty storefronts stood out like missing teeth in a smile. Farther west the gospel churches awaited Saturday to send out their message of hope in joyous song. Theo's window featured a new display of the works of Harlan Ellison thrown together with what can only be described kindly as reckless abandon. Decker was tempted to knock on the door—but decided against it.

He turned east—toward the city. Passing by the Axis Grill he had a memory flash. A condominium being built on, around, and through an old church on Annette Street had a glossy handout with photos of "romantic Dundas." The shots were taken from a high angle at night and carefully lit so as not to show the wide variety of cheap convenience stores, to say nothing of the choice selection of used appliance shops. The photos made Dundas look like a chic Paris street on the Left Bank just waiting for the right hour of the night for the cafés to open and the bohemian nightlife to spring into action.

Decker never trusted photographs. In fact, he didn't like them.

They were based on an intrinsic lie. They stopped life for an instant. But life—while there is life—never stops. Is never a matter of instants of time. Life is fluid. What happens at any given moment only has meaning in relationship to what happened before and may happen after. Only in death is a photograph truthful. When there is no "there" there, a photograph is an honest thing.

He looked up and down the old street. Nothing called out to him.

Eddie was within walking distance, but he caught a taxi and headed downtown to his studio.

Decker paid the Bengali cabdriver and climbed over the large mounds of snow between the street and sidewalk. He was happy to see that the condemned sign had been removed from the front door. His key, however, didn't work the lock. No doubt they'd changed the locks to prevent the occupants from getting in when the building was condemned—and, of course, hadn't bothered restoring the originals.

Decker went around the building's north side, hopped up on the Dumpster there, got hold of the bottom rung of the fire escape, and hauled himself up. For an instant he worried that his hand would stick to the frozen metal—but it didn't. He pushed open the side window and entered his studio.

The forty empty chairs that were filled every Sunday, Monday, Wednesday, and Thursday for his classes seemed to silently welcome him back. He wondered when he would teach again. He'd contacted his assistant to put his classes on hold. Maybe he should start up soon—get back to his life.

To his truth-telling business? He had no idea how that would play out.

He looked around and wondered if Yslan and her boys had been in here. No doubt they had.

He pushed open the office door and flicked on the light. Yslan had left the *Globe and Mail* and the *Toronto Star* open to reviews of *At the Junction*. "Not bad," she'd scrawled across the former.

Considering that a cranky old Irishman controlled the reviews of Canadian television, it wasn't bad.

They liked the show's approach—"Wry," "Sardonic," "Witty," "New direction for Canadian television." They weren't crazy about the director's work—no kidding. The guy had all the imagination of yesteryear's Heritage Minute—*"The tri-breasted warbler common to most northern woodlands . . ."* They also weren't nuts about the casting of the actors who played the reenactments. Right again, Mr. Irishman—it was almost impossible to get casting directors in this town to move away from the ten folks they endlessly used. They did, however, like the leading actor—and didn't find him too distant or off-putting or private. Decker had trained this guy from the time he was seventeen and guided him through his ten years in Hollywood—and he was a real talent. Nice that the critics saw that, but a fluke that the casting directors allowed Decker to get him into the room. Actually not a fluke. Through Trish he had informed them that if they didn't see this guy there would be no show. Why these folks made you play the death card over and over again to get anything done in this town is something that needed asking.

Decker checked to see if anyone mentioned the Mountebank voiceover warning at the top of the show—no one had. Just a reminder to Mr. Yolles that the voiceover existed.

Decker was about to dump the newspapers into the shredder when a clipping from the *Wall Street Journal* fell out. "U.S. DRUG AGENCY PROBES CALATREX" was the heading. In her precise scrawl Yslan had printed, *"You owe me again, Decker."*

He headed into the kitchen. He slid the USB keys out of his pocket and threw them on the counter.

He looked at the slender things just lying there, then picked up the one marked Stanstead and hid it beneath a loose floorboard beside the door frame.

"Later," he said to the air. He had to stop doing that. People would think he was even weirder than he actually was.

He stepped back into the studio. The light on the message

machine was blinking—he unplugged the machine. He needed a bit of time alone before his world began again.

He converted the couch into a bed and stretched out on the lumpy mattress. He put his hands behind his head and watched the snow fall through the shafts of street light—and didn't remember when he fell asleep.

And his night was gratefully dreamless.

In the morning he contacted his assistant and informed him that he was going to start up classes again. His assistant was pleased and said he could get a class together for that evening. Decker thought about that then said, "Sure."

"Six to ten thirty?"

"Yeah, the usual," Decker replied.

"How many actors?"

"Sixteen—and as many auditors as there are chairs. Messages?"

"A guy named Eddie keeps calling. You need his number?"

"No. Got that, thanks."

"See you tonight. Welcome home."

Decker hung up and thought about that. Is this really my home? He didn't know. He lunched at the Swan on Queen Street, then walked back to the studio. The city seemed vaguely welcoming today. It hustled and bustled by him, but it acknowledged him, saw him, and he saw it. *Home?* he wondered.

He called his assistant for the names of the actors taking class, and as he walked across Bellwoods Park he plotted the session. He'd do the Betrayal Game with them. It was an acting game that Decker had developed years ago. Four actors are given the following scenario: They all work for a clothing store downtown. The store has not made money for three years, and they are planning to turn the corner with this year's spring line. But as they gather for the monthly meeting they pass by the competition's window and everything, every piece, every idea, every design concept is there on full display—and their supply of clothing is not due for six more weeks. They are effectively done, finished, kaput, and all because one of the four betrayed the other three. The Betrayer is selected by secret draw. The object for those who have been betrayed is to determine who did this to them. The object for the Betrayer is to have someone else blamed for his or her perfidy. As the audience watches they have to separate the innocent from the guilty. And as the audience agrees that a person is innocent, that person is pulled out of the scene until there are just two people left—one who has been betrayed and one who is the Betrayer.

His assistant set up the parameters of the game, and then Decker came in to introduce the intricacies—the back stories that are the givens. As he spoke to the assembled sixteen actors and the twenty-odd auditors, he took note of the attentive faces in the seats and of Eddie sitting at the very back to one side—an empty chair to his right.

For a moment he didn't think he could proceed. Then he sucked it up and started the game.

In each of the first three scenes Decker identified the Betrayer long before anyone watching or any of the actors in the scene. And in each of those first three passes when there was only the Betrayer and a lone betrayed person left on the set, Decker allowed the betrayed person to punish the Betrayer—each succeeding scene with more and more vigor.

In the fourth and last scene of the night it took Decker longer to find the Betrayer. It was the immensely talented girl with the oddly spelled name, Tawtiawna, and when he finally spotted her, he looked back at the audience to see who else had picked Tawtiawna out of the group.

Eddie sat very still.

Decker quickly turned back to the scene and removed two of the betrayed actors, leaving only a betrayed middle-aged actor and the talented young actress Betrayer.

The look of shock on the middle-aged actor's face was real. Tawtiawna had completely fooled him. The look of "I'm caught" in Tawtiawna's entire being was even deeper and more truthful.

"Ask her why—single word—Why?" Decker prompted the middle-aged actor.

"Why?" the actor asked Tawtiawna.

"Deeper," Decker said.

"Why?" then a pause, then, "Why? Why? Why? Why? Why?"

Decker heard a whimper behind him. He turned to the audience. Eddie was wide-eyed, tears streaming down his face. All eyes turned toward him—even the actors looked in his direction.

"Because of my daughter," Eddie shouted.

Decker whipped around to face the scene. "Use that line."

"Because of my daughter," Tawtiawna said tentatively.

"Again," Decker said. "Stay on that line. Just that line and no more. Your drone note against his," he ordered, then turned back to face Eddie and the empty chair beside him. Over his shoulder he heard the actors work.

"Why?"

"Because of my daughter."

"Why?"

"Because of my daughter."

"Why?"

"Because of my daughter."

"Why?"

"Because of my daughter."

"Why?"

"Because of my daughter."

"Why?"

"Because of my daughter."

"Why?"

"Because of my daughter."

"Why?"

"Because of my daughter."

"Why?"

"Because of my daughter."

And Decker sensed it before the actors did, but they were slowly, inexorably—finding their way to forgiveness.

And through their artistry, their gift, Decker found forgiveness too.

Henry-Clay Yolles stood in the massive front entryway of the Treloar Building and listened to the phantoms as they skittered away from him. Now that he was the owner of the damned thing they'd better damned well skitter. But he knew they weren't disappearing—they were simply hiding, waiting for him no doubt, on the roof from which, in 1929, his grandfather and a granduncle had held hands and jumped.

Harrison turned off his computer and leaned back in his chair. Another day gotten through, another day without an attack, another threat detected and disarmed. He flicked on his scrambled phone and hit three digits.

On the other end Mr. T picked up the phone.

"I'm listening," Harrison said.

"Decker's back to work, we're on him."

"Good." Harrison knew he shouldn't ask, but he couldn't resist. "And Hicks?"

"She's on the case."

It wasn't what Harrison wanted to know. "Sure. But him and her?"

"If it ever was, it isn't any longer, boss."

Harrison hung up. The lights on his other phones were blinking. He looked at them for a moment . . . but chose not to answer.

Yslan hit the shuffle command on her iPod and a Journey tune came up. She hadn't listened to Journey for ages, since *The Sopranos* ended with this very song.

She leaned against the cool window of her hotel room and allowed the music to move her—move her to thoughts of the little girl she'd been and the private name she'd had for herself, and to Decker. As she slowly rocked to the music she began, for the first time in her life, to do what Decker would have called voyaging.

*  *  *

There were four or five inches of fresh powder snow on the side-walk. It was a clear, cold night. The new snow puffed up to their knees as Decker and Eddie walked past the churches on Annette Street.

Neither spoke.

Both knew that the ghosts of their respective children walked with them, just out of sight.

Decker knew that Yslan and her guys were not far away, and he sensed that others—as of yet unidentified others—were watching too.

But for now he didn't care. He was content just walking with his friend, toward what used to be Eddie's home and now would be their home.

He looked around him—the churches, the police station just up the road, the old library, the turn-of-the-century Heintzman House, the roads laid out on old riverbeds, a solitary lamppost from which a fourteen-year-old boy had been lynched. Secrets, many secrets, but a place where things come together—where divergent streams meet—where Decker would wait for the return of his son and Eddie would continue to work to get his daughter back. Here, in the Junction.

DAVID ROTENBERG has published five mystery novels (the Zhong Fong detective series set in modern Shanghai) and the bestselling historical fiction novel *Shanghai, The Ivory Compact*. He has directed plays on Broadway, in Shanghai (where he directed the first Canadian play in the People's Republic of China), in Cape Town and in many regional theatres in North America. He is the artistic director of the internationally renowned Pro Actors Lab in Toronto whose unique acting techniques are used by actors in Canada, the United States, the United Kingdom, South Africa and the People's Republic of China.

He lives in Toronto, in the Junction, with his wife, Susan Santiago, and is currently at work on the second novel in the Junction Chronicles series.